ROMA TEARNE

The Swimmer

Harper
Press

Harper*Press*
An imprint of HarperCollins*Publishers*
77–85 Fulham Palace Road
Hammersmith
London W6 8JB

Visit our authors' blog at www.fifthestate.co.uk
Love this book? www.bookarmy.com

This Harper*Press* paperback edition published 2010
1

First published in Great Britain by Harper*Press* in 2010

ISBN 978-0-00-730159-1

Typeset in Minion by Palimpsest Book Production Limited, Falkirk, Stirlingshire

Printed and bound in Great Britain by Clays Ltd, St Ives plc

Mixed Sources
Product group from well-managed
forests and other controlled sources
www.fsc.org   Cert no. SW-COC-001806
© 1996 Forest Stewardship Council

FSC is a non-profit international organisation established to promote the
responsible management of the world's forests. Products carrying the FSC
label are independently certified to assure consumers that they come
from forests that are managed to meet the social, economic and
ecological needs of present and future generations.

Find out more about HarperCollins and the environment at
www.harpercollins.co.uk/green

Barrie

. . . years
Later in the same fields
He stood at night when eels
Moved through the grass like hatched fears
Towards the water.
                          Seamus Heaney

A people does not carry the memory of
its humiliations as an individual does.
                          André Chamson (1940)

SOMEONE HAD PLACED THE CALVES AT the entrance to Unthank Farm. The farmer, arriving at his usual early hour, discovered them. All three, pushed up against a barrel of hay, with their throats slit, in the way animals were butchered by the Halal butcher in Ipswich. It was August, hot and with the promise of a golden month ahead. Shocked, the farmer called the vet, who in turn reported the matter to the police, but the calves were already dead. A small item in the local newspaper recorded the incident which otherwise went unnoticed.

Unthank Farm spreads out towards the edge of the city of Ipswich. It is the largest farm in the area. A few days later, a rambler out walking some thirty-two miles away on Dunwich Heath, came across a dog with its throat slit. The dog was a German shepherd and it lay on the edge of the road that runs in a straight line down to Dunwich beach. It was still alive. The rambler bent and examined it. The animal had a collar but no name disc. The nearest house was some distance away, its rooftop just visible. Assuming it must belong there, he picked up the feebly struggling animal and staggered back along the road. But the house, when he reached it, looked empty. It was large, built in red brick and with an abundance of Scotch pines and thick under-growth in the small copse behind. There were no cars in the drive, no signs of activity, no radio playing. The man hesitated. The dog was obviously cared for, its collar looked new, but the rambler was on his way to meet a group of other walkers and was already late. Placing the animal on the front doorstep, he rang the bell. There was a long pause. Then he rang the bell again, listening out for the sound of footsteps. Still nothing. Moving back, he was about to call out when he noticed one of the windows had been smashed. Clearly someone had broken in. The rambler peered through the jagged glass. He saw a room lined with bookcases and a few pieces of what looked like 1950s furniture. He saw some paintings on the walls but they were too far away and the room was too dark to make them out properly. He stepped back. The place was probably alarmed. It wouldn't do to be caught like a thief, he thought. Just at that moment the dog made a rattling noise in its throat. Blood gushed out. It struggled, moaning softly. Then it was still. The rambler saw that it had died. Suddenly he did not want to be in this place another second. He had a mobile phone deep in his rucksack, he would call the local police about the break-in and the dog. But first he would get the hell out of here, he thought, his feet crunching hastily on the gravel driveway.

Twenty minutes later the vet from Orford arrived with the police. He was the same one who had examined the calves at Unthank Farm. The marks on the dead dog were similar to those on the calves. A slit across the throat. It was also clear that the house had been broken into. But although the rooms had been ransacked, at first glance nothing appeared to have been taken. The police began the process of lifting fingerprints and contacting the owner, William Letsby. Letsby had left his dog alone in the house for only a few hours while visiting friends in the Ipswich area. When asked his occupation he told the police he worked for the Home Office. The officer, glancing at Letsby's ID, realised he was fairly high up in the Department of Immigration. He could also see that the man was very distressed about his dog and trying to hide this fact. Apologising, glad that nothing had been stolen, he left as soon as possible. He would be in touch, he said, in the event they caught any suspects. Meanwhile he was sorry about the dog.

Orford is a sleepy village of some beauty abutting the marshlands on one side and the estuary on the other. There are mighty tides that sweep in from the sea. Banks of sludge and silt laid down over the ages by all the marsh rivers lie unnoticed on the riverbed. The wading birds do nicely, as do the eels. Occasionally, when the tide is out and the water in the surrounding inlets appears to drop to almost nothing, you see them: eels, the length of bootlaces and the colour of green glass, twisting in the twilight.

Appearances can, however, be deceptive. People have been known to drown here. Two miles to the east, a matter of minutes by car, is Orford Ness, a one-time MoD establishment used for atomic weapons research. Now it is a benign and deserted haven for wild birds. Visitors in a small but steady stream come to visit it all year round, to walk, and observe the wildlife. This flat land with its extraordinary skies and matchstick forests is steeped in history. It is perfect country for painters, perfect crow country. But it is not a place with a high crime rate, and the vet was puzzled by the two incidents. Nothing like this had happened before. The police wondered if the animals had been the victims of a vixen. The vet knew this was not possible as the incisions looked to have been made with a knife. A local journalist filed copy about the Orford Ness animal killer but the editor did not print it for fear of causing panic amongst his readers. Besides, a circus had just moved into town and there were other, more interesting stories to print. And so the matter was dropped.

Then on the following Thursday two houses on the A1094 out of Aldeburgh were broken into and a large black retriever was found lying in a country lane. It too had been killed with a single cut to the throat. Nothing had been stolen from the houses and although a couple of windows had been broken no one had been seen entering or leaving. By now the circus was in full swing and the editor of the local paper did not run this story either.

The journalist who had filed the report was a married man, bored by the fact that nothing ever happened in Orford. The editor told him to stop complaining, forget the animal killer, and write a feature on the circus instead. But luck was on his side. While he was poking around the caravans, there was a commotion. One of the performing monkeys had been found dead. Its throat had been slit. The journalist's eyes gleamed.

The day was marked by a warm breeze carrying the smell of ozone and fish, the sea was jewel-like and sparkling with the sun spilling over it. A small plane from RAF Mildenhall droned overhead, children played ball on the shingles. By nightfall the beach would be crowded with people returning from the circus, heading towards the fish-and-chip shop or the pub. But for now Eddie Sharp's matinee performance was about to begin. Minus one small monkey.

No one would talk to the journalist. His eager, wolfish face made the circus folk wary. The monkey was buried quickly before the flies and the stink took hold, and the unease was quietly papered over.

In the centre of town a book launch was under way. A bestselling crime novelist was discussing his latest novel before a small audience. The journalist poked his head through the door of the bookshop. The launch had been advertised as 'Fiction Noir' with a picture of a corpse on a red background on the poster. The shop was packed. Solving a crime was better than Sudoku. There's nothing here, thought the journalist, and he headed back to the office.

'Not enough for a story,' said the editor, shaking his head. 'Talk to the police, see what they think. They won't want you alarming anyone while the circus is here.'

The journalist was expecting this response. He had just been trying it on. The editor, who understood him all too well, eyed him speculatively.

'Take a break, John,' he said easily. 'Take your son to see the big top.'

John frowned. He didn't welcome advice about what to do with his kid, but he decided it mightn't be a bad idea to take another look at the circus that evening, when it was dark. Something was nagging at him; perhaps a return visit would clear his mind. And what could be more natural than taking his four-year-old son?

'It won't finish until after his bedtime,' his wife protested. 'And he'll be bad-tempered tomorrow.'

But the journalist insisted, and as it had been years since she had been to a circus, his wife agreed.

'I'll be back in a minute,' John announced when they were settled in their seats. His son was clutching a balloon, staring solemnly at the empty ring ahead.

Sawdust and bright lights, with a hint of tiger musk. John slipped out. The caravans' entrances were obscured from view. When he tried to push past the barrier, he was stopped. His press pass was useless against the wall of hostility he encountered. He slipped back into his seat just as the drum rolled.

'What are you up to?' his wife hissed.

John shook his head, placing a finger on his lips.

'Sshh!' he mumbled as the show began.

The applause was deafening. No one heard the scream. No one inside the tent, anyway. By the time the story was out, it was too late; the show was over, the trapeze artist had folded himself down to the ground, the sawdust was soiled with sweat and the tent had emptied. John Ashby, freelance journalist for the *Suffolk Echo,* heard nothing until the next morning when his editor informed him of the event.

A circus woman in her mid to late thirties had been attacked in her caravan. A kitchen knife had been held to her throat and the threat of rape whispered in her ear. She had not seen the man's face but his hands were dark-skinned. Later, she told the police that all her travel documents, including her British passport, had been stolen.

Ria

1

I REMEMBER IT WAS TOWARDS THE middle of August. Thursday the eighteenth, in fact. That I remember so clearly, so painfully still, tells me that I have never for one instant truly forgotten what happened. Great waves of tenderness sweep over me even now, and I am still able to feel within myself the faint, dreadful stirring of what so overwhelmingly and completely engulfed me then. That night the heat held me in a stranglehold. I remember swallowing it in huge gulps and sighs as I listened to the soft gasp of the river. A vast yearning, an unknown expectation was poised to grip me, so that some time later I thought my heart itself would burst. But first came the beginning.

Towards midnight on that evening I woke with a start to the crackle and dance of white static on the television screen. I think I must have fallen asleep with my fingers wrapped around the remote control. It was stiflingly hot, unusual for East Anglia. I remember I wiped small beads of perspiration from my face with the back of my hand, thinking how unlike Britain this was, to feel so hot. I must have been disorientated, confused rather than frightened. No, I wasn't frightened at all on this perfectly ordinary summer night. Car headlights swept up and down the length of the garden like giant eyelids lighting up parts of the river, dipping into wetland mud before vanishing. The summer renters from Italy had returned after an evening out. I heard them slamming doors in a reckless way, laughing, happy.

'*Si, va bene,*' one of them said, faintly. '*Capisco, capisco!*' and then they went inside.

I switched off the television without moving from my chair and the surface of the night appeared once more as an undisturbed skin. Except for a small liquid sound, quickly suppressed. So small was it that I continued to sit, glasses in hand, straining my ears, still half asleep, only half listening. Then I padded across towards the open window where the air was filled with summer fragrance. And I heard the sound again quite distinctly. A splash, some movement, then . . . nothing. The river licking itself, perhaps. Fully awake now, I stood bandaged in the folds of the thin curtain, glad of the high hedge that screened the garden on one side from my neighbours. And I heard it again, that sound, soft and rhythmic, like oars, moving through water. It was coming from below, from the direction of the river. An animal perhaps, cooling off. From where I stood I caught a glimpse of the water. A horned moon cast a dim light over it. In the distance, not quite discernible, was the vast shingle waste of Orford Ness.

One of my tasks that August was to do something about the inlet from the river that lay at the end of the garden. Over time, slowly and due to lack of use, it had become a swamp of leaves and drowned insects. There was no one to swim in it any more; no children escaping from parents, no adolescents messing about in boats. Since I returned to the house it had become merely a thing of untidy beauty. Only Eric came past occasionally in his boat, looking for places to leave his eel-traps. Eric had farmed the land and fished these waters for as long as I could remember. He lived at Fruit Tree Farm. When my Uncle Clifford decided to split his farm and sell it because of ill health it was Eric who saved the land from developers by buying it at a decent price. It all happened long ago, when I was still at school and the house we call Eel House came to be mine.

I was still living with Ant when Clifford died, still hoping I might have a child, still craving for love of sorts. We were in the middle of doing the rounds of the fertility clinics with dreary futility. First Ant was tested, then I. There were months of endless temperature charts ahead of us before I was forced to acknowledge that no technology on earth could help an old uterus. I was told bluntly that the eggs would not stick, whatever that meant. I was thirty-eight and, it would appear, punished by inexplicable infertility. When it sunk in, when at last I said the word *barren* out loud to myself, staring into a mirror, I began to notice that infertility was on the increase in Britain. Everywhere I went, I met women who could not hold a fertilised egg. There we all were, girls with bodies that still looked young but had grown old internally.

'It's always been this way,' the doctor told me, when I protested. 'Women's reproductive rate slows down with age.'

So why hadn't I realised there was an epidemic of childlessness? The papers wrote about insecticides and too many chemicals in the soil. Women, they told us, were filling up with harmful poisons. It would take years to reverse the current trends. Teenage pregnancies are best, the papers urged, contrary to everything they had been saying for years. If only it were that simple.

Ant left me. He was desperate for a family. If I couldn't help him then he was sorry but he would be forced to go elsewhere. Who says men don't have biological clocks? His callousness was breathtaking. In the long, sleepless nights that followed I began to think of Eel House. Throughout what was left of that miserable year the memory of it shifted uneasily within me. Like a tennis ball passed over the net, a plan went backwards and forwards across my mind. Once, many years ago, I had been happy there and now it was as though a fragment from that time had begun working its way to the surface, dislodging the earlier hurt, buried for so long. Suddenly my homesickness could not be contained and I wanted to go back. I remembered East Anglia as a place of both love and betrayal, of far-away summers and family fictions. A place where my beloved father had walked with me in the matchstick woods, and the place where, after his death, I returned to briefly in despair. Eel House belonged to me now, it would be easy to go back. On an impulse I wrote to Eric, who replied with a single word.

'Come!'

So I turned back towards the east and my past, wanting to see again those wide watercolour skies and soft reed-grey marshes that blended so perfectly with the sea. Hopefully, looking for peace. I was forty-three years old; a poet whose work, even before Ant left me, dealt with emptiness; the colour of it, its smell.

The tug of the water being pushed aside grew louder. It wasn't an animal; there was too much control, too many regular pauses, as if something, or someone, was taking their time. The moon came out from behind a cigarette-paper cloud and I caught a glimpse of the row of wooden fence-posts rising up like the river's rotten teeth, and then some spray as an arm rose and fell and turned again in the water. My first thought was that I ought to warn whoever it was that this inlet was dirty and had been stagnant for a long time. Swimming in it would only churn the mud up. My second was that the door into the house was not locked. Whoever was down there could easily come in. I was alone, of course. Earlier that evening Miranda, my sister-in-law, had rung to say they were leaving London the following morning for their annual visit. In the morning, too, the cleaner would arrive, but now, at midnight, I was alone. With the darkness and the soft paddling of human limbs in the water below.

The movement stopped and then resumed, stroke by stroke, rhythmically. Silently, avoiding the furniture, the small occasional tables, the standard lamp, the foot stool, I moved across towards the French windows. I could get a better view from here. By now I was fully awake, breathless with suspense. Like a young girl, alert and taut, interested. Even my dress, caught in the moonlight, scrunched up and white, felt insubstantial, as though worn with the crumpled haste of youth. The moon was so good a liar, I remember thinking fleetingly, as I edged towards the window. Why was I so unafraid?

The man – no woman would have ventured into such filthy water – reached the end of his length and I saw a pair of hands rest against the grass before he heaved himself up on to the bank. I squinted, trying to catch sight of a face, concentrating hard, wishing I knew where my glasses were but not daring to move too much in case I was spotted.

The straw-coloured moon was just slipping behind a cloud as I saw with some surprise that he was bare to the waist. He had been swimming in his trousers. In the semi-darkness I could see he was young and as he turned and picked up the shirt that lay on the grass I saw he was very dark and somehow, I felt, even from this distance, foreign. He turned sharply as though he had heard me move, but it was in the wrong direction. I wish you could have seen me in that moment, unafraid and a little astonished by my own calm acceptance of an intruder on my property. An owl hooted and the man looked up at the sky, unhurried, as though he had all the time in the world, as if the garden itself belonged to him. What cheek, I thought in reluctant admiration, as I watched him button his shirt and search for his shoes. The moon disappeared completely and when it reappeared he was moving in long strides through the soft August night. A small, gloved wind stirred the trees. There was a noise downstairs, in the hall perhaps? I could hear my heart beating. What should I do if he was in the house? There was no telephone in my study. To get to the renters next door I would have to go through the front door and down the drive. My feet would crunch on the gravel. I would be heard. Again, the smallest of noises; I was certain it was coming from below. Suddenly I was rooted to the spot; belatedly, I was frightened.

After the business of the will and the house, after the years of animosity, my brother Jack and I were finally on speaking terms. During the years of our disagreement he had pestered me constantly to sell the house. Ostensibly the reason he had given was that I should not live in such isolation in this house.

'For God's sake, Ria, sell the bloody place,' he was always saying. 'What does a woman in your position want with a mausoleum like that?'

What he meant was, what did a woman of forty-three, an unloved spinster like me, want with a house that by rights should belong to a family like his. Eel House had not been left to him but to me. There had, however, been a clause in the will. If it were sold, he would have half the money from its sale. My brother Jack was a strange, restless man, frequently angry, sometimes a bully. We did not know what to make of each other, so that, ignoring the sub-texts of our disagreements I had inadvertently ignored his warnings about safety. Only yesterday he had told me I needed new locks on the doors and windows.

'I suppose you're waiting for me to sort it out,' he had said.

Bitterness from childhood flashed between us. I was weary of it. I had offered him every access to the house. I told him that he could use it at any time and that I would share everything with him. It was not as if he were poor; he had been left our London home by our mother. All I had was Eel House and the small amount of dwindling savings from my days as a university lecturer. Nonetheless, Jack wanted me to sell up and split the money. But for once I stood up to him. Our mother was no longer there to take his side. Miranda had always, to her credit, stayed neutral, so I told him firmly I would never sell the house. It was the beginning of a feud that was to last for years, until Ant left and Miranda, feeling sorry for me, rang up.

The truth was I hadn't cared; either about his never-ending resentment, or my own safety. These days I was past caring about anything much, except perhaps for the fact that I had not completed a poem in nearly two years. Everything had dried up inside me.

Now, belatedly, fear stirred within me and I hesitated; tomorrow morning might be too late. Of course, I didn't think this. When you are frightened all your mind has time for is the fear itself, and by now I admit I *was* frightened. It took some effort for me to open the door and head for the landing. I held an open penknife in my hand. It was laughable. Everything creaked. All those boards that were usually silent moved with me as I crept downstairs. Several times I froze, straining my ears. The moon was still behind the clouds; there was no light on the marshes. I was convinced someone was in the kitchen. What I needed was to get as far as the hall in order to find the telephone. The phones being portable, none were ever where they should be. Too late to be thinking about this, now.

Slowly I inched my way along the hall, barefoot, skimpily dressed, clutching that ridiculous penknife. What if he was a rapist? Don't be stupid, Ria, I told myself, you're too old to interest a rapist! I tried not to think about the incident that had occurred a few days ago in

Aldeburgh when a woman had been held at knife-point. The woman had been a circus hand, but still, the police had urged people in the area to lock their doors. I reached the telephone just as the church clock struck the quarter. The only number I could ring at this hour was the police, but I was reluctant to do so. This was a small community; word would get out. People knew my brother Jack. He was bound to hear of it. He would tell me triumphantly, finally, I was losing my nerve! I would play into his hands at last, and the insidious process of ousting me from the house and putting it up for sale would begin. I hesitated. I swear the only reason I didn't punch in the number was the thought of Jack's smug face and in that moment, while I stood uncertainly, without warning, the outside light flickered on. I flattened myself against the wall and held my breath. There was the unmistakable sound of gravel and then, footsteps, fading away. I don't know how long I stood there, rooted to the spot, but eventually the light switched off again. The moon reappeared showing its damaged side, barely above dream level. I blinked and found the switch in the hall.

Nothing, there was nothing. An unmistakable sense of disappointment flooded over me. The penknife was still in my hand. I closed it, turned the key in the back door, (yes, it *was* unlatched) and pulled down the blinds. Then, getting myself a drink of water from the jug in the fridge, I went upstairs and fell into an exhausted sleep, not realising I was still clutching the telephone.

The following day was Friday and I awoke late. Sarah the cleaner had let herself in and was just finishing downstairs.

'You're tired,' she said when she saw me emerge. 'Late night?'

'Yes.'

I went over to make some tea. My weekly organic box was on the work surface. There were the last of the broad beans, field mushrooms and asparagus. There was no fruit. I had asked for cherries, some raspberries, but there was nothing. Not even apples. Sarah was vacuuming the stairs. I could hear her banging the nozzle against the banisters with more vigour than seemed necessary. I knew she had stolen the fruit. Every time she came she stole something, however small. It was a token of . . . I'm not sure what. Some suppressed rage.

I knew she didn't like me. Once I had confronted her with some CDs I'd found in her bag and she had pretended to be dumbfounded.

'I've no idea how they got there,' she had said.

As if it was my fault. I know she stole money, too, but I had no way of proving it. Since it wasn't possible to get another cleaner to come this far out of town, I continued to keep her on, but I didn't leave anything of value lying around. I was on the point of looking in her bag for the missing fruit when she walked back into the kitchen and glared at me. Sighing, I picked up the paper and went into the dining room. Jack, Miranda and their children would have left London by now. I could hear Sarah going back upstairs to put clean sheets on all the beds. Then she would wash the kitchen floor and then, thank goodness, she would leave. It was almost ten. I sipped my tea and suddenly, without any warning, I remembered the swimmer. My God! How could I have forgotten him?

Solitude creates a peculiar inner life. Unbroken silence, frightening to begin with, soon becomes a way of life. At mealtimes there is only the clatter of one set of crockery, the crunch of your own teeth on food, the sound of yourself swallowing. When Ant was no longer there to bounce my thoughts off those things that had been suppressed for years began to turn endlessly in my head. There was no one to shout, Stop, stop, you're going crazy. If you are unloved, as I was, husbandless, child-less, you develop a way of thinking and being that is haphazard. Life pares down, sex becomes something other people engage in, like dancing. However much you longed for it, all you had was yourself. This was how I was at forty-three. Years before, when Jack first brought Miranda home (Ant had not yet made his brief appearance in my life) I could tell he thought of me as a born spinster.

'My sister is frigid,' I imagined him saying, making her giggle.

Hard to think of her giggling now, but in the early days, I used to be able to tell simply by the way Miranda looked at me, she was thinking, Oh yes, frigid. Definitely! I was not frigid. Someone had to suggest sex before they could call you frigid. There was no one to do that then or now.

In some sense life closed down for me after the shock of my father's

16

death. Until then, I've been told I was a chatty, friendly child. Happy, too, I believe. Now and then glimpses of that girlhood flit across my dreams; sunlight on an otherwise shadowed life, insubstantial like light, vanishing as I wake. The woman I am today is still possessed by that invisible child.

Last night's appearance of the swimmer had the quality of those dreams. I remembered a mosaic I had once seen in the archaeological museum in Naples. That too had been of a swimmer. Thin arms, rising slightly, slim hips, head poised as he bent to retrieve his clothes. What nonsense the night throws up, I thought. In the daylight it was unimaginable that I had been frightened. Stirring myself, I decided to tidy the garden before Jack arrived.

'I'm off then,' Sarah said, coming in, making me jump.

She stared at me, her face resentful as she waited for her pay.

What the hell was she angry about? I'm the one whose fruit had been stolen. I hesitated.

'Sarah,' I said, handing over her money, 'I'm afraid . . . I'm sorry, but I'm not going to need any cleaning for a while. The house is going to be full for a month. It's a bit pointless trying to tidy up.'

She had a bullish look. She wasn't going to make it easy for me.

'I'll tell you what, I'll contact you after the summer, shall I?'

'Are you giving me the sack?' she asked.

'No, no, Sarah . . .'

God! The woman made my flesh creep.

'I'm just suggesting we have a bit of a break.'

'You'll lose me,' she said threateningly.

'Yes, I see that.'

'I'm not going to wait around. There are others who'll want me.'

I looked at her helplessly.

'I'll take a chance,' I said.

I should have sacked her months ago.

'Please yourself then,' she said.

And she left, taking my fruit and who knows what else with her.

It was eleven by now. Jack would be here by four. The house smelt of the eucalyptus polish that Sarah insisted on using. Sunlight poured in through the kitchen window. Relieved to be rid of her, I went upstairs.

In the shower I thought once more of the swimmer. Warm water flowed over me. I felt a spurt of energy, the first in months, and the stirring of a possible poem. The emptiness I carried around within me receded slightly. I felt moulded in wetness and light. When I was younger, during that awkward adolescent stage, Uncle Clifford used to say I had the look of Kate in the novel *The Go-Between*. What he meant was, I think, I looked a bit like the actress who played the part of Kate in the film version. I can't remember her name but she had blue eyes (as I do), and fair, wavy hair, like mine. Why am I saying this? What difference can it possibly make, except perhaps to present the picture of what I once was, what I might have been, had the circumstances been right? Tall and willowy, Ant had said, in our moments of passion. With a sensuous mouth. For some reason I thought of this now.

It is important that I describe the fabric of that day and the days that followed. After I dressed, I went outside into the garden and picked some white Japanese anemones. The sky was cloudless. That summer, the heat had built up in layers, slowly, beautifully, like daily washes of transparent colour, hinting at how it would be remembered in years to come. The greengages were luminescent in the light, heavy with juice, golden like the sun. I walked towards the place where my swimmer had stood, beside the willow, just where the bank sloped into the water. Dragonflies skimmed the surface of the water, iridescent beetles looking like prehistoric creatures moved along the riverbank. I stared. I'm not sure what I had expected. There was no trace of any presence. The air buzzed with invisible activity. Some of the long grass looked slightly flattened, although that was probably my imagination. I walked back towards the house thinking, I ought to cut it today.

By lunchtime the garden was beginning to look better. I had cut the lawn closest to the house. Perhaps Jack's children could be persuaded to help me with the furthest bits where neglect had cultivated weeds. The fish I ordered from the local fishmonger arrived and I made some soup. Then I took my lunch out on to the terrace where the sun lay trapped in its own bubble of heat. From here I could see the inlet glistening and snaking towards the river. And in the distance, if I squinted, I could make out the barbed-wire fence and the tomb-like structure that was all that was left of the military base of Orford Ness. The best view of it was from my first-floor study window, where I would often gaze mesmerised at its melancholy, desert-like bleakness. The sun retreated momentarily behind the Scotch pines, sending sharp pinpoints of lights on to the trellis of roses. I sat finishing off the wine from last night and once again I felt the beginnings of a poem bubble up. I must relax, I decided, closing my eyes. I must not get too anxious, or think of the disruption of the impending visit. Perhaps, I thought hopefully, they would go to the sea every day, leaving me free to work for a few hours. Although the sea was within striking distance, hardly two miles away, there was no view of it from the house. It might just as well not have existed. Eel House had no connection with it. Out of sight, out of mind. Even our gardens had a lushness not usually associated with the coast.

The afternoon moved slowly on. Guiltily, I wanted their car to break down, or the children to fall ill. I resisted an urge to drive out towards the fens and not return, to walk with the wind in my face and the reeds rustling beside the water's edge. But the soup was almost ready and I had a loaf of bread in the oven. At three I glanced at my watch; they would be here in three-quarters of an hour. Going back out into the garden I cut handfuls of flowers; roses and some tendrils of honeysuckle. Then I filled a vase and went into the sitting room. It was a room I rarely used, except when I had visitors. Because of this the door was nearly always closed and as I approached from the kitchen with my huge jug of flowers, I registered, though with no special significance, that it was now ajar. I placed the jug on the top of the small Bechstein piano I had inherited. As I did so, a piece of sheet music drifted to the floor. I picked it up, stuffing it back into the seat of the piano stool. Then I plumped up the cushions and hurried out, for a car had driven up towards the front door. Jack, Miranda and the children had arrived early.

'When are you going to have this kitchen refitted?' were my

brother's first words as he walked in. 'I can't understand how you can live like this.'

I took a deep breath.

'Very easily,' I said. 'It's a nice kitchen. It's got character!'

Jack snorted. He placed two boxes full of groceries on the table.

'We didn't think you'd have anything civilised in your larder, so we've brought a contribution,' he said.

I raised an eyebrow and Miranda frowned.

'Jack!' she mumbled.

I thought she might kick him. The children came rushing in, full of some talk of a grass snake. They looked around the kitchen as though I was invisible.

'I'm starving,' Zach said.

'Hello, you two!'

I was determined to keep all irony out of my voice.

'For goodness' sake,' Miranda said, 'at least give Aunty Ria a kiss.'

She was already sounding harassed; probably she and Jack had been quarrelling on the way here.

'We should have stopped off for something to eat,' Jack said. 'I told you she'd have nothing.'

'Welcome to Eel House,' I said.

Two weeks seemed like a long time.

Later we had supper on the terrace overlooking the water. There had been some talk of driving into Snape or even Aldeburgh, but in the end I cooked a mushroom risotto followed by sea bass and fennel. Needless to say, they ate the lot. Afterwards, Jack pushed his plate away and looked speculatively at me. My heart sank as he helped himself to more wine.

'Well? Have you had any more thoughts on the house?'

I groaned inwardly. I had thought the subject had been dropped.

'Look, Jack,' I said, 'we've been round this so many times. I don't care if this is a good time to sell, I don't care if the kitchen is anti-quated, I don't care about the money. Please, let's not start it all up again. I'm simply not going to sell.'

There was a small silence.

'So you want me to service your boiler,' my brother said.

'No, I don't. That isn't what I said!'

He looked at me. Perfectly calm, indolent, ready for another argument, loving it. Yes, I thought, here we go. It was what he used to do when we were growing up and he'd return from boarding school wanting something that belonged to me. Later, he used to get money out of me in this way, slowly, draining away my savings, wearing me down, weakening my resolve. Well, he wasn't going to do that any more. Love might never have existed between us for all the show there was of it now. We were children from the same womb, fathered by the same man, but separated by a shared past.

'It will probably blow up and kill you,' he said.

I stared into the distance of the darkening garden, my face tightening. His nastiness always took me by surprise.

'Sell the house, Ria,' he said again, softly.

In the twilight I could see his teeth as he spoke. They were small and even, and very white. The children were watching us, fascinated.

'Who would like some raspberry tart and cream?' I asked.

'Yes, please,' Sophie, my niece, cried. 'Can we have it while we watch television?'

'You should cut the grass by the river,' Zach said. 'It's not a good idea to allow it to grow so long. Anyone trying to get out of the water in a hurry might have trouble.'

'Why would you want to get out in a hurry?' Sophie asked.

'Because of the current, stupid!'

'Stupid yourself.'

'Zach,' Miranda said.

'If you're planning on swimming,' I said, 'perhaps you could clear it for me?'

'Nah!' he said.

I wanted to say that a bit of exercise might help him lose some weight. But I'm not his mother. As far as I could see, all they appeared to do in their spare time was watch endless television and play computer games. But this, too, wasn't my business.

'Why don't you fence the river off?' Miranda asked, slicing up the tart. 'After all, you don't swim in it, do you?'

I shrugged. I could have told her that I liked having the river at the bottom of my land. I liked the way it moved, as though it were a sleek animal, lean in high summer, flushed and heavy in spring and autumn, cold and uninviting in winter. If I fenced it off, I would not see the extraordinary birdlife that lived around it, nor would I be able to wave to Eric on his trips upstream, on warm, moist nights, his low battery light encircled by moths as he hunted for pebble-black eels. I could have told her this, but I didn't.

'You'd get a flat in London for half the price of this place,' my brother reminded me.

Still I said nothing. He wanted a share of the money to fund his political activities.

'Why are you such a loser?' he asked. 'Think what you could make – enough to buy two houses.'

'Jack!' Miranda protested. 'I'm sorry,' she said, turning to me.

'Look,' I said, as pleasantly as I could, 'shall we stop baiting Ria for the duration of this holiday? I'm just not selling, Jack. Get this into your head. I'm not interested in the monetary value of this house, nor am I interested in funding your fascist politics, okay? Now, who wants coffee and who wants tea?'

Jack laughed. How the hell was I going to get through the fortnight? Miranda was looking at me with something like kindness. Lately I had begun to feel a great deal of sympathy for my sister-in-law. There have been moments, when she was pregnant with the children, for example, when we'd come close to seeing eye to eye.

I went back into the kitchen to fill the kettle.

'We're thinking of going to Cromer,' Miranda announced, coming in after me with the pile of dirty plates. 'Just for a few days – give the kids a bit of beach. Fancy coming with us?'

I held my breath. *When* were they thinking of going? We cleared the kitchen together.

'You need a holiday, too, Ria,' she said after a while. 'You work far too much. In that way you're like Jack.'

I laughed without humour and filled the dishwasher, scraping bits of food off the plates. I would not cry.

'Actually,' Miranda continued, lowering her voice, 'I'm a little worried about him.'

I was surprised. My brother's marriage had always seemed to me to be run along the lines of a business. Nothing emotional was ever aired. What was she worried about?

'He's getting far too involved in politics. We're spending vast amounts of money and I'm worried. You know how stubborn he is. I was wondering if you might talk to him.'

'Me! You must be joking!'

'Yes, I know . . .' her voice trailed off.

If Miranda was appealing to me, then things must be desperate.

'I just want him to take it easy. There are a couple of people who have joined who are . . . well, a bit extremist, you know what I mean? We've had a few odd-looking types visiting. Anyway,' she glanced around quickly, 'what d'you think about Cromer?'

'Ria, I need to use the Internet,' Jack announced, walking in with the empty wine bottle.

He poured himself a whisky.

'I presume you did get it installed after last year's fiasco? Let's forget Cromer, Miranda. I'm thinking of hiring a boat for a few days.'

The sound of the television drifted out through the open window, mingling with raised voices and the odd thump. The children were fighting.

'Oh God!' Miranda cried, wiping her hands, 'I'd better go and see what they're up to.'

'Yes.'

A kind of hollow despair enveloped me. In just a few hours my house had been stripped of its privacy. Alone in the kitchen I poured myself another drink and walked outside, moving swiftly towards the wild part of the garden. Beyond the river, and before you reached Orford Ness, were the matchstick woods. They were hidden now by fingers of dusk. The air was much cooler here and the trees were outlined sharply against a darkening sky. Nothing stirred. I heard the faint sound of traffic from the road beyond the trees, but that was all. The renters next door seemed to have disappeared too and silence enveloped me. I breathed slowly, feeling the tightness in my chest slowly easing.

Every summer of my childhood had been spent in this house. It had belonged to Uncle Clifford, our father's brother, and his wife Elsa. By the time he was six, Jack was allowed to come with me. Our parents put us on the train at Liverpool Street and Uncle Clifford met us at the other end. There followed a month of blissful neglect when we roamed the fields and helped on the farm. I was meant to look after Jack. I remember how once we had got lost in some field before finally finding our way back to Eric's farm. I had been scared, but as the eldest it had been my responsibility to get us home. Peggy, Eric's wife, had given us two fresh eggs each when we reached her kitchen. We had carried them triumphantly back to Eel House. It was the beginning of a ritual that marked all our summers after that. Towards the end of August, before the weather broke and we returned home, our parents would join us. I was delighted, knowing that at last I could have my father all to myself. Even in those days Jack was a bit of a mother's boy, less interested in the outdoor life. As soon as Mum arrived he stopped trailing around with me and the pair of them would go to the cinema and afterwards to tea in Aldeburgh, or on a long drive to visit friends. Mum was always buying him toys, which he broke almost instantly, whereupon she would promise him more treats. Dad disapproved hugely of such spoiling, but Jack was a precocious, rather bright child, so I suppose he got away with it. Meanwhile, Dad and I would go rambling in the matchstick woods, looking for fossils. We would pack a picnic and leave in the morning, returning at dusk when the light fell differently and the woods took on an air of enchantment. On other days we two would go out in the boat with Eric. Eric was Dad's great friend. Dad and Uncle Clifford and Eric had all grown up together. They used to call themselves the Three Musketeers. 'One for all and all for one,' they used to laugh. After our fishing trips we would return with eels for supper. Later, Jack and I would play board games with my parents and Clifford and Elsa, laughing and cheating, ganging up against each other; Dad, Jack and Uncle Clifford against Mum and me and Aunt Elsa.

Where had all that easy affection gone? I sipped my wine. Once, I had believed that the farm and the fields, and Eric's eels, would last for ever. Sighing, I closed my eyes and the poem that had been fermenting in me all day turned restlessly. It was getting late. High above the land a harvest moon moved silently while all the stars appeared like germinating seeds in the wide East Anglian sky. As I went back to the house I could hear the television. Clearly no one was tired.

'Oh, there you are,' Jack observed. 'I wondered where you'd got to.'

He sounded subdued. He and Miranda had pulled two chairs out on to the old flagstones and had opened a new bottle of wine.

'I hope you don't mind, Ria,' Miranda said, 'but we opened one of your whites.'

'Where are the children?' I asked.

'Playing some computer game. They can't stand being out because of the bugs.'

You've brought them up to be townie wimps, I thought, but I didn't say it. I was more alarmed by the fact they were using my computer.

'It's okay,' Miranda said quickly, seeing my face. 'They're using my laptop.'

Thank God, I thought. The poem inside me had begun calling, insistently.

'What happened about your boat idea?'

'Oh yes, I forgot. We've got one! Tuesday, for a week. Come, if you like. We're going to sail across the Broads from Wroxham.'

He was looking at me intently.

'Thanks,' I mumbled. 'But I have a poem in my head that I'll have to attend to.'

I laughed nervously. Jack seemed to accept my excuse.

'At least you're working again!'

A momentary benign feeling descended on us.

'We'll leave about midday,' Miranda said. She sounded a little upset. 'If that's okay? We'll leave some of our stuff here, travel light, be back in a couple of days.'

It was a quarter to ten.

'I'm knackered,' Jack said at last. He yawned. 'One thing I must say, the beds are wonderful here, even though the plumbing is antiquated.'

'Who's going to prise those two away from the laptop?' Miranda asked.

'Moan, moan.'

'Oh, shut up, Jack. You're the one who's been complaining.'

Again the tension was back. We were doing what we always did. Taking small bites out of each other, never addressing anything with honesty. I wanted to scream.

'I'd like my study back so I'll tell them, if you like.'

I put on a fake smile.

'You're not going to work, are you?' Miranda asked, amazed.

'Of course she is. Can't you see she's dying to get rid of us? Go on, Ria, go back to your masterpiece!'

'Well, I haven't actually done anything today.'

If I wasn't careful there *would* be a fight. Jack must have thought the same thing because he rose and took his chair in.

'I'm off,' he said. 'What time's breakfast?'

My study was a tip. Somehow they had managed to knock over a glass and scatter the cushions. There were books on the floor and paper from the printer was everywhere. My good intentions evaporated completely. Furious, I closed the door. Then I cleared the mess and turned the television off. I no longer felt like working, but I didn't feel like going to bed either. Upstairs, on the third floor, in the room above my study, the children made thumping sounds as though they were fighting. Taking up the book I had been reading I settled down on the sofa. The poem that had peeped out had taken fright and vanished. I could hear Miranda's voice followed by Sophie screaming. Then Jack joined in and there was a stampede towards the guest bathroom. Miranda began calling me. Oh God! I thought guiltily. I sat pretending not to hear, feeling trapped. To think I had ever wanted children! Towards midnight things quietened down. The floorboards stopped creaking, the house was settling at last. I sighed and switched off the light. Was it safe to go to my bedroom?

People have said to me that at least I have a brother, at least I have a nephew and niece. Long ago, soon after Sophie had been born, I had volunteered to look after her while Jack took an exhausted Miranda out. It had been a sort of peace-offering on my part. Sophie had been only a few weeks old and I had not long heard I would never have a child of my own. That evening, after they had left, I picked Sophie out of her cot and held her against my cotton T-shirt. Then I put her mouth against me. I had wanted someone to suck my breast. I went into the bathroom with her and locked the door, naked to the waist. I wanted to feel what it was like to nurse her. I wanted to feel the tug and demand of another life. But after a moment I heard a noise and Sophie began to cry. Scared, in case Jack and Miranda had returned, I rushed out. I blushed, recalling the long-forgotten incident. Loneliness expands wherever crowds gather, Eric used to say. Thinking of him, I wished I could have gone over there tonight, but it was too late now.

Closing my book, I went across to the open window. Immediately the scent of late honeysuckle and jasmine came wafting towards me. Somewhere in the depths of the garden a nightjar called. Just after Ant left me, taking all hope I had of love, I had heard a nightingale pour its fluid notes across this garden. I had stood on this very spot, mesmerised by it, wondering for a confused moment who the singer was. I have never heard a nightingale sing since.

A slight breeze moved the muslin and the trees rustled. It had become so muggy that there would probably be a storm soon. I yawned, slowly. If I turned in now, I would wake refreshed. Next Tuesday, when they left, I'd be able to have a clear day to work. The poem would, I hoped, return once peace was restored. Turning, I reached out to close the window in case of rain later, my eyes scanning the garden idly. I froze. There was my swimmer! Good God, I thought, astonished, for there he stood, bold as brass, bare-chested at the water's edge. What a nerve he had, trespassing in someone else's garden, *again*. As I watched, to my amazement, he moved towards the honeysuckle and bent to smell it. He was towelling his hair with his T-shirt; I could see the whiteness of the cloth against the dark garden. Then he pulled it over his head. I shrunk back further into the room, but he wasn't looking in the direction of the house. I saw him edge towards the water and stare beyond it. Something had obviously caught his attention for he stood perfectly still, looking in the direction of the woods. Almost instantly I heard the nightjar again. An owl flew past and my swimmer jumped. I could have told him the garden was full of nightlife and that over by the trees there were a family of owls, but I did not make a sound.

He turned his head as if he had read my thoughts, but he was still looking in the wrong direction. Then, bending down, he did up first one shoe and then the other with casual indifference and a second later he vanished from view, going presumably around the side of the house. I continued to stare out of the window, unable to move, straining my ears. There was a slight pause and unmistakably, I heard a door open. Could any burglar be this reckless? I hesitated. Damn, I thought, belatedly, the back door was unlocked, again. What if I went downstairs and confronted him? He had looked quite young. Not that it mattered if he was carrying a knife. But would you swim first, before you committed a crime? By now I had moved to the landing and I heard once again an unmistakable creaking of floorboards. There followed another silence. I waited. My study door was shut. I opened it a fraction of an inch, on the verge of going out when I heard a soft step. I was struck with paralysis. He was definitely in the house. I shivered. Something thrilling and fearful passed over me. Holding the empty bottle of wine in my hand I crept downstairs at the same moment as the outside light came on. Instantly I hurried down the stairs and into the kitchen just as the timer plunged the garden back into darkness. In a flash I had switched on the kitchen light. I gasped, there was no one there.

All this had taken only a few minutes, but any thoughts of sleep had vanished. Locking the back door, I checked the windows. Then I filled the kettle and was about to put some tea into the pot when I noticed the lid of the bread bin was slightly open. I closed it, changed my mind and opening it again peered in. It was empty. There had been a freshly baked loaf inside. I knew this because I had baked it myself only this morning.

2

TUESDAY, AUGUST 23RD. ON THE MORNING that Jack and Miranda left for the Broads I awoke to them having breakfast noisily in the garden. I was exhausted. They had now been here for three days. Last night I had again waited up until midnight hoping to catch sight of the swimmer, but the garden had remained undisturbed. Then, just as I dozed off, the outside light came on and woke me. It was him! But by the time I crept downstairs he had vanished. There were damp marks on the kitchen floor.

'There's no bread,' Jack informed me, his mouth full of muesli.

Miranda handed me a cup of tea.

'You look tired,' she said.

'Of course she is!' my brother said, waving an empty cup in her face. 'Workaholics usually are!'

He laughed a braying laugh and I wondered how Miranda could bear living with him.

'More tea, more tea!' he shouted childishly. Obviously he was in a good mood. I looked at him over the rim of my mug. Ant always maintained that Jack had a touch of Asperger's Syndrome. It was the only way he could explain my brother's sudden mood swings. Eric thought otherwise. Jack, he had once said, was disturbed for other reasons. Sunlight glinted through the trees. We had not had such an astonishing summer as this for years and it was going to be another hot day.

'You need a wash, Miranda,' Jack said. 'You're sweating, already.'
And he laughed.

'I've got seven mosquito bites,' Sophie complained.

'Aunty Ria, have you seen how weird the spiders are in this house?'
Zach asked. 'They're enormous, like in the Caribbean!'

'That's global warming for you,' Jack said.

He was eating and drinking with an odd, manic speed. Miranda
seemed not to notice.

'I read somewhere that the insects in Britain will become more
like Mediterranean ones as the place hots up.'

'Ugh, how will they get here? By swimming the channel?'

'No, Sophie, I think they'll just evolve differently. Like your Aunty
Ria has!'

'Mum!' wailed Sophie. 'I hate spiders.'

Go, I thought. Just go. We'll never get on.

'Stop winding her up, Jack,' Miranda said. 'There was some bacon
in the fridge, Ria. I hope you don't mind, but I've used it.'

I nodded, not wanting the subject of bread to be brought up again.

'Of course, help yourself.'

In all, my swimmer had appeared three times. Last night the images
of him had played themselves over and over again. His visits were a
puzzle, I was becoming mildly obsessed by them. Perhaps, I thought, I
ought to write a poem about the mysterious way in which he visited
and then vanished. I yawned. I had meant to wake at six, begin working,
but not having managed this all I wanted to do now was sit in the sun.
Miranda was probably right and I needed a holiday. The coffee was lukewarm. Could it be, I frowned, returning to my earlier train of thought,
that I had *imagined* some of it? The facts were few. At some point in the
night the outside light had come on and the bread was missing. That
was all. I had no proof the swimmer had taken it. I had no proof that
he had come into the house, even. I glanced at Jack, but he was concentrating on the map spread out in front of him. My baby brother has a
round, slightly chubby face. Curiously unlined. Empty, Eric always said.
Like a man who could not comprehend what was lost. I yawned, again,
distracted. Hmm, I thought, but had I actually seen the swimmer?

Miranda was looking at me, quizzically.

'You're out of it, aren't you!' she said. 'Would you like me to do the shopping before we go?'

'Oh no, I shall go into town a bit later on.'

Tonight I would try a small experiment.

'We could go through Bury,' Jack was saying. 'On the A14, that's probably the quickest way.'

'Are you sure you won't come with us, Ria?' Miranda asked.

I felt a certain desperation on her part. Fleetingly, I was sorry for her. Neither of us understood the preoccupations of the other.

'My sister lives in a time warp,' Jack declared, to no one in particular.

I ignored him. There was an electronic beeping and he started searching his pockets wildly. Miranda watched, expressionless. When he finally located his phone it had stopped. The air was filled with transparent light.

'Damn,' he said.

I laughed. He was frantically searching through his numbers.

'Damn!' he said, once more.

In his pixelated, globally driven life every eventuality depended on electronic devices. His iPhone, his iPod, his chargers, his cables; modern-day worry beads, all of them. Poor Jack. Was this the only way to survive what had happened to us as children? So no, I didn't want to spend a few days with them on a river.

'What time are you leaving?' I asked, instead.

'We have to pick the boat up by four at the latest, and we've got to find moorings before dark . . . so let's say we leave around eleven?'

I would go shopping, I decided. A delicious sense of freedom brought on by their imminent departure spread over me. And I would buy bread.

By midday the house was mine again. The silence settled slowly like dust on the sunlit surface of the furniture. I tidied the detritus of the last few days in a desultory, half-hearted way, and went out. Orford is much smaller than Aldeburgh, a village really, with one main street. In reality it is an island, surrounded by marshland and the estuary running into the sea. For the past two years the heavy rains have brought extensive flooding to the area and house prices were going into a decline. Those who could had begun to move away. Others, like me, who chose to live close to the river, kept a supply of sandbags at the ready for the next deluge. As Orford has no tourist attractions it seldom gets crowded even at the height of summer. The smart London visitors come for the festivals and are interested only in Aldeburgh. They hardly ever venture as far as us. Which suits the xenophobic residents of Orford perfectly.

I went to the fishmonger's and picked up the fresh crab I had ordered. The greengrocer was selling samphire and watercress, so I bought some. Next I went to the bakery. I bought a loaf of bread, hesitated for only a moment and bought some scones.

'Your family's arrived, I see,' Eileen said.

I nodded.

'How's the politics?' she asked.

I frowned. Jack's semi-right-wing political party was of no interest to me. Eileen's face was studiedly blank.

'He thinks we should stop campaigning against the developers building the marina.'

If the marina and the proposed block of flats alongside the riverbank were built, apart from the flood risk they would face, the lanes in Orford would become completely clogged with cars.

'Oh, does he!' I said.

So Jack was talking to the locals now, was he? Poking his nose into things that were nothing to do with him.

'Don't worry. The builders won't get permission,' I said.

I didn't tell Eileen, but I had written a piece for the local newspaper on the subject. So far, it didn't look as though they would run it. The circus and the assault that had followed used up all available column inches.

Eileen packed up my scones. She nodded a little grimly, I thought. Then she slipped a pot of cream into the bag. I knew she would talk about me later. Everyone in Orford is like that. The landscape collects conversations as effectively as a bucket. I have known most of the people here since I was a child. They all know what happened to us. They know about our fight over the ownership of the house, and that I had come back to bury my secrets. I knew there were those who thought of me as the woman who had everything; there were others who felt sorry for me, but in either case I no longer encouraged friendship. In my experience, those who extended the hand of friendliness usually gave out private information at the drop of a hat and I trusted no one.

'The children have grown a lot,' she ventured, and I agreed, they had.

It was one o'clock. I bought some apples and a small pork pie and drove across the bridge to the other side of the riverbank in the direction of Orford Ness. When I was a teenager I used to sit for hours staring at this shingle desert of military ruin. The horizon remains the same through one hundred and eighty degrees. I used to love its other-worldliness. From here it is possible to catch a glimpse of Eel House as a faint smudge in the distance. Over time, the National Trust volunteers had grown used to seeing me sitting on the edge of its desert-like landscape, lost in thought.

The sun had become very hot while I walked and, because of the lack of rain, the marshland had taken on a brittle aspect. The smell of rotting vegetation in the dykes mingled with a drift of sea-air. All around me the reeds gave off a dry, hollow sound. By now I was lightheaded with hunger and something else. There was a strange suppressed anticipation in the air. At the edge of the marshes, there was a small hollow in the ground where I always sat and slipping into it now I ate my lunch. Silence stretched in every direction across the cloudless East Anglian sky. I watched a couple of waders fishing in the stagnant pools that had spread out from the river. Overhead a few gulls sailed confidently on the air. A fly buzzed in my ear and I could hear the faint sounds of crickets. Slowly, hardly aware of what I was doing, I closed my eyes.

I must have been asleep for ages, for when I woke the sun had moved lower in the sky. My face felt burnt and I suddenly remembered the food in the hot boot of the car. It was three o'clock. Hastily I retraced my steps and drove back. I was beginning to feel slightly sick and hoped I had not got sunstroke. At home I made myself a large mug of tea. Then I went into my study and worked with a solid concentration and an enormous sense of relief. For two years I had been working on a collection of poems. Working and re-working, trying to find the clear stanza that stands for a lorry-load of elaborate prose. The collection was about water and the way memory travels through it. I had wanted a high, pure sound, an elegiac note, of life poised between two states. My past and all it represented was what interested me most, but I had been stuck for months and the collection had got nowhere. This afternoon, as I rewrote some of the clumsier passages, a sense of calm began to break over me. I worked solidly for nearly three hours. When I finished, my headache had gone and it was seven o'clock. Going downstairs I made a salad. At seven thirty Miranda rang. They had arrived to find the boat was as enormous as a double-decker bus.

'Jack can hardly steer it,' she laughed. 'And he's in a terrible mood, but the kids are pleased because they each have their own bathroom!'

'How large is it?' I asked.

'Well, the only boat available was one that sleeps twelve. So what could we do, having got here!'

'We've only just managed to find a mooring,' Jack said, taking the phone off her. 'Miranda is hopeless. What . . . shut up, Zach, I'm speaking.'

His voice broke up slightly.

'I can't hear you,' I shouted, wanting to laugh with relief that he was so far away.

'. . . but unfortunately it's on the furthest bank with no access to the towpath. So we can't get off and go to any of the restaurants on the other side. If Eel House wasn't so uninhabitable we wouldn't have had to come to this bloody place.'

Suddenly I lost it.

'What d'you mean, Jack? You didn't have to come, you know what it's like here. Why didn't you have a holiday somewhere else, instead?'

'Fine,' Jack said, very clearly. 'We won't bother, next year.'

'Stop it, you two,' Miranda shouted. 'We've frozen chips, beef burgers, Coke and a bottle of whisky. We could have some fun, if we tried, you know?'

Outside, a spectacular sunset was unfolding and I felt the satisfied tiredness of having done a good day's work. Miranda's voice came over faintly.

'We've got the boat for an extra week, if we want it.'

I heard Jack say something in the background. Something in me snapped. I was fed up with his rudeness. He talked to me in the same way my mother used to.

They rang off, with Miranda still trying to smooth things over, and I went back to preparing my supper. In the years since my mother's death I had become a different kind of person. There had been a time when my mother's constant stream of boyfriends invading my privacy, and Jack's pushiness, would have reduced me to a state of desperation. I had wanted a life of my own, then, away from them both. I had wanted someone to share things with, as only my father had done. Now that was all over. I no longer had anything to share and I was relieved to discover that the desire for belonging had finally gone.

The last rays of the sun caught the windowpanes as I cooked my pasta and dressed it lightly with olive oil. A sentence was threading through my head. It ran like music, rising and falling. Suddenly I needed to write it down. Covering the pasta, I quickly went upstairs and sat at my desk. In the last-nights-of-summer darkness that arrived more swiftly each evening, hardly daring to breathe lest I lose it, I sat absorbed for another two hours. The effortless ease with which I worked told me that *this* poem was going to be perfect, and as I wrote I smelt the drift of roses coming in through the window. A blackbird sang and sang again, the sun set and night descended while I remained absorbed.

When I had finished the rough draft I put on a CD. Then, sitting by the window, listening to Verdi, I fell asleep for the second time that day. I had completely forgotten about my swimmer of course and my plan to catch him in the act of stealing. Once again it was after midnight when I woke. The Verdi had long finished. The garden was completely silent, there was no moon tonight as I opened the window and breathed in the scent of newly opened jasmine flowers. The river glinted now and then. The starless sky made it impossible to distinguish water from garden. Nothing moved, there was no sound. I felt a small nudge of disappointment as the church clock struck one. The house next door was closed. Either the renters were asleep or they were out again. Well, that was that, I thought ruefully, aware of some disappointment. It was a simple enough explanation. A passing youth had decided to cool off by swimming upstream and then had discovered the house. Perhaps he had been on his way back from the pub, perhaps someone had even dared him, so that, in a moment of bravado, he had wandered in and stolen a loaf of bread. As I was the subject of some curiosity in Orford, what could I expect? Lucky he didn't take anything valuable, I thought, pulling a face. Better lock the back door. The bare skeleton of the poem still glowed inside me. At least the swimmer's appearance had given me the kick-start I needed. Reaching for the catch, I was about to close the window when I froze in my tracks. Someone was playing the piano downstairs with the soft pedal down.

The back of my neck went cold. I stood confused, staring into the darkness. Jack, the only person I knew who could play the piano, was miles away, moored up on the Broads. And Jack didn't play jazz. The music went on and on, faint and familiar, jauntily inviting me to move in time to it. There was a small delicious run of notes and then it came to an abrupt end. I heard the lid come down, followed by footsteps going out into the hall. The kitchen door opened and shut gently. Moments later the outside light came on. Instantly I was galvanised and rushed downstairs. But when I reached the back door the garden was in darkness once more. I switched on the light. The kitchen was exactly as I left it, the pasta was still covered, the bread was in the bin and the forgotten bag of scones stood untouched on the work surface. Exasperated I went into the sitting room but the piano remained as it always had and it was then, at that moment, staring at the music on the stand, that I remembered there had been a piece of sheet music on the floor two days before. Without another thought I rushed to the front door and opened it, going swiftly around to the back of the garden. All was silent. No footprints on the grass, no rose petals fallen off the bushes, nothing had been disturbed. I felt sure the swimmer had not used the river path tonight. I waited, uncertain. Suddenly, realising how vulnerable I was, and with my fearlessness now tinged with a vague dissatisfaction, I went indoors. The rest of the night stretched ahead of me. I knew I would not sleep so, making a pot of tea, I sat down to make a plan.

*   *   *

My plans were all in vain. The following evening there was a thunder-storm of spectacular proportions. I suppose it had been building up to this with all the heat. Lightning flashed and rain fell heavily. It went on for hours. Miranda rang during the worst of it.

'Can you hear it?' I asked.

'Sort of. It's lovely here. We've had a busy day. Zach has got the hang of steering and won't let anyone take a turn! So he and Jack argue all the time.'

She sounded a little drunk.

'Did you manage to buy food?'

'Oh yes,' she said vaguely.

I could hear her sipping her wine.

She rang off and I wandered restlessly around the house, unable to settle to any work. I found myself going towards the piano and staring at the closed lid.

'What's wrong with me?' I muttered.

Maybe I had overworked myself last night. The draft of the poem I had written in an alcoholic haze wasn't quite right yet. What had seemed luminous and neat in the darkness was a little clumsy. I would have to work on it much more. Perfection did not come without pain, but I wasn't in the mood tonight.

After about an hour the rain began to ease off and the air cooled slightly. I shivered and threw on a cardigan. It was not the weather for swimming. Pouring myself a generous glass of wine I went back up to my study where force of habit made me drift towards the window. I was still struggling with an idea. This long overdue collection of poems was turning out to be about the absence of parental love. I stared towards the dark point where the water flowed. Bitterness had stopped me from writing objectively, I thought. Then, perhaps because of the peculiar mood I was in, for the first time in many years I began to go over what had happened in that single most significant moment of my life.

I was ten years old and the school summer holidays had arrived. My father was due to have a small operation. Six-year-old Jack and I were sent to Eel House. This very room had been my bedroom, then. In those days, when the farm was at the height of its productivity, an extra pair of hands at harvest was always welcome. We kissed our parents goodbye. My father was going to the hospital the following morning and with us away my mother would be free to nurse him back to health. I remember them standing on the step waving.

'Look after Jack,' my mother called, anxious as always about her darling son.

'Don't forget to write, Ria,' my father said, his smile going all the way up to his eyes.

He had the bluest of eyes, like a shimmer of cornflowers. The sunlight on them seemed to sharpen their colour. I have inherited their brightness. Jack has brown eyes like my mother. At Saxmundham station, Uncle Clifford was there to meet us. He was older than Dad, more serious, quieter. Both Jack and I were very fond of him.

All through that long holiday my brother and I played by the river and helped out in the fields. I wrote home twice but was told there was a postal strike so no letter came back. My mother rang several times, but on each occasion we were either out playing or at Eric's farm for supper. Several times during those weeks he took us out in his boat to set the eel-traps and once or twice, very early in the morning before the sun was up, we went to check the baskets.

There came a night, one that remains very clearly in my memory, when for some unknown reason my uncle and aunt insisted we stay over with Eric and his wife Peggy. They seemed upset. Eric had looked a little subdued too. We could go with him on another early jaunt upriver, he said. Jack was excited but I remember I didn't want to go, and the next morning I caught a glimpse of our uncle and aunt driving off in the direction of town.

'Where are they going?' I asked, puzzled, but Eric had his face turned away and didn't hear me.

The weather continued to hold, the land grew rosy and then golden in the heat. Jack and I lost our pasty look and turned a gentle nut-brown. We had taken to running around in our bare feet and even Aunt Elsa didn't try to stop us. Preoccupied with worries of their own, both our uncle and aunt left us to our own devices. From time to time, in the weeks that followed, as we loitered in the overgrown country lanes in search of treasures, or took our kites to the beach, I wondered vaguely what was the matter with them, but then forgot about it. Suddenly one morning my aunt woke me with a grim look on her face.

'Your mother wants you back,' she said shortly.

'When?' I asked.

'Why?' was Jack's predictable reaction.

Uncle Clifford had brought the car round already. Our aunt, I saw with surprise, had even packed our bags in the night.

'But I don't want to go,' Jack wailed. 'I don't want to go back to school.'

I knew school wasn't for a few more weeks. Something about my aunt's mood alarmed me.

'What's wrong?' I asked, but she shook her head and looked away.

I knew she didn't like my mother. Probably they had had a row, I decided. We rushed to wash and have some breakfast. By now I was a little uneasy and Jack was in a bad mood. We had arranged to go to Orford that day and have a kite-flying competition with my friend Heather. I remember Jack howling and refusing to put his shoes on. He loved Heather and was bitterly disappointed.

'Be a good boy, darling,' my aunt said, bending to do them up.

She mumbled something about growing up, but wouldn't say more. Then, just as we were getting into the car, she ran out and gave us each a fierce hug, after which she held me at arm's length and peered hard at me. She looked as if she had been crying.

'Come back, Ria,' she told me softly. 'Whenever you want. This place belongs to you.'

That I hadn't said goodbye to Eric was all I could think as my uncle drove us to the station to board the train bound for London. Our aunt had packed us sandwiches and some of the delicious home-made lemonade we had been drinking all summer long.

The journey home was tedious and we had to change trains twice. The views from our carriage window went slowly from the flat landscape I loved to a grimy build-up of houses and factories. After what seemed like ages we arrived at Liverpool Street and saw our mother waiting for us on the platform.

'Where's Dad?' Jack asked.

'Is he still in hospital?'

'Come on,' Mum said. 'The car is in a twenty-minute space.'

'How's Dad?' I asked when we were in the car, but she was busy negotiating the traffic and didn't answer.

We were home in fifteen minutes.

'I feel sick,' Jack said.

'I told you not to drink all that lemonade,' I scolded, rushing up to the house.

But once in the front door we both came to an abrupt halt for the sitting room was filled with flowers.

'Why are there so many flowers?'

'Where's Dad?'

'Mum?' I asked, suddenly frightened, seeing the look on my mother's face.

She sat down heavily and looked at us both helplessly. Then she grabbed Jack, who squirmed but allowed her to draw him towards her. She was looking at me, fixing me with a look I took to mean that I was in trouble.

'What's wrong, Mum?' I asked.

The pit of my stomach seemed to be falling away. My legs had begun to shake.

'Mum?' I asked again, my voice rising with panic.

There was a fraction of a pause as she drew Jack to her more closely so that he made a small noise of protest.

'Children,' she said, 'I have some bad news. There was a complication with your father's operation. He got peritonitis.'

She stopped and seemed to choke.

'Where is he?' I shouted. 'Mum? Mum?'

'He's dead, Ria,' she said in a small voice. 'We had the funeral last week.' And then she began to cry.

It was how I heard the news of what had happened to my beloved father; on the day that my childhood ended.

* * *

The air had become warmer and the scent of stirred-up earth and grass, and dust after rain, filled it. The sky was rosy once more and in the early twilight a sharp fork of geese flew clacking between the trees, silhouetted now by a watery light. Tomorrow the sun would be high in the sky again, the heat would return for a week or two longer, even though a few autumnal minutes were already wiping away the summer. What lingered was a softness of light. I was just about to reach out for the switch of my table lamp when I saw him. My swimmer! He was much earlier than before, moving slowly across the surface of the water. I stood open-mouthed and astonished. Then I turned silently and let myself out of the kitchen door, rounding the corner of the house before I stopped. The swimmer had reached the bank and was clambering up it. He had his back to me as once again he began to dry himself with his shirt. I stood waiting. Under the darkening summer sky I could see that he was not a local boy. I watched as he shook his dark curly hair and water sprayed out. He had been swimming in his trousers again and now he reached for the shoes he had thrown down in the long grass. He was putting them on when something made him turn slightly. I stood rooted to the spot and watched as, lifting his head, he listened. Then slowly he moved his head and saw me. For a whole minute we stared at each other without speaking. Both of us shocked. He was the first to break the silence, surprising me by holding up his hand, one foot in a shoe. He looked ready to run.

'Excuse me,' he said, in perfect, though accented, English. 'I'm very sorry. Please. I won't do it again.'

I saw he was terrified and in the light fading from the sky I saw that he was also very young.

'It's all right.'

There was a silence. The boy, he was surely no older than eighteen, stood waiting as though he had been stunned.

'I don't mind you using this stretch of river. It isn't private or anything,' I said. 'Just filthy, that's all. And your mother might not be so happy with you swimming in it.'

I was talking to keep him from doing a runner. He continued to stare at me and then he smiled with sudden force and I saw he wasn't so young after all.

'Are you from around here?' I asked.

He shook his head and in one swift movement pulled his wet T-shirt on. I hesitated.

'Did you come into my house last night and play the piano?'

'No . . . I . . . no!'

'I think you did,' I said.

My voice sounded unfamiliar, as if I couldn't breathe properly. I was stalling for time.

'I might have called the police, you know,' I said, conscious of trying to sound amused. 'You might have got into a lot of trouble. Were you going to steal anything?'

What a ridiculous thing to have said! The swimmer shivered. He stood with his head slightly bowed. Silent, reminding me again of the image of the Roman swimmer I had seen in Naples. I hesitated.

'You play the piano well.'

He didn't move.

'Would you like to come in and play it again?'

He said nothing.

'You can, if you like.'

He looked at me full in the face. In the growing twilight I could not see the expression in his eyes but I had the distinct feeling he was sizing me up.

'Are you going to ring for the police?' he asked.

He sounded Indian.

'No,' I said. I looked at him in what I hoped was a stern but friendly and motherly manner. 'Not if you promise you won't steal anything. Where are you from?'

One part of my mind was amazed at the ridiculous nature of this conversation. The swimmer hesitated as if he too were thinking something along these lines. Then he seemed to make up his mind.

'I'm not from here. I'm from Jaffna in Sri Lanka,' he said, and now I could see he was shivering violently and I thought, he's frightened. 'You know where that is?'

A single blackbird trilled a long note into the rain-dampened air.

'Of course,' I said. 'Where the tea comes from. Are you on a visit or a holiday?'

'Neither, miss,' he answered gravely. 'I am a refugee.'

Sitting in my kitchen he told me his story in perfect but halting English. He had come to Russia by plane and then overland in a lorry that had been waiting at a pick-up point along an empty stretch of coast road. The conditions had been cramped, the driver had demanded more money than he had and the journey had been terrible. His name was Ben and he was twenty-five years old. He told me this much while he ate the cold chicken I gave him and drank a glass of beer. The driver of the lorry was an aggressive man. Having taken the last of their money he began dropping people off randomly. It had been Ben's turn halfway along the Unthank Road. It was how he became separated from the people with whom he had travelled from Moscow. Not that they were his friends, but at least he had spent some of the worst hours of the journey with them. Left by the roadside he had walked in circles for five days with no money and no documents, sleeping rough, eating when he could, trying to keep clean. He had been petrified of being picked up by the police. He had heard stories that, if that happened, he would simply be deported. And if he returned to Sri Lanka, he feared he would be killed.

Then he had found a farm and burrowed down in one of the outbuildings. The farmer discovered him one night, but instead of calling the police had offered him the chance to pick sweetcorn. In exchange for a bed and food and, the farmer promised, a work permit. Ben could not believe his luck. This was where he lived for the moment. The work permit hadn't materialised and he had yet to make contact with his mother to tell her that he was safe.

He finished speaking and drained the glass of beer. He had eaten the small amount of food I had put in front of him with ravenous haste. I wondered when he had last had a proper meal. Under the electric light he looked terribly young and vulnerable. It crossed my mind that he might be lying about his age.

'I want to get to London,' he said. 'I want to find proper work.'

'What sort of work?'

'I am a doctor, but because of government restrictions I have never practised . . . well, hardly at all.'

He moved his head rapidly from side to side. I felt he was with-holding something.

'I began working as a nurse in the hospital in Batticlore. Then an opportunity came for me to leave. It was becoming dangerous for Tamil men of my age to stay. The insurgents were rounding them up for their army.'

He paused, looked around the room, taking in his surroundings for the first time.

'So I left.'

The light flickered, distracting him.

'You have a loose connection in your switch,' he said, finally. 'I can fix it for you, if you like.'

I had been listening to him, spellbound, and didn't know what to say.

'I would like to do that . . . as payment for this meal.'

I waved my hand.

'There is no need to pay, it isn't anything, just a little chicken.'

He stood and picked up his plate awkwardly. I had a feeling he was thinking about the stolen bread. In that moment there was within me a stirring of something exciting, something undefined and exotic. Before he could open his mouth to protest, I took the plate from him and put it in the sink.

'But if you want to pay me,' I told him, smiling faintly, 'you could play a little of the jazz you played last night. Without the soft pedal!'

Instantly he lowered his eyes, embarrassed.

'I'm sorry!'

'No, no. I really mean I'd like to hear the piano being played.'

I spoke briskly, turning and leading the way into the sitting room.

When I relive that moment now I am always reminded of a story I once read by Jean Rhys. My swimmer sat gingerly down at the piano. He opened the lid and stared at the notes. Then he placed his hands gently on the keys. I noticed his fingers were long and thin. Confused, there grew in me again the conviction that he was younger than twenty-five. He sat with head bowed, then suddenly he was galvanised into action and he began to play. I am no judge of music, nor have I ever learnt to play the piano, but I was struck by his velvet touch. The piano had not been tuned for years. Apart from the odd occasion when Jack played it, it hadn't been touched.

For nearly an hour I sat listening, spellbound. Ben played as though he was a blind man who had found sight. He played with no music. I suspected he was going through a memorised repertoire and it made me wonder what journey he had passed through to go from someone who knew this kind of music to become a refugee who carried his trainers on his back. He played on and on, gaining confidence, never looking at me, hardly aware of my presence. Some of the pieces were familiar; pieces like 'Honeysuckle Rose' and 'Maybe', others were clearly music from his own country. Then, just when I was beginning to think his supply of jazz was inexhaustible, he turned to something else entirely. A piece of music I was familiar with. Schubert, I thought, uncertainly. I remembered Aunt Elsa used to play it. The melody ran on, hesitant and haunting. He was playing differently. In the light from the lamp I could see his face as he stared across the room and now I had the distinct feeling he was playing for someone beyond me, some invisible presence I knew nothing of. The next moment he bent his head and the music came to an abrupt stop.

'What was that?' I asked, breaking the silence.

He looked at me as though from a great distance.

'Schubert's last sonata,' he said, tiredly. 'Your piano needs tuning. I can tune it for you, if you will let me.'

'In payment!' I teased and unexpectedly he smiled for the second time.

'Yes, in payment. For all the times I used your river and your garden, and . . . I stole a loaf of bread one night.'

I thought of Jack's family, his children who had everything they wanted. I thought of my own comfortable life. It was not the last time I was to think this way.

'You are welcome,' I told him, quietly.

Neither of us knew what to say after that. He stood up and I saw his T-shirt had dried.

'You know the river is polluted, don't you? It isn't what it used to be, years ago.'

'I can dredge it for you, if you like,' he said.

'For payment!' I teased, and now we were both laughing.

He nodded.

'I'd better make sure I cook something really good in that case,' I said.

'There is no need,' he said, perfectly seriously.

We were both assuming he would come back tomorrow. And that was when I noticed he was becoming anxious to be gone.

'I'll start early,' he said. 'Do you have a lawn mower? I could cut the grass by the bank.'

He seemed relieved.

'I can come while it is light,' he said and I understood that he had dreaded sneaking into the garden.

He went swiftly after that, the outside light coming on as he left. I watched from the door. At the top of the drive he turned and I saw him raise his hand in a gesture of farewell. I saw his white T-shirt fluttering through the trees and the next instant he was gone. I stood watching a moment longer before I let out the breath that I had not known I had been holding. The garden was still, the outside light went off and once again I smelt the fragrance of honeysuckle and roses. Summer seemed to linger, the storm might never have occurred. Overhead, the Milky Way stretched like an endless satin ribbon across the darkening sky. For no reason at all, I felt inexplicably, deliriously happy.

3

THURSDAY, AUGUST 25TH. EARLY MORNING SUNLIGHT is best. I wasted it by oversleeping but awoke refreshed and filled with energy. Lying in bed like a hostess planning a dinner party, I decided my day's activities. First a trip to the fishmonger in Aldeburgh. The sun streamed in through the cracks in the shutters; I knew that when I opened them, they would reveal a blue sky. A seagull called faintly. Today was for work, I decided, with sudden optimism. With a flash of certainty I saw how my collection of poems might shape out. Ideas that seemed to have been unanchored for most of my life floated towards me. Traces of my father's presence nudged me. I had swum in apathy for years but now possibilities spread their wings. I would begin again. Getting out of bed, humming to myself, I went into the bathroom. From outside the window the green hinge of summer opened, wide and seductive, while beyond the river the fields were a smudge of blue flowers. I showered and went downstairs, drank a coffee swiftly and went to fetch the car.

I drove fast with the smell of the sea threading my thoughts. The circus that had been in town a few days earlier had gone now, leaving a slight sense of unease. There were a couple of policeman walking on the beach which was otherwise empty of people. As yet no one had been charged with the attack on the circus woman. Aldeburgh is a sleepy town caught in a 1940s time warp; there is no pier, no seaside paraphernalia, no marina. Only the shingles, shelving steeply to the water's edge, a few fishing boats and the seagulls. I stopped the car and walked the length of the beach.

On what was to be the last summer of his life, my father had decided to make both Jack and me better swimmers. That summer he had brought us daily to this spot, to plunge us screaming into the water, laughing and shivering as the waves broke over us. Jack had protested and at one point started to cry, but my father had bribed him with the promise of hot chocolate afterwards at his favourite café. I remember hugging Jack as he clung to me but, thanks to Dad, he was now a much better swimmer than I was. On that last day of summer I remember the pebbles we found. I have them still, on the windowsill. Afterwards we visited the bookshop and Dad bought us each a book. Mine was *The Mill on the Floss*. I have it still, inscribed with his message: *To my darling daughter who reminds me so much of Maggie Tulliver.* Today the handwriting remains as fresh as it had looked on the day he wrote the words. In the lonely years that followed I don't know how many times I stared at those words. Looking back, I see how my literary tastes were formed in that little bookshop. We used to always be laughing. Even when we returned home late and my mother was cross with us, Dad had the knack of jollying her out of her bad mood. Often, after his death, when my mother tried first to find another partner and, when that did not work, turned slowly to alcoholism, when Jack went his own way in silent grief, I used to wonder where that summer had vanished. I did not know then what I know now; that a way of life can disappear in an instant.

On that terrible day, after she had broken the shocking news to us, Jack and I went to our respective bedrooms and stayed there in silence until the following morning. Neither knew what the other was thinking; neither cared. We were sealed in shock. It was the beginning of the end of our family, for by the time we emerged through the wall of silence we had changed, for ever. Jack and I would never hug each other again. From now on he was my little brother only in name. I blamed myself. I was the oldest, I should have taken care of him, should have comforted him on that first night, gone to him when I heard him crying. But I did not. A great, terrible tidal wave of grief had engulfed me. I was drowning in it and I had become mute. I wanted my father so desperately, so inarticulately, my heart was so broken, that I simply closed in on myself. I did not cry for years. Funerals are for crying but we had witnessed no funeral. Mother withdrew. She made matters worse by expecting us to act like adults from then on. She stopped shouting at us, stopped telling us what we should do, letting us go to bed whenever we wanted, quarrel as much as we liked. Suddenly there were no rules. It would be years before I recognised the guilt she felt. By the time we went back to school, a month later, the three of us had formulated a way of circling the empty void of our lives; dead planets around a sun lit by the memory of Dad. There was some money left in a trust fund and a year later, when Jack was seven, my mother used it to send him away to boarding school. Now there was one fewer pair of eyes to reproach her.

It was in that year of living alone with her that I wrote my first poem. Filled with suppressed grief, but also a curious optimism that I now see was more to do with being young than anything else, it reduced my English teacher to tears. She printed it in the school magazine. The headmistress read it and entered it for a national competition where it won second prize. The story was about a fossil that had water poured on it, bringing it back to life to reveal a previous existence. During the writing of the poem I dreamt of my father every night. Mum knew nothing of any of this; even after I won the prize I kept it hidden from her. She had begun to drink and was often drowsy when I got back from school. It was a few more years before I found out that she had fallen out badly with Uncle Clifford, who disapproved of what she had done to us children. She would never visit Eel House again. Meanwhile Jack did well at boarding school. He grew with startling rapidity and took up weightlifting. At the end of his first year he came home for the summer just as we had to have our cat Salt put to sleep. I remember he came with us to the vet. There were dogs being restrained by their owners and cats that howled. Jack and I sat on either side of our mother waiting our turn. The room smelt of disinfectant and damp dog. We did not speak. The vet came out and recognised us.

'Hello, my dear,' she said, and she put her arm around my mother.

I could see my mother beginning to cry. The vet took us into the back and took Salt out. Then the vet began stroking her. Hurry up, I thought. Get on with it. Our mother began a long story about Salt's life and what a character he was and how she was going to miss him. When the vet gave him the injection, Mum stood stroking him and sobbing so loudly that I thought everyone in the waiting room would hear her.

'Give your poor mum a hug,' the vet told me.

I swear there was disapproval in her voice. Jack was examining a chart on the wall. Throughout the whole business he had whistled softly, under his breath. Later, I caught him in the garden pouring boiling water on to a line of ants.

'Look,' he said, when he saw me, 'come and see how they're struggling.'

And he laughed in a voice that was already beginning to deepen.

The changes in Jack were unnerving. He began to look more and more like Dad, but there the resemblance ended. He would fly into sudden, violent rages that erupted for no reason at all, which Mum ignored and which terrified the other children he played with. One day a neighbour called round. Jack, who knew the neighbour's disabled son, had tampered with the brakes of the boy's wheelchair. It had rolled on to the road with the boy still in it. Luckily, there had been no cars and someone had come to his rescue.

'He might have been killed,' the neighbour said.

'You've no proof it was Jack,' my mother said, feebly.

'I know it was Jack,' the woman insisted. 'I don't want him coming round again, Mrs Robinson. I'm sorry. I know your family has had a lot to deal with. I think you should get your children to see a counsellor, perhaps?'

Jack was hiding upstairs.

'Did you?' I hissed.

In answer he kicked me. Downstairs there were raised voices.

'Just look at them,' the woman was saying. 'Can't you see how disturbed they are?'

I remember I was far more shocked than Mum, but when I tried to talk to her she became vague and would not look at me. Something had gone terribly wrong with us all and there was nothing I could do about it. In hindsight, this was when I noticed how Jack loved to simultaneously bully and be kind to me. What I didn't know was that everyone at school was frightened of him too and that my mother received letter after letter of complaint about his behaviour from the head teacher. This was something that came out much later.

We lived with our individual preoccupations in this way while all the time our collective skeleton languished in a hidden cupboard. In the end, the sea at Aldeburgh saved me. When I was fourteen I went back to Eel House, and my uncle's farm. I went back without Jack. He was spending the summer with friends from school, living a different existence with a different family. Who could blame him? Secretly I was glad to have the place to myself. My life had not so much gone downhill as stagnated. When I arrived another shock awaited me. Both Aunt Elsa and Uncle Clifford seemed to have aged terribly. None of us mentioned Dad. It was as if my father had never existed. On one rare occasion, after a particular angry phone call to my mother, my uncle told me gruffly that although Mum had behaved disgracefully he believed I would find it in me to forgive her one day. I said nothing. I was already hating my mother in a way that was beyond speech.

It was Eric who eventually talked to me about what had happened. All through the summer when I was fourteen we would go out eeling while my uncle grumbled that he wanted to make me a farmer not a fisherman. Eels were Eric's passion. We would go out in his boat on the hot summer nights, mooring up in places where the water curled around the base of a willow tree. Then, after we had eaten the delicious supper of fresh fish he had cooked on his little camping gas stove, Eric would tell me eel stories. It was he who introduced me to the Sargasso Sea.

'Imagine, Ria,' he would say, 'a sea without shores, without waves, without currents. That's the Sargasso for you!'

I listened mesmerised as he talked about a place of utter darkness, where starfish and sea cucumbers crept. My imagination was
fired by a place full of weed-harbouring monsters.

'The eels swim there, Ria,' he told me. 'They are programmed to
swim three thousand miles in order to remain faithful to their
ancestral life in the matter of reproduction!'

I had no idea what he was talking about, but the stories fascinated
me, nonetheless.

'And then,' Eric said, getting into his stride, 'after they finish repro-
ducing, spent and exhausted, far away from home, the fire of life
goes out of them and they die. That's life, Ria.'

We would sit staring at the night sky with its Milky Way running in
a silent ribbon above us. And it was on such a night as this, without
fanfare or fuss, that he began to talk about my father's death. The
conversation slipped in easily like oars dipping into the water. All conversations with Eric were like that. He told me that death, whenever it
came, was always sudden, always a shock. You could not prepare
for it, he said, no matter how hard you tried.

'Your Ma was only trying to protect you both,' he said. 'She wasn't
being wicked, just foolish, maybe. We're all foolish at some point or
other. Don't listen to other folks.'

We sat in companionable silence. For the briefest of moments I
felt a kind of peace.

'How's Jack been?' he asked, finally.

I shrugged and Eric looked at me sharply.

'You're both out there in the dark, aren't you? It's too much for
you to have to deal with on your own.'

Then he talked of other things too. He told me about the brother
he had lost years before and he told me that having been born on
the farm meant his roots were firmly buried in this little patch of
land.

'The land you are born on is so important, Ria,' he said. 'People
take it for granted these days because travel is so easy. But it never
was in my day and I have never wanted to be anywhere else.'

I had no idea how old he was.

'You'll come back, luv, when you've grown,' he said, nodding his head, certain. 'Your dad loved it here and this place belongs to you, you'll see.'

I nearly began to cry but I took a deep breath and looked at my hands and then the tears went away again. Only the lump in my chest stayed where it was and I remember thinking I would have to learn to breathe with it always there.

One day Eric gave me a photograph that my father had taken of me. In it I was sitting on the steps at the back of Eric's farm, holding a doll. I must have been about five at the time, because I still had my hair in long blonde plaits. Later, as an adult, I had the photograph enlarged. It sits on my desk now, that figure of a little girl, smiling up at the sun with her father's shadow across her face.

'He'll always be with you, Ria,' Eric told me, busying himself with his eel-traps. 'You mustn't fret. Time is the famous healer.'

As I grew older, even after I moved away from him, and first my aunt and then my uncle died, it was Eric I loved the most. When the will was read and it turned out that the house had been left to me, it was Eric who wrote first.

I love Eric. Always in the background of my life, his presence nevertheless underpins it completely.

I had walked the length of the beach and was now on Main Street. This stretch never fails to remind me of those long, lonely years after Dad's death. I was going to call them the barren years, but in fact barrenness came later. The breeze blew unstoppable and fresh, straight off the North Sea. Today it was warm, but in winter it could be very cruel. I bought my fish and returned home.

Looking back, that day proved to be one of the most productive of the summer. I finished the poem and later even managed to do a bit of weeding in my vegetable patch. The sun had given my tomatoes an intensity of flavour. I picked a few and some runner beans, too. I decided to grill the fish with dill and parsley. It was all planned. The basil-soaked olive oil, the fresh bread. The pudding was to be apricots, halved and stoned and tossed with slices of watermelon and late strawberries in a dressing of my own invention. I had a bottle of wine chilling in the fridge but then, remembering how my swimmer had drunk his beer so thirstily, I put the last of Jack's cans to cool. I was excited. It was years since I had cooked for a man. At six o'clock the phone rang. It was Heather. I sighed. Heather is my only friend left in Orford. As a child, Heather hated her own mother. She used to want to be part of our family and our mother was very fond of her. Later, when everything went cold at home, Heather would still sometimes visit us. Occasionally she even used to cook for us, making cakes that she knew Mum and Jack liked, fussing over them and bringing presents from the farm. I remember after one such visit Mum saying Heather should have been her daughter. I think I stopped believing that Heather was my special friend after that.

'How's the visit going?' she asked me now.

Heather knew all about Jack. She knew I dreaded these annual visits and she knew about the long-running battle over Eel House.

'They've gone away for a few days.'

Instantly I regretted telling her.

'Poor Jack,' she said. 'Have you driven him away?'

'Of course, not!'

I was back on the defensive.

'How about supper over here, then?'

'I'd rather not, if you don't mind. I haven't done any work for ages and I'm on a roll now.'

'Of course, of course . . . um . . . well, never mind . . .'

She made a sound as if she was gulping down some food and all the irritations of the past few days gathered in me. I could tell she was hurt by my refusal of dinner. The hurt was constantly in her voice and the more she tried to hide it, the more distant I became towards her. But, I suppose living alone had made me waspish.

Why am I friends with Heather? When we were children her parents ran the farm on the other side of Orford, along the Unthank Road, the unfashionable side of town. We met each summer but then, after Dad died, apart from the odd visit, we went our separate ways, I to Cambridge and Heather into marriage to a difficult man, another farmer. She had three children in quick succession. The process aged her. We kept in touch spasmodically, but never met up again until my mother died. Then she tried to resurrect the friendship with the absence of the years lying unspoken between us. As a reunion, it was not successful. Mother had just died after a long and rambling descent into dementia. I had been the one to look after her, until Ant put a stop to that and I was forced to put her into a home. More guilt. The transfer killed her; of that I remain certain. We had about two months before the end when I tried belatedly and unsuccessfully to address the past, and then she died. Heather came to the funeral and fussed over Jack even though he had done nothing for Mother for years. She blamed me for the feud over Eel House, telling me that, as we only had each other now, I should try to sort out our differences. I never forgot that remark, made on the steps of the crematorium.

'Try to understand him, Ria,' she had said, in her kindly voice.

I had been too shocked to defend myself. Looking at Jack's handsome face, I suspected him of complaining about me. I never really forgave her after that.

These days, now that her children have grown up and left home, Heather has drifted away from her monosyllabic husband and started throwing herself into local politics. She has a large circle of acquaintances to whom, when I first arrived in Orford, she introduced me. I think she hoped I would meet a suitable man. It was kind, but the ploy didn't work. Neither her male friends nor I were interested. After a while she gave up and we continued our lukewarm relationship, regardless. The trick of intimacy evaded us both.

There was a short, awkward pause.

'Did you get the local paper?' she asked.

'No, I forgot. Why?'

'You know about the calves that were killed?'

'Probably a fox,' I said.

'A fox can't slit throats,' Heather said quickly. 'Anyway there's been an attack at the circus. Did you hear about that?'

'You think it's related?'

Heather loved a good crime story. In this, as in so many other things, she and my mother were similar.

'Of course! The woman's passport was stolen, you know.'

'So? What are you saying?'

'Well, obviously it's worrying. Clem has become paranoid. He thinks there are terrorists in Suffolk. Muslim terrorists!'

Clem was the husband. Paranoia was his speciality. I laughed.

'So the terrorists go around slitting up animals? What for? Doesn't make sense.'

She was silent.

'Yes, I agree. So what are you doing this evening?' she changed the subject.

I had the feeling she wanted to catch me out, and this both annoyed and made me nervous.

'I'm really exhausted, Heather. And I simply *must* work.'

She rang off a few minutes later, her disappointment hovering like cigarette smoke in the air. To dispel it, I tuned in to the local radio station. There was nothing new. They were still talking about the animals that had been found with their throats slit. There was also speculation that the woman who was attacked had been part of a drugs ring. There was no mention of Heather's terrorist theory. I went back to my cooking.

My swimmer arrived just as I was pouring a glass of wine. The halibut, creamy white and melting at the touch, was almost cooked. He entered the kitchen silently, lifting up the latch. With the practised hand of a burglar, was my first ironic thought. He was wearing a clean T-shirt and had a folded piece of paper in his hand.

'I have brought some music,' he announced.

I could see straight away that he was keen to play the piano, so I took him into the drawing room. As I set the table in the garden, music drifted out through the open window like wisps of scent. All my irritation over Heather, the vague anxiety she had induced in me, evaporated instantly as I listened to Ben playing French jazz and managing somehow to make the piano sound both unfamiliar and mellow. Confused, I felt the light from this summer evening fall sweetly through the tangle of trees. Roses bloomed. I stared at the old garden table set for two and, as if on cue, the phone rang, and rang again, insistently. The music faltered, almost stopped, then continued regardless as I hurried into the kitchen and closed the door. I picked up the handset and moved towards the small scullery.

'Yes, yes, I'm fine. I was listening to some music,' I said.

'You're out of breath,' Miranda remarked.

I took a deep breath.

'I didn't hear you ring,' I said as calmly as I could. 'Are you having a nice time?'

The piano stopped and I heard footsteps approaching the kitchen but Miranda was still talking. I suspected she was trying to make amends for Jack's brusqueness, but I could have done without it just at the moment. On and on she went; how wonderful the weather was, how dreadful the children were, how they squabbled, how crowded the Broads were, the ghastly day-trippers. I listened, saying as little as I could, not wanting to prolong the conversation, wanting her to finish.

'Jack's meeting someone in the pub,' she said. 'Honestly, Ria, sometimes I think he's trying to take over the world!'

I had no idea what she was talking about.

'You know what he said this morning? How nice it was not to see any black faces on the Broads!'

I felt my jaw tighten but managed to say nothing. Finally, thankfully, she rang off. My hands were sweating.

Ben was sitting quietly at the kitchen table, waiting for me.

'If you give me a screwdriver I'll fix your light,' he said.

'That was my brother and his wife on the phone.'

There was a pause.

'You don't like them?'

'Oh no,' I said. 'It's not that . . .'

I was rummaging for a screwdriver and when I turned around he was staring at me with a puzzled look. I was aware of the velvet brownness of his eyes. I looked away abruptly.

'Actually, you're right,' I said. 'I don't much get on with him. We are . . . quite different.'

He nodded and said no more, just fixed my light.

Later, as we lingered over the halibut, I asked him tentatively about himself. How had he learnt to play the piano so well? The last light flickered on the leaves. I felt detached as though a part of me had been severed sharply from my body. The evening drew together as he spoke.

'In my town, before I left,' he said, 'people were nice to me. They told me I had a talent.'

He shook the hair from his eyes and smiled. He needs a haircut, I thought.

'They said it sadly, as if they were really thinking, What a pity he'll never get anywhere in this place. He's just a Tamil boy. There are thousands of them.'

'Is that why you left?'

Again he shook his head. He had left, he told me, because of the war. Why else would anyone want to leave their home?

'I am the only child of my mother,' he said. 'I have two cousins from my father's side of the family. The cousin closest to me in age was in the year above me at medical school. One day he was asked to leave his course. We think it was because someone saw him talking to a journalist. After that, he worked as a male nurse at the hospital. No one dared teach him any more.'

Ben paused and sipped his beer. I waited. His eyes had darkened.

'One morning, my cousin went to the hospital to work as usual. He didn't know the army had arrived to begin an offensive in the area. As he cycled up to the entrance, an army officer shouted to him to stop. So he stopped and started taking out his ID. The officer shouted at him to raise his arms above his head. My cousin tried to get his hand out of his pocket but wasn't quick enough and the soldier shot him in the face. At point-blank range. Some of his friends saw it happen.'

Ben stopped speaking and for an immeasurable moment the evening too became suspended in the spaces left by his words. I felt a small shock, like electricity, jolt through me.

'At the same time this was happening, my cousin's younger brother was at school. He knew nothing about it. An air raid started and planes began dropping bombs. No one had been able to get a message to my uncle's house after the shooting. My aunt still had no idea her eldest son was dead. The head teacher at the school told the children to leave the building. The teacher decided to take them out the back way into the countryside, where he thought it would be safer. He urged them to go quietly and quickly, with him walking ahead and the children following in single file. But an army helicopter spotted them and started firing. The children broke into a run, heading for cover. My little cousin was the smallest child. He couldn't keep up with the others. The teacher was screaming at them to hurry, but my cousin slipped. He must have been petrified. He was hit. They left him where he had fallen and when the air raid was over the teacher went back and found him. He was not dead. But when they brought him to my uncle's house, he was senseless and this is how he has remained. I don't think he will recover, and my aunt has lost her mind.'

Shocked, I didn't know what to say. Remnants of food lay on the plates.

'And you?' I asked, finally.

He nodded and finished his beer. I had no more left, so I offered him a glass of wine instead. When he smiled his thanks a small dimple appeared in his cheek.

'I am a qualified doctor,' he said. 'I trained during the short space when they dropped the restrictions, but after what happened my mother didn't want me to stay in Sri Lanka. I had witnessed too many things. I knew how the innocent civilians were treated, how medical aid was withheld from the hospital doctors. I witnessed the way children had their limbs amputated, without anaesthetic, using only a kitchen knife. I had seen too much and because of this our family was marked. It wasn't easy for me to leave. There were money difficulties too.'

He hesitated.

'It cost twenty thousand euros for the flight to Moscow. Then another ten thousand for the overland trip by lorry.'

I was staring at him. What he was telling me seemed disconnected from what he was: a refugee-medic who played French jazz. And now, he told me, he would wait for asylum status. He had applied to the Home Office, two weeks ago.

'They haven't replied yet,' he said. 'I don't know how long it takes.'

He sounded confident and I wondered why it hadn't occurred to him that his application might be rejected or that he ought to plan for that eventuality. I began asking him.

'Have you actually *been* to the Home Office?'

He shook his head. I felt he didn't want to discuss it. The farmer had sent the letter in for him, Ben said. The same farmer who was paying him a little cash and letting him sleep in the barn. It was all illegal, of course.

'But how will they contact you?' I asked, puzzled.

It didn't make sense.

'At the farm. The farmer will let me know when the letter arrives.'

'There are centres where you can stay,' I told him, tentatively. 'I think there's one that's opened in Norwich. At least you'd have a proper bed and food.'

'That only happens when you are registered. I have to be patient, to wait.'

There appeared no doubt in his mind that the letter would arrive any day now and meanwhile the only thing he missed was playing the piano. And the chance of a proper shower.

'That is why I try to swim every day.'

'Have you been here a lot, then?' I asked him.

He shook his head sheepishly.

'I have only been coming here for a week,' he admitted. 'Before that I used to bathe in the river further upstream. But it takes longer to get to and there are others there. I wanted some privacy.'

I digested this fact in silence.

'You can come here any time,' I said, finally. 'And play the piano. No, really,' I added, not understanding the look he gave me. 'I would like that!'

I wanted to tell him he could have a shower too, but it seemed too intimate a thing and I had an acute sense of his wariness.

'I would like to clear your garden by the river in exchange. And maybe you would like the grass cut?'

His face became closed. He looked suddenly stubborn. I could see it was necessary for me to accept the offer. Only then did he relax. He told me that he felt as if he had been walking through a page of history. To have his country's history inscribed on him was a disquieting sensation, he said. I was appalled by his matter-of-factness.

'How long have you been here?' I asked.

'It feels like years!'

In fact it had only been about four months. He was moving in some mysterious current of destiny, quite alone, as alone as a man dying, he told me. And travelling with him was the soul of his dead cousin.

'It has been a long journey,' he said softly, folding his hands together, intertwining the fingers. His voice belied the sorrow in the words. His wrists were slender. Once again I began wondering how old he really was when, without warning, he told me another story. That of the journey.

'The air in the lorry was stale. After a while it became difficult to breathe and some of the women started to cry. We were banging on the sides, begging for the driver to stop, begging for air.'

I shuddered. He had sat in this way for hours as day and night became indistinguishable and the miles fell away unnoticed. It felt as if he were travelling through nothing but unbending time. On and on from one horizon to the other. The truth was, he no longer felt in the world.

'I tried to imagine the sea,' he said, shaking his head. 'But it was useless.'

The darkness in the lorry had blanked out every thought except that of trying to breathe. Even his grief at the last glimpse of his mother's face had been blotted out, and in this way he had travelled, across endless land, feeling ever more mortal and insignificant as he went. Like the swimmer he was, he had moved further and further from the shore, until at last he understood the meaning of 'no return'.

'I have crossed a line,' he said. 'Even if my application for asylum fails, I know that I have crossed that line.'

I stared at his young, still unfinished face and saw how his experiences would slip into the fabric of his features. It would happen slowly, unobtrusively at first, but then one day someone would take a photograph and suddenly the change would be noticed.

'There was not a single one of those miles that was not filled with memories,' he said, very softly.

He was frequently conscious of not wanting to die. Which was not the same as wanting to live, he said. Then, just as he had thought he was on the brink of death, the lorry began throwing them out, one by one.

England had come to him in this way. Cold air filled with the smell of seawater. He remembered breathing deeply, thinking he would never again take breathing for granted. And, turning, he had seen the sea and his heart had filled with such longing for his home that he realised why it was considered a sickness. All that first day he had walked, keeping the sea in his sights, never knowing where he was until at last he found himself on the outskirts of a town. He had been the only one of the original group in the lorry who spoke English and he supposed this had saved him, although from what, he did not say. He never found what had happened to the others. He walked all night and finally stumbled on the farm. Now all he wanted was refugee status. The farmer had registered his letter and Ben had kept the proof of postage, along with a copy of the letter itself. I didn't know what to say. It was simply a question of waiting, he told me.

'I'm not able to earn enough money until I get my papers.'

It worried him that his mother knew nothing of his whereabouts. The farmer had given him stamps and paper and he had written home, but he didn't know if the letter had even got to her.

'Look,' I said, swallowing, 'you can have some stamps. Why don't you write, giving this address?'

He glanced at me with a faint smile, shaking his head. Again I sensed an iron stubbornness, lurking.

'You are kind, but you can't do this. You don't know who I am. Let me do those jobs for you, first.'

There was an awkward silence. It was growing dark, he needed to get back, he told me.

'I can't come tomorrow,' he said. 'We're going to the sea to pick samphire. I don't know what time we'll finish.'

I wanted to tell him to be careful of the tides. I had read somewhere there weren't any tides in the Indian Ocean and that people there had no idea of the dangers they brought. But I could say nothing.

'Look,' I said instead, hearing my own voice as it repeated itself, 'come any time you like. I work late. If the light is on, come in. I'll leave the kitchen door open.'

'You don't lock your doors, do you?'

I laughed.

'We wouldn't have met if I had!'

He smiled instantly and I felt another jolt. His smile went on for longer than I had expected, exuding some other kind of life that I had no knowledge of. He rose then, and helped me take the plates into the kitchen as if it was the most natural thing to be doing. This too unnerved me, so I turned my back as I filled the sink with water.

'Thank you,' he said when we had finished the washing up. And then he left.

I watched from the upstairs window as he walked away. The grain tower's black shadow stretched over the earth, far into the fields, and now his shadow moved towards it, joined in and parted again. All of it felt like a dream. I was aware of feeling both transfixed and weary at the same time. And then an inexplicable happiness, seductive and heavy, rose within me for the second time that day. But because of the mysterious suddenness of this emotion, because of the moonlight and the wine, the sense of having witnessed something of his journey, and after my own emotional famine, I was frightened.

Too much too quickly, a voice repeated in my head. Life is not like that.

4

FRIDAY, AUGUST 26TH. TO BEGIN WITH his story kept reverberating in my head and I could not stop thinking of the way he had talked about his home.

'On my last afternoon I noticed all kinds of things,' he had said. 'Things I hadn't cared about until then.'

It was impossible to hide my curiosity.

'What sort of things?'

But he had been unable to say and when pressed spoke reluctantly only of sunlight and how sad it was in the afternoon. He had noticed the way the bats flew out at sunset, two by two, swooping low, and the smell of the hibiscus and, later on, the sounds of the rain on the galvanised roof, thundering on and on before stopping abruptly. The conversation had marked me in the strangest of ways, for all of it was outside my experience. There remained, too, the business of the Home Office. Without telling him I searched the Internet for information, but all I came up with was the government party line; smug, determined and unmovable. Next I discovered other sites protesting against the treatment of illegal immigrants but they too were vague and unhelpful. There was nothing I could do. The truth was I had never taken much notice of the things written about asylum seekers.

On Saturday morning Jack rang unexpectedly. He had decided to extend their stay for another week. He sounded vague.

'How's Miranda?' I asked, but he ignored the question.

From this I suspected he was networking rather than spending time with his family. Same old power-hungry Jack, I thought wearily, party politics even when on holiday.

'Well,' I said, 'try to enjoy the weather, at least.'

He surprised me by laughing. Whatever he was up to had put him in a good mood. For the rest of that day I buried myself in my work. I had woken in the middle of the night with another, newer, poem spilling out. Poetry is for me both a creative and thinking process. Perhaps this is why I am so slow at producing anything. The new poem was, predictably enough, about my swimmer. I worked steadily all morning. At lunchtime I made myself a plate of salad and cheese and went outside with a tray. The sun was at its highest and the garden was hazy and bleached by heat. Once again I walked down towards the river and sat on the bank watching the water.

'We hardly have time to raise our heads when the trains pass,' Ben had said.

An image came suddenly into my mind. I had been on a train on my way up to London as it flashed past a level crossing. Looking up, I had seen the low-lying watercress fields in the distance, caught in a burst of sunlight. A few workers in orange jackets had straightened up to shade their eyes and watch us pass. Somehow I had felt they were all immigrants.

On Sunday I began to feel a little melancholy. It was blisteringly hot and the only fan I possessed was old and rather slow, making more noise than cool air. My poem was going well enough, but the heat made it impossible to concentrate for long. By mid-morning I was exhausted. The hours stretched endlessly ahead and, unusually, I regretted my lack of friends. I stared aimlessly out of the window. On an impulse I decided to go into Aldeburgh, to visit Heather.

The sight of the sea lifted my spirits a little. Ribbons of seaweed threaded the shingles, light refracted on the waves. Ahead on the horizon two white-funnelled boats moved slightly. Across the sparrow-coloured beach, here and there, were buried smooth white stones. I began filling my pockets and a bit further on I found an exquisite seashell washed up by an unknown tide. I stuffed the shell in my pocket. A line kept turning slowly in my head. People of no account, no name, no documents, no graves . . .

Heather was standing in front of her farmhouse, talking to a man as I drove up. Hera, her black Labrador, barked once and bounded towards me.

'Ria! Hello! This is John Ashby,' she called. 'He's a journalist. Maria Robinson, our local celebrity poet!'

I winced.

'Why don't you join us for some tea in the garden, John?'

The man put away his notebook and glanced at me.

'Thank you, but I won't, if you don't mind. I'm due back at the office, really.'

There was a tiny pause. I saw him exchange glances with Heather.

'But many thanks for that info,' he added, nodding at her. 'And I'll be in touch if there's any other news.'

'What's he doing here?' I asked as we went inside.

'Oh, he was just passing,' she said easily. 'Wanted to ask me some questions. I've known John for ages. He used to come and talk to me about the Ipswich murders some years ago. You won't remember them, they were all drug-related. It was when you were with Ant. Come into the kitchen, I'll make a cuppa.'

'What's he trying to solve now?'

Heather looked at me solemnly.

'Well,' she said, her hand hovering over the kettle, 'for a start there's been another dead calf. Did you know that?'

I shook my head. She had an air of slight amusement, I thought.

'Oh, Ria, honestly! You live on another planet. The calf was left on the roadside near one of the farms – not ours, thank God – with a swastika drawn in blood.' She had moved towards me as she spoke and her eyes were round and sparkling. 'So you see!'

'What?'

I was nonplussed.

'Well, first there's the three calves,' she said, ticking them off on her fingers. 'Then there was the woman at the circus with her passport stolen, and now more animals have been killed. It's obvious, isn't it? There must be a terror cell somewhere around here. Like Clem said.'

She's mad, I thought. But at the same time I felt uneasy.

'Why, if there are terrorists around here, would they want to make themselves known by killing animals?'

'I know. That's the missing link. But I'm working on it! I've talked to your brother; he agrees.'

'*Jack?* You've talked to Jack? What? Did you call him on the boat?'

'Well, yes. Why not?'

'Why not? Why not?' I wasn't aware that I had begun to shout. 'Because he's a right-wing fascist. He'll wind you up.' I paused abruptly, then asked, 'Do you often talk to him?'

'Yes,' she said, a little smugly. 'We have, shall we say, certain sympathies.'

I stared at her. Something was stirring at the back of my mind.

'And you shouldn't use such words to describe him.'

I was speechless.

'Oh, Ria, don't look so shocked. Your brother isn't a fascist. He just wants the best for this country. He and I happen to agree on certain issues. It's not so terrible. This country *has* had terrorist attacks; we *do* need to be more vigilant and less trusting. I'm not telling you anything you don't already believe. So why the shock and horror?'

I swallowed. There was something I needed to tell her.

'There's one thing I do know,' I said. 'Jack doesn't *have* any ideology. He's just interested in power. He couldn't care less about this country. He's interested in control. Something got destroyed when Dad died. He functions on . . . he doesn't want . . . he . . .' I couldn't go on.

'Ria, something happened to you both, not just Jack. You're very hard on him. He's a sincere man; I don't think you see your brother for what he is. He's clever and funny and handsome too. I don't think even Miranda understands him,' she added softly.

Astonished, I didn't know what to say. It occurred to me that she had always rather fancied Jack. I remembered her telling me once that she used to write to him when he was at boarding school. She began to slice some ham and bread.

'I hear you've given your cleaner the heave-ho!'

I nodded, feeling deflated. An unresolved thought hovered and then vanished.

'I don't suppose you've eaten, have you?' she asked, then continued before I could answer, 'honestly, Ria, you'll fade away!'

She put everything on a large tray and we went outside. The heat, even under the shade of the tree was stifling. Further away towards the fields the sun fell heavily on the pastures, and the grass was dry and lifeless. It doesn't look in the least like England, I thought. There were beads of perspiration on Heather's face, which she wiped on her napkin, and suddenly I felt sorry for her. Long ago, when we had been children, she had run behind the tractor with me. A slight figure with long legs; she had been my first real friend.

'D'you want some eggs?' she was asking.

Maybe I was too hard on her. Old friends, what did that expression mean? Did we need to have things in common?

'Do you still boil your eggs in the kettle?'

She smiled, and for a second I saw traces of that slender child, but then it was gone again. Well, there had to be someone you shared the past with, to keep it alive, I thought.

'No,' I said. 'God, how long ago did I use to do that?'

Driving back through the shimmering afternoon heat I saw the journalist again. He was sitting in his car with the windows open and his hat down over his eyes. When he heard my car he sat up and stared out of the window. Then he raised his arm. There was something ferret-like about his features that I didn't much like. As I accelerated I saw him open the door of his car and get out. I was certain he was going back in to see Heather.

I was beginning to think I would never see Ben again. On Sunday I stayed up late in the hope he would return for a swim and some supper but there was no sign of him. The renters were packing to leave. Their car was parked in the lane that led up to their house and they were loading it noisily. Perhaps this had put him off, I thought worriedly. Someone had been working the field beyond the river and the scent of hay drifted across the garden. Madame Alfred Carrière, my old white French rose, gave off a trail of fragrance along the back of the house and all around the dry dusk air was filled with muted birdsong. But although the evening presented itself as polished as glass, beautiful and serene, all I felt was an awful sense of loneliness. Pouring myself a gin and tonic I went indoors and turned on the television. Two pigs had been found killed in the same way as the calves, with their throats slit. Local farmers were now seriously worried about their livestock. I was just about to switch channels when the phone rang.

'What are you up to, then?' Miranda asked. 'Everything okay?'

I wondered if she had heard the news.

'Of course. I've been working all day.'

The lie slipped out easily. There was a pause.

'Jack's out at the Six Bells all the time,' she said flatly. 'And tomorrow he wants us to entertain some people on the boat, can you imagine? I'm fed up with him.'

I was alarmed.

'How long are you actually staying for?'

'Not sure really. The kids have made friends so I guess we'll stay for a couple more days. You don't fancy joining us, I suppose?'

'Oh, Miranda, I can't. I'm on a roll with my work. It would be a pity to be distracted.' Again the lie.

But then, after she rang off I could not settle. Suddenly I felt sorry for her. Why was Jack leaving her on her own so much, and what was the real reason that Heather had rung him up? I frowned. All I really wanted was for Ben to reappear. I was being ridiculous, rushing to the window whenever I thought I heard the splash of water. Nothing stirred. There was never anyone there. A burst of singing was followed by laughter from over the hedge. The renters were leaving and the whole world seemed to be enjoying the evening.

That night I slept fitfully and on Monday morning went into Aldeburgh again. Another scorcher lay ahead. The shingles down at the water's edge glittered like brown sugar. The light was almost too painful to bear and the day itself seemed unnatural and useless.

I walked aimlessly. Out at sea a group of fishing boats, some blue, some grey with sails of brilliant white, drifted westwards on an ocean of bright green. The sails sat transparent as wings on the water. I stared. In the splintered, extraordinary light, the whole scene seemed to my dazed eyes to have been conjured up from some foreign place. Perhaps it was time for a change, I thought. I had no ties here, perhaps what I needed was to move abroad, get away, start over again. I could go to Africa, I thought or, I hesitated, I could go to Sri Lanka and work in the war zone. Blushing, I looked around me. Fool! Turning my back on the sea, I returned to the car and drove home, cursing my stupidity.

All that long, hot afternoon I tried and failed to work. So much for the run of creativity, I thought, pouring myself more white wine. Once again someone was disturbing my hard-won peace. Restlessly I kept going over our last conversation. Then, as the afternoon turned into early evening I began to worry that something might have happened to him. The image of the migrant workers in the watercress field recurred and I wondered uneasily if I ought to go over to one of the farms near Unthank and make a few enquiries. I could of course have visited Eric, but Eric would know the instant he saw me the kind of mood I was in, and I didn't want his questions. In any case, I had no clear idea on which farm Ben worked. At six o'clock I poured myself a very large gin, thinking grimly I was drinking far too much. It was the only comfort of the lonely.

'Idiot,' I cried out loud, catching a glimpse of myself in the mirror. 'Stupid cow, what were you hoping for? Did you think you had something in common with a refugee, then? A young man nearly half your age?'

My reflection stared back at me.

'Or was it sex? Is that it? No sex for five years has left you gasping for it, hasn't it?'

I swallowed and my reflection swallowed along with me. I'm going mad, I thought. Solitude had finally begun to unhinge me. Barren and sexless, and now, unhinged. But I want to be touched, I thought, my face hot with the admission. Memories of Ant, of what we had done together, were returning. This way lay insanity, I thought, closing my eyes. Was this the sole reason for my interest in the swimmer? I could not bring myself to say his name. Shame spread across my neck. I was mesmerised by my reflection. When had I become so ugly?

'Why should a man eighteen years younger than you are be interested in having sex with you, Ria?'

There, it was out. Like sickness. I sipped my gin, wanting to weep. When my father died it had been anger I had felt. Cold rage that everyone, my mother included, mistook for a lack of feeling. Actually, I had wanted to kill her. For years the desire had sustained me. Until the discovery of my body's own betrayal. Acceptance had been terrible; harder still was the dead hopelessness that followed. Until finally I was able to fall asleep without weeping. So why had I allowed myself to become unsettled now? Why had I not protected myself better? I sloshed another large gin into my glass and tried not to think about Ant, happily married; with his pretty, empty-headed wife and his twin girls. Last Christmas, tracing me through my publishers, he sent me a card. Printed on it was his e-mail address and a link to his social-networking page. Middle-aged, balding and smug, he had invited me to become one of his friends. Suddenly the thought of it set me laughing. I stood in the kitchen and shook. My life as a farce! That was what I should be writing about. Outside, the garden darkened imperceptibly. A bat swooped low from under the eaves. The invisible wound had not healed. It was seeping blood once more. Perhaps, I thought wildly, perhaps I could pay him for sex! The idea seemed hilarious. Oh God! I thought.

I was sitting at the kitchen table and did not hear the step or see the shadow that fell across the flagstone floor.

'Why are you crying?'

Ben had entered silently and was standing over me. I started and he thrust something at me.

'This is for you,' he said. 'I have been collecting for some time and I didn't know what to do with them.'

Caught off guard, I could only stare. He was holding a brown paper bag.

'There was no one to give them to, but I kept finding more. So now I would like you to have them.'

He went on looking at me, his face unsmiling and anxious, as though he had done something wrong, or had been caught out. Fleetingly confused, I imagined it was how he looked when his mother had told him off as a child.

'Why are you crying?' he asked again, with a puzzled frown.

He had looked this way when I had caught him swimming. I wiped my eyes.

'What is it?' I asked, faintly. 'Why don't you sit down?'

'Open it,' he said. 'Carefully.'

Some geese flew overhead with a slow sawing like rusty blades. I undid the paper. Inside was a string of broken bird's eggs, about thirty of them, blue and white and scribbled and speckled brown, reminding me of a rhyme we used to sing as children. I gasped. God knows how I looked with my eyes brimming over and my mouth slackened and out of control. The shells were strung together into a necklace, graded by colour. They were utterly beautiful.

'Do you like it?'

'Where on earth did you find them?'

He shrugged.

'If you look, wherever you walk there are broken things lying on the ground.'

He did not take eggs from nests, he told me, only those that had already fallen and were broken.

'I have been collecting them ever since I left Sri Lanka. There were several on the grass verge when we stopped in Russia. The rest I found here. So I thought, why not? And I began to collect them again.'

He had always collected things, from when he had been a boy. But whereas in the past he had given his collections to his mother, or later on to his friend, now there was no one to give them to.

'Until I met you,' he said seriously.

When he had been a boy he had loved wandering across the fields at the back of his home. Collecting was part of preserving memory, he told me.

'There was a canal near our house. When I came home after school I would find all sorts of things: small animals caught in traps, birds that had damaged wings . . .'

He would bring them home, much to his mother's annoyance, and look after them until they were well again. Around this time he had thought he would become a vet, but later on he had decided that he wanted to become a doctor.

'When I went to medical school, the animals in the back yard remembered me from one holiday to the next,' he said.

There was a silence during which I began to feel exposed and embarrassed.

'Why were you crying?' he asked.

'Oh . . . it's nothing.'

'People don't cry for nothing. Why?'

I took a deep breath, my face was hot. I wanted to crawl away in middle-aged shame.

'When you are alone a lot, as I am,' I began, 'you get to speculating about stupid things.'

I paused, but tears continued to spill out of my eyes. He waited, watching me, solemnly in the way a child watches an adult, adding to my considerable shame. He looked so wholesome, so strong, so . . . I could feel that at any moment I might break into a howl. I was busy concentrating on keeping my voice steady. At last I sighed deeply and attempted to pull myself together.

'I was . . . I wondered what had happened to you, how the samphire-picking had gone. If you were all right.'

I pushed my glass away, utterly embarrassed, now, aware he was smiling.

'You were worried!' he said, as if the idea had only just dawned on him. 'My mother used to be worried. You mustn't worry!'

Shut up, shut up! I thought. Don't you dare talk to me like this.

'I said I will be back and here I am! We picked samphire for three days. I wanted to bring some back for you, but they were watching us, so I brought you the eggs instead. Tomorrow I have no more work, so I can clean the banks for you.'

He grinned.

'Oh, no, no,' I said hastily. 'Really, there's no need, absolutely not. I'm just glad you are okay.'

I couldn't look at him. All I wanted was for him to go. And I also wanted to put out my hand, touch his arm, make him sit down. I did none of these things. Instead, I asked him if he would like an omelette and a glass of wine.

'An omelette, yes. Please. But not the wine.'

'I've no more beer left,' I said.

'It doesn't matter. Will you eat with me?'

He was looking disapprovingly at my empty glass. Then he picked it up and sniffed it, crinkling his nose at the smell. I laughed.

'Don't you like gin? Look, why don't you go and play the piano while I get the food ready? I'll call you.'

I felt unhinged. The necklace of broken eggshells lay on the table. I moved them carefully to one side. I would have to find a suitable place to put them. In my study perhaps, or on the mantelpiece in my bedroom, away from the prying eyes of my brother's family. Then with sudden energy I took out butter and garlic. I cracked four eggs and went outside to pick some parsley. Suddenly I too was ravenous. Through the open doors I could hear the sound of the piano. He was playing that piece of jazz I had first heard him play, only now he sounded confident. I listened, marvelling at how, in so short a time, my house had an air of being lived in.

Roses bloomed across the garden wall and the evening was very warm and soft. I set the table outside while a quarter moon rose amongst the pines beyond the river. Placing a few tea lights around on the paving stones I went in.

The music had changed and quickened. He was playing a tango, snatching at scraps of movements, making me want to dance. Unable to resist, I drifted towards the doorway and watched, struck by the way the music gripped him. He swayed slightly and I saw a kind of isolation had encased him. At the same time he looked a little stern, removed from everything, a person from a precarious world with no clear future. I wondered when last he might have played this piece of

74

music and who might have heard him. He was connecting me with his past through it. An unseen hand struck a match in the sky. A pale phosphorescent streak gleamed and went out as he finished playing and turned to me with a dazed look. I felt he was still elsewhere.

'Come and eat,' I said, and he nodded, closing the lid of the piano. We were both silent over supper, remote from each other.

'Tell me about your home,' I asked eventually.

'If you will tell me first why you were really crying when I came in?'

I was silent, listening to an almost forgotten sound within myself. As if my heart, stopped for so long, was beginning to beat again.

'You are lonely,' he said. 'Like me?'

He sounded surprised. Then he leaned towards me and placed his hand over mine. I was struck by the youthfulness of his arm.

'I feel out of the main part of the world, too,' he said quietly, sipping the wine he hadn't wanted.

'Once my life was in the centre of things, but now . . .' He shrugged. 'Now I no longer can be counted. This is very hard to accept when I had not been born into such circumstances. Do you understand?'

I nodded.

'War does that. It picks you up and moves you to places with no future.'

Once, he said, people had deferred to him. He was capable of taking decisions, people looked to him with trust. Now all he could do was wait passively. What was the use of his existence? he asked softly. He smiled, with the suddenness that I had noticed before. He was like some exotic bird, inadvertently here on our northern shores.

'My mother,' he said, 'calls me her swimmer!'

He took a thin wallet out of his pocket. It was worn and falling apart. Inside were some passport-sized photographs that he spread on the table. His mother, the dead cousin and the other, irreparably damaged, and living with his aunt and uncle. There was one other picture, of a young girl with wide, startled eyes, like a faun. She must have been about seventeen.

'Your sister?'

He shook his head, silenced.

'No.'

Still, foolishly I persisted.

'A relative?'

'No,' he said steadily. 'She was just a girl I knew. In my village.'

'What happened to her?'

'Nothing. She is still there, I think. But I am here.'

I pulled a face. He had silenced me fairly effectively.

'Well,' I said with a brightness I no longer felt, 'I have some ice cream. We could have it with raspberries.'

What I really wanted was another drink. And then I wanted to howl. I could feel an exaggerated nervousness in the quickness of my breathing and I was thrown, aware of his unhurried gaze. River-light lay in the distance, starlight above us as he reached out and put his hands on my shoulders. This was so far from my expectations, so beyond my hope, that I froze, astonished. Time halted; this first touch made me blind with excitement. I felt the trees tremble above me like great dark waves in the sky. When I could see clearly again I saw he was standing up. He was saying something. It sounded like:

'Even God can't change the past.'

Still I couldn't speak.

'I am here now. I won't see her again and even if I do, the moment will have passed,' he said.

I could not identify the tone of his voice. There was something other than sorrow in it, some acceptance, I suppose. He made a small gesture with his hand.

'Too many things have happened, I have known too much, there isn't any way I can share that with her, or anyone else over there.'

He shook his head as if shaking some thought away.

'I am talking too much,' he mumbled.

I felt ashamed and in an agony at what I had stumbled on.

'I am forty-three,' I said bluntly, before I could stop myself. 'We shouldn't even be having this conversation.'

A moth danced around the candle flame. We both watched it, dazzled. Half-blinded, I was aware only of the movement, for the second time, very quick and delicate, of his hands on my shoulders.

And then he was touching my hair. I heard him trying to say with coherence that he thought it was beautiful, and suddenly the astonishing fact of someone touching my hair and finding it beautiful was simply too much for me. Overcome, I stood up and moved towards him, hardly aware of what I was doing. And as he held me I felt the whole of the front of my body turn molten and quivering, and wanting. Shutting my eyes against the gold of the candle, I felt an extraordinary sensation of nakedness. We stood under the stars and he kissed me. I think he was speaking to me but whatever he said was incomprehensible and it was a moment longer before I realised he was speaking in another language.

'You are different tonight,' he said at last in English, amused by my bemused state. 'You look different from the first time I saw you.'

We sat for a long time like this, under the stars, with the pine trees outlined like woodcuts in the distance, and I knew without a shadow of doubt what I was about to do. I knew and did not care, for the loneliness in my life, undisturbed for so long, was greater than caution.

Afterwards he curled up close to me like a child, his hair ruffled, his face creased by sleep. The hours that had passed were locked in tenderness. All at once I felt as though a wind was blowing over my soul, taking with it the dusty dreariness of the day.

'I am almost eighteen years older than you,' I had told him again at the last moment, and in the dim light of the moon I caught him smiling.

'These are not conventional times,' was all he said as he silenced me with a kiss.

The picture of the girl in his wallet floated once more before my eyes. Watching him sleep now, I thought of her, again. Curiosity consumed me; pain, I knew, would come later. I determined to ask no questions. I could not know how many women he had had, I told myself; why should I? He slept now with all his life hidden from view, with memory and hurt, and loss sleeping beside him. I was mesmerised, remembering how he had hung over me tenderly, with the patience of someone who had found a wounded animal in the fields, staying with it, not leaving until it could run again. Remembering, I moved my hipbone slightly and touched him gently. My stomach curled against his buttocks but he continued to sleep without moving. Holding him, I had the strangest feeling that I had come home at last. In the night I had cried out: 'There is no future in this.'

To which he had replied: 'We don't know that!'

Insect sounds drifted in from outside. I went over it again, under cover of the night, a miser considering his wealth. At the moment when we had joined I had become shyer. My throat had made strange noises. Limb by limb, lip by lip, by sex, we joined together in that dark, starry, night. And after that I wept on him, my eyes closed as he finished, as he took me into the ending as if leading me into another world. A metal spring gave a startled jerk within me, a quiver far down that by the smallest fraction released its tension. For in that moment even I had begun to see possibilities. One day soon, perhaps, the entire spring would uncoil and fly wildly, shattering me with feeling. I must have closed my eyes for a moment, for when I opened them again light hovered behind the skin of the sky. He was gazing at me.

'I've been wondering about you,' he said, and I held my breath.

An enormous silence followed in the centre of which was our exploration of each other. Behind the rim of the sky I knew an exuberant sun waited to burst out.

When he woke again he was in a hurry to be gone. He had nothing to shave with and although he had no work that morning he did not want his absence reported or talked about.

'I'll come back tonight,' he promised, refusing breakfast, refusing the offer of a shower, wanting only to be gone.

And, silent as a cat, swifter than a sparrow, faster than a breath, he went. With the speed of a swimmer. Leaving me with a bewildering sense of happiness and confusion, with my world in turmoil, with fear a pulsating fist in my mouth.

'What time will you be back?' I called, but he had gone and I heard the outside door close softly.

I rushed out of bed and went to the window but there was no sign of him. The day was waltzing into loveliness. A corncrake was screaming over and over again in the reeds, cornflowers shimmered and somewhere in a distant field a tractor droned on and on. What day was it? What time? I sighed and went into the shower.

In the coolness of the water streaming over me I tried to take stock of what had happened. My body was still that of a youngish woman. Middle age did not show on it, yet. Forty-three is not so old, I said out loud, willing myself to believe this. The telephone was ringing. Jack, I thought. Miranda. What on earth would they say, had they been here? Suddenly I could not bear the thought of their coming back. Perhaps they wanted to tell me that they were returning today. Panic-stricken, I rushed naked out of the shower, dripping pools of water, but the phone had stopped ringing. I would have to put them off somehow, I thought. Frantically I rang Jack's mobile but there was no answer. It was too early for them to have rung; the children would still be asleep. Relax, I told myself, and returned to the bathroom to finish dressing, then I went downstairs to make coffee.

For the rest of the morning I tried and failed to work. Nothing had prepared me for these events. The tension was all gone. There was a dark bruise on my arm and another on my neck. Like trophies of an unexpected victory, I thought. In the mirror my face glowed and my hair shone a burnished gold. I went into a delicious daydream. Blushing, for I could hardly believe my new-found vanity, I wondered what it had been like for him. Was he thinking of me now? Oh, foolish heart, I thought, remembering the girl in the picture.

At midday I gave up trying to work. I wanted him back. I simply wanted him to take my clothes off; to do with me whatever he wanted. Without the haze of last night's alcohol, without the darkness, I wanted him back in my body. But he did not come and insecurity swiftly returned. Did he mean what he had said? Was he one of those unreliable men, never doing quite what they promised, always leaving one short-changed? I had known others like that and, young though he was, Ben was still a man.

There was nothing for it but to wait and see, I told myself.

5

TUESDAY, AUGUST 30TH. BEN DID NOT return as promised. I kept checking the field in front of the house, but there was no sign of him – or anyone else, for that matter. I was deeply disappointed. Calm down, I told myself, stop being stupid; there *will* be a good explanation.

That evening Heather rang once more.

'I don't want to alarm you,' was how she began, 'but there's been another burglary!'

I had fallen asleep. Her voice sounded shrill in my ear.

'At the top of the heath, by the crossroads. There are two houses? This is the second burglary in a few weeks!'

She sounded triumphant and I struggled to wake up.

'Ria? Are you listening?'

'Yes, yes.'

'You don't sound awfully concerned. It isn't far from you.'

'Well, I . . .'

'And you never lock your windows, Ria. Jack told me!' she added.

At that I woke fully. Had she been talking to Jack, again?

'When did you talk to him?'

'Jack? Oh, I saw him a few days ago, actually. Stop being so touchy, he was just worried for your safety. Anyway, the point is . . .'

'What on earth was he doing visiting you?'

There was a small pause. My mind was racing. The idea that had evaded me for days returned as a certainty. Heather was having an affair with Jack; I was both astonished and triumphant. Had he just left Miranda and the kids on the boat? Without a word? Did Miranda know? Heather was still talking.

'Just statistics,' she said.

'What?'

'He came to meet John Ashby. The journalist. John's writing a piece about the increase in anti-social behaviour amongst immigrants. In Ipswich. And Jack wanted to talk to him. He was only here for a few hours.'

'Does Miranda know?'

'I'm sure she does. Stop fussing, Ria. What's the matter with you? Do you want to hear about the burglary or not?'

'Yes.'

'Well, it started as a break-in, I guess, but they must have disturbed the owner. So they beat him up,' she said flatly. 'And killed the dog. Nasty business.'

I had gone cold. What if Jack had come back and seen Ben? And where was Ben, anyway?

'Heather . . .'

'Yes?'

'Is there something going on between you and Jack?'

She laughed. 'Of course not! Why d'you ask?'

Liar, I thought, certain now.

'Look, Ria, be serious now, please. Why don't you get a dog? We could give you a puppy.'

'Doesn't sound as if they're much protection.'

Miranda *was* suspicious, I was sure. Jack was immersed in politics, but she knew there was more to it than that.

'The odd thing is, nothing was stolen,' Heather continued.

What a nerve! I thought. Still what did I care? It was their business. I wanted to get off the phone and I wanted Ben to appear.

Later, I heard the story on the news. Heather had got it wrong.

Something *had* been stolen. A quantity of euros and a passport had disappeared. The dog had had its throat slit.

Ben did not return and that night I slept fitfully. I was both cross and anxious. The next day I awoke with the sun full on my face like the touch of a hand. I had been quite drunk when I finally crawled into bed and had forgotten to close the curtains. Where *was* Ben? Another wasted day, I thought dispiritedly. Here we go again. I was weary of my collection of poetry. I felt it was never going to get written at this rate. Perhaps the problem was that I had nothing to say any more. Perhaps this new friendship was just an excuse and the time had come to give up writing altogether.

Assailed by doubts all over again, I went out into the garden where the river unwound as though it were a roll of flat, bright zinc. A fish jumped into the air, its scales caught in a brief flash of light. Then it was gone.

'You're up early,' a familiar voice called.

I jumped. It was Eric, rising stiffly from the bottom of his boat.

'God, Eric! You gave me a fright. How long have you been here?'

'Since about five.'

He was looking at me quizzically.

'The eels are coming in nicely.'

'D'you want a cup of tea?'

He moved his traps up into the boat.

'I'll put the kettle on,' I said, suddenly relieved at the sight of him.

'So, how're you?' he asked a few minutes later.

He held a half-mended willow eel-trap under his arm.

'Look, this was the problem,' he continued, showing me a hole in the bottom of it.

Eric still wove his own eel-traps by hand. It was a craft peculiar to this part of the world but now largely dying out. Partly this was because there were fewer eels and partly because it was so much easier to buy the plastic, mass-produced traps. Eric's traps were more fragile and needed frequent checking. They took a long time in the making and demanded dexterity and skill. What they lacked in cost-effectiveness they made up for in beauty. And being constructed of willow, they blended completely with the colours of the water. The eels went in at one end and were caught when a partition closed. You couldn't get traps like these any more. And lately you hardly even found eels on this stretch of the river. The creatures that had swum here for hundreds of years were in decline.

'Mind if I fix it here?'

I pointed to the kitchen table and handed him a mug of tea. Then I put some bread to toast. I always thought of Eric as a sort of ghost person, almost extinct, not quite gone, but no longer appreciated. Like a dying species, walking the surface of the earth with an intuition that would die out with him.

'You all right?' he asked. 'Haven't seen you around for a bit.'

He spoke casually, concentrating on his weaving, sipping his tea, making slurping sounds. As always, his presence calmed and comforted me.

'Where's that fascist brother of yours? And his brats?'

In spite of how I was feeling, I laughed. Eric couldn't stand Jack. Years ago, when Jack had been in his early teens, Eric had taken it upon himself to talk to him about our family. He had talked about Dad in the same way he had done with me, but it had been useless. Jack hadn't wanted to listen and Eric, not wanting to make matters worse, dropped the subject. But then, some days later, when he thought no one was looking, Jack started throwing stones at one of Eric's dogs. I had been with Eric at the time and had seen what happened. Eric had gone over to Jack and ticked him off. Jack, to my everlasting shame had hit him.

'Oh, Eric!' I said now. 'He's just confused – as you're always telling me. They've gone to the Broads for ten days.'

He grunted and crunched loudly on his toast. I made some coffee for myself.

'I see you've met that young man, Ben, then,' he said casually. 'Do us another piece of toast, love, will you?'

I nearly dropped the teapot.

'You *know* him?'

'Mmm. He's just been fixing some of my fencing, why?'

'He works for you?'

Eric shook his head and finished off the rest of the toast. Then he drained his mug of tea and pushed it towards me for a refill.

'He works on the other side of the river. Foster's farm,' he said laconically. 'Queer folks. They've got some immigrants in a couple of barns and get free labour in exchange for filling in the Home Office forms. So they say.'

He went back to his weaving.

'I should get Ben to fix this for me,' he muttered.

'Wait a minute,' I said, confused. 'You're telling me you know Ben? The Sri Lankan?'

'The doctor-boy? Yes, of course I know him. He's always sneaking over to do little jobs for me in his spare time.'

I stared at Eric.

'He never told me.'

'Perhaps he didn't know you knew me,' Eric said, reasonably. 'How did you get to meet him, then?'

I swallowed. I could have sworn he was trying not to laugh.

'I saw him swimming across the river,' I said. 'He came on to the bank and so I spoke to him.'

My face was becoming hot with embarrassment. Eric's shoulders were shaking.

'Pinching stuff from your pantry, eh!' he said under his breath. 'Naughty boy!'

'*What!* Did he tell you that?'

'Talks about you!'

'Oh, *really*?'

'Hmm,' Eric said.

Then he looked straight at me and burst out laughing. I was so furious that I could only glare at him, but this seemed to amuse him even more. Throwing back his head, he hooted with laughter, until seeing the look on my face he tried to stop.

'Ria . . .' he began.

Putting down his basket, he looked solemnly at me.

'Oh God, Ria! Don't look at me like that!' And he started laughing again.

Then he stood up and came around to me. Bending, he took my hands in both his, forcing me to look up at him.

'Ria,' he said, 'the boy can't stop talking about you! I'm not sure what you've done, but . . .' he looked thoughtfully at my hands, 'since he's met you, he's become a different being. Transformed, I'd say.'

I was speechless with resentment. Clearly, even though he couldn't keep his word and visit me, Ben had no qualms in talking about me to everyone. Eric continued to watch me, his face serious now. He sat down again.

'You're looking good,' he said. 'I haven't liked the way you've looked for a long time.'

I didn't know what to say.

'When you were a little girl,' Eric continued, 'after your dad died, you changed overnight.'

Still I said nothing, caught halfway between exasperation and interest.

'You left your uncle's farm a little girl that day and came back all grown up. And completely silent.'

He hesitated.

'And the next time I saw that brother of yours, he had turned inward in a different way.'

He shook his head very slightly.

'He was too young to work anything out, whereas you, well . . . I've watched you struggle, Ria, don't think I haven't. You deserve to be happy.'

Embarrassed, I was silent. Eric hadn't talked about these things in years. I had no idea he still felt so strongly about what had happened.

'And another thing, while I'm at it: I'm glad you left that idiot Ant,' he said. 'I never liked him! You can do better.'

'He left me, actually!'

Eric made a gesture of dismissal.

'This time you've met someone different, Ria,' he said. 'This man will be good for you, you'll see. He brings a wider horizon with him.'

Something shifted in my heart. The morning readjusted itself. In the room, light stretched across the worn floor. Disjointed emotions rushed at me. Eric looked steadily into my eyes. Witness to all of my childhood, what better person to understand how I felt than him.

'Well, I must be off,' he was saying. 'I expect your swimmer will be along soon!'

And, picking up the willow basket, with a wave of his hand, he left.

The rest of the morning passed slowly. I cleared a small part of the garden, dead-heading roses and tying back some of the more unruly honeysuckle. All the time I was thinking of my conversation with Eric. And I wanted Ben more than ever. Towards eleven I heard a car draw up. The rising heat made it impossible to work in the garden. It would soon be lunchtime. Ben was clearly not coming. Swallowing my disappointment, I went in just as the front doorbell rang. It was a policeman, making house-to-house calls about the burglary. Had I seen anything suspicious in the last few days? I ushered him into the sitting room.

'Walker, Sergeant Walker, madam,' he said, showing me his ID.

He mopped his brow.

'Nice piano, you've got. Cool in here.'

'Yes,' I agreed.

And no, I hadn't noticed anything. Wasn't the burglary close to Dunwich?

'That's correct,' Sergeant Walker said, still eyeing the piano.

'Do you play?' I asked.

'Well, yes. But I don't have anything as grand as this!'

'Have a go,' I said, opening the lid.

I've no idea why I did it. It was completely out of character. Sergeant Walker hesitated. He looked sheepishly at me and touched the keys. Then he made a sound of appreciation and began to play a waltz in a minor key. For the second time that day, I was astonished.

'Venezuelan,' he said, when he came to the end of it. 'A waltz. I used to have a wife who was Venezuelan. You lived here long?'

'About three years.'

He nodded and I guessed he had heard the story before.

'Of course,' he said. 'The poetess. You heard about the burglary at the top house?'

I nodded, but I had no information for him.

'Nasty business. The guy's in hospital with a broken arm and the dog's dead.'

'Have you caught anyone yet?'

'Not yet. But we will.'

He gave me a considering look, then smiled suddenly.

'Go to the theatre much?'

'No.'

'Pity. I've got some tickets for the local rep.'

He sighed in an exaggerated manner and I waited.

'Make sure you've locked the doors at night,' he said as he left. 'I know what you country folks are like!'

I felt the sun beat down on my eyes. All summer seemed to rush forward in a single sultry breath.

'I'm a Londoner,' I retorted.

He grinned.

'Nice piano, though,' he said again. 'Here's my card, if you think of anything.'

And then he was in his car.

'The man who was burgled, is he out of hospital yet?' I called, but he had shut the car door and didn't hear me.

An enormous silence descended into the thickening heat. It was beginning to give me a headache so I lay down on the sofa. Desire, sharp as a splinter, seemed to be piercing my heart. I longed for my swimmer. It was no use fooling myself, I thought. My life, the world out here, everything had been transformed overnight. On Monday night I told him I wanted to go with him up to London to visit the Home Office. What I really wanted was to find a way to sponsor his stay in Britain. Uncertain of his response, I had broached the subject tentatively, fearful of offending him, not wishing to take him over. But in the end, when I did so, he had turned towards me, putting his dark hand against my white arm. He had smiled, without much excitement, and I was struck by the fact he did not beg for anything.

'You are like the bird shells I collect,' he said finally.

There was a certain randomness to his conversation, I told him teasingly, but he replied seriously.

'No. I'm wondering why you want to help me like this. Something has happened to you, too.'

At that, I told him about my father, and how the loss of him was inscribed on my life. How it had stultified it. He listened intently.

'I've been to counselling, I've tried writing it out of my system, but nothing works completely. So now I've given up.' I shook my head, feeling slightly self-conscious. What was my problem, compared to his? 'When my last relationship failed, I said to myself, no more. Better to live alone!'

He sighed deeply.

'Why?' he asked. 'Why didn't she tell you? What was she frightened of?'

'Grief, I suppose. She didn't want to deal with it. It wasn't what you did in her family.'

'And your grief remains?'

We both were silent, thinking.

'I can feel it,' he said, at last, laying a hand on my heart.

I nodded, staring into the darkness, waiting.

'And anger, too. I think you are angry with men?'

I was taken aback, but before I could say anything he told me about his mother.

'I have escaped,' he said. 'And she remains in hell. Leaving her to her fate was not easy. It took an act of will.'

I could imagine him steeling himself, making the decision, sticking to it. Knowing there was no way out.

'She had protected me in so many ways.'

He was staring up towards the ceiling, his face unreadable.

'She walked through life bare-footed in order to give me the best of everything.'

I tried to imagine what it must have been like for her.

'On that last day, before I left, she said, "Be a good boy in Europe and take care of yourself, for me, and don't forget to brush your teeth!"'

I squeezed his hand.

'I looked at her face and saw how the stones on the road she had walked on must have bruised her feet.'

I felt his words entering me like acid. I felt too, he had moved away from me again, to some remote spot where I could never follow. Despair started up again in me, but then he kissed me, full on the mouth and with strange insistent gentleness.

'The war can't stop because of all the people who have been hurt by it,' he said. 'Too many people have been killed, too many people have been left behind who remember those who have died.'

Because of this he felt there was no single power that could stop it.

'If I'm sent back,' he told me, 'I will be killed. One or other of them, either the army or the terrorists, will know I tried to escape, and they will hunt me down.'

I had wanted to ask him what he planned to do if his residence status was denied, but I was afraid to.

'I am a person lost in transit.' He laughed. 'Maybe when enough of us have died, some foreign government, one that is more powerful than us, will take notice.'

'Not you,' I told him.

I put my hand over his mouth.

More than ever, I had become determined to help him. Now, lying on the sofa, exhausted, I closed my eyes. He had told Eric about me. I felt extraordinarily touched by this.

I must have dozed off because the next thing I knew was the touch of something warm against my lips. Confused, I opened my eyes to find myself looking deep into Ben's dark eyes. He must have let himself in through the back door. He was looking at me as intensely as a cat watching a bird.

'Have you eaten?' he whispered. 'I was afraid you had eaten.'

'No. I've been clearing the garden all morning and then I got tired. Where've you been?'

He nuzzled his face against my shoulder, like a young animal. His skin smelt of hot earth, fresh and very youthful.

'Look what I've got,' he said triumphantly, holding up a trout.

'Where did you get that?'

'I've been fishing. I want to cook it for you,' he said. 'The way we sometimes cook it at home. Let's go outside.'

He seemed in a great hurry, ordering me imperiously to fetch foil and cooking implements. Then he made a fire.

'Why don't we grill it?'

'No, no. I want to show you my way.'

We went down towards the river where the willow tree offered some shade. Ben slit its throat and gutted the fish with ease. Then he dug a hole, covered the fish in foil, buried it and left it to cook on the bed of charcoal. He was whistling, like a little boy whistles: loud, clear and pure. He looked so serious that I began to laugh.

'What's the joke?' he asked, absent-mindedly.

'Ah! That reminds me, before I forget,' I said. 'I hear you are friendly with an old friend of mine.'

'Who?'

'Think!'

He pretended for a moment not to know.

'Eric,' he said.

'You never told me.'

I tried to sound accusing. He looked at me and grinned. He didn't have to tell me everything, he teased. Then he came to stand in front of me and began to slowly undress me. Underneath his flippancy I felt the tenderness of someone very young, rising towards me.

'I'm astonished,' I told him seriously, taking his face in my hands, 'to be doing this with you. I am astonished to find so many of life's experiences in just a few short days.'

Moments before we joined, my shyness returned. Instinctively understanding, he came to me. Time stood still. There rose from deep within me a glow. What seemed like hours passed until finally, reluctantly, he dropped away, leaving the traces of love, the snake-skin of semen against my leg, kissed dry against the summer air. We lay entwined, brown against white. Between gasps I told him I had not been naked in the open air since I was a small child. He looked at me seriously, thinking about it, and then once more he was burning in me, turning and growing like molten glass. I stopped thinking. A lip folded back on itself and this time I was weeping on him as it began again.

Afterwards, I felt we lay together in a place out of time. We stared up at the cobalt blue sky. Eternity stretched around us. Maybe, I thought lazily, exhausted and uncaring, to understand sex fully one has to risk being destroyed by it. Small, dark-winged birds were lining up in their thousands on telegraph wires, preparing for a long flight south. Through the chalk-white heat of late afternoon I saw small signs that autumn was on the march. Tomorrow it would be September.

'For so long,' I murmured, 'for as long as I can remember, sex has only shown me the things I could not have.'

I stopped abruptly, wishing I hadn't spoken, for how could I describe the long lonely years, the child I had made in my mind's eye, without ruining this moment of peace? I might have told him that while the whole world was making babies I was engaged in useless acrobatics. But while I hesitated he turned his face slightly towards the river. For a moment or two the reflected light of it, with that curious blinding power, was full in his eyes. Looking at him, I was dazzled by the sight of it. For quite some seconds I was speechless. When he looked down at me I was startled by the sadness in them.

'There are too many children, now,' he said quietly. 'We have lost the art of loving for the sake of loving.'

Was that what he was doing? I dared not ask. All that hot afternoon I remember the air was full of the sweet young scent of him as we comforted each other. We had forgotten about the fish, but when we dug it up it emerged, salty and crisp on the outside and soft inside, so that we made a late lunch of it washed down by white wine. Ben drank glass after glass and it was my turn to tease him about how quickly he had got used to drinking wine.

He did not have to go back until much later on. The hours drifted unchecked. I told him about Eric and my father and what the farm had looked like when I was a child. The day was ours entirely. Towards five o'clock we strolled back to shower and I went into my study to work while he played the piano. Hours went by in this way, with the sound of his music drifting in through the house. He played some jazz and then a piece of music I recognised.

'What is it?' I asked, coming in.

He grinned and played it again, a lilting melody.

'A waltz?'

'Your policeman friend played it,' he said, laughing.

I frowned. How did he know, he hadn't been there?

'I was,' he admitted. 'I was hiding in the kitchen!'

For some reason this disturbed me.

'You mustn't slink around, Ben,' I admonished. 'You'll scare me.'

Solemnly he promised he would not do it again and I thought what a child he was, for all his tender attention to me.

'I couldn't let him see me,' he said reasonably. 'They took someone into the police station last week, thinking he was a Pakistani.'

'What? Why would they want to do that? It's just a crop of burglaries, isn't it? Why do they want to look for Pakistanis?'

He shrugged, carelessly. The other men on the farm had heard rumours of a foiled terror attack in Ipswich, he said. He was speaking casually and I frowned.

'You must be careful,' I said. 'No, really, Ben, it's not funny. Promise me you won't go skulking around?'

I went back to my study. It had been so long since I had worked in a house with another human being in it that I was beginning to feel I had lost the thread of what I was writing. The Schubert now being played was more real than anything I was capable of creating at the moment. Perhaps, I thought, the time has come for me to give up. I had written seven collections of poems. Maybe there was no more to be said.

A little later on, as I sat doing nothing, listening, the phone rang. It was Heather. Ben stopped playing. I could feel him listening in the background.

'Are you working?' Heather asked.

The sound of her voice panicked me.

'Yes,' I lied.

I tried to keep my voice as normal as possible, but even so she gathered something was different.

'You all right?'

'Yes, why?'

'Oh, nothing. I presume you heard the news?'

I told her I had been too busy to turn the radio on and she told me that there had been another burglary in Appleford and another dog had been found killed in the same horrific way, with its throat slit. No one knew why.

'Who was that?' Ben asked, coming up behind me as I put the phone down.

He put his hands around my neck and smiled at me through the hall mirror.

'You have a very, very, slender neck,' he said, pressing his hands gently against my skin.

Then he began kissing me all over again, his face hard against my throat. The next moment we were lying naked on the floor.

6

MONDAY, SEPTEMBER 5TH. BEN HAD THE day off and arrived at seven. The weather changed, subtly. A late burst of summer heat embalmed the air. Not surprisingly, Ben still had heard nothing about his application for refugee status. I had been nagging him for days to let me ring the Home Office, but he had turned lazy and wouldn't co-operate. I had the distinct feeling he wanted to shelve everything that was unpleasant and that this oasis of calm was all he needed. Every effort I made to get him up to London was met with evasion and in the end I realised I would have to go alone. I decided I would take the train the following day.

I walked barefoot to my herb patch and picked some parsley. There was a smell of cut grass everywhere and I could feel the heat rise from the paving stones. Ben was absorbed in playing the piano. I wanted to make him a summery soup, green and cool, and very English, before he went back to the farm. He had to be up early and dared not stay the night in case he overslept. In any case, I told myself, we both needed a pause to take stock of where we went next. For a week we had done little but devour each other. When we were together it was impossible to think of anything else. I felt we needed to make some decisions, sort out a more permanent arrangement.

Thrushes were calling to one another. The evening sky looked as beautiful and as incomprehensible as the love that had found its way to me. I headed towards the riverbank. I remember thinking, just in case it did rain, I should bring in the rug we had lain on earlier. So I walked towards the trees to pick it up. My sandals were scattered carelessly across the grass. I sighed. Happiness coursed through me, my body ached sweetly. The sound of the piano followed me. I remember thinking he could not get enough of the piano, or me. Folding the rug I picked up my shoes and was just turning away towards the house when something caught my eye. There on the narrow path across the water, close to the trees, was a parked car. The river was low; there had been no rain for weeks. But now, in the few minutes since I had walked towards it, the sky had slowly become overcast. A slight breeze had sprung up, rustling the reeds. I heard the creaking beat of wings and watched a formation of birds move slowly towards the horizon. Puzzled, I stared at the car, wondering again what it was doing there. Not many people knew of this stretch of marshland. Uneasily, for we had spent the last hour making love in the open air, I hoped we had not been seen. The birds had disappeared from view and faintly, in the distance; I could hear the sound of thunder. There was a stagnant, warm smell of rotting vegetables and river water. Now that the harvest was over, rain would not matter. I glanced back at the car as with the smallest of movements a man stepped out of it. He lit a cigarette and leaned against the bonnet. He seemed in no hurry. I moved quickly behind the willow tree and watched. Something must have caught his attention too because he walked towards the edge of the water. A few large drops of rain began to fall and I screwed up my eyes. The man was peering down. Then he went back to the car, took out a camera and began to take photographs of the river after which he bent low and fished something out of it. The rain increased slightly and the air was beginning to smell of wet dust as the man hurriedly returned to his car. He reminded me of someone, but I couldn't think who it could be. A second later I heard the engine rev up and with a small wheel spin he was gone. I hurried back to the house with my rug over my head and forgot all about the incident.

Ben had stopped playing the piano and was looking out of the window for me.

'Let's go to the beach,' he said.

'We'll be soaked,' I laughed.

He was laughing too. He loved the rain, he told me and besides, once it rains beaches all over the world empty of people in a moment. There would be no one there. So, wanting to give him whatever he desired, wanting to keep him happy, we went to a beach near Dunwich. The rain was falling in soft grey veils by now, the sun had completely vanished and the sea was transformed. My heart had taken wings. Ben ran from the car like a child. He thought the wet shingles were wonderful. The beaches in Sri Lanka, he shouted, were so different from this place.

'Stones, hundreds of stones!' he yelled.

And he laughed, dancing on the shingles. In the distance the disused power station appeared before us shrouded in mist as we ran towards the water's edge, shouting at one another. I told him about the town that had slipped into the sea. And how, on a day without wind, local people said you could still hear the fifty-two bells chiming under the waves. He looked at me eagerly, the thought catching his imagination.

'Really?' he asked.

I thought how he must have been when he was a little boy, in the years before he had worries. I remember thinking, I'm so happy! A dog bounded, barking, towards us, then turned abruptly at the sound of a shrill whistle and ran off. Ben was busy searching amongst the shingles. We were both soaking.

'Let's sit in the car till it eases off,' I pleaded.

In the car he handed me a pebble.

'I lost my rucksack,' he said. 'I left it in one of the fields and couldn't remember where I had left it. I had a lovely river stone for you in it. But this is better.'

Some people have the knack of finding things, I thought, smiling. They find things others never see in a lifetime, no matter how hard they search. The pebble, whitened by the sea, was clumsily heart-shaped. He had found it in a mass of grey-brown shingles and now it sat in the dark of his hand.

'For you,' he said, and kissed me.

'I shall have to start a collection,' I said. 'I'll call it Ben's museum!'

He looked at me solemnly. Then he shook his head and folded the heart into my hand and kissed it, finger by finger.

'Everyone has to be young once,' he said. 'Sooner or later.'

His shirt was wet; he was shivering slightly in spite of the heat from the car. I wanted to go into a café for some tea, but he refused. With a flash of insight I understood that he was embarrassed by his clothes and possibly also by his lack of money. I saw too that the swiftness of our passion had masked many things and that this was not necessarily a good thing. Sighing, I suggested we go back to Eel House. Tomorrow, I thought, when I was in London, I would buy him some clothes and a new rucksack.

That night after our light supper of watercress soup and salmon pasta, before he left, Ben and I made love once more.

'You're wasting good piano-playing time!' I teased him.

'The piano does not need my attention at the moment,' he retorted. 'It has had my company for hours!'

I told him he was becoming too bold for my liking and he laughed, delighted. While I had been cooking he had played almost all the music I possessed and I promised to get him some more when I went up to London. In the silence that followed, within the quick, delicate movements of his hands, I felt he was working things out for himself. An inexpressible sweetness took hold of me. Finding him had been a small miracle. I doubted he would ever know how much it meant to me. I held his face with both my hands, very lightly, like a precious object, thinking, You are still too young to see this moment for what it is. Like all else on earth it will be of such short duration. Yes, I thought, this is you and this is what is happening! And as we started the in, out, the long, beloved torso, lowered, lifted, lowered, the delicate, blunt, long caresses, I wanted, with a desperation I cannot describe, for it to never end. And as he began to draw out all that had been so wrong in my life, I saw he was to be my undoing. No, I did not want it to leave me.

'Tell me about your mother,' I said in the pause that followed.

His eyes were closed. In the dim blueness of the room, with the soft sound of rain outside, his thick curly hair gleamed and sprung up under my caress.

'My mother?' he murmured.

'Hmm.'

'My mother used to draw faces. We had her drawings all over our house. My grandfather, before he died, my father, before he disappeared, me . . . before I left.'

'How did she bear to let you go? How will she cope without a word from you?'

He was motionless, his face unreadable.

'It is not possible to have everything,' he said, at last. 'She is a courageous woman.'

'Would you like to ring her?' I asked suddenly.

He looked startled.

'It's not possible,' he said. 'It would be too expensive.'

'I'm not talking about the cost. Would you like to phone her?'

He hesitated. His eyes were open now, watchful.

'What's the time difference?' I asked briskly.

Here at last was something I could positively do.

'Five hours . . . four and a half . . . depends,' he told me, reluctantly. 'I don't know if the phone will be working . . . if she will be in the house . . . if . . .'

He was making excuses, I told him.

'Well, it's too late tonight, but if you can get here by six tomorrow you can ring her then. Okay?'

He didn't answer, turning his face away so that I leant over him, pulling him towards me, wanting to kiss him. Still he did not move. Only when I tugged at his hand and found his mouth did I feel the saltiness on his face as he hugged me to him, fiercely.

Afterwards, before he left, when I had gone to pour him a glass of wine, I found him staring at my bookshelf.

'There's trouble in Pakistan, you know,' he said. 'They've tried to kill some Sri Lankan cricketers.'

I kissed him. He seemed to have become remote in the few moments I had been away. Suddenly, for no reason, I was afraid.

'The wars everywhere will begin to join up. People will write about them, make up stories. But what's the use? It won't change anything.'

He did not want to talk about love any more. I could see that the moment had passed. Terrified, seeing him slip away from me, I wanted to hold on to him, but I didn't know how.

'Leaving wasn't a simple thing,' he said, sipping his wine. 'I stood on a tarmac stairway and smelled the air and looked over the land where I was born.'

We were silent. He, I supposed, because he was remembering, and I, because of a terrible feeling of exclusion. Whatever experiences had defined him, I would never be wholly part of. A feeling of hopelessness came over me, but then he caught my eye and took hold of me and kissed me.

'I didn't know people could have such blue eyes,' he said.

'Why don't you stay?' I asked lightly. 'I'll get you up at dawn.'

He hesitated, thinking no doubt that he would be missed, but it had begun to rain again and I could see that he was exhausted so it was, I think, a little against his will that he stayed. As I closed up the house for the night I noticed my answerphone flashing. It was a message from Heather's friend, the journalist John Ashby. He wanted to arrange a meeting with me later on in the week.

Tuesday, September 6th. I went up to London to the Home Office. I had wanted to make an appointment, but no one ever answered the telephone. It was maddening. First you were presented with a series of automated options and if you chose to 'hold for an operator' you were eventually cut off. I had tried the number on and off for a couple of days and in the end had given up. The website, too, was out of date and difficult to use. I had tried downloading a form but only half of it printed and I could not get a reply to any e-mail I sent, either. So I had booked a ticket on the six forty-five train to Liverpool Street. Ben must have been up working for two hours already, helping with the milking. All night it had rained and I had lain awake, worrying about him. I felt that the conversation about his mother had upset him.

He had left in the early hours. The rain had begun the process of bringing the leaves down; yellow spotted willow lay in a carpet on the grass as I walked with him at dawn towards the river. He kissed me once and then he pushed his way through the hedge into the field beyond. Just before he disappeared from view he turned and waved.

'Go back to bed!' he called, softly, and then he was gone.

I watched him disappear, a familiar feeling of desolation descending on me once more. The certainty came upon me in that moment that I wanted him to live at Eel House.

Last night I had tentatively brought the subject up.

'It's too soon for you,' he had mumbled.

Lying in the darkness, watching him, unable to sleep myself, I was aware I was being idiotic. It was far too soon for both of us, but impulsiveness had taken hold and I was consumed by his plight. I knew I would do anything to help him.

Later, sitting on the six forty-five train to London, I watched the light burst out of the sky. Last night Jack had rung me sounding his normal self, irritable and rushed. They were planning to be back in two days, he said. I needed to find out what the position was at the Home Office before I could say anything to anyone, even Eric. Jack with his xenophobia would have to be handled carefully. The whole subject of Ben would need to be broached slowly, for if there were no hope of Ben staying legally in Britain, Jack would be the first to denounce him.

I glanced at my watch. I had read that the queues at the UK Borders Agency, as it was called these days, were horrendous. I wanted to be there when the doors opened.

The train passed a forest made charcoal by the light on the horizon. Space is the luxury of Suffolk. It hangs in quiet stillness over the flattened fields. The morning was like honey; summer's lease was almost over. All I had was Ben's proof of postage, and a copy of the handwritten letter he had sent. He had been reluctant to give them to me and this had started me worrying again, in case he felt I was taking him over. In the end he had let me scan them so as not to relinquish the originals.

'Don't, whatever you do, tell them I'm working, will you?' he had said at one point.

'Of course not! And in any case, you're hardly being paid anything, so it isn't really employment!'

'I know. But don't tell them.'

'How do they think you are living?'

He shook his head, looking angry. It was the closest we had come to a disagreement. I could feel the tension between us. We need to live together, I thought. Iron out our differences, deal with them.

'Don't tell them,' he warned again, and in the end I had promised, furious with a system that was so cruelly confused for any refugee trying to comply. I only had one question. How could I sponsor Ben? After my visit to the Home Office I had an appointment with my financial advisor. I had decided to withdraw some money, and open a separate bank account for Ben. Without his knowledge. It broke my heart to think of the indignity of his poverty. I was going to put money into the account every time he did a job for me.

The morning light appeared unstable after last night's rain. The train passed close to the sea, never quite allowing us more than a glimpse of it, but with an underlying sense of its presence behind the matchstick woods. We passed a bleak war memorial and a silo tower and then a graveyard of machinery glittering in the sunlight. I bought a coffee from the trolley and took out my bundle of papers. I had decided that I would temporarily give up trying to work on my book until I could clarify Ben's legal position. We passed Wickham Market. High banks of greenery flashed by. The carriage was almost empty, save for two men working on their laptops. I caught sight of my reflection in the window. My life was on a landslide beyond my control, I thought ruefully. The train stopped at a small local station and several people got on. One of them was reading a newspaper.

SOFT TOUCH BRITAIN, screamed the headline. JOBLESS IMMIGRANTS STAY HERE AND GET £715 A WEEK BENEFITS.

Underneath, I could just make out:

Tighter borders are what are needed with fingerprinting of every visa applicant wishing to travel to the UK. We are also cracking down on illegal workers, with more enforcement raids than ever before.

I shivered. How desperate would you have to be before you wanted to live in this hostile country?

At Ipswich the train began to fill up and a row broke out between the elderly passenger near me and the ticket inspector. The man was travelling on a senior, reduced-fare ticket but had forgotten to bring his card with him.

'You'll have to pay the full price,' the inspector told him.

'I'm so sorry,' the man said quietly. 'I've just returned from abroad. When I left I emptied my wallet out and then forgot to put the card back in. I can ring my wife and get the reference number for you. You can check it on your system?'

The ticket inspector licked his lips. He was already shaking his head.

''Fraid I can't do that,' he said with some satisfaction. 'You'll have to pay the full fare.'

'Look . . . I'll just phone . . .'

'Suit yourself. It's either seventy-two pounds thirty, or you get off at the next stop. You have to travel with the rail card, otherwise it's illegal.'

I was listening to this exchange with amazement.

'I'm only doing my job.'

'Well, can't you do it with a little imagination?' I asked before I could stop myself. 'Can't you see this gentleman isn't lying?'

The man glared at me. Then he ran his hand smoothly over his greasy hair.

'Oh, it doesn't matter,' the passenger said hastily. 'They're all like this nowadays.'

He paid for a second fare and the inspector had swayed off down the train.

'It's called running a society,' the elderly man said. 'There's something Kafkaesque about life in Britain nowadays.'

We were passing slowly through Suffolk, and its landscape of flooded fields. The sky brightened across the horizon. High white clouds were reflected in mile after mile of shining dyke water, so that the marshes seemed to stand between the clouds and nothing. It continued to threaten rain. My tea trembled in its plastic cup as I thought of Ben.

At the Home Office I entered by a side door that looked as if it might be an entrance to a warehouse. People shuffled forward in a queue, quietly submissive, confused. Mine was the only white face amongst them. I had worn a cream linen dress, thinking I needed to be formal, but now felt uncomfortably out of place I took a ticket and joined the line. The room was painted a lurid green. A plastic rack stood against the wall. It was stuffed with leaflets in every shade imaginable. They were numbered but some of the numbers in the series were missing. A listless man, an African with close-cropped hair, walked over and began picking some of them out absent-mindedly. The number on the board flickered and changed. Forty-seven. Mine was fifty-three. I sat staring ahead, conscious of curious eyes on me. The African man returned with a handful of the leaflets and handed them to his small daughter who instantly began to sort them by colour. The door to the lavatories opened and closed and a woman in a burka came out. She had three children who clung to her, screaming. The girl at the reception desk looked up from her telephone call and frowned slightly. She had rings on every finger, I noticed. Then the number above me flickered and changed again. Forty-eight.

I went back to thinking of Ben. I tried not to dwell on the life he had lived before me. It's all in the past, I told myself, wanting reassurance. Instantly and perversely, I was lit by the fear that nothing had changed, really. The small girl beside me finished sorting out her pamphlets. She walked over to the rack and began stuffing them into the lower pockets. She was not quite tall enough to reach and most of them fell on the floor. Her father walked slowly over to her and gently began to put them back, but the little girl began to scream in frustration. She wanted to tidy them up herself. Her father picked her up and whispered in her ear. Then he carried her as far as the large patio window and together they watched the traffic rushing past outside. I picked up the newspaper on the low table and read: *Asylum applications in 2007 were at their lowest level for 14 years, according to statistics.*

The board above me flickered. When I looked up again the African and his child had disappeared into one of the consultation rooms. The number on the board was fifty-two. I was next.

The woman who waited for me in the cubicle was young. She was protected by a sheet of toughened glass. I sat on the plastic chair but could not move nearer. It was screwed to the ground. There was a minimum of privacy. The woman raised her head slightly, then went back to staring at her computer screen.

'Could I have your reference number, first.'

The notice on her desk told me her name was Vicki and she was a 'Processing Officer'. Like meat, I thought. Her face had the blankness of a certain kind of youth, unlined and expressionless. I suspected she would remain this way, no matter how much she aged. Life would not mark her; she would not let it. She was frowning.

'Sorry,' I said and I handed her the copy of Ben's letter.

'This isn't enough,' she said flatly. 'And it's a photocopy.'

'I know. I didn't want to take the original away from the person. He is in some distress at his precarious state. I didn't want to add to it. I've got a proof of postage too, if that's any help.'

I could hear my voice. It had become slightly pleading.

'We don't take account of photocopies.'

'Yes, I understand, but I was wondering if you could look up the serial number and check you received his letter?'

'We don't acknowledge photocopies. You'll have to bring the actual document and he has to actually fill in the form.'

I was silent.

'Have you looked at our website?' she asked. 'It says quite clearly *actual* documents only.'

'The website is down,' I began.

The girl shrugged.

'You should have phoned the help desk.'

'No one answers the telephone,' I said.

A helpless rage was creeping over me. The girl's pink and white face, her expressionless eyes (had she been trained to keep them this way?), her small clean hands, everything about her gave me offence.

'You'll have to come back,' she said. 'Bring the right documents next time.'

All around were notices warning against hitting an officer. Abuse, it was called. I swallowed. The woman's face was as high and as impenetrable as a blank wall.

'So this is a wasted journey?' I asked. 'I've come all the way from Ipswich, wasted the entire day, queued, for nothing?'

She looked at me as though I were insane.

'You could have rung.'

'I just told you the lines were always engaged. I couldn't get through.'

'Yes, we are experiencing a high volume of calls,' she agreed, changing tack.

I took a deep breath.

'Look, I've travelled up from East Anglia, I've tried to phone, I need some advice. I want to make an appointment for someone to talk to my friend. We can't access the forms, he's sent a letter, that's obviously got lost . . . can you not understand?'

I had caught her on some raw spot for she turned on me, stung.

'I understand, perfectly. It is you who do not understand. I'm doing my job . . .'

'Obeying orders?' I said.

'Don't speak to me like that,' she rejoined.

For a moment there was a brightness in her small eyes, a flash of some emotion. Then it was gone and she clicked the computer screen blank.

'Let me give you an advice pack,' she said smoothly, reaching out across her desk.

I glanced at the advice pack. It was of the same tertiary colours as the leaflets with which the African child had played earlier. Written in large print, the questions in it had no bearing on real life. We would have to start the whole process again, just as I had feared. As I left, a dark-skinned woman was ranting at one of the officials. Her voice went on and on, getting increasingly out of control. Two security guards came towards her but she would not stop. I saw her small frame heaving with the effort of her rage. They got hold of her arms and hustled her out of the door. I could hear her voice growing faint until it disappeared altogether. Turning my face away, I walked out of the building.

The whole operation had taken only two hours but such had been the trauma of the experience that I felt as though I had been there for days. I suspected that, for most, leaving this no-man's land was an impossibility.

While I had been in the building it had rained heavily. London steamed in autumnal grey as the train travelled east. Ben was coming over to make his phone call this evening. I had wanted to be home by five, now it would be closer to six.

Essex passed in a wash of rain-polished light screening an invisible sun. The sky cracked open into floating lakes of greyish blue. I watched it, thinking of the last few weeks and how, already, they had slipped into the past. Staring out of the rain-streaked window I thought, I am like an animal that has found its mate at last. This then is how it happens, I thought, glancing at the person sitting opposite, quietly reading. He, she, all these people here in this carriage, knew nothing of my transformation. And I thought, with renewed determination, somehow I would find a way to help him.

As we approached Ipswich there was a holdup and I saw a man taken off the train by the transport police. The passengers in my compartment strained their necks to watch. The man was black, and young. He was led on to the platform, handcuffed. I saw him twist his head frantically from side to side. I was reminded of a dog straining at the leash. The guard blew his whistle and raised his arm and the black youth turned towards the moving train. There was a slight scuffle and his eyes held mine for a moment. Then we had moved on and he was no longer discernible through the rain slanting against the window. We passed over the bridge that took in a derelict corner of Ipswich. A group of tramps gathered in a doorway surrounded by empty beer bottles. In less than an hour I would be home.

Ben had not appeared by the time I got back so I made myself a cup of tea and unpacked my shopping. I had bought some Middle Eastern salads and a couple of fillets of John Dory. I went to the fridge and took out a bottle of wine and the summer pudding I had made yesterday. The rain stopped abruptly and the evening was again streaked with a soft glow. I wondered whether it would be warm enough to eat outside but decided it would not. I picked up the phone and listened to my messages. There was one from Miranda, confirming their return. Suddenly I was depressed. I made myself a gin and tonic then decided to take a quick shower. As I stood under the spray, the day and all its difficulties returned. I thought of the boy taken by the police. Where would he be now, in what cell, for what crime? Suddenly overcome, I raised my head to catch the warm water and began to cry.

He came while I was drying myself, bounding up the stairs as though he had lived here forever. I could see he was excited about the phone call.

'How was London?'

I made a face.

'We need to talk. You're going to have to start all over again, fill in the forms. It's going to take a bit of time.'

He was watching me as I dressed. Then he came up to me and started taking my clothes off again.

'You're not listening!' I told him, laughing, for my mood had changed instantly at the sight of him. 'And you must make your phone call first.'

'Okay,' he grinned. 'But afterwards,' he warned, 'no objections!'

While he rang his mother I prepared food. Cooking for someone who was constantly ravenous gave me a peculiar pleasure. He was both child and man. I smiled as I chopped parsley, fried the onions and sliced mushrooms. The quiet hum of his presence in the house, the weight of it, his voice talking now in another room, all of this changed everything. Preoccupied with cooking, setting the table, pouring wine, nevertheless I kept a steady dialogue going in my head. Tomorrow, I would ask Eric to come over. I wanted to see the two of them together.

His call must have lasted about ten minutes. I could hear his excited voice faintly through the closed door until finally there was silence and he emerged.

'Mmm, smells good,' he said, leaning over my shoulder looking into the pan with the freshly fried John Dory.

'Well?' I wanted to know, 'what did she say?'

He took both my hands in his and kissed them. Then he stuck his finger into the pan and broke off a piece and put it into my mouth.

'Stop it,' I said. 'Don't be bad!'

'I'm hungry,' he said, helping himself to a plate. 'Let's eat quickly.'

'Why quickly?'

'So we can go to bed,' he whispered, grinning cheekily at me. 'Then I will tell you all about it.'

'No, tell me here,' I said. 'I'm still cooking.'

His mother had not answered the phone straight away. He had become afraid something had happened to her or that the house had burnt down. Feeling sick, he had been about to put the receiver down when someone had picked it up. He could hear noises in the background: a voice speaking in Tamil, a dog barking. The noises were both familiar and far away at the same time. It had been strange hearing them in this way.

'Yes?' a voice asked at last and it held traces of his other life.

'Amma?' he asked, hesitantly. The pause that followed was intense.

'My God, it's Ben! My God!' the disembodied, loved voice said.

He noticed how she pronounced the word God with a long slow sound on the 'G'. He knew it was how she had always pronounced it, of course he did, but hearing it from where he was now gave it a new poignancy. He felt his heart constrict with pity for that voice and for all it represented. He had tried so many times to ring her, he said, but he had had no money to use his mobile phone and the public phone boxes just chewed up his money and would not connect him. He had sent four letters too, but she had never received them either.

They did not speak for long; he had not wanted to waste my money, he said. When I protested, he could have talked for longer, he shook his head.

'It was enough time,' he told me.

Enough to find out that she was all right. And how many people now knew that he had left.

7

WEDNESDAY, SEPTEMBER 7TH. THE TEMPERATURE ON the thermometer began rising again. Large thermals corkscrewed into a sky that had temporarily regained its earlier summer blueness. Ben was due to have two days off and I was desperate that he should spend them with me. In order for this to happen, I needed Jack and Miranda to return, take their belongings, and go straight back to London. In the meantime, the farmer had bussed all the men who worked for him to some remote farm to help with fruit picking. I wasn't very happy about it, but there was nothing I could do. In order to distract myself, I decided to decorate the kitchen. I began by taking everything out of the old wall cupboard and preparing the room for painting. We had discussed the possibility of Ben putting up new shelves, and I suppose I was hoping that when my brother returned and saw the mess he would promptly leave. It was while I was cleaning down the walls that the police came. It was the same man who had played my piano. This time, however, he was in less jovial mood and he came with two other officers.

'Did you hear anything last night?' he asked.

'No. Should I have?'

He looked at me grimly.

'Well, I would have thought you'd have heard the police sirens, at least! Were you in?'

'Yes.'

'You must be a heavy sleeper. We arrested two squatters in the house next door to you. You heard nothing, then?'

I shook my head, frowning. Ben had left at two and after that I had slept an exhausted, uninterrupted sleep.

'An arrest, you say?'

The detective was looking casually around the room.

'That's right. In your neighbours' house.'

'There are only renters there. Well . . . they've left. They seemed perfectly ordinary!'

The sergeant looked at me, nonplussed.

'They left a week ago,' he said. 'The squatters were South Africans. You never saw anything untoward?'

I shook my head. Such had been my preoccupation with my own affairs that I'd barely registered the new people. He was writing in his notebook.

'You don't know the owners?'

'Never seen them. There have always been renters.'

'You don't happen to know the names of the Italians, by any chance?'

I shook my head and he laughed.

'Of course not. You poets like to keep yourself to yourself!'

I didn't like the look on his face, but the telephone ringing shrilly interrupted my thoughts. It was Heather.

'Look, I can't talk,' I said. 'The police are here. Yes, of course I'm fine. I'll ring you later.'

'There were five people living in that house, but you never saw them coming or going?'

Again I shook my head. The sergeant shot me a look.

'They broke in and were using the house.'

'What for?'

'Two of them had swum across from the other side of the river,' he said, ignoring my question. 'Must have crossed your land and walked into the house.'

I digested this in silence.

'I was in London all day yesterday.'

'What time did you get back?'

'Oh, about six thirty-ish.'

'And you didn't go into the garden, I suppose? Why should you? It was still raining.'

I nodded.

'And what did you do for the rest of the evening?'

I turned away and began filling the kettle. 'Tea?'

'Thank you, that would be nice. You were saying, what did you do for the rest of the evening?'

'Oh yes. Well . . . eh . . . I had a bite to eat and then I went back to work. I hadn't done anything all day because of going up to London to see my editor.'

'Ah, poetry!'

He smiled at last.

'Read any of her books, Joe?'

Joe stopped writing and shook his head sheepishly.

'No, sir. Have you?'

'I'm more interested in her piano, Joe,' Sergeant Walker said easily as I handed them mugs of tea.

'I'm afraid I can't really tell you anything,' I told him, but he had strolled out again.

His voice came towards me, muffled, from the hall.

'Nice painting,' he remarked, emerging holding one of Ben's old trainers, discarded recently, after I had bought him new ones.

'Whose are these?'

'My brother's,' I lied.

'Mind if I borrow them?' he asked, throwing me.

'Well, if you want, but he's due back shortly and . . .'

'No worries. I'll have them sent back tomorrow.'

I would have liked to ask him why he wanted them at all, but my heart was thumping loudly and I could not.

'You live alone, don't you?'

'Yes.'

'Just you and that damn fine piano, eh?'

'Well, me and my poetry, actually.'

He laughed and I saw him relax.

'Ah, you have me there! But I tell you what, I'm going into the station in Aldeburgh now and I'll pop into the bookshop and buy a copy of your latest.'

I smiled stiffly. We had been playing an elaborate game that was now over. They finished their tea and went, telling me to ring if I should hear or see anything suspicious, cautioning me about security or answering the door. I nodded. I was shaken but glad that at least Ben wasn't around. I wanted to ask him if he had known anything about the break-in.

Several hours passed. I finished the final coat of paint and began to clear up. I put my brushes to soak. My back was aching and I decided to make a pot of tea. It was now three o'clock. Looking out of the kitchen window, I saw a man bending over the vegetable patch. I knocked on the glass and as he straightened up I recognised him as Heather's friend.

'Hello,' he said, walking towards me, holding up his ID. 'I think we've met before. I'm John Ashby.'

He smiled through discoloured teeth. I stood glaring at him, a vague idea turning in me, but I invited him in anyway.

'Nice place, this,' he said pleasantly. 'Decorating?'

I nodded.

'What d'you think about what happened next door?'

He jerked his head in the direction of the garden.

'How do you mean?'

I suddenly realised I didn't like him.

'They were terror suspects, you know.'

'Oh, really? The police never said.'

'Well, they were. Why d'you think they were arrested?'

'They were squatters. They'd broken in.'

'You heard anything?'

'I've already been asked that. It's so remote from this house, we can't even see over the fencing, let alone hear anything.'

'We?'

'I mean me, or my brother, who comes here sometimes.'

'He lives here?'

'My brother? No. The house is mine. What exactly do you want?'

'Oh, just a conversation with you, really. I left you a message, did you get it?'

Again I nodded. I felt uneasy.

'Just wanted to ask you a few questions about your writing. I noticed you hadn't appeared at the literary festival this year and I wondered why. I love your work. Wasn't there a poem in one of the Sunday papers, not long ago?'

'The festival was months ago,' I said. 'I don't have a new book coming out, which is why I wasn't at it. But why the interest now?'

Belatedly I wished I hadn't asked him in.

'You only get invited if there is a publication. I'm in the middle of writing another collection.'

I was talking too much. He was not writing anything down, just looking at me a little insolently.

'Look,' I said, trying to hide my annoyance, 'if there isn't anything else I can do for you . . .'

'Actually, there is. I've a hunch about something. The men who were arrested . . . you know the police think it's part of a bigger plot, don't you?'

'How do you mean?'

'It'll be out on national news tonight, you'll see. There've been two Pakistani men apprehended already. I've a hunch that what happened, what's been happening in this area for some time now is all part of the same thing. Look at the way they've butchered the animals, huh? Bit suspicious, don't you think? Halal and that sort of thing?' He gave me a knowing look. 'I'm telling you, I smell a rat. Look at this, here –'

He pulled out a piece of fabric. It looked like a strap for a bag of some sort.

'See this? It's off a rucksack. Not far from the scene of the crime.'

'What crime? The squatters in the house next door?'

'Oh no, no. I found this beside the first dead dog. The one that was killed a few weeks ago. So you see, the police have only part of the evidence. Only I know there is a crime yet to happen!'

He paused, significantly. I hadn't a clue what he was talking about.

'I knew there would be trouble when they opened that detention centre in Ipswich,' he said, when I didn't react.

I stared at him in disbelief.

'Have you talked to the police?' I asked.

The man was making my blood run cold. All I wanted to do was to get rid of him as fast as I could. And underneath all of this, something else was still bothering me.

'These people aren't stupid, they just feed us red herrings all the time. To keep us happy, you know. But this time, I've worked it out!'

That's it, I thought triumphantly. That's where I had seen him. Across the river, standing by his car, smoking a cigarette. And then I was filled with horror at the thought he might have seen us, Ben and I. I edged him towards the door.

'Look,' I began, but he'd finished.

'Here's my card,' he said, and then he raised his hat and was gone, swiftly, walking across the gravel and out through the gate. I waited until I heard his car start and and only went inside when he had driven off.

That night he brought me a heap of feathers found in the woods at the back of the farm. He had found them on his walk over the fields. It had been an easy day, he said. All the time he was going over the phone call to his mother in his head and because of this he worked faster, got less tired.

'Because of you, I was happy!'

On the way he had heard fire engines, he said. 'There were police cars as well. Going towards Dunwich.'

'I've got something to discuss with you,' I said, changing the subject, and I told him that I wanted him to leave the farm.

'I've looked at the forms for the Home Office and tomorrow I'll go through them with you. It's not too difficult. We'll fill them in together. But now I want to tell you something else.'

I spoke quickly before he could interrupt.

'I want you to come and live here with me until we get your illegal status changed.'

He was watching me intently and I braced myself for objections.

'My brother and his family will be passing through tomorrow on their way to London. I shan't tell them anything at this point.'

'I will not come tomorrow,' he said instantly.

'Look,' I said, not wanting him to misunderstand, 'Jack is a very odd man . . .'

I stopped. He was looking at me blankly; I didn't know how to go on. Whatever I said would come out wrong, I feared.

'We are not close,' I said, at last. 'It's best if I say nothing until I know what the situation is. Do you understand?'

He nodded. I remembered I had bought him a white shirt but had forgotten to give it to him.

The gift surprised him and he immediately put it on. It was a good fit.

'I hate these T-shirts,' he said. 'When I left they were new and represented my hope. Now they just remind me of the journey.'

We were both silent, both thinking. I guessed he was thinking of his mother.

'I would like to buy you something, too,' he said at last. 'Maybe one day I can.'

'One day,' I agreed briskly, aware of the touch of melancholy that had invaded us both. 'But first we must sort out your status here, and then we must get you back to being a practising doctor.'

He nodded. Suddenly I was struck by the thought that he was simply humouring me. This country owed him nothing, he said quietly. A sense of exile was branded in him. At that a chilling thought, that really he wanted to return to his country, hit me forcefully and I felt my heart tighten with fear. Don't go, I wanted to cry, but instead all I said was:

'I want you to clear your things from the farm. I've got a funny feeling about the place.'

'It's not bad. Stefan is not a bad man. We get plenty to eat and at least I've had a bed there.'

'Well, you don't need it any more. You've a bed here, now!'

Ben grinned. He reached over and took my face in his hands.

'I can work for you,' he said. 'I can be your gardener and your cook. Your houseboy!'

'Shut up!' I said sharply.

I kissed him and in the tenderness of the moment I forgot I had meant to watch the evening news.

Thursday, September 8th. Jack and Miranda returned en route to London. They both seemed subdued and I guessed they had been quarrelling. Miranda looked as though she'd been crying and the children were being tiresome. They arrived noisily, hungry and chaotic, ready to spread their things all over the house. I was jumpy and desperate for them to leave.

'Is there anything to eat?'

'Can I have a sandwich?'

'Sorry, Ria, they're starving,' Miranda apologised.

Today, more than ever, my relatives seemed like people from another planet. I watched them, unable to think of a single thing to say. There was food in the fridge. Adult food for two. Champagne and salmon, some left-over duck, home-made ice cream.

'Good God, Ria!' Miranda cried, astonished. 'Have you been entertaining?'

'Ugh, I hate duck,' Sophie said.

'Could we have a barbecue?' asked Zach.

He was batting a ball around the kitchen.

'That's enough, Zach,' Jack shouted. 'No, we've got to get back. Good lord, Ria, you've painted the kitchen!'

'And put shelves up!'

'Can we go on the computer?'

'Yes! Let's download *House*! C'mon.'

'Children!'

'Now look,' I said, 'I'm afraid my study is out of bounds for you two. I've got work all over the place in there and I don't want any of it muddled. Why don't you go outside?'

I stopped. Both children looked crestfallen and Miranda was staring at me.

'You've done something to your hair?' she said faintly.

'You're looking good!' Jack added at the same time. 'As if you've had a holiday. Have you?'

I laughed.

'*Have* you been entertaining?' Miranda asked, peering at me.

'No, of course not! I told you, I've been working. Now, what time are you leaving? I want to cook you all lunch before you go.'

In the fraction of a pause that followed, the telephone broke in with an insistent ring. My heart leapt but I went out calmly into the hall and answered it. It was the journalist from the local paper, trying to get hold of me again. While I talked to him I could hear the murmur of voices in the kitchen. The subdued sound meant they were talking about me. I told the journalist that today wasn't convenient as I had family present. But he was insistent so I agreed to meet him one day next week. Afterwards I wondered which day I had agreed to. My main preoccupation was getting Jack and Miranda to leave as quickly as possible. I wanted Ben back.

To my surprise, there was no resistance from either of them. Perhaps sensing my mood, they seemed happy to have a quick lunch before leaving. We sent the children out into the garden.

'I think it's done them some good,' Miranda said. 'They haven't seen any television for weeks!'

I refrained from reminding her that the first request on their lips had been for the computer. Oh hell! I thought. She was only trying to be friendly, after all. As soon as everything is settled, I decided, I would take Ben to London. To see them on their own territory, and I would insist we became a family once more. Humming to myself, preoccupied with thoughts of the future, I made lunch. Jack was busy repacking the car, hurrying backwards and forwards through the kitchen, moving the stuff they had left behind.

Miranda lowered her voice.

'He's been to see that friend of yours,' she said.

'What?'

'You know – Heather whatshername. They're getting a dossier together. There has been a spate of passport and identity card thefts in East Anglia which have been linked to all the illegal immigrants around here. Jack wants to present the information at the party conference next week, as a possible angle for the next election. Immigration is a hot topic, he says.'

She paused.

'He's insane, Ria!'

I swallowed. So he wasn't having an affair. Or was he?

Miranda was looking at me steadily.

'Ria,' she murmured, 'are you okay?'

'Of course.'

She hesitated and I was struck, perhaps because of some heightened emotion within me, by the sweetness in her. There seemed about her a vulnerability I had not noticed before. Until this moment I had felt very little for her. But now I was aware of a faint stirring of warmth. She likes me, I thought with surprise. I saw how she had inherited a set of circumstances and how she was doing the best she could with them. I could trust her, I thought. I would talk first to Eric. Tell him of the changes I was making to my life. And after that I would tell Miranda about Ben. Naturally Eric would be pleased. Jack would be a problem, but Miranda would be the one to help me. And Ben, I thought, going off into a daydream, would discover a ready-made family to help with the loss of his own.

So far was I into my imaginings that I hardly heard Miranda.

'Ria, Heather's been telling Jack about a man who visits you at night . . .'

'Mmm?'

'Ria . . .'

Startled, I looked up. I was about to answer when we heard a bang. It was very loud and sounded as if it came from the garden. We both jumped. Instantly Miranda rushed to the window but there was nothing to be seen. She started calling the children, who were nowhere in sight.

'Where are they?' she cried, her voice rising in panic and Jack dropped the box he was holding and rushed outside too.

'Sophie! Zach! Where are you?'

The boot of his car was wide open. The willow trees were moving gently in the breeze. Miranda and Jack started along the side of the house towards the river. I turned to follow them and at the same moment I heard raised voices. Someone was shouting.

'Stop, armed police!'

'Stop!'

There was the sound of scraping and panting and then heavy foot-steps as a figure emerged running higher up in the field beyond the trees. It was Ben. I could see him clearly as he zig-zagged across the rough grass, the whiteness of the shirt I had given him fluttering in and out between the trees. I think I screamed, although I couldn't be sure. The sun must have been in his eyes for I saw him raise his arm against it. He appeared to be calling something.

Above and behind me, I heard another yell. As I turned I saw to my horror a man with the barrel of a shotgun levelled in front of him. I screamed again, but the sound of my voice was shattered by the blast of the second shot. I saw Ben, blown backwards, in the act of trying to wildly wrench the pain from his eyes and then his body, convulsing like a rabbit, turned over and over until at last it lay still.

'Oh my God, my God!' I said. 'Oh! Oh! My God!'

I stood gasping for a moment longer, weeping. Then I began to run, raising my hand in an agony of whiteness against the sky.

Anula

8

SIX O'CLOCK. HORSEFAIR BUS STATION. IT is over. I am going back. Tomorrow when the sun is once more briefly in the wintry sky, for a few, short, daylight hours, if no snow falls, the river will flow again like a ribbon of mercury. The water meadow will return to a pale sodden green and although the grass will remain still flattened from my last pilgrimage to that spot, winter will edge a few minutes closer to a lighter hour. Tomorrow, what has been lost will be restored, outwardly at least. Trains will pass swiftly in the distance. Crows will sit on telephone wires, sheep will huddle under bare-branched trees. But I will be gone, my plane lifting through the heavy skies, turning and banking over the bitter sea. Over the snow-capped Alps, across Turkey, over Damascus and the Arabian Sea; across India then down, down, flying beside the Indian Ocean, homing. That is how, in a very few hours, I will go towards my journey's end. Returning to the place that betrayed me, leaving the dead where they do not belong. Leaving this corner of a foreign field that is forever Sri Lanka.

Sitting in the coach speeding towards the airport I watch my reflection in the window. Caught between a backdrop of a forest of trees the reflection is of a person I no longer recognise. The trees flank the roads for miles, close growing, forming a wall with no room to breathe, seeing me off, indifferent. Then they peter out. The trees at home don't suffocate each other in this way. Occasionally I glimpse the land beyond the sea. Occasionally we pass houses with low red roofs, a chimney trailing smoke. No washing hangs out to dry, no flowers bloom. The streets are empty, monotonous. We have been travelling for about half an hour. The bus is almost empty. She drove me to the central bus station very early, in a place called King's Lynn. We left at dawn.

'I will wake you,' she told me, and I agreed, dully.

The reality is I have not slept for weeks. At least, not in the way I used to, not in that innocent, trusting abandonment of the past, when waking up was always a moment of refreshment. That kind of peace is over. But at five she came as she had promised and knocked on my door, then paused a moment and opened it. She came in and hesitantly sat on the end of my bed. It was the first and only time she did this. I was careful not to react. It was dark. All I could see was the outline of her body swathed in a dressing gown, head bent. I have to admit she looked frail; ill and ill at ease. I had been with her, in her house, for twelve days and in all honesty this was the first time I really considered her. It is a shocking admission. Until this moment all I had space for was myself. I *still* only have space for myself, but in the early hours of this, my last morning, I noticed how she sat, waiting for me to speak. She had the patience of a beautiful animal, I thought.

'Would you like to drive past the field?' she asked in a low voice.

I was grateful for her thoughtfulness.

'Yes.'

'It won't be fully light, but if we leave early enough, you could . . .' she tailed off.

I had bought flowers yesterday specifically for this purpose and she had guessed as much. Perhaps she had worried I would try to find the place myself and then get lost, or try to do something worse. I could see that she had become, in this short time, an anxious person, someone who would never trust that things would be normal again.

'I will get dressed now,' I said.

We left the house in the strange half-light that I now recognised so acutely as characteristic of this country. The sky was yellow with cold, very wide and empty. I am in the north of the world, I told myself silently, staring out of the car. When I was a small child, one girl-child amongst so many others, I had a book of pictures of Lapland. One of my father's friends from the university had brought it for me.

'This child will travel far,' said the man, whose name I can no longer recall. 'She is clever, very clever. Who knows, she might even become prime minister!' he had laughed.

I was the cleverest in my family. After Ben was born, my father said I had passed on my genes to him.

'Don't neglect your intelligence,' the old professor had said, but then I met Percy and fell in love. The book on Lapland and all it stood for faded in the heat of this new love.

Being good Catholics, we had married in the big cathedral in Jaffna. And then, easily, with no sense of my fate, no warning, I became pregnant. When you long for a child, things like fate don't disturb the surface of your dreams. Wanting a child is so big a desire that nothing can possibly overshadow it. In spite of the intermittent war, none of us thought it would get so bad that the hope for new life would vanish.

The bus is speeding through another town. It stops. I have no idea where this place is. I don't want to say his name. I have stemmed the flow only briefly and any stray thought might cause it to break through. Outside, as though from a great height, I watch as new passengers join the coach. A head of hair, golden in this pale morning, another, short and reddish and then, behind it, the dark, curly head of a youngish, dark-skinned man. He must be about twenty-four. Instantly I feel my chest tighten and I gasp for breath. Is this how it will be for the rest of my life? Am I consigned to spend what is left seeing what I have lost in every place I pass? The bus begins to move, the new passengers settle in scattered seats, and soon we are speeding on to a faster road with fields distanced by metal barriers.

It was September when they told me. It has taken me this long to get permission to leave. Someone, a man, rang up. I couldn't understand his accent. It was English; I knew that, of course.

'Mrs Chinniah?' he asked.

'Yes, yes.'

'Mrs Chinniah? Is that Mrs Chinniah?'

The urgency in his voice was subtle, but I heard it nevertheless and it made me shiver. I maintain, one always knows. The horizon had already begun to tilt. There had been no one in the house. I had been listening to the faint sound of shelling all day further up the coast. And then it had stopped. A bird sang melodiously in a tree in the wooded area behind the house. It had been singing off and on all day and had made me think of my swimmer, my beloved Ben. The truth was, everything made me think of him. The whole world was tied up with him, the sun, moonlight on the sea, a small animal scurrying across the garden, a bird in flight, a fish arcing through water. Oh God! When he left for England he had left those things behind as a reminder for me. Lest I forget. Painstakingly, on his instruction, I had released all the animals he had healed, all those birds with broken wings that he had cared for. I let them go back into the wilderness behind the house. Some of them refused to budge, some kept coming back for food, looking for Ben, thinking perhaps that he would return.

'Mrs Chinniah, are you alone in the house? Is your husband with you?' the man had asked.

'My husband has disappeared,' I whispered.

I could say that without a tremor in my voice. It was possible for me to speak of Percy as though I'm not involved in any way. He disappeared twelve years ago. After every ceasefire I still hoped he would return. Of course it never happened, but the hope remains, regardless.

'Is there any other relative with you?' the voice asked next.

I registered it as a kindly voice. Like a priest. Like Father Anselm. So because of this, forgetting the person on the other end couldn't see me, I shook my head.

'Tara has gone to the post office,' I said. 'We have to draw out money. It has been impossible to do anything for days now because of the shooting and we owe the rent for this place.'

The funny thing was I didn't ask the man's name. I didn't stop to wonder why he was ringing me, anyway. The palms of my hands were sweating and I couldn't stop talking. I didn't want to know. Already I was on the threshold of grief, already, in some way, deep within my body, I understood.

'Mrs Chinniah,' he kept repeating, 'this is Scotland Yard here. From London. I'm terribly sorry but I have some very bad news for you. It is my duty to inform you that there has been an unfortunate accident. Your son, Ben Chinniah, has been killed.'

Those were his words. I felt them race through me like quicksilver, like the cyanide the boys take when they are caught by the army. Race through me and spill out on to the concrete floor I was standing on. Outside, the bird was still singing and I could hear it through my screams.

'No, no, no,' I screamed. 'No, no, no.'

I wasn't crying. Tears take time to gather, moments have to pass before they are released from the eyes. Screaming comes first. Had I known what it would be like when they finally came crashing against me, I would have held them off for as long as I could. But I didn't know.

He kept talking to me. I didn't understand what he was saying. All I knew was that I was holding the phone but my face was close to the ground. I could see an ant hurrying across by my feet; I could hear a jay in the tree outside. I could hear the man saying my name over and over again.

'I will ring again in half an hour,' the man was saying. 'When your daughter comes. I want to talk to someone who can take down a contact number.'

I don't really remember what he was saying. I remember the tone of his voice, but that was all. It was how Tara found me, crouched on the ground.'

'Aunty, what has happened?' she asked.

I saw her face through a blur; everything was a blur now, everything would be this way, forever. I was saying his name over and over again and she took the phone out of my hand. I could hear her voice rising and falling as she talked and then from nowhere there were other people in the house. That is all I remember for some time.

When I surfaced there were many people in the room. I had no idea who they were. Everyone was talking in subdued voices. I can see it very clearly, the way it all happened, the way I was gripped by grief, the way my mind ripped apart with disbelief and my breathing lowered itself to a pant. I remember crying for someone to take away the pain. It was so physical. It still is, only now it is worse than I believed possible. Now I am charged by invisible forces to keep reliving every detail of that moment. I am charged to tell everyone I meet, everyone who will listen, the details of that day. I am impelled to speak of how those hours slipped away, how rain clouds gathered but did not fall, how the bird that had sung came closer to the house to sing so sweetly and so fearlessly that all in that house of death heard it and marvelled at its song. What I have grown old in possession of was gone. There was nothing else of importance. These are the things I need to talk of, for ever, until the end of my life, to whoever will listen. It is my only task, now, a part of mothering that no mother imagines they will ever do.

Yesterday, when Ria took me for a walk, as we wandered across the town in silence, I saw a woman pushing a small pushchair with a boy in it. The child could not have been more than three; the woman saw me looking at him and she smiled proudly. Ah, I thought, you do not know what things you might have to face. The boy wriggled his legs excitedly, forcing me to think of Ben.

Other people took charge. Other people who were more capable, shocked, yet more detached, intervened. I was incapable. The day turned a sickly green as though I was viewing it from the bottom of a well through the ferns that grow there. When the sedative wore off I found I was still screaming. It is difficult to describe the way in which I cried. Someone said the sound was that of an animal in pain. I heard them talking outside the house in Tamil. Tara was with me all the time. She was crying as well, and in some corner of my mind I was aware that for her, too, the future as she knew it was over.

The school teacher came. He talked to the doctor. They were talking about moving me to some other safer place, but I would not move.

'Amma, we must move from here, in case they start shelling again.'

'I cannot leave,' I cried. 'Go without me.'

I pulled back the curtain into the alcove that had been Ben's room. The curtain was green; all his books were placed neatly on the shelves he had made. There were pictures of Tara on the wall, pictures of them both. Pictures of them smiling. There was a small statue of the Virgin Mary and next to it was a framed photograph of his father, taken long ago, before Ben was born, before Percy was a father. And at that moment, my heart's blood ran cold, for there in front of me were the few clothes he had left behind, the T-shirts, the cotton trousers, the trainers with holes in them that he didn't want to throw away. I had washed and ironed the clothes for his return. Folded and mended the holes in them, cleaned the old trainers. So that everything would be in order for when he needed them. I remember the screaming beginning again. I remember the sight of my son's clothes was the worst of all. Like a signature, handwriting that could never be erased. And I remembered too that in the roof, on a small ledge, was a trunk with other things from our broken lives, things from his childhood: his toys, his first shoes, his certificates. I turned towards the picture of Our Lord, his heart bleeding, the thorns surrounding him, but the face of Our Lord was turned away from me.

It was at that moment that the darkness descended. Pitilessly, unbending, running through me like poison.

'Anula?' Tara said. 'You knew when he left it was dangerous. You knew, you knew!'

But he had been gone for months. He had survived the journey, he was working, waiting for his papers to come through, he had rung me. I thought I would see him soon. I thought he would send for Tara as we had planned.

'Be happy, son,' I had said as I kissed him goodbye. 'Please, for my sake.'

Grief zig-zagged across my mind. There was so much of it, so many oceans, all surging towards me, it might have been better had

I simply given in and drowned. But no, cunningly, I floated in this sea of grief and did not die. I could not drown. Memories rushed forward, rolling and flattening out against my totally lucid brain, giving me word-pictures again and again. So that, even as I struggled to deal with one image, raising my head above the waters, I was knocked back by another. Remember, remember, my mind screamed. My mind had turned into a monster.

We had been planning his departure for a long time. Longer than a year. Ever since his cousin was killed and the army questioned Ben for hours, I been terrified they would kill him too. He had known he would leave one day. He had survived his father's disappearance and had learnt to live with the fear of losing me. None of this stopped him from working. He was clever, conscientious, and he passionately wanted to practise as a doctor. Jaffna needs doctors, Amma, he used to say.

'I want to heal people, not kill them!'

That is what my son used to say. He had managed by dint of keeping very quiet (we moved several times to avoid both the Tigers and the army) to survive. We had good friends. Since Percy was taken, there were those who looked out for us. The priest, the school teacher, people who saw Ben as someone who could help give Jaffna a future and therefore wanted him to survive. Yes, there are such people in the world. Even in Jaffna. And so he grew into a tall young man, so like his father that it made my heart swell with pride to look at him. In this way I indulged myself in love in this time of war. But it was obvious to all of us that he would have to go if his life wasn't to be truncated. Sooner or later he would get caught, sooner or later the army or the Tigers would catch him.

The night he left me was moonless. The smugglers had chosen it carefully. In the darkness wild jasmine bloomed and our sense of smell grew stronger. He would leave in the dead of night, he told me.

'Don't get up, Amma,' he said, and I smiled in spite of my fear.

Did he really think I would not get up! How little do you know me, my son, I thought.

I had made some *arpe* and *vade* for the journey. And I had filled a plastic bottle with king coconut juice. I was packing his food as I had done all his life; as if he was going to school. I wrapped a little rice in a plantain leaf, but he looked at the parcel and shook his head.

'I can't carry all that,' he said.

I could see his mind was firmly fixed on other things and not his eventual hunger. All boys are like that. Think only of the moment, deal with the hunger later on, when you get back home, after class, ravenous, demanding instant food. Again I smiled, remembering. My little swimmer!

We had been busy all day with the preparations for his departure. I had not had a moment for introspection. This trip, this last desperate dash in search of safety, had taken every ounce of energy in planning, every rupee I could muster. I had sold everything: my wedding thora, my remaining bangles, my wedding ring.

'Don't do that, Amma,' Ben had said when he realised what I was planning to do.

He looked at me disapprovingly.

'It is nothing, Ben,' I told him. 'Human life, *your* life is more important. This jewellery is only a symbol.'

He had been unhappy for days, had begun to mutter that he wouldn't go, and I had panicked. I knew he was marked. It would be a matter of time before the Tigers hunted him down. Young, fit, intelligent, perfect fodder for their bloody cause. Over my dead body, I thought.

'Get him out,' Father Anselm said, 'as soon as you can.'

So I sold my jewellery, knowing that Percy, had he been with me, would have approved.

Finding the money was the easiest part. The next thing we needed to do was to find a courier who was trustworthy. Father Anselm helped. He knew of a man who was safe and eventually the whole thing was set up. I can't describe the tension, the bitter-sweet triumph. Enough to say I just handed over the money. It felt as if I was handing over my life. After that, there was nothing more to do except wait for the papers to arrive. A passport – false, of course – an entry visa written in Russian. Was it believable? we wondered, staring at the script. I looked at my son's curly head as he lay sleeping. He was unfazed by all of it. Having made up his mind that this was what he had to do, he simply got on with the job of preparing to leave. I could not be so calm. I knew that to leave the land where you were born was not a thing to be done lightly.

Father Anselm was my solace, both at that moment of departure, and later too, when everything spiralled into blackness.

'No, no, Anula.' He shook his head gently. 'Don't think of it in that way. Wherever the moon shines, *that* is the same world you share with your son.'

Dear Father Anselm. That was what he said. Wherever the moon shines. Father Anselm had been a child during the Second World War. He said there was a song the soldiers sang.

'I'll be looking at the moon, and I'll be thinking of you.'

He sang it sadly for me.

And so, slowly we inched our way towards Ben's departure and I thought by the time the final morning arrived I was prepared. Everyone we knew had been visiting us in a steady stream for days. In spite of the shelling and the curfews, our visitors arrived to say goodbye to Ben. He was well loved. Many remembered Percy and how he had risked his own life over and over again for others, and Ben was his son. So they came, bringing gifts most of which had to be left behind. I found myself eating *vadi* for days after. Tara was at our place almost constantly now. Ben would take her into his room behind the green curtain and I could hear them laughing and I would marvel at how the young can live so much in the moment, however dangerous the situation was. This is what it is to be young, I told myself. Neither side in this war could take that away. Youth, I told myself with satisfaction, triumphed, every time.

The day of his departure was interminably long. I was weary of holding together my emotions, feeling the weight in my heart, helplessly, knowing that my grief was in abeyance. Outside the small bungalow the heat expanded in the slow, sad air. Later I realised that the silence was due to the sudden withdrawal of the army. All fighting seemed to have stopped. This is crazy, I thought. Why does he have to leave? The day inched by. Returning exhausted from the well that afternoon, I sat on the step at the back of the kitchen. Ben had gone out on an errand. He had been in and out of the house for most of the day, muttering to himself, distracted, ticking things off on his list. Avoiding my eye. All around the light seemed to be filled with an unbearable poignancy. It was as if what was going on inside me was happening outside too. Everything was holding on, everything trembled with the thought that this was his last day. I rested my back against the hot brick wall and closed my eyes. Flies buzzed. A gecko scratched the air in bursts. I waited. It felt strange to be resting in this way. I could not remember a time when I had sat so still. Never had I missed Percy as I did at that moment, sitting under the green shade of the murunga tree. Everything that has gone before, I thought, was made null and void by this day. I kept going back to the beginning, to that other sunlit day when I left my father's house to marry Percy. How happy we had been, how we had laughed with the hope we were filled with.

'Aunty,' a voice said, breaking into my thoughts.

It was Tara, coming to sit down beside me. She was twisting a thin gold ring that held a garnet, round and round one of her fingers. I didn't remember seeing it before. Glancing at her I saw she had been crying again.

'He's gone to get his shoes from the mender's,' Tara said, not looking at me.

'Are you skipping school today?' I asked.

Tara was seventeen, tall for a Tamil, beautiful, with sleek, long black hair. She had tied it in a plait that lay neatly along her back. When she finished her exams she had wanted to go to medical school, but unlike Ben the chances of her doing that in today's climate were slim. She nodded without looking at me. Her eyelashes were wet.

'School has been cancelled because of a burst water pipe. If everything stays quiet it will be mended by Monday.'

Neither of us said what we were thinking, that by Monday Ben would be gone and our world would be another kind of place. I could feel her shivering slightly.

'He'll be fine, Tara. You'll see. As soon as he gets to England, he'll write.'

She nodded and I knew that she, too, was thinking of the long journey ahead of him. I felt her terror coming towards me in a wave. Neither of us could speak of it. Long shadows fell across the yard on the dry red earth. Just beyond the trees it was possible to glimpse a burst of yellow flowers from the jacaranda tree. It caught the light at an angle so that it appeared like a wheel of fireworks. I remember looking at it as if for the first time in my life.

Tara stayed with me until Ben returned from his errands. Then before we had our early evening meal she went home.

'No, no, Aunty, there is food at home for me,' she lied.

I knew she was giving me the last evening with Ben alone. Ben, too, seemed to have decided. He would walk over to her house after our meal to say goodbye. Everything was ready. His clothes were squeezed into the smallest of rucksacks; his false papers were beside them, along with a pen and a diary. There was a small packet of boiled sweets, the same sweets he used to like in fourth grade. That much hadn't changed. My face was stiff with self-control. The food I had prepared earlier was simple and his favourite. Some rice, a little fish I had managed to get that morning, a pol-sambol and some curd. I could hardly eat and I suspect he too was struggling. But he hid the fact and pretended to eat with relish. Night had fallen like a stone as we ate. There were three houses on the road where we lived and from the verandah I could see the cautious glow of electric lights.

'They know I'm leaving so they decided to end the war,' Ben said, pulling a face, laughing. 'I'm going to meet Tara, now, Ma.'

'Be careful,' I said, uselessly.

He nodded. The soldiers that rode on motorbikes along the main road, their machine guns strapped to their hips, were one of many constant worries. They would suddenly swarm an area, surround a house or a group of people out walking, demand to see their ID, and after that, who knows. If the mood took them, they might put a bullet through your head.

'Don't worry.' Ben grinned. 'It's too late for them to get me now!'

We had not talked properly. Communicating with your son is something that is done almost subliminally; anxiety, like love, passes between you without the need for speech. He knew I was frightened of his journey, just as he had known of my constant worry about his safety. To have sons in this part of the country is no longer a blessing. I knew he worried for my safety too, alone without Percy and soon without him, that he was trying not to think about leaving Tara behind. To love is a dangerous thing in Sri Lanka.

While he was gone I started to sew the dress I was making for Tara. It was my secret present for her birthday. Ben had made her a necklace of blown birds' eggs. They were of mottled browns and reds, all strung together on thread. He had been collecting broken birds eggs for ages with this in mind, I suppose. The necklace was complete and looked very lovely. I was to give it to her when he left. At midnight they both returned to stand in the doorway, silently. Looking up, I had the strangest sense of their completeness and their quiet together-ness. This moment was their best, I thought. They should have got married even though she was still a schoolgirl. Instead he was leaving. Who knew if she would stay faithful to him? But this moment I felt was perfect. Ben must have thought so too, because a moment later he fetched the bird-egg necklace and took it out to her on the verandah. The murmur of their voices was breaking my heart. Later they went into his little alcove and closed the curtain. There were just three hours left. I hoped they would get some sleep. Packing away my things, I went into my room and lay fully clothed on the bed where once Percy and I had slept. It no longer felt like a room for two people.

I must have dozed off because the next thing I knew Ben was shaking my shoulder.

'It's a quarter to, Amma,' he whispered and my heart leapt like a fish.

Tara was standing in the kitchen, subdued again; her dress crumpled, waiting.

'Do you want some tea?' I asked, trying to be calm.

We strained our ears. There was the faintest sound, a scraping of something. We froze, but it was only Father Anselm.

'Ready?' he whispered, coming in.

Ben nodded. He picked up his rucksack.

'Where have you put the money?'

'Here. In my shoes.'

'Why not in your rucksack?'

'No, Ma. It's safer in my shoes.'

I didn't argue.

'Drink some water?' I begged instead. 'It might be some time before you get clean water. And always try to clean your teeth.'

My heart seemed to be lodged somewhere in my throat. Breathing was difficult. Tara was pushing something into Ben's hand. It was, I guessed, a medal of Saint Christopher. And then, what we were all listening for, what we all secretly dreaded: the knock on the door.

'Look after yourself, Ma.'

'Don't worry about her, son,' Father Anselm said. 'I'll make sure she is safe. You take care and get in touch as soon as you are able, huh?'

Tara was crying as he hugged her and then he turned swiftly to me and enveloped me in one of his bear hugs.

'See you later, Ma,' he said in Tamil, as he used to do when he left each morning for school.

And he smiled his lopsided smile and raised his hand in farewell. And then he was gone, following the guide, through the back door and out across the compound, past the faint glow of the jacaranda tree, deep into the thicket of trees.

9

SIX THIRTY. THE BUS IS SLOWING DOWN.

'Cambridge city, park and ride,' the driver calls out.

I notice he has a husky voice. Ever since this monstrosity of grief has taken over my life I notice all kinds of irrelevant things. Colours appear brighter, voices louder, birdsong more piercing. While all the time life continues regardless, each day arriving with unstoppable regularity, even though I have ceased to want it. The bus draws to a standstill and I see my reflection again, high against the wintry trees. I look terrible, like a circus lioness, broken, like an eagle without wings, speechless as a violin with no strings. The driver leaves his seat and opens up the base of the bus, taking luggage out, putting suitcases in. A small group of people crowd around him, three, four. For a moment I am distracted and wonder to what far-flung corner of the earth they might be travelling. I will never travel this world again, I think. From now on I can only go backwards in time.

When I was a child, an astrologer told my mother I would go to far-off places none of our family had ever visited.

'Do you mean Trincomalee?' my sister had asked, giggling.

'What nonsense,' my mother had said, sounding annoyed.

The idea of either of her daughters going further than the next village was not to be contemplated.

'No, no,' the astrologer said, shaking his head seriously. 'Much further than that.'

He waved his hand in the air to denote distance.

'Overseas,' he said.

But he had not looked happy.

'The man is useless,' my mother had said, after she had paid him and he had left. 'I'm not going to recommend him to anyone.'

'You never know,' my father had smiled. 'She might. After her marriage, now the war seems to be over. Percy might decide to go abroad.'

My mother had not been pleased with that. If she had thought Percy might have had itchy feet, she scolded, she would not have approved of this marriage. Ah, Percy!

A passenger climbs on board, moves slowly in somnolent mode towards a seat. She is a woman with a shawl around her shoulders, and she sits opposite me in the aisle seat. She places a large plastic bag beside her and takes out a flask. I watch through the reflection in the window. The bus starts up.

'This is the seven-twenty National Express to Heathrow Airport,' the driver says into the microphone. 'You are instructed by law to wear your seat-belts. Please also take a moment to read the safety regulations.'

The woman pours tea into the lid of her flask and begins to sip it. She sighs.

'How do you switch this cold air off?' she asks out loud.

No one answers. We are moving through another town; houses blind as moles, doors closed, curtains drawn, unwelcoming.

'Are you all right?' asks the woman with the flask.

Home is no longer home, I think. The words rise, gloved and folded, opening out, first through my stomach, moving across my body, up through my throat, exploding silently in my brain. Catching me unaware again. Help me!

'Excuse me, are you ill?'

I become aware of the woman leaning towards me, her watery green eyes fixed on my face. I bend forward, straighten up, try to arrange my features, try to control myself. She is holding something out to me and it is a moment before I realise it is a paper hanky.

'Do you feel sick?' she asks again, seriously. 'Shall I get the man to stop the coach?'

I shake my head, grief, held in for several hours now, is beginning to burst its barrier. I stare with heavy eyes, dimly aware that I am crying.

'No,' I say in a voice I don't recognise as my own. 'My son has died.'

It is the first time I have uttered the words out loud. Others have said them to me. The man on the telephone, the neighbours, the ambassador who sent the car and met me at Kataynika airport, the officials here in England, the lawyer, Ria, all these people have said it. Over and over again, as if I needed to hear the words, as if hearing such words once was not enough. And in all that time, even though my mind was screaming his name, even though the sound of it brought the blood to my mouth, I could not utter a word. There flashed before me an image from long ago: the little torso lying along my left forearm, the nape of his neck in the crook of my elbow as I soaped him. And how, when I told him how wonderful he was, he would look up at me and listen to the sound of my voice, intently. His one-week-old eyes, shining pools. Then I would feel him relax, as slowly, calmly, he would kick his silky limbs in the water of the blue plastic baby bath. My little swimmer! My son. Help me, God!

The woman is staring at me, mouth slightly open. She is not English but I cannot place her nationality.

'Madonna!' she says.

Her voice is warm and soft; horrified. And through the blur of tears, I watch as she offers me a sip of tea from the lid of her flask.

It was a low building they took me to. Low and grey. There were no windows. I will never forget. All my life lay there. When I got out of the car I could not make my feet walk. This then was where they were keeping him. I had not been aware that, until this moment, in spite of everything I had been told, still I had hoped his death was a lie. Such was my desperation to be with him that I had focused only on the journey. I looked up at a sky filled with terror and saw my hope die. Ultimately love has no power, I thought. Ria sat without moving in the car. She had already seen him, of course. It was she who had seen him fall; she was the chief witness.

Ria was his friend. Or so she says. The last person to know him. I nodded to myself. The very thought of the woman, Ria, fills me with a blinding rage. When I first set eyes on her, her coldness, that icy remoteness, was terrifying. The coach speeds silently through a wintry sky that lightens and lightens and makes me think of the broken birds' eggs Ben used to collect as a child. The memory brings something else to mind but the thought hovers and then evades me. I stare at my hands. They tremble.

'Have some tea,' the woman urges.

She hands me the flask, moves her bag up on to the overhead shelf and settles in her seat. When she smiles, her lower jaw, which is bigger than her upper one, sticks out, giving her a strangely resigned air. She is Italian, she tells me. The last thing I want to do is talk to her, but her face calms me, very slightly. The light outside the window is brightening. I am leaving, I think, again.

I will never forget that building. There had been no grass, no plants growing, only earth that had been turned, like a newly dug grave. The bus lurches and stops before some traffic lights. It waits then moves off again, speeding along a smooth dual carriageway. My mind is playing its new game of hide and seek. Like a wound that bleeds, it occasionally stops, only to start up more vigorously again. I must expect this to happen all the time from now on.

Ria, I think, my mouth filling with grief. Maria. My son was in a relationship with her.

I hear my breath, uneven and hot. Now it isn't simply my hands that are shaking. How had Ben got involved with such a woman? She herself never said a word, but I could work it out. It didn't take much; the row of blown birds' eggs, the photographs of my son, the clothes, brought by her, washed and ironed, folded. I shake my head. What had they had in common? Questions thrust their way into my consciousness. I noticed her eyes first, so blue and brilliant, almost vitriolic; I couldn't look at her for more than a moment. I had the

THE SWIMMER

strangest sensation of looking down into a dark empty pit at something that was no longer quite human. My next thought was of Tara.
Waiting for him at home. I remember thinking, What shall I tell *her*?

'Ria saw them kill him,' I could say.

However terrible it was for her to see it happen, by the time we
met at the airport she was composed. There she stood, at the barrier,
waiting, with a man from the police commission. And a lawyer too.
He will be paid, but not by me.

I shiver, remembering. Arriving has been terrible, leaving will be
worse.

'I am leaving him,' I whisper inside my head.

The woman in the next seat glances sharply at me. Have I spoken
out aloud? I don't know or care. Closing my eyes, I begin tormenting
myself again.

'Can you imagine?' I ask myself. 'Here was a face that I had created.'

Limbs that had been made with the minerals from my own body,
love that had created love. Here were the eyes that had opened their
gaze for me, closed forever.

I stop, confused. Am I speaking out loud? I can't tell the difference. Continue, continue, I think. A mouth that smiled first at me,
unsmiling now, lips that had spoken their first words, a hand so small
that once I held it in the palm of my own. Now motionless. How
could a few shots vanquish him so completely? Will I ask these
questions forever? For the rest of my life?

'You have to find a way of explaining this to yourself,' Eric had said.

I open and close my eyes, again. Not so fast, I say to myself. They
had laid Ben on a slab. He was waiting for me to identify him. When
he was born I had no need to do this, you murderers, I wanted to
scream. He had gone straight into my arms, straight to my breast.
Loved, safe, protected. I am crying again in a way that hurt right
down in my heart and my stomach. Help me, I want to say. I am in
a dark place next to a dark place. I, who hardly ever shed a tear, even
when Percy disappeared, now cannot stop. The Italian woman puts
her hand on mine. It is warm, soft. Instantly I open my eyes and the
tears stop.

'They shot him,' I say. 'Not once, not twice, but several times. Just to make sure.'

The coach passes silently through East Anglia. The Italian woman sits without moving.

I saw the photofit of the man they were looking for.

'See,' they said, 'see how we made the mistake. See how similar they looked.'

It was nonsense; there was no similarity. Could they not see from the way his hair grew, straight up and glossy black, the shape of his beautiful mouth, the smoothness of his skin?

I had gulped for air. I would never have enough air to breathe again. Never.

'Of course, they did not have any time to notice. Shoot to kill. Kill first, think later.'

The woman beside me sits, head bowed, still holding my hand. I must be talking to her.

'In my country,' I say, hearing my voice rising at the mention of home, 'they kill because of war. You expect them to kill; you are surprised if you don't get killed. Here, they kill out of terror.'

The woman looks shocked.

'Do you have a lawyer to fight for you?' she asks. 'Is he going to take the matter up?'

Now I am crying so hard that I don't answer.

'Whatever you decide to do about this, you must not see it as an alternative to grieving,' the woman says. 'You must let yourself lament this terrible chapter in your history.'

I hear her voice through the thick fog of my struggle. All I want, I tell her, or maybe I just think it, is to hear his voice just one more time. Just once; then I will be satisfied. See him walk towards me. He used to say my name with that question in his voice. She is nodding. Then she hands me some paper hankies.

'What has been lost cannot be comprehended easily. Maybe you will never understand.'

How many ways, I wonder bleakly, would I be crucified by this loss? What power did motherhood have to create such pain? Had I been burnt all over, had I had petrol poured on me, had I been tortured, it could not have been any worse. The bus speeds through a landscape of flat indifference. It is haunted by absence. Bare trees on dead earth. Flocks of birds rising as one from the ground. The whole country is a requiem, I think. This is England. This place I have visited so often in my dreams, this country whose history had so completely been entwined with ours; now, the resting place of my son.

'Will you take him home? Will they send his body to your country?'

At that the floodgates really open. I tell her there is no question of it. The Tigers would see him as a betrayer of their cause, the army as a terrorist. So no, there was no safe place to bury him at home.

They had led me into a waiting room. Two of them beside me; a policewoman, a pretty young girl with blonde hair, and one other in plain clothes. I remember a green carpet on the floor and a potted palm in the corner, a smaller version of the sort that grow wild at home. I glanced at it. Everything my eyes alighted on filled me with horror. In some parts of Sri Lanka, in the rich Singhalese gardens of the low country, palms grow to magisterial heights. But here, in this room, the pot that held the palm was dry and needed watering, the leaves were dirty green. It will die in this place, I thought, certain. The policewoman was talking to me. Someone, she didn't know who, had paid for Ben to be embalmed. Her radio crackled. I must have answered because she nodded very slightly. I could see the tension in her face and I wondered what her own life must be like. She was nothing like the police in Jaffna. I could imagine this woman, when she took her uniform off and put her hair down. I could imagine her going dancing with a boy, laughing, eating, doing all those things necessary in order to make human life bearable. Then, as I stood woodenly, shivering in my thin sari, wearing the coat Ria had given me, I heard another sound in the room next door, at first unidentifiable.

'It won't be long now,' the woman in plain clothes said in a low voice.

She had her arm on my shoulder. I could see she did not want me to feel alone. I could see she thought that what I was about to do was a terrible thing and her heart went out to me. Pity crept out from under her uniform in spite of all her professionalism. But a paralysing fear was wrapping itself tightly around my body and I wanted none of it. I wanted no arm around me, no hand touching mine, no word of comfort as I waited to do what I had travelled seven thousand miles to do.

We went in. I do not remember the room at all, except for the fact there were no windows, no natural light. And there was the smell, a strong antiseptic odour when the man in the hospital green stood before me. His lips moved, he was speaking. The policewoman had stayed outside; only the other woman and I approached. Bracing myself, my mind a fearful blank, I walked the immense distance towards the table. The liaison officer was beside me. Unawares I squeezed her hand and I must have said something because she bent towards me and I smelled a faint perfume.

'Yes,' I said again. 'Yes, this is my son. Ben.'

There was nothing in my voice, no feeling, nothing. My heart balanced on its hinge. Yes, it was him. We were meeting again, as we had always said we would. He lay sleeping, as I had seen him sleep so many times in his life, when I would shake him awake, telling him he was late for school, or his interview, or later on for work. Sleep transcended all time zones, I realised. But for the darkening around his mouth and the closed eyes, if I too closed my eyes he might still be asleep. Here lay the end of my journey. It is I, your mother, I wanted to say. What have you done, Ben, while I have been waiting for news of you?

Something came out of my heart into my throat and then into my eyes. I stood staring down at him and then I heard the woman beside me say:

'Take your time, love, stay as long as you want, go out and come back in, if you want.'

I heard her words turn dry and useless in my head. A tight band was holding me together. I shook my head, knowing that while I was here, with these people, kind though they might seem, drones in this lightless room, I would be unable to think.

'Are you sure, my dear? Would you like to sit down next door and then come in by yourself?'

I shook my head. There was nothing here for me. Nothing could come out of this place that was any good. In order to talk with Ben I knew I would have to leave. Turning, a sound rising in my throat in spite of all I did to suppress it, I let her lead me out.

They gave me his things. His clothes, the wallet that Tara had got for him on the black market. A plastic bag with his clothes and his shoes. It was as though I was back home again, standing at the door, bending over the small parcel that was Percy's clothes, left there by an unknown hand. Blood-stained, torn clothes, giving me all the evidence I needed of the violence that I suspected but would never prove. So now I was receiving clothes again, in some other place, like a benediction from strange hands. I sensed sympathy in the way the pen was handed to me. I signed my name as proof of who I was. Ma, he used to call me. They did things correctly here, I saw. And I saw, too, that in the end, it amounted to one and the same thing.

10

SEVEN FORTY-FIVE. OUR COACH IS speeding along a smooth dual carriageway. In the distance I see a large town sprawling for miles. There is a big board above the road, warning of delays. I see the sign for London. The passengers on this coach have fallen asleep. Even the Italian woman has closed her eyes. Above us, flashing past on a steel bridge, I see a man walking briskly. He is followed by a large black dog. For a moment both man and dog are silhouetted in a burst of light. Then they vanish. I have flown halfway across the world, travelling through treacherous stretches of jungle in Sri Lanka, careless of danger, forgetting that the urgency was mine alone and that it would make no difference to Ben, whatever I might do, however fast I go. Now every mile we travel is taking me further away from him.

'Amma,' his voice admonishes me, 'Amma, don't beat yourself with a stick!'

It was the expression he used whenever he saw me become agitated.

When I came out of the mortuary, the woman, Ria, had thrust a tissue into my hand.

'Mrs Chinniah,' she said.

It was the first I knew of my own tears. The police were carefully sympathetic. They were wary of me as if I was some sort of unexploded bomb. After all, they were going to be sued, weren't they?

For getting the wrong man? For thinking my beloved son was a Pakistani Muslim; a terrorist who steals passports and makes bombs. For thinking he had been slaughtering farm animals when all the time it was some white criminal who was framing the refugees. My Ben, who loved *all* animals. There were two crimes, I wanted to scream. And none of them involved my son. The lawyer, hired by Ria, had been grim-faced and determined. Justice, he told me, would be done. Now there was nothing left to fight for, they talked about justice. Ria, her face a perfect, neat symmetry of emptiness, watched me, frowning. Ben would have talked to her about me, of course and I imagined she was trying to work me out. Try, I thought, grimly. What had my son to do with her?

The sun has temporarily disappeared. A large notice advertising fresh eggs flashes by. Grief clots heavily inside me. I dare not move in case it escapes and takes on a life of its own. The coach travels onwards, carrying us through a landscape of vast fields and endless skies. Time passes, minutes move seamlessly. I can tick them off neatly from my life.

As we left the mortuary, Ria asked the driver to drop us off at Saxmundham.

'I've left my car in the car park there,' she said in a low voice.

It was all she said.

'Yes, of course.'

I remember I licked my lips like an animal in a trap. The moment stretched like an elastic band, tightly around my head.

'We'll see you Monday at ten, then?'

Still I continued to stare out of the window.

'Mrs Chinniah?'

It was the lawyer. I couldn't think what his name was.

'Yes,' Ria said quickly. 'Yes, ten on Monday. We'll be there.'

At Saxmundham we changed cars and the lawyer shook my hand. I couldn't look at him. I couldn't speak.

'Not far,' Ria said, glancing at me, as she got into the driver's seat.

The road we took wound its way through empty countryside flanked by fields and leafless trees. They reminded me of a child's drawing. The earth, I thought, had killed itself. It was black and petrified and poisoned. I remembered my father saying long ago when the war first began, we would always love our country no matter what, because we had our childhood in it. We cannot change the way things are, I thought dully.

'Have you eaten?' Ria asked.

I shook my head and she sighed.

'You should eat.'

'I can't.'

She frowned.

'Tomorrow will not be any easier, Mrs Chinniah.'

Why did she keep calling me Mrs Chinniah? I felt a savage stab of rage. I had no idea where it came from, but as if she understood Ria gave me a sharp look. I hate you, I thought. She slowed the car down and turned into a narrow lane. I thought perhaps that we had reached her house but instead I saw a flat colourless expanse of water. It had begun to rain slightly and a late afternoon sun was struggling to break through the tight drum of the sky. Ria drove the car up a pebbled path and stopped. Turning off the ignition, she wound the window down and through the wind I heard the long, keening cry of a lone seagull. It was my undoing, this cry, flying straight to my broken heart. Surely Christ had stopped at this god-forsaken place?

She said nothing while I cried. I must have sat there weeping for twenty minutes or so, but all she did was sit motionless, staring out at the sea through the windscreen of the car. She was cold, you see. A cold, white woman without feeling. I cried as though I hadn't cried already, as if I had only just heard the news. As if the person who had sat so obediently on the long journey here was another person, entirely. After a while, as her silence grew, I began to speak.

'Everything I have ever prayed for,' I cried, 'all throughout these long months, was only that I might see him again. It was all I wanted, going to Mass every day, taking communion whenever I had the chance, hoping to hear word, to see him one last time before I died. And now, God has granted my wish.'

She continued to look elsewhere. The sea rocked very slowly. It smelt of melancholy.

Still she sat, motionless, her face covered slightly by her delicate blonde hair, saying nothing.

'There's a town near the house where I lived as a child,' I told her. 'My grandfather worked there and my father too. When the war flared up again, this place was prosperous; there was a university department, a train station. Many families used to take the train from there to Colombo. There were always people saying goodbye to relatives going down south to find work.'

I don't know why I was telling her this, but I felt, by some tension in the way she sat, that she was listening.

'Then the government reinstated an old rule: no Tamils could continue their studies at the universities. In retaliation, the Tigers mounted a series of attacks on Colombo. I was pregnant with Ben. I can't tell you . . .' I paused, made a gesture, hesitated, not knowing how to express all I had felt. 'This was my first pregnancy, this baby meant everything to me, my whole life was tied up with him. The war was a reality and my father was worried. He wanted us to leave, but where could we go? Percy was only a sub-post office clerk. We had no money, no connections either in India or the UK. I remember my father saying, "One day this war will overwhelm our people. It will destroy this country, make it unrecognisable. And the day will come when we shall see the sea from this verandah." I laughed. This was impossible, I told him, but he was right. One day the government ordered the air force to bomb Jaffna and the university. They flattened the railway station, and from the verandah it is possible to see the ocean, now. Just as my father predicted.'

I stopped talking. Exhaustion drifted over me in waves. Ria moved slightly.

'I want to show you something,' she said, finally, and the next minute she had opened the door of the car and was striding out.

The beach was covered in large brown and white pebbles. This made it peculiarly difficult to walk on, but I followed her. There were a few people walking dogs and some children running along beside the water. Everyone was bundled up in clothes and hats. The cold edged my grief like a bed of thorns. The wind whipped through my thin coat. Ria strode determinedly towards the line of waves. Then she turned to me, her face pale, frowning. I thought how cold she looked, how cold she was, so much part of this landscape, really.

'Look over there,' she called, pointing. 'That's Dunwich. There is a whole town under the sea. Can you see the cliffs?'

I nodded.

'Well, once Dunwich was a medieval town with fifty-two churches.'

'What happened? Was there a war?'

'No, only a war with the sea. There was a terrible storm one day.'

'Like the Tsunami,' I said. 'That destroyed everything in parts of Sri Lanka.'

Ria nodded.

'Yes, I know.'

The light was beginning to go. The sky, which had seemed pale and insipid, had suddenly become stained with blood red. The sea changed.

'This place,' Ria said, and at last she was looking straight at me, 'this is where I came. Afterwards. There was nothing else I could do, you see. They called the ambulance, there were police officers everywhere, I . . .' She spread thin hands out. 'I was superfluous. There was nothing for me to do or say. I was nobody.'

I was struck by the phrase.

'So I came here.'

She swallowed.

'That day,' she hesitated, 'when they took Ben away, before I could ring my friend Eric, I came here, wanting to hear the bells that legend says ring under the waves.'

I saw her lips twist as she tried to keep them in a straight line.

'Did you hear them?' I asked.

I spoke reluctantly. I knew she was trying to share something with me, but I couldn't bear the idea of intimacy now. What had Ben seen in her?

'No,' she said, with an impatient gesture of her hand. 'No. I just wanted to show you this place.'

I knew perfectly well she had brought Ben here. I should have gone up to her, taken her hand, perhaps, maybe, even kissed her. A better woman than I was would have done that. But my son was lying in a windowless room and it was beyond me to summon up the smallest gesture of affection towards this stranger. So instead, we stood staring at the sea; together, yet not.

An early darkness descended, brought down like a curtain, closing up the gap between land and sky and sea. Soon the lights in the town came on one by one and the tips of the waves became ghostly white against the gathering gloom. It was only four o'clock, but already it was dark.

'We should go back to Eel House, Mrs Chinniah.'

'Please don't call me that,' I said, anger rising like the waves. 'My name is Anula.'

'We should go back, Anula. You must be cold.'

Again I was aware of some hesitation on her part, but it was easier to ignore it.

By the time we drove back to her cottage it was pitch black. I had no sense of where we were. The rest of that evening remains a blur. I know at some point she made food, but what it was, and whether I ate it, I have no idea. She offered me a drink of whisky. I shook my head, declining.

'Would you like a glass of wine, instead?' she asked. 'It might help you to sleep?'

Suddenly the one thing I wanted was to be alone. I wanted Tara; I wanted to die, to drown myself in the sea we had just left; to find the church that lay beneath it. As if she could read my thoughts, she took me into the sitting room where she had lit a fire. It was warm and very beautiful in the room. I looked around at the photographs on the piano. I was looking for a picture of Ben. There was a piano. I wanted to ask her if he had played it, but at the same time I didn't want the answer. I felt I was burning up with a fever.

'How long have you lived here?' I asked, instead.

'Permanently for almost four years and before that very occasionally whenever I could. I used to come here as a child. My father's brother owned it, and when he died it came to me. I was lucky.'

I digested her words with barely any interest.

'Mrs Chinniah – Anula,' she corrected herself, 'you should not be here. It is monstrous, this thing that has happened. It *is* a case of mistaken identity. The police were in a rush, the lawyer thinks we have . . . I want to do the best I can about what has happened, to bring them to justice, to make them admit their error. I am sorry you are being put through this, I'm sorry and angry and devastated all at the same time. If I have to spend the rest of my life doing so, I will bring them to justice . . .'

She trailed off and it was my turn to be silent. A great rage was hijacking my grief. What was this woman saying? What did she know about being devastated?

'Ben used to play the piano when he was younger,' I told her, abruptly, reining in my rage.

Ria placed the bottle of wine by her feet, now she poured herself another glass and offered me some again. I nodded. We had bought him a secondhand record player, I told her. And after that he found some records. They were all jazz. He'd play one record over and over again, starting from the moment he woke up until he went to school. Then he'd play it again as soon as he got back home and he'd start improvising it on the piano. Or he'd play one section of the record, one chord, one progression, then he'd do it on the piano. Then back to the record. Then back to the piano. How we laughed! Percy used to throw up his hands in despair; the neighbours, some of the jealous ones, complained because you could hear the sound of that record and that piano a long way away in the evening. People asked us how we stood it. It wasn't living so much with a person, Percy used to say. It was more like living inside an instrument! We began in a way to be affected by the rhythm of the music so that we too tapped out the tune when he started playing, or, in the case of Percy, he would whistle it over and over again until I shouted at them both to stop driving me mad!

'The truth was,' I continued, 'whenever Ben touched that piano, he made it sing. I have never seen anyone play like that. You should have heard him!'

There was a long, significant pause.

'He never forgot how to play it, did he?'

Ah, I thought, so he *did* play for you. And then I looked at her with a kind of pity and also of triumph for I could see how far she had travelled with him, how deep her attachment and therefore her wound must be. And, I thought with bitterness, what kind of a woman was she, not to have given a single thought for Tara, waiting for news from Ben.

'He never stopped playing it,' I said. 'Two weeks before he left we were invited by Father Anselm to go to the big cathedral to a gathering there. Our church is bombed out, you understand. There is no church, just two or three of us gathered together in the jungle. But the cathedral is different. At the back there is a piano left from the old days; when Mass used to be said at Easter and at Christmas. Father Anselm wanted Ben to play for us, for one last time.'

I stopped. Could it be that Father Anselm *knew* Ben would not be coming back? That the significance of his departure was perhaps more than the rest of us realised? Nobody will forget the way he played in that back room of the old cathedral, with the priests sitting there in their shirt sleeves, and a handful of nuns tapping their feet and nodding, and with me, beside them, smiling and smiling as if my heart wasn't really breaking.

'All I know about music is that most people don't really hear it,' I told Ria. 'Ben hadn't been near a piano for almost a year. He was at a tense and troubled crossroad in his life. But that day, when he began to play, he and the piano stammered, started one way, got scared, stopped; started another way, panicked, marked time, started again. They seemed to find a direction, but then they panicked again. Until finally, unexpectedly, almost in a dream, he seemed to find, right there beneath his fingers, the blues. In the darkness of the tropical night, with all the stars out and his trip to England only a moment away, he was telling us the tale of how we suffer and what things make us happy. We sat listening, mesmerised by the music, listening to the tale that is the oldest in the world. It seemed like the only light we had in all that darkness.'

A log fell off in the fire, a shadow crossed Ria's face.

'I was well aware that night that the world was waiting outside, as hungry as a tiger, while trouble stretched above us, wider than the sky. And as I watched him playing that night, I saw what it meant to be a Tamil. How one day, in some way, he would pay the price for being one. In the indigo light, with all the stars shining as they had for millions of years, I saw too that in the scale of things my sorrow hardly counted for anything,' I said.

Ria sat with her head bent. I'm not sure how much she had understood, but she looked beaten. Something vile and uncontrollable rose up in me. It felt like vomit. Good! I thought, and then I said goodnight to her and went up to bed.

11

Eight o'clock. Trumpington. Traffic jam somewhere in Cambridgeshire. A thirty-minute wait. The stationary traffic forms a long, docile line. No horns blasting, no abuse being shouted, nothing falls off the lorries, nothing breaks or buckles. Instead there are grey, faceless buildings, and a sea of red brake lights.

You would think the identification was the worst that could happen to me. You could think it, but you would be wrong. It was my first night in this country but my nightmare was only really just beginning. When what little there was to be said had been said, Ria and I went to bed. The room she had put me in faced the river. I could hear it licking and sucking faintly, almost, but not quite reaching the sea. I lay on the bed like a rack of bone, listening to the long dark night as it passed into infinity. I felt it press against me. I felt I was suffering from a form of sleepless extinction. An owl hooted somewhere in the trees. Maybe it had been hooting for centuries.

Eventually I must have fallen asleep. When I woke I had no idea what time it was. A strange light, stitched through with phosphorescence, greeted me. The silence was as remote as the death I was facing. Had I the experience, I would have understood that snow had fallen in thick blankets around this flat landscape. Unknowing, I went shivering to the window and saw the black-and-white television-set light that came from outside. 'Snow fell undated', the expression came to me from the dredged-up line of a poem I had once read. Memory has its own way of revenge. Emptiness cut through me. Ria slept, exhausted, in her room on the floor below. The house slept with her. I had never seen trees without leaves, never seen their construction so clearly laid bare. One frost-crippled leaf dangled on a branch. I am fifty-two, I thought. An old woman. Yesterday I had not known snow.

I can hardly speak of what happened next. How do I justify it to myself? How to explain that I moved from one dreamlike state to another? Now, when it is too late, sitting on this coach, I think of Percy. I need absolution from Percy. All the violence I had ever witnessed was beginning to fuse together. Think of it, Percy, I beg, silently. I was alone, at the end of the earth, mesmerised by the falling snow. What would you have done? I watched as some flakes fell heavily earthwards while others wheeled around in the semi-darkness. Then I opened the window a fraction and felt the air, tensed up and bleak on my face. Gradually the sun rose, glittering but power-less against such cold. The wind from the day before had died and I heard a high, nasal chatter, ebbing and whimpering into silence. It was a bird moving from branch to branch, flicking the thin powdery stuff on to the ground. I stared crazily at it. The light and the sky and the shadows and even the room I stood in were all against me, I thought. The sheer remoteness and desolation of this place hit me with such force that my legs trembled. Everything had gone except misery.

I closed the window and began to dress, folding and pleating my sari, slowly. My hands looked black against the unnatural snow-light. Come back, come back, come back, my heart cried. I did not hear the soft knock on the door.

'Can I come in?' Ria asked from the other side of the door.

I could not speak.

'Anula?' she opened the door a fraction. 'I've brought you a cup of tea.'

She hesitated. We both stood looking at each other. For the smallest fraction of a moment I think we might have embraced, but then the moment passed, unattended. We are, I suppose, proud women. That is what we have in common. I took the tea from her, nodding my thanks. Unwilling to speak.

'I have a friend downstairs.'

She sounded uncertain.

'I'd like you to meet. His name is Eric. He's . . .'

Again she hesitated. She was nervous.

'He knew Ben.'

I could feel my ability to act politely slipping away.

'Well, come down when you want,' she said finally. 'I'll be in the kitchen.'

And she left quickly, with a downward sweep of her eyelashes. Wearily, for what else could I do, I washed my face of tears and went down. Outside the kitchen I hesitated, listening to the voices.

'There's ice on the car,' Ria was saying.

A man's voice answered, softly. I was startled to hear it. The cold rushed around my ankles, my sari was thin like tracing paper. I opened the door and went in, and instantly there was a scraping of chairs as they both got up.

'You must be freezing,' Ria said.

Was she trying to sound concerned to impress the man?

'Let me get you something warm to put over . . . that.'

The man was very tall and he stooped slightly. He was watching me silently. I remember thinking I liked his face. It was bright with a kind of terrible sympathy. I noticed he had very sharp blue eyes and I had the strangest feeling of having met him somewhere else, long before. Confused, I felt he had stepped off the pages of the Hardy novel I had once loved and the title of which now escaped me. When he spoke, his voice was very soft and a little slurry. I could not guess his age.

'I am Eric,' he said. Holding out his hand. 'I would have known you were the lad's mother, anywhere.'

I couldn't trust myself to speak.

'He was like a photocopy of you!'

Stunned, I could only stare at him.

'Yes,' Ria said. 'Ben's mother, Anula. That's right.'

She gave me a cardigan to wear and a pair of socks. There was a pause while she took three mugs from the dresser. There was a basket at Eric's feet.

'What d'you want me to do with this?'

I could tell by the way she spoke they were comfortable with each other.

'It's for the lady,' he said. 'It's hers.'

And he gave me another sharp, bright look. He reminded me of a sprightly bird.

'What sort of basket is it?' I asked faintly.

It had been woven with some sort of green twigs. I wondered what kind of basket could be so long and thin and with such a small, narrow opening.

'Not a basket,' he corrected me. 'It's an eel-trap, made of willow. I was teaching your lad how to make them, so he could give it a go in the spring. As it was, there was no use for that,' his voice trailed away.

We were silent.

'But he'd started to make one,' Eric said. 'This is it. Never finished, but I reckoned you'd like to have something. And the willows, you know, weeping willows . . . Do you have them, in your home?'

I looked at him. Something moved the hard lump in my chest. A fragment of stone fell away. It was too small to make a difference, but still, I felt it happen. We were silent together and then spoke at the same time.

'I've never seen snow before.'

'I'll get you a pair of thick shoes,' Ria said.

'The river's frozen over. No eels today!'

Eric smiled faintly.

'It's what January used to be like,' he said. 'No proper winter weather. The sort we used to have. When the milk froze in the bottle and the icicles formed on the inside of the lavatory!' Icicles were not something I knew anything about.

'We haven't had this kind of bitter weather for a long time,' he said, getting out a pipe and tapping it. 'Ten years or more, maybe.

There's just been warm winters, with the forsythia coming earlier and earlier. Shouldn't happen, but it does.'

I nodded, not knowing what to say. We sipped our tea.

'Have you heard about the warming, in your part of the world?' he asked.

'Yes. We know all about what's happening to the rainforest and the desert in Jaffna. But there is a war on in my country.'

Killing is what preoccupies us, I wanted to say. We'll think about the world later.

There was a pause. The telephone rang and Ria went out. I felt the atmosphere lighten.

'It's happening here, too; here in Suffolk,' Eric said. 'The sea is moving in, year by year, inch by inch. No one in the government does anything much. This summit and that summit, but the sea doesn't care. We've got freak tides and the rivers are changing. We don't get many eels any more. This was the place where the old eel catchers used to live. There've been eel catchers here for two hundred years. Now I'm all that's left!'

We sipped our tea.

'And the winters that I knew as a lad are gone,' Eric said. 'Now and again, things go back to how they were and we get a real winter, with snow and such like. And then we'll have a spring that isn't silent. It's a joy when that happens.'

He finished his tea.

'It's the earth's way of saying goodbye,' he said unexpectedly. 'It knows there is no future. It's nature's way, slowly, looking backwards, like Persephone.'

I was suddenly alert, mesmerised by his voice. Ria came back in. Then she made fresh tea.

'Only people take it to mean there is no crisis, no warming,' Eric continued. 'But I tell you, there is!'

'Eric has lived over at Fruit Tree Farm for ever, haven't you, Eric?' Ria said.

I was startled by the change in her voice. She likes him, I thought, and then I decided. So do I.

'I was born there. All of us were. I had six brothers and sisters. Not all of them survived childhood. My older brother and I took over the farm. The rest are all dead now, of course. I was the youngest.'

He held out his mug. I could see he was a frequent visitor here.

'There were Bessie and Dick and Ted, and one that died young. And then there was Franny, she was the wildest, and Marge. And last of all, me.'

His eyes twinkled and I was distracted.

'You come from a large family?' he asked. 'Over the way? Where you're from?'

Ria laughed. It was the first time I had heard the sound in months and this, too, startled me. It was the first conversation that I was involved in that didn't feature Ben. The laughter brought on a different kind of pain. Ria was watching me.

'There were two of us,' I said. 'I was the oldest.'

I too am all that's left.

'Eric has an extraordinary local knowledge,' Ria volunteered. 'He knows all about the tides, the winds and the weather histories in the whole of his patch.'

Eric nodded. He looked faintly pleased.

'I'm sixty-two,' he said.

'He knows the stories of the inhabitants, living and dead, and the birds and fish that lived and thrived here, or died throughout the twentieth century, don't you, Eric,' Ria said. 'Distance doesn't mean the same to Eric as it does to most people.'

I know all this, I thought with sudden anger. I can sense it. I felt disturbed. The conversation had moved away from Ben. As if already he was no longer part of the landscape, already a ghost. But strangely, I felt comforted by Eric's presence. I didn't want him to go away, I did not want him to leave me alone with Ria. As if he understood, he looked directly at me and then turned to Ria.

'What's happening, Ria? What has to be done?'

'Nothing today. We've got to wait until Monday morning to see the solicitor and . . . the other things.'

I swallowed.

'So there is a space to breathe, then?'

Ria nodded.

'Why don't you both come over to the farm for lunch?'

'I can't,' Ria said. 'I'm waiting for a phone call from Jack. He might be visiting, briefly.'

Eric frowned.

'Hasn't he said enough?' he asked. 'Hasn't he meddled enough?'

He looked suddenly angry. There was tension between them I didn't understand.

'I can drive Anula over, though,' Ria said. 'If you want?'

I was extraordinarily pleased but didn't want to put them both to such trouble.

'I could walk,' I said.

'Don't be silly. I'd drive you.'

She seemed galvanised, suddenly.

'It isn't far. Eric's farm is worth seeing. It will be a good thing for you to do.'

She was trying to be nice, I thought, but then she added:

'I'll come back and wait for my brother Jack.'

Ah! I thought; it isn't like that at all. She just wants me out of the way. Well, it suited me, too. I did not want to see her brother. Eric looked from one to the other of us.

'Good,' he said, standing up.

Then he began to put his hat and coat and gloves on. He wound his scarf around his neck and slipped on some large rubber boots.

'I'll see you at one, then,' he said.

And he left with a wave of his hand.

Eric's farm was not far but Ria had a steady stream of phone calls which delayed us and it was past one before we left. I had spent the morning staring blankly out of the window at the snow, waiting. The light hurt my eyes. At one point Ria handed me a newspaper with the report of the shooting, but I didn't want to look at it. I had heard somewhere that after a stillbirth a woman was given tablets to dry her milk. Perhaps tears were like mother's milk and the tablets Ria had got from the doctor were drying my tears.

I could have walked to the farm, but Ria insisted on driving me anyway. I noticed the snow had flattened the appearance of the fields, making them similar, removing all distinguishing features. As we drove up to the farmhouse a dog began barking and rushed towards us in a flurry of kicked-up, powdery snow. A moment later Eric appeared, walking slowly, along the side of his house. When he saw us he raised his arm in greeting and headed towards the door, holding it open for me. Ria would not stay.

'I'll be back in a couple of hours, if that's okay?' she said. 'Ring me when you're ready to come back.'

I sensed her desire to be gone. The dog followed her back to the car, wagging his tail, no longer barking. Then when she had driven off it came back and whined to be let in.

'Will you take a bowl of soup with me?' Eric asked when he had hung up both our coats.

I was busy looking around his kitchen. It held traces of the woman who must have once lived there. A pair of faded curtains that had seen better days, an embroidered picture on the wall, a wedding photograph of a young man and a girl. The girl was laughing up at the camera, the man, no more than a boy, looked solemn. I felt my heart flex unaccountably. Hanging over the stove, which was very old and blackened, was a cloth heart tied with a colourless ribbon. *Be My Valentine*, it said in faint stitched letters. A saucepan simmered. I remembered him saying he had been born in this house. Continuity presented itself to me without preamble, the blessedness of it, the simplicity. Eric held two dove-white bowls in his hand. His expression was unreadable. Everything in the room was yellowed with age. I had a sudden, clear picture of the green curtain that separated Ben's room from the rest of our small bungalow. Sunlight filtered down through the trees and a monkey screamed with the piteous sound of a child. The day shifted gear. The blinding light from the snow outside was adding to my sense of unreality.

'It can only get easier,' he said, so softly that I barely caught the sense of his words.

There was something terribly sweet about his voice. I trembled.

He put another log on the fire and we both sat quietly for a few moments.

'In Sri Lanka,' I said, 'when I was a child, we used to cook in clay pots on an open fire.'

The saucepan on the stove grumbled and bubbled. A black-and-white cat was curled up on the brick ledge nearby. Eric bent his head towards me. He still had a full head of curly hair. It was white but once it would have been black. The watch on his wrist was beautiful, I thought irrelevantly.

'Did you live in the countryside?' he asked.

I could hardly catch what he was saying.

'Yes.'

We continued to sit watching the flames. At last I broke the silence.

'You knew my son . . . well?'

'I did. Not straight away. He was working at the next farm over, but one day I saw him swimming in the inlet near Ria's house. I was checking my eel-traps, we got talking, you know . . .'

He picked up a bottle from the shelf behind him and poured wine into tiny, beautiful glasses. The liquid was golden.

'I heard music coming from Eel House, another time,' he said. 'Blues music. It was drifting out towards the river. Way upstream. Ah! I thought, and I went to have a look. It'd been a long time since I heard music coming from there. Try some of this,' he added, raising his glass to his lips. 'It's red onion wine.'

The wine was sweet, not a bit like onion. Again we sat in silence. He put his hand out and touched the folds of my sari, curiously.

'I've never seen one of these up close,' he said.

He smiled apologetically, and in spite of myself I smiled, too. He had the most piercing gaze. I saw a confusion of grief in it, mirroring my own.

'Isn't it cold, wearing it?'

I shook my head.

'It's what I'm used to. It's what I am.'

He nodded, as if satisfied by my answer. Then he poured out the soup. He cut two chunks of bread and placed a small square of butter, some knives and two spoons on the table. He wouldn't let me help him.

'No, you rest,' he said.

The dog was whining again but he ignored it. We ate in silence with the only sound being the slight spitting of the fire and our spoons scraping against the bowls. I suspended all thoughts for the moment. Like a pilgrim on the way to Adam's Peak, in the centre of Sri Lanka, I rested in this oasis of calm.

'He was a long-distance crosser, was your lad,' he said, finally.

The tone of his voice was gentle. It was many years since I had heard such an expression.

'Like the geese,' he said. 'Or the egrets and the coots. They come from all over the world. Like the eels, too. Beautiful creatures, all of them.'

He finished his tiny glass of wine. His face in repose was still handsome. It was the same face, I suspected, that had been loved when he was a child. He reached for the bottle and offered me more wine. When I shook my head he poured himself some instead. I felt a confusion of emotion struggle within me. He understands, I thought. He knows how I feel.

'The rivers used to be full of them in the summer – the eels, I mean. Some people didn't use to like them, they were afraid of the thought of them, I think. But eels are beautiful creatures, you know. Did you know they swim all the way over here from the Sargasso Sea?'

His voice was a caress. I shook my head.

'They do! All the way. Can you imagine? I used to wonder what the Sargasso Sea was like when I was a lad. Mother used to say, "Well, go, then! Leave the farm and go find it!" But I never did, of course. Too frightened to leave. Little skinny chicken, I was.'

He chuckled. The sound was startling. Like a bell clearing the air.

'Know what I mean?'

I nodded.

'Well, it didn't stop me dreaming. On spring nights, when it was warming up and the water was still, I used to row my boat along the river, just around here. Not far from Eel House. Ria's Uncle Clifford used to let me put my traps along his stretch of water.'

He paused.

'I became an expert at catching them.'

I was listening properly, now, trying to imagine the river in warm weather.

'They were beautiful when they first arrived. We used to call them glass eels on account of the fact they were so transparent. Like old-fashioned green bottle glass. When they started out from the Caribbean they were quite small. It took them about three years to get here.'

It was clear that this notion still amazed him.

He stopped speaking and gave me a curious look which I couldn't respond to. Then, with a small, modest gesture he put his hand over mine. I sat very still as if my survival depended on it. Since my arrival in this country, touch had been mostly absent. Now, with no warning, I began to cry. Eric sat with my hand covered by his, never moving while the fire crackled and spat, until at last I raised my head and found him looking at me. I wiped my eyes and blew my nose and still he sat without speaking.

'I'm sorry,' I said, making a useless gesture with my hands.

'I was thinking,' he said.

'What?'

'That you must have looked like this when you were small; when you fell over, when you were unhappy. This would have been how you looked. Young and full of despair. Full of passion.'

I was so taken aback that I didn't say anything. Then I asked, did he mean childhood unhappiness was preparation for this terrible day? He shook his head.

'No.' He smiled. 'I simply meant you would have looked beautiful even then. I hope you don't mind me saying this.'

He reached up and touched my face, wiping away my tears with his two thumbs. Speechless, I stared at him.

Grief had unhinged me. What happened next was beyond comprehension. There was no shame; not at that moment, anyway. When he touched me I felt a rush of excitement in my throat. I had not realised how physical, how taut my feelings were. Or how much I needed to be held. I stood at the edge of an oasis, my heart quivering with its grief, desperate for some relief. I had the curious feeling that Eric too was weighed down by some mysterious and wordless pain that had nothing at all to do with me yet was connected in some awful way. Perhaps it was this thought that loosened my sanity finally, this recognition of a kindred spirit. Dumbly I reached up and brought his face towards me. Who will understand that moment? Love had been murdered and only love would suffice. I felt him resist me and then it happened and he was kissing me. Nor did it strike me as anything more than curious, afterwards, to find myself in a room at the top of the house with Eric beside me. A sharp light fell slantways across the threadbare carpet. The soft white sheets, the plumped-up duvet, the faint fragrance of the washed cotton, gave my tired, wracked body warmth; it was comforting, like a bird's nest. If I told myself I had no knowledge of what I did, I would be lying. I did. Percy, what would you make of me now? I must be honest, it was I who made the first move. It is astonishing how need transcends all else, miraculous how the old ways of loving survive.

Sitting on this coach with my locked-up secret, I see that it was a kind of blind loving. Afterwards. I would be filled with shame, shocked into a dead-ended silence. Afterwards, I would think, oh God, why? How? But at that first moment, with the soft amnesia of snow outside, it was another matter. I have to remember.

I have to remember how he tried to save my sanity. At least he tried, Percy. When he entered me, I just thought, It's not so bad, really, just something going in and out of me somewhere far down my body. So what? I thought, brazenly. Who will know? The dog whined outside the door. Truly, I felt nothing then. I had stopped thinking of Ben. Yes, that's the brutal fact. What we were doing was lessening the pain. It was the end of the story; only it wasn't. If I felt nothing to start with, that didn't last. Lust entered the room with stealth and tore the celibacy off me. I must admit, it was a relief to stop the grief. Defiance that had been knocked out of me, because of who I was and how I had lived, returned. I stopped thinking. Desire, anguished and fearless, overflowed in me. If he was taken aback, he didn't show it. It had been years for him too. We were in this together. At last, after decades I was engaged in something I had not known I missed. Of course, I didn't think like this at the time. That would have been real madness. No, I didn't think at all.

He entered me in silence. I was the one who made the noise. There were goose pimples on my exposed arm, whether from the cold or fright I have no idea. I remember at one moment, I think perhaps when his hand strayed helplessly to my breast, I opened my eyes and saw fragments of things. A bit of curtain, a yellowed wall, the edge of a mirror. A thin shoulder. But at least, one part of my brain screamed, at least he was alive. I didn't care, you see, that I was a widow, betraying a dead husband, a mother waiting to bury her son, a guest in Ria's house. We were in a hurry and slow at one and the same time; ending and starting again almost without pause. How hungry for sex must we have been? It was astonishing. Finally – it felt like a long finally – he tired before me and fell back, grey-faced and exhausted, on the bed. Still shame did not come to me. I could look at him at last and what I saw was this. His body was very white and long and there was the thinness that came from old age. I reached down and placed my hand between his legs, and then I saw him gazing into my eyes as though they were precious stones. Before I could speak he placed a finger on my lips.

'Don't say anything,' he said.

The sky had darkened.

'There will be a fresh fall of snow, soon,' he said. And then he said, 'All of you is very beautiful.'

There was a curious softening and mounting ache in my limbs. I must have fallen asleep because I don't remember much after that. The next I knew was Eric sitting beside me on the bed, holding out a bowl of soup, without a word, just a small sideways smile. He handed me a spoon with this smile still on his face and I ate. This was the first food that I had actually tasted since the accident. Was I enjoying myself, now? Guilt knocked but did not enter as he kissed me again.

'I don't know why . . .' I began, after I had finished eating.

'It doesn't matter, why.'

He took the bowl out of my hand and shook his head.

'Between us,' he said, 'there is no need for explanations. You are beautiful,' he said again.

Percy, I thought. As yet I felt no sense of the betrayal.

Later, he helped me dress with a tenderness locked into his fumbling fingers, holding my sari while I wound it around me. Snow was falling again and it made me cry. Things were coming back, like spiders, slowly out of the corners. Seeing how it was going to be for me, quietly, tactfully, he distracted me by telling me about his passion for eels. I listened passively, watching his hands. I wanted him to touch me again. Perhaps, I remember thinking, I am finally going mad.

'They came all this way, only to be caught in traps,' Eric said.

Startled, I looked at him, but he was still talking about the eels.

'I told your lad about them. He was interested. "Maybe I can catch some," he said.'

I breathed in sharply. I didn't want to talk about Ben.

Overhead, geese plotted a line across the sky. Eric was looking at me steadily. He took my hand in his large warm one and the dog whined, jealously. There was a hard, merciless piece of guilt forming inside me. I would have to deal with it, soon.

'I took him out in the boat at dawn to check the traps. He was in the middle of weaving one of his own when it happened.'

He poured more wine out and as I stared tears fell from my eyes in huge drops on the table. Like the monsoon, with the same tentative beginning. The tablecloth was checked with faded baskets of fruit. Once it must have been lurid, I thought. Hysteria threatened. Eric's hand, gnarled and roughened, squeezed mine.

'There have always been migrants in the world,' he said. 'It's one of the wonders of nature. But there's a risk attached to the journey. Always. We don't think of that.'

I nodded. There were fine lines on his face.

'He brought you here. This *was* his home, however briefly. It will be yours now. Forever. Because of him.'

A clock in another room chimed. Time hesitated. Eric sliced his hand through the air. Certain. I could see he wasn't going to stop talking until he was sure of me. He put another log on the fire and then he came and knelt by me, rubbing my hands with his.

'I can see you're going to, but you mustn't think badly of what happened,' he said. 'We have shared love. If it has helped in any small way, then it is a good thing.'

I said nothing, hanging my head, staring at his hands.

'Tomorrow is Sunday. I'll get Ria to bring you here again. Or I can fetch you?'

Seeing the look on my face, he shook his head.

'Don't think . . . I'm not expecting . . .' He broke off, looking helpless. 'There is nothing you can do except wait until Monday morning. I want to show you some of the countryside under snow; the places where your son roamed. That was all I meant. It will make the waiting a little easier, perhaps.'

I told him Ria would probably want me to stay at her house.

'Don't worry about Ria. She will want you to do whatever makes you feel comfortable.'

He put both his hands on my arms and shook me very slightly.

'She's devastated, too,' he said. 'I know she's being very detached. But when it happened, she came here. She had run off to her place on the beach and then, not knowing what to do, she came here. Homing. She didn't want to speak to that bloody brother of hers.'

I was momentarily distracted, puzzled.

'Jack,' Eric said. 'He's . . . ah, well . . . he was messed up long ago. Through no fault of his own. Maybe we could all have done more . . . but, well, it all happened so quickly and we didn't react fast enough, and then it was too late, the damage was done. He's a strange man . . . he always wanted to hurt his sister, his wife – everyone. Ria was her father's favourite and when he died I think Jack resented this. Who knows, really? He's lost. They both are, because of what the mother did.'

I was getting cold and had begun to shiver. Eric glanced quickly at me. His eyes were like bright marbles.

'Ria is . . . not like him. Jack was shocked to hear how much . . . how . . .' he hesitated, swallowing. 'She loved your lad,' he said softly.

I knew my thoughts were showing on my face.

'You find her lacking in feelings, perhaps? But, you know, it's her way of dealing with it. She shuts down. Ever since she was little. It's her way of surviving.'

He fell silent.

'She is suffering too,' he said at last. 'I know it isn't the same, of course I do. I haven't been a farmer for all these years for nothing. I have seen the mothers.'

He looked directly at me, then. I saw he was exhausted too, and worried about what we had done. And I saw also that there were no regrets in him.

'I'm not good with words, but for what it's worth, I know how you feel,' he said again.

'There was someone else in Jaffna,' I told him. 'Someone who thought . . . who hoped . . .'

I couldn't go on. Eric sighed.

'That's all right, too,' he said. 'The boy was only trying to survive. Like all of us, just trying to survive, really. Ria knows, anyway, about that girl. It's painful for her.'

I shook my head.

'He did what he had to do. It's a part of his life.'

The dog rose and whined, then sat down again and yawned.

'If you stand watching the shoals of fish as they pass,' Eric said, 'that is all you'll ever see. But you must look at the patterns they make, the way the currents flow and how many pass through the corridor of departure on their journeys elsewhere. And only then do you understand that some will survive. And these ones are like you and I, living on to tell the story.'

The fire suddenly flared up, lighting his face in profile. He rose and stirred it and then he fed the dog and after that the cat. The walls of the kitchen were tobacco mellow with age. Yet the soup had been delicious and the floor was swept clean.

'Look to the land,' he said when he had finished his tasks and filled the kettle. 'That's what I always do. My son was killed in Afghanistan. When my wife died, and then, after, when the boy died, I just kept going. And I looked to the land. It's all that endures.'

But our land was war torn, I told him. There was nothing there any more.

'No,' he disagreed. 'The land is still there. Hurt – that's what it is. Damaged by bloodshed. But still there. What has happened in this new century is wrong, but it will pass.'

He placed a mug of tea before me.

'The twenty-first century is full of non-places,' he said with distaste. 'There are waiting rooms and stations and airports. There is no fixed place called home any more, so they tell me.'

It shocked me to see how handsome he was.

'People carry their home in their heads. It's how things are now, and we have to live with this change. To find home wherever we travel is a gift.'

He looked tired. I felt he had loved Ben.

'Your son was trying to do this. As you will, because of him. It's the only thing left.'

The dog sat up suddenly and pricked his ears, listening to a sound out of our range.

'When the war was over, half the dead were in foreign places. Those that survived knew they would have to migrate in their mind's eye to those places.'

He took his pipe out of a pocket. Watching him, I was reminded of Percy. I thought of him smoking his pipe, squatting on the verandah, staring at the tamarind tree in the furthest part of the garden. He had known that peace would not last for ever.

'You're right,' I said out loud. 'I am in a state of transit between different worlds. My home is a thing of the past. There is no return to it.'

'Make your home wherever you and those you love have walked, Anula,' Eric said. I almost smiled at the way he pronounced my name.

Tobacco filled the room with comfort. Just for a moment, I had been given respite from the darkness. What more could I ask for? I thought. The dog barked, there was the sound of a car. Ria. The sunlight moved a little. In some other life I might have looked for some sort of future with the man sitting opposite. In some other place.

'There'll be even more snow later,' Eric said. 'I can feel it in the air. Tomorrow.'

He did not mention what we had done, how we had touched each other's nakedness, but I knew he was filled with a sort of wonder. And I thought of the transparent glass eels he had talked of, carried on currents each year towards the cold waters of the spring tides, to the rivers of England; and how some of them returned and some of them did not.

12

EIGHT THIRTY-FIVE. TOWARDS STANSTED. GRIEF WEARIES the mind in inexplicable ways. It sticks close, becomes your second skin, suffocating you slowly behind closed doors. But guilt is a different matter. Guilt burns a hole in the psyche, spilling adrenalin restlessly, always watchful in case the truth is uncovered. Until that moment I had been awash with grief, ebbing and flowing steadily. It had weakened me with its strong current. But now, in an instant, that changed. In the car, going back with Ria, we were both silent. Small talk had never been an option. Unsaid things shook like water in a bottle between us.

'How did you get on with Eric?' she asked.

We drove through the dying light. Feathery tree-skeletons dotted the fields. It had stopped snowing but the daylight had almost gone. The wide, flawless landscape had become static. Low clouds suggested further snow some time soon. Sensations of all kinds assailed me; I was in a state of shock. I wanted to talk to Ria about Eric. I wanted to say, in a different sort of life, anything might have been possible after today. But in a different sort of life I would not be the person I was now. What I had now wasn't what you would call a life.

'He was very kind,' I said instead.

I couldn't look at her. Madness was propelling me towards further deceit. Petrified, I sat without speaking.

'Did he talk to you about the animals that migrate here each year?'

I nodded.

'It's his special subject. Did he tell you about his dead son?'

'Just that he died in Afghanistan.'

'I don't think Eric ever got over his death. He was tortured, you know. And then beheaded. There was no body.'

'*What?*'

I glanced at her profile. She was giving nothing away.

'Probably he didn't want to detract from what has happened. He's that kind of man. I've known Eric for a long time. He told me once . . .' she hesitated, 'he felt the world itself had died with that boy. It was such a horrendous event. He was taken hostage, you know. There had been nearly a year of agony before they killed him. Not long before they did, while there was still hope, Eric's wife died. He said he was glad she had been spared the grief.'

'He never said a word.'

Ria smiled. I felt her relax very slightly.

'Eric is a complicated person. Probably he didn't want you to think he was encroaching on your feelings.'

I digested this in silence. What have I done? I thought. As we approached the house, I noticed something move by the line of match-stick trees.

'Oh, look,' Ria said, pointing. 'Look over there. A deer!'

The animal stood motionless. The more I looked at this beautiful creature, the sadder I became.

'A young deer. Its mother must have been killed, I suppose.'

'Look how still it is,' I said.

'It's petrified by the headlights.'

She slowed the car, but the deer continued to stare in our direction. Then, as she cleared the windscreen, suddenly, it was gone. The snow was veiling the dirt and the death that was everywhere. Hiding reality, pretending it didn't exist.

Her brother was in the sitting room reading the newspaper when we arrived. There was a fire made up in the grate.

'I have to go soon, Ria,' he said, without looking at me.

He was a man in a smart suit, the sort of man I had seen in Jaffna when there had been some peace talks.

'This is Anula,' Ria said.

Next to him, she suddenly appeared frail.

'My sister is very upset by what has happened,' he said when she left the room. 'Hence her generosity.'

He smiled thinly. I presumed he meant the money for the airfare and the visa. He wanted gratitude, I saw.

'Not just that,' he corrected me. 'I mean, she's had to guarantee your trip too.'

Of course I knew. I told him she had insisted she would help. That I had not asked.

'Yes, well,' he said.

I could hear him rattling the loose change in his pocket. What did he want me to say? That I would pay her back? I had no money. Did he not know I had paid for Ben to leave and so had nothing? He was silent, staring at the fire and then his feet. I could hear Ria clattering cups in the kitchen. Shame spread its heat over me. I was a beggar in this country, unwanted, despised. I stood, caught in the dim glow of the fire, not knowing what I should do. Ria came in with a tray and switched on a light.

She went back out again.

'I will try to pay her back,' I said, speaking softly, so she wouldn't hear.

'Good!' Jack said, shortly. His voice was like his sister's. 'These are difficult times for all of us, you know. With the fall in the stock market and problems with investments,' he mumbled.

'What do you mean, Jack?' Ria said sharply, coming in with a jug of hot water.

'I mean we are all a lot poorer in this country at the moment,' he said crossly.

'I don't know why you need to tell us that,' she retorted.

Jack made a small, irritated sound and checked his watch.

'Look, can we stop fussing and have this tea. I've got a long drive ahead.'

She nodded instantly.

'There's going to be more snow tonight.'

'Exactly. I don't want to be cut off,' he said. 'I've work tomorrow.'

He went soon after that, gathering his coat and briefcase. His mobile phone rang once and he answered it impatiently. I noticed that everything he did, every gesture, had an undertone of irritation. I had begun thinking in Tamil. My mind had switched into another mode and I could not think of a single thing to say in English. As he was leaving, kissing his sister briefly on the cheek, nodding in my direction without looking at me, the doorbell rang. I stood up and moved towards the hall as a draught of cold air was let in.

'Oh, hello,' I heard Jack say. 'What are you doing out in this weather? Ria, it's Eric. Sorry – can't stay, long drive and all that.'

I froze. The front door closed and I could hear Eric talking to Ria quietly. There was a sound of a car skidding as it turned and then the sound of it disappeared into the distance.

'Anula,' Ria called out, 'Eric's back to see you!'

No one knew what to say.

'You left this behind,' he said, without looking at me, giving me my handbag.

It was my best handbag, but in the reality that I was in, it looked small and shabby. I was ashamed.

'I was thinking I'd call for you tomorrow,' he said in a low voice, 'and we'd go for a drive in the snow.'

'Would you like a glass of wine, Eric?' Ria asked, reappearing with a bottle.

'I'd like that,' I said awkwardly. 'What time?'

'You'll need to wear something else,' Ria said.

We spoke at the same time. She poured the wine. In the firelight I was shocked to see how sick she looked.

'Sorry,' she said, pulling a face. 'I feel sick.'

And she went out, quickly.

'Anula,' Eric said.

He turned towards me, but I was looking at the ground.

'Look at me.'

'I didn't know what I was doing,' I whispered.

'Listen,' he said. 'I came here because I was worried about you, knowing what you must be thinking. I don't want you punishing yourself. Let's talk tomorrow? Can we?'

Still, I couldn't look at him.

'Anula, we did nothing wrong. There isn't anything to be ashamed about, you know. We haven't hurt anyone. Anula?'

He moved nearer to me. Already I loved the way he said my name, but I was also trying to hold on to thoughts of Ben.

'Not now,' I murmured.

I felt sick with a myriad of emotions. We could hear the sound of Ria's movements in the other room.

'She's not feeling too good,' Eric said. 'I'll go now. Will you promise me one thing? Will you promise me you will not judge any of this until we speak tomorrow?'

I could promise him nothing. Seeing this, understanding, in part, he put his hand on mine. Then he bent over and kissed me on the cheek. I knew he understood more than he said, I knew, too, that he was suffering, but the judgement I was rapidly making on myself blocked his words. He could see there was no talking to me.

'Ten o'clock,' he said, squeezing my hands. 'Okay? Tell Ria I said goodbye.'

And he left.

The rest of the evening was terrible. Under any circumstances, even if I were not a woman who lived in a different culture, what had happened would be in bad taste. I wanted a priest; I wanted to confess to someone. Ria had made something to eat, but neither of us had any appetite. All I wanted was to rest a little until the morning came. She understood and gave me some pills. I knew she kept them in the bathroom cabinet upstairs. I knew where the rest of them were. Ria had hollows around her eyes, made darker by the firelight. We spoke a little but only of trivial things. She told me that she had not seen such a snowfall as this since she was a child. I told her that I had first heard about snow in books from England. I looked at her obliquely. What would she say if she knew what I had done today?

177

We did not mention Ben. Accident had brought us all together but then abandoned us, unconnected.

On the television that night the news was all about the war between Israel and Hamas. I saw bodies of children being removed from the rubble created by Israeli war planes. If you closed your eyes slightly, the images could be of Jaffna. Women crying as they do the world over, men watching in stunned silence while others held up machine guns as victory signs; dancing in the street. There was nothing new here. A small child, covered in blood, carried in her father's arms, rushed screaming towards a waiting ambulance. I watched, impassively. The child had dark glossy hair, just like Ben's. If you took away hope, I wondered, if you destroyed everything precious, if you showed no mercy, did you make a suicide bomber? My heart was a stone. To have nothing is a million miles away from having very little, I thought. Ria sat beside me. I thought of the endless wiping out of generations at home. Love that could never return. Images of the Israeli flag being burnt outside some embassy in London flickered on the screen. The camera panned the road outside Downing Street. Perhaps, I thought, if we had fought harder, if more of us had been slaughtered, the world might have noticed?

'At least we can fight for justice,' Ria said.

Startled, I looked at her.

'I mean, if we can get to court,' she said. 'If it is possible, I shall do it. I want people to know what happened. The disgrace of it.'

I didn't want to comment. In her very first phone call she had told me her plans to bring the police to account.

'I will fight for it!' she had cried. 'I promise.'

I wondered if she believed this was still possible or whether, like me, she now knew it was a hollow hope. The dead could never be vindicated.

The news finished and she poured herself a glass of water. Then she turned to me.

'What will you do when you get back?' she asked. 'How will you manage?'

She looked a little wild. Tension coiled in me, hysteria bubbled up. I wondered if I might get to her bathroom cabinet after she was asleep.

What I did was no longer of any importance to me, I wanted to shout. Why do you care? I wanted to scratch the calm off her face, make her react. Maybe it was myself I wished to hurt? The urge died as suddenly as it arose.

That night I did not sleep. Hours went by; occasionally I went over to the window and looked out, but there was never anything to see. Snow fell invisibly in the darkness and the temperature dropped further so I could not even stand by the window for long. Several times I wanted to leave my room, but the light under Ria's bedroom door stopped me. I had forgotten about Tara. All night I tossed around in the darkness. Several times I saw the light in the hall go on and once I heard Ria in the bathroom. She's ill, I thought. Grief has sickened her and revealed me as a different kind of woman. Unscrupulous, without morals. The truth was out. On and on I went, unable to think of Ben, trying to forget Eric. And the worst of it was, I wanted him, again. Tomorrow, I decided, I would get the tablets from the bathroom and without fuss would end it.

The coach has come to a halt, stuck in another traffic jam. Someone is asking the driver how long we will be. The passengers seem restless, anxious to move on to their final destination. All of them except me. I sit trying to make sense of the things that I did and didn't do.

The next morning, as promised, Eric arrived. Ria and I had both woken at the same time. I'd say neither of us had slept much. Ria gave me a pair of trousers and a pullover. She gave me some tights and socks, she gave me gloves and boots. Then she made us both breakfast, which neither of us ate.

'I'm going to spend the morning working,' she said.

But then she pulled a face.

'Well . . . in theory,' she qualified.

Her eyes were red-rimmed and I thought she must have spent the whole night in tears.

'Eric is being very sweet to you,' she said.

Does she know? I thought, petrified.

'I think he liked Ben, that's all,' I told her.

'If he didn't like you, he wouldn't bother this much. Eric isn't

179

polite. He hates my brother, for example. He can hardly bear to say hello!'

I made a small sound of denial, which she didn't hear.

'Why shouldn't he like you, anyway?'

I knew her motives were admirable, but as I could not match them, I hated her for it. Suddenly it seemed to me that all I had ever despised in my own people, my hatred of their deceit and their destructiveness, their jealousies, their prejudices, applied to me too. I was filled with self-loathing. I went searching in Ria's bathroom, but the bottle of tablets had gone. There was nothing to do but face Eric.

He was dressed in an old-fashioned suit that made him look smarter, younger than he had yesterday. He took his cloth cap off and unwound the scarf around his neck. Then he handed both of us a white flower.

'It's a hyacinth,' he told me. 'I was growing them in my green-house and I noticed a few days ago that they were beginning to come out.'

I didn't know how to thank him, so I reached up and kissed him on the cheek, awkwardly. To cover my confusion, I told him I knew these flowers. We had our own varieties growing in the canals near Jaffna. Ours were water hyacinths and they grew wild but they smelt the same. Ria didn't say anything. The scent of the flowers was strong in the warmth of the kitchen. The light from outside sharpened across the kitchen table. There was a feeling of suppressed violence in the room.

'What will you do?' he asked Ria, as I put my coat on and pulled on my boots.

'Oh, I shall try to work.'

'Why don't you go back to bed, love?' Eric said, and I was struck by the tenderness in his voice. 'You'll do no work today.'

She shook her head without looking at me.

'No, I must try.'

I thought of all the things she must be longing for. For the funeral to be over, for me to leave, for her to get her own life back, or the pain of this relationship to die down, for another to take its place. Just like me, I thought bitterly. I've become like some white woman. Eric was watching me.

Outside, the snow was falling more slowly. It would go on all day in this way, Eric said.

He turned the heat up in the car. In the few minutes that he had been inside, snow had covered the windscreen.

'I saw your deer,' he told me.

She must have spoken to him after I went to bed. Had they talked about me, too?

'It's lost. Mother killed by poachers, no doubt, and the rest of the herd's probably rejecting it. Not sure how long it will survive. I rang the rangers, they're going to take a look, see what they can do.'

'Where did you see it?' I asked.

'Just by the copse, leaving my house, you know. On the brow of the hill.'

In another life I would have marvelled at the way he spoke; the lilt in his voice, the storybook words. Our ex-colonial lives had been marked not only by violence, but also by the romance of the English language. Far more than we were prepared to acknowledge. My father would have loved to visit; Percy, too. And here I was, instead, sleeping with a stranger. It was a nightmare.

'The snow is beautiful,' I murmured.

'You were brought here,' Eric said, 'by your lad. Think of it like that. He's opened up this part of the world for you. And brought your world to me. Though that's less important.'

I felt myself beginning to shake. There were animal tracks all the way down to the frozen river.

'Would you rather we didn't go back to the house?' he asked.

'Oh no,' I said before I could stop myself.

Suddenly I desperately wanted him to touch me again. Appalled, I knew what else I wanted. Terrified, I wanted to run away.

'There's nothing wrong with you,' he said. He spoke very gently. I had heard him talk to the dog in this way. 'You're just stunned. What do you expect? That your mind can take in everything all at once?

It isn't possible. You found some comfort. By chance. It came your way. Don't question it. Accept. You have hurt no one.'

We were driving through a white landscape of breathtaking beauty. Snow hung like fruit off the bare branches.

'When my son was killed,' Eric said, 'everyone was sympathetic. The papers were full of the tragedy of the war in Afghanistan. I had public support. The locals all knew me, knew my son. They had known my wife, of course; some of them had even come to her funeral. So everyone was kind to me. They cooked me food, they did my laundry for me. Some of the lads, mates of my son's who had got back safely, were already helping on the farm. And there was a woman I knew in Snape. She was called Ellen.'

He paused. I said nothing, staring out of the window. We were turning into the lane that led to his house. The dog had heard the car and was barking. When we stopped, he first opened the door before helping me out into the cold. Snow fell on my face, on my lips and I licked it without thinking. He was watching me with a small smile, inscrutable. I wanted him to finish the story of his son, but the dog was racing around in the snow, joyously wagging its tail. It recognised me.

'Floss,' Eric called.

He whistled and the dog came back obediently and shook itself all over the flagstones.

'Something to drink,' Eric said, and he put the kettle on.

He took out a small fruit loaf and began to slice it.

'My neighbour at the next farm baked this today. Try some.'

He put out butter and mugs and a jug of milk. Then he poured us both some strong, bitter-tasting coffee and buttered a piece of the fruit bread.

'I wanted you to taste the fruit from my trees,' he said.

I had not heard such a tone of voice for years. He took out his pipe and began to clean it. I waited.

'Well, Ellen thought, I suppose, since I was, you know, a widower, just lost my only son, perhaps I needed comfort. I didn't look too upset, you see. I looked as if I was just, well . . . lonely. There was no proper funeral because he was killed overseas and there was no body to bring back. I didn't shed a tear at the memorial service, and afterwards I seemed to carry on in true British fashion. The war was still raging. But it was elsewhere.'

Eric paused and emptied his pipe. Then he began to pack it with tobacco.

'Ellen was very good to me. She was always cooking me little tit-bits I didn't want but ate anyway because I didn't want to hurt her feelings. We went on like that for a few months.'

He smiled and lit his pipe. Then he drew on it and puffed out the smoke. Instantly I breathed in the tobacco and something stirred within me.

'It was winter when my son was killed. A winter just like this; heavy snow cutting off the farms, making it difficult to move around much. Weather from Siberia, everyone said, I remember. I had cows in those days, so there was milking to be done. The trucks came for the milk daily. Ellen was there for me, helping in every way she could. Then finally the snow began to thaw and the rivers to flow again. The weather was still bitter and now there was rain, too. In all this time I said nothing about my son, never even mentioned his name. Something was locked in me. Something had got stuck.'

He sat quietly, the smoke from his pipe filling the room. The whole world was steeped in silence as Eric continued his story. He told me that spring had come before he felt anything. One morning he had been out with the tractor and the air was filled with the smell of earth. Fresh, clean smells. It had been a warm day, an exceptionally blue sky. He remembered it as if it were yesterday. Willow trees were beginning to grow leaves again. He had heard a cuckoo, the earth was on the move, restless to recharge itself. Eric, too, felt restless. He knew Ellen should not be there, doing his washing, cooking his food. She should have moved on and found her own life. She might have done, if he hadn't been encouraging her with his silent acceptance of her presence. But he saw that she had been useful in bandaging up his emotions.

'I was standing there, looking over the land, I remember,' he told me, 'whenever a formation of planes flew overhead. It was what they always did at that time of day, practising, I suppose, for the future. The war was hotting up. More and more young men were being killed and needed replacing, and I guessed there were secret plans for some big event. Anyway, the planes flew over like a flock of birds and I watched them disappear over the horizon. And suddenly, at that moment, something broke in me. Broke completely. I cried as I have never cried before. Or since. I cried for all the lost innocence over that horizon.'

He stopped talking and re-lit his pipe.

'Later,' he said, with a sad smile, 'I told Ellen it would not work between us.'

We sat in silence. I had eaten the bread without noticing. The dog whined in its sleep and Eric sighed and stood up. He took my hands in both his and looked at me.

'You are grieving in your own way,' he said. 'Not as others might expect you to, but in your own way. What happened between us . . . it need not be spoken of. Not because there is shame attached, but because it is something just for you . . . what little light I can give. Soon you will be gone. Take comfort where you can; one love does not cancel out another. You'll see.'

And then he led me upstairs to the little room with its funny crooked windows and its amazing view of the flat, white land.

I am thinking of that moment, now, from the distance of this journey in the coach. That was all it was, a moment. Gone in a flash. Love of a kind, comfort too. I did not think of Ben. I had suspended thought. What was in that loving, that I never had before? Expectations, perhaps; hopelessness, certainly. He told me he was an old man, I said I was a woman nearly so. I know that touch was what I craved. I had never wanted anything in my entire life quite so much as him. The room was warm and familiar this second time. We were slower. He was looking at me; we were looking at each other with all awkwardness gone. He told me his son had died ten years ago and I guessed that Ellen had left him not long after that. How did he, a man from the other side of the moon, understand my needs?

There was no rush, he said. Days and years would follow, so why rush now? Fiercely he filled me, gasping I held him. Something luminous passed between us and there were tears on both our faces, perhaps for different reasons. But I knew he was giving me his heart. Afterwards, he stroked my hair, we got up, dressed in gloom, went downstairs. Like an almost-lost species. What we made together, together we murdered too.

'Rest is what you need,' he said to me when he drove me back. 'Do nothing, think nothing. Rest. I'll see you tomorrow, after the lawyer. We can walk out in the snow. If you want to see the land clearly, you must walk. No good sitting in a car.'

That was what he said.

13

NINE FORTY. LONDON STANSTED. THERE must be an airport close by. A few passengers prepare to leave. I hear the roar of planes overhead but the cloud is too thick to see them. The Italian woman is asleep. She offered me something to eat but I could not bear the thought of food. At least not this English food, which was what I presume it was. Had it been a bowl of hot rice, that would have been another matter. At the thought of rice and how I used to make it for Ben, I nearly start weeping again. The road we travel on is featureless and I go tirelessly over the events of the last days.

As soon as Eric left me, my secret grew into a monster of depravity. I saw clearly that I was an unnatural mother. It was in this mood that I went with Ria to see the lawyer on Monday morning. Neither of us was in any fit state to deal with him. Ria looked dreadful and I felt utterly crazed, unable to concentrate. My treacherous mind kept oscillating between thoughts of Eric and Ben. My heart was breaking with grief, but then, suddenly, my mind would switch and I would find myself consumed with longing for Eric. So great was it that I was certain I could not go on. I toyed with the idea of getting Ria to take me to a doctor for sleeping pills which I could take in one swift gulp. I could hear trains passing and I thought of sneaking out at night to throw myself on the railway line. I was going mad. There was no peace.

The solicitor wanted to talk about compensation. How much could be procured for the one life I had created. Distraught, I wanted to scream at the man. At least the anger had a decent feel to it, but I hated all of them in that office with their quiet calmness, their lack of confusion. At home when they kill it is with noise and commotion. Here they fill in a form after the deed is done. Murderers, I wanted to scream. You came, you conquered, you destroyed. Bastards, I wanted to cry. But I said not a word, shivering in my chair, obedient as a slave while my dead child, mistaken out of fear and killed in terror, lay on a slab. And all the time, in the back of my head, running in tandem, was my own crime.

Everything was still contained; nothing had broken its banks for the moment. Ria bent towards me, a concerned look on her face.

'Anula, do you understand? You do agree we should prosecute the police, don't you?'

I was a huge fish dying in the water. A piece of Ben's blues began to play endlessly in my head. I tapped my foot in time to it. Ria and the lawyer exchanged glances.

'Mrs Chinniah,' the man said heavily, 'suing the Suffolk Constabulary is not an easy matter.'

I stared at his jowls. I wanted to tear the flesh from his face with my bare hands. Then I wanted to kill myself.

'They are not going to give in easily, you understand. They will plead not guilty. They will say that they were under impossible stress to protect the British public from threat of terrorism. They will tell the jury that their officers are highly skilled, trained to act only when they are absolutely certain. On the morning of the accident, they will say, they had been following your son for some considerable time because someone – and they will not tell us who – had seen him swimming across the river, day after day, even at night. They had traced the footprints of his trainers and matched them to *one* of the footprints on the riverbank. Of course, there will be other footprints belonging to the men who were the real terrorists living in the house next door to Eel House, but they will not tell you that. Your son, they will say, bore a close resemblance to the man they were hunting.

The man they were after was the ringleader, they will say. Extremely dangerous, probably armed. They will tell you that several people in the area had had their passports stolen and witnesses had described a man very like your son. In short, they will say, it was a very, very, unfortunate incident. Regrettable, deeply upsetting, terrible, but ultimately inevitable, given the circumstance. That is what they will say.'

I burst into tears.

'Mrs Chinniah,' the lawyer continued, 'your distress will be as nothing to them. The police, with the backing of the government, the Home Secretary, the Prime Minister, his spin-doctor, every single one of them, will be adamant. The shooting of your son was terribly regrettable but really not anyone's fault.'

No one spoke as I continued to sob.

'Mrs Chinniah, you must not expect pity. You must not expect compassion, except in the abstract. Grief means very little in the end. The police will be fighting for their reputation, their image in the public eye. Please understand, the media will be behind them, the government too. You are nobody in this country; your son should not have been here in the first place. The jury will know that he was an illegal immigrant, someone who came here to take the jobs of the British residents. That's the thought that will be in the back of their mind. No one will say anything. In this country, what is unsaid is the most powerful. Do you understand?'

He stopped. His face looked grey and corpse-like. I could see the sweat seeping out. Flesh, hair, skin, I thought, crying hopelessly.

'You will be taking on the establishment, Mrs Chinniah,' the lawyer said, again.

The quality of mercy is not strained, I thought, remembering how I had learnt that speech long ago, in fifth grade. Ria moved restlessly in her chair. I presumed she had been told all this earlier.

'You *must* see what your position is, you *must* be realistic,' the man continued, his hand moving up and down as if he were pumping water from a well. 'In the scale of things, your son, your suffering, counts for nothing!'

He sounded less certain, now. Perhaps he, too, was exhausted.

'My swimmer,' I said.

'I beg your pardon?'

I was weeping so much, so pathetically, that I could hardly speak.

'We used to call him that because he was such a strong swimmer,' I said at last.

There was a silence.

'Yes, well,' the lawyer said. He seemed taken aback.

'Look, it is my duty as your solicitor to tell you these things,' he said. His voice had become very slightly softer. 'It would be unfair to let you assume it will be easy. We know now there were two sets of crimes being committed at the time, but it's taken this long for that to become clear. There were the people from the Clean-Up Britain Party, trying to implicate the Muslim community in a series of animal killings and burglaries, and then there were the terrorists themselves. It was all so confusing. It still is.' He paused. 'The reality is, we have a fight on our hands, and it won't necessarily be a fair fight.'

'Ah! The CUB Party,' Ria said. 'We've always been told they have no political clout!'

She too spoke softly. Her mouth had twisted into a thin, uncompromising line. The lawyer glanced at her. Then he gave a startled laugh, without mirth.

'Quite,' he agreed.

There was another silence.

'They're everywhere,' he said flatly, turning to me. 'You will find them in our border towns, you will find them in our cathedral cities; on our streets, in our schools. You will find them living amongst people who have come from the far-flung corners of our empire.'

Ria was nodding.

I had no idea what they were talking about.

'He was not an illegal immigrant,' I said finally. 'He was waiting to hear if the Home Office would look at his case, wasn't he? He didn't want favours. We were told long ago that anyone who was part of the British Empire had a right to come to this country. We were told England was the Mother Country. Don't you understand?'

They were watching me with pity in their eyes. The lawyer picked up his pen and drew a line on the white sheet of paper on his pad. Then he drew another and another. From where I sat, the drawing had taken on the shape of a bird. Was it a cormorant? I puzzled dully. We had cormorants on our canals. Without thinking, I leant forward in my chair, but when he saw this he lowered his eyes and threw his pen down. Then he screwed the paper into a ball and tossed it into the waste-paper basket. Ria would not look at me either. Silence grew in the room like fungus. I had stopped crying. Dried tears, like war paint, streaked my face. If I could have ended it there, in that room, I would gladly have done so. The lawyer was looking at me intently now.

'Look,' he said. I could see the time had come for him to talk reasonably. 'Don't think I'm not on your side.'

Looking at him, I saw beneath the surface how it must be for him. How it was for every living creature. How fear was greater than love. How fear made you do things you could not account for. Why do we pretend it is otherwise?

'It isn't that simple,' he sighed. 'You *must* see that the kind of Britain you had believed in is somewhere in the past. A Victorian idyll, a place that no longer exists.'

He looked out of his depth. Did he have a wife? I wondered. Did he make love to her as . . . No, I thought, shaking my head, don't go there. They were looking at me, warily.

'This is a country that had a kind of peace for sixty years. The people here are complacent. Even the severity of this endless recession hasn't dented that. We are an insular nation, fearful of what foreigners might do to us. Shadow-boxing as we go, waiting for a real kind of patriotism.'

I stared at him. He sounded earnest, but was he really laughing at me?

'Your son strayed into this world; I'm afraid it was to his cost. What happened, happens every day. People are being shot all the time; mistaken identity is part of life,' he added, glancing at Ria.

She was sitting with her eyes closed. Who knows what she was thinking, the cold fish, I thought, fury erupting again. I couldn't think of anything to say, either. There was a faint stain on the lawyer's shirt. He must have spilt tea and then tried to wipe it off. I stared steadily at the spot.

'I'll put everything in writing,' he said. 'I needed to tell you how bad it could get, that it wouldn't be a quick process, that it won't be pain-free. Now you know –' he stood up and held out his hand to me – 'the rest will be easy.'

He shook my hand, and I gazed at his lips. As a child, I used to draw. My father would encourage me by saying it was a good thing to have the observational skills that came from drawing. There were pencil drawings of my family all over the house. My father used to show them proudly to our visitors.

'Look,' he would say, 'see what a talented daughter I have. She will go far!'

I had not drawn any faces for years. Suddenly, looking at this man's colourless skin, his bloodless lips, his cold blue eyes, I knew exactly what I needed to do.

'Ria,' I said urgently, so loudly that she turned, startled, 'I want to see Ben one last time. I have to draw his face.'

My voice was completely calm, determined. They were both looking at me, aghast.

'Mrs Chinniah . . .' the lawyer said gently, 'I don't think that will . . .'

But he got no further, for it was Ria, pale, tearless Ria, who interrupted him.

'She must!' she said. 'You used to draw, didn't you?' she asked, turning to me. 'I know. He told me you did.'

Now we were looking at each other properly instead of avoiding each other's eyes. Everything was naked. A ledge appeared on which we stood together. And for an instant an incomprehensible feeling rose between us and hovered uncertainly. The ledge we moved on swayed slightly. I knew then, if I could not draw my son I would simply die.

Ria was talking with some urgency in her voice. I was too exhausted to follow the argument. My whole body yearned to sit beside Ben and draw him. All I needed was twenty minutes.

'It might not be possible,' the lawyer said.

He sounded flustered.

'Look, I'll do what I can, but . . .'

He was frowning.

'I suppose it might have some publicity value,' he added.

He glanced doubtfully at me. I felt a thread of warmth – approval was too strong a word – break free and extend itself towards me. Underneath the coldness, I felt there might be some kind of heart beating within this man. It was Ria's turn to be stubborn.

'She *has* to do this.'

The man was already talking on the telephone, his tea-stained shirt turned away from view.

'Sit down a minute, Anula,' Ria said.

I heard contradictions in her voice. I dared not ask her what Ben had said. I needed to keep a clear head for the job in front of me.

In the end it was easier than any of us expected. The details remain hazy. All I knew was that I would be able to draw Ben.

'Tomorrow morning,' the lawyer said, showing us out. He looked relieved.

Outside on the pavement there was a small group of reporters.

'Can you tell us how you are feeling, Mrs Chinniah?'

'Have you only just arrived in Britain?'

'Is this your first visit to this country?'

'What is your opinion of Britain's immigration policy?'

The lawyer pushed them away grimly.

'No comment,' he said.

'Were you Ben's girlfriend?' a woman asked Ria.

'Mrs Chinniah,' asked another, mispronouncing my name, 'can you tell us something about Sri Lanka? What do you think of your country's suicide bombers?'

I couldn't believe what I was hearing. Ria bundled us both swiftly into her car. She was crying quietly and without fuss. Tears did not distort her face. I was calm. We drove off, leaving the reporters behind. There was a police car escorting us, so that, apart from a few flashbulbs going off, we were left to drive away unhindered.

'This is unbelievable,' Ria muttered, and then she headed towards the beach. Snow fell indifferently. The sea was a grey, foaming mass edged with white. Seagulls breasted the waves, losing themselves in camouflage.

'I'm sorry,' she said. 'I'm ashamed and sorry, but at least you're going to be able to draw him.'

And now she cried for the end of everything. I touched her arm timidly. What was lost, I wanted to say, was innocence. At that moment I wanted nothing more than to tell her everything. Who knows, I might have done so had she responded in some way, but she did not seem to feel my touch. And a second later, the moment had passed.

We parked the car halfway along the sea front. It was the North Sea I was facing, grey and very rough and unforgiving.

'He never saw the sea in winter,' Ria said.

The wind whipped her words away. Bitterness gilded her words. Three people were walking on the beach, huddled together, all dressed in black; dark, like the weather. Ahead of us was a deserted Martello tower. Seagulls screamed and the sea heaved. I wanted Eric.

'Will we see Eric, tonight?' I asked, unable to stop myself.

Luckily she did not hear. She had turned away and was facing into the wind and the sleet, her coat tightly wrapped around her body as she walked away from me. Her head was bent. I followed, my orange sari a kite flapping behind. The cold was so bitter I could not stand it for more than a few minutes. She had walked very fast and had become a mark moving away from me across the shingles. Because she was so tall, her height made all her movements seem effortless and fast. Like a piece of machinery, I thought. In spite of this cold I felt a powerful sense of Ben's presence and an idea began forming in my mind. I wanted to scatter his ashes near water. He had been born within sight of water; now let him rest beside it.

Ahead of me, Ria had stopped and now stood waiting. The snow was coming down harder as I hurried towards her. Suddenly, with my decision made, the world began to shrink. Ben had been here, walking on this patch of earth. I would be forever connected with it because of this. Just as Eric had said.

He was waiting at Eel House as we drove up.

'Oh, Eric,' Ria murmured.

I felt a harsh thrill pass over me. I wanted to tell him about my decision to draw Ben, but Eric appeared distracted. He had found an elderly woman waiting to speak to us. She was a journalist, sympathetic, very different from the others, he felt. She had left her card with him in the hope that Ria would contact her.

'I'll do it now,' Ria said. 'You coming in?'

He shook his head. I sensed he was upset but I couldn't think of any way I might talk to him alone.

'Come in for a minute,' Ria said. 'I'll just make this phone call.'

In the kitchen he stood looking at me helplessly.

'I have to see you,' he said. 'I have to talk. Will you come over to the farm? I know this is a nightmare for you . . .'

We could hear Ria on the phone. It was midday.

'When?' I asked.

'I'll come back later – about three?'

I nodded.

'I feel very bad about all this. I must talk to you.'

'She'll be here at six,' Ria said, coming in. 'I'll do the talking, if you like.'

'It won't be necessary,' I said. 'I can talk for myself.'

I could sense rather than see Eric looking at me.

'I would like to draw the fields from the window of Eric's kitchen,' I said. 'Would it be possible to do that?'

I was looking at Eric, but it was Ria I was talking to. Never in my whole life had I been so devious. All sense of right and wrong seemed to have left me. Anything was possible. I am a hard woman, I thought. Death has made a monster of me. Tomorrow I would draw my dead son and today I was capable of such cool brazenness. It was shocking. The images of all those who had loved me rose before me. Percy, my father . . . Ben, of course. But it was Eric I wanted. Death had made me lose all sense of decency, I thought.

'Why don't you go,' Ria said. There was a kind of weariness in her voice. 'If Eric doesn't mind, that is. I want to lie down. I've a headache. I don't feel well.'

I thought her voice complaining.

'I don't mind,' Eric said. 'You could come now, if you liked. I'll bring her back in a little while.'

'Whenever,' Ria said, tiredly.

And she went upstairs.

As soon as we were driving off in the car I turned to him.

'What is it?' I asked.

He was silent for so long that I wondered if he had heard me. We drove up to the farm. He stopped the Land Rover and sat for a moment with the engine running. Then he put his head down on the steering wheel and did not move. I was shot through with a ridiculous and paralysing thought that he was never going to move. For more than a minute I sat staring at him, stunned and cold and without thought, then with a sinking feeling I realised he was crying.

'What's the matter?' I asked.

'I am sorry,' he said at last. 'I am so sorry for any pain I caused you. I have no idea why I behaved in this way. I have no excuse. Only that I saw in you . . . something of what it had been like for me . . . when Kevin died . . . It was unspeakable . . . but that's no excuse.'

I was silent, numb.

'When I saw you, I was shocked. You didn't even look old enough to be his mother. You were so . . . so raw, so dazed by what had been done to you. Everything shocked you; the cold shocked you, Ria's silence shocked you. You looked like a child, lost, bewildered. I saw your son in you. As others must have seen Kevin in my face afterwards.'

He shook his head.

'It brought it all back . . . so vividly. And I thought . . . yes, she will understand.'

Still I said nothing, hardly daring to move.

'Thinking of myself, I was. And now I see I have confused you even more. You feel guilty. I know what you are thinking: that you have been disrespectful of the dead. You are so alone, so far away from home. And I have done this to you!'

He shook his head helplessly. The dog in the back of the car began to bark in protest. I reached out and switched off the ignition. The car was becoming colder. I touched his arm.

'Let's go inside,' I said.

Remembering those two hours before I left him, I think of them as the sweetest in those dark days. Now it was I who took charge. We had entered a pact together, I told him. It would last for the smallest moment in time.

'What you have given me,' I said, 'is the means to get through these few days. It is I who should be thanking you.'

He touched me then, and I saw how well he had hidden his frail-ness. Accustomed to giving all his life, taking had profoundly disturbed him. He was full of a kind of pain, hopeless and bleak, he said. All night he had tried and failed to deal with it, and when he could no longer bear it he had gone to Eel House in search of me. That afternoon we agreed would be spent without words of regrets. And then he took me back to the beginning, to the white room at the top of the house. And now it was I, for he was too distraught to move, who knelt and peeled away his clothes. Once long ago I had knelt this way for Percy, touching him, marvelling at his transformation. So this was how my life had gone, I thought. For a moment I glimpsed the young girl I had once been, there, in that room, alone with Eric. I looked at his bent head. Skin less supple, eyes that had witnessed too much, gazing at me now. Ah! I thought. This, too, is a moment of joy. All that slow, bitter-sweet afternoon he held me in the pit in which I had sunk. And some-where between the beginning and ending I understood at last it was a far better thing to travel, however briefly, amongst the shooting stars than never to see one.

When I got back, Ria was up and wandering around in a dazed sort of way. She held a glass of some foul-smelling drink in her hand. I think she might have been crying. To be honest, I don't remember. I was leaving the remembering until later.

The journalist was sympathetic. We sat by the fire and drank tea. Ria began by telling of her visit to the Home Office.

'He had sent his form off to the Border and Immigration Agency,' she recalled, 'but they had not replied.'

She was holding a piece of paper in her hand.

'That was the reason I went up there,' she said. 'But this was all I came away with.'

The paper was folded in several places and I took it from her. It said, 'Proof of Postage'. That was all. I tried to imagine it in his hands, sitting in his wallet. I imagined his hands as he looked at it, but I couldn't.

'And this is the form we were going to fill in,' Ria said.

At the bottom of the document was a sentence written in capital letters. WORKING FOR A SAFE, JUST AND TOLERANT SOCIETY, it said. I burst into tears.

'He had been sleeping rough at the farm,' Ria said. 'Working illegally. I wanted him to have some sort of stable situation before the winter came. That was when I went up to London.'

He hadn't said anything of this to me when he rang. I had a gathering sense that there had been many things he had not told me. I had imagined a thousand times that moment when he was no longer within my sightline and the horror of his journey had overwhelmed him. Now I caught a glimpse of what it must have been like for him.

'Sometimes,' the journalist told me, 'when people travel these vast impossible routes, the trip itself is so incomprehensible that in order to survive and protect their sanity they re-invent themselves. And they think their real story is too terrible to be believed. I've seen this happen, over and over again.'

Ria was nodding in agreement.

'Imagine what it would be like to be living in a world without structure or geography or mercy,' the journalist said.

'Write this down,' I told her, galvanised. 'He left because there was nothing and found himself in another place with nothing for him, either. There was nowhere that he could call his home.'

I shook my head in disgust. At home we thought that sending our children to England was the only solution.

'I work part-time at a refugee centre,' the journalist said. She sounded as sad as rain. 'The people there say they are treated well by the public until they admit they are asylum seekers.'

'Ben travelled seven thousand miles for a better life,' Ria said. 'But the essence of it hardly changed at all.'

No one spoke.

'When he phoned me, he said he wanted to come home.'

Too late, the words had slipped out. I heard Ria breathe in sharply. The journalist looked as if she might cry. She had the kind of face that in another life I might have wanted to know better.

In the darkened garden a bird gave a piercing cry and something shifted inside of me. I realised I had been calm throughout the whole afternoon.

'If there is a justified fear of persecution, everyone has the right to apply for asylum,' the journalist said. 'This was set down in the 1951 UN Refugee Convention. No country has ever withdrawn from the Convention.'

Ria stood up. There were razor blades in her laugh.

'The government has been trying to define their obligations to refugees as narrowly as possible,' she said. 'I wanted to marry him. We were at that point when . . .' Her voice faded away.

Startled, I couldn't look at her.

'You didn't know this?' the journalist said, turning to me.

I shook my head, trying to cover my distaste. The woman's eyes were bright pools of green, younger than the rest of her face, alive to possibilities. There had been someone like her who had worked with the torture victims in Jaffna. After the army had done their worst and the Tigers had almost finished off the job of destruction, these women from London had worked with the victims and their families. I had even gone to see them, hoping stupidly they would help me find Percy. I had spoken to one of the women. Like leaves, those eyes had been, leaves in sunlight. This woman was of that type. Had she noticed that Ria and I were tearing chunks out of each other? As though we had started a war of our own?

'No,' I said, my eyes downcast too. 'We only talked for a few minutes. Perhaps he thought it was best not to tell me.'

'I had only just suggested it,' Ria, conceded. 'I'm not even sure he wanted it.'

She too sounded subdued.

'I'm sure he did,' I said. 'If he said so. Ben always meant what he said.'

I was lying. For the first time I was realising I knew nothing about anyone, not even myself.

'People can change very drastically under the circumstances your son had to deal with,' the journalist said. 'They need so badly to readjust to the new shiftless life they have been catapulted into.'

Ria spoke directly to me.

'He told me,' she said, in a voice so sweet that I was silenced, 'you said he must clean his teeth every night. It was the last thing you told him, he said. So he was determined to keep his promise. Throughout the whole of his time travelling, even when he lost everything, he managed not to lose his toothbrush.'

In all we had talked for four solid hours when the journalist made a move. Ria asked her when the piece would come out in the paper.

'I don't know,' she said, 'but I'll ring you when they tell me. It could be on Saturday.'

Then she turned to me.

'How long is your visa for?'

'Two weeks. I'm going back after the funeral.'

She handed me her card.

'If you ever want to contact me, this is my address and e-mail.'

The word e-mail was the trigger. I had thought my crying was over, but the word reminded me of Ben.

Later we had had some food, more or less in silence. In the light of the open fire I saw the strange beauty of Ria's face and wondered why I had not seen it so clearly until now.

I was bone tired and didn't want to refer to Ben again, so I asked her about her brother instead.

'He's called Jack,' she said, and I heard a different hopelessness in her voice. 'He never met Ben. He never knew anything until it was over.'

I waited for her to go on.

'I'm afraid his reaction would have been the same as all those people we were talking about just now. Fear of a disruption to his life.' She shrugged. 'He's not a bad man; just not very highly developed. Complicated thought scares him. He likes to keep his life simple.' She made a face. 'Uncomplicated stories to go with the uncomplicated life he wishes to have. Only . . .' She laughed without mirth, and left her sentence unfinished.

We were not looking at each other, yet in a mysterious way, it was all, all right. A picture of a kite, sharply defined against a blue sky, crossed my mind. Someone was holding the string, pulling it taut until suddenly, with no warning, it went slack and collapsed.

'I told him to be careful when he left,' I said. 'Look after yourself, was what I said.'

Ria nodded.

'He was moving in here the day he was shot,' she answered.

In the firelight I saw again the strange beauty of her face and wondered why I had not seen it so clearly until now.

14

NINE FIFTY-TWO. HATFIELD. COLLEGE LANE Bus Station. It took another
day, but Ria got permission. I would be allowed to draw Ben. Cold air
cut at my throat as we drove. There were crows patrolling the white
fields, scavenging for small animals. The ground was covered with them
and occasionally, through the sound of the engine, I heard the boom
of a gun going off in the distance. We drove on, keeping the Martello
tower and the sea on our left.

'What is it?' I asked, unable to bear the sound.

'The farmers,' Ria said.

This morning she was silent again and I was keeping sane
by thinking of Eric. Half a mile later we turned off and headed
towards the centre of Orford. The undertakers were on the outskirts of the town. At the back was a low garage of brightly polished
black empty hearses. Ria brought the car to the front entrance.

'I'll come in with you,' she said. 'But I'll leave as soon as I've introduced you. Shall I come back in an hour?'

When I didn't speak, she looked sharply at me.

'Will you be okay? Are you sure you want to do this?'

I nodded. The palms of my hands were sweating and my whole
body was freezing.

'Yes,' I said, and we went inside.

And that was it. The drawing is here in my bag now, on its way home. I shall frame it and put it up in the alcove that was his bedroom. I shall draw the green curtain over the doorway as he used to and close the last chapter of my life. I shall do these things very soon. But on that morning, with the snow lying frozen outside, as I sat in the room with its sickly flowers I drew him blindly and did not think of the future. Unhappiness is hard work and I was exhausted. My mind wandered along a path of its own making. The undertaker moved around quietly in his office next door while I drew. When it came to it, I drew my son with a skill I had forgotten I possessed. Time had both altered and halted his face. I tried to capture it with an unwavering line. Drawing is like poetry, my father used to say. It is possible to say everything in a line. I tried to keep this in mind; I tried to draw with my whole heart. Gazing at his face, I noted his hair had not lost its dark sheen, crow black and springing up. Remember, how you used to smooth it down? I told him. He and I carried on a conversation wordlessly. Of course, I can't remember what we said. Goodbye, I expect. Perhaps it was here, as I drew him into my memory through my fingertips, while other people came and went through other doors, banging lids and whispering, that I understood Ben had left me long ago.

'I had to lead my own life, Ma,' he told me. 'Now it's your turn to lead yours.'

Outside, snow began to fall lightly, magically, as the undertaker stirred his mug of tea.

'What can I do now, Ben Putha?' I asked out loud.

I could see the slight glint of white teeth between his lips. Through my blurring eyes I imagined he was smiling at me.

'Stop worrying, Ma. It's all over now. You don't have to worry.'

In a tree, somewhere, a bird sang brightly. Yes, I could be less vigilant now. The Suffolk birds were melodious, I thought. The undertaker cleared his throat and stood watching me.

'Are you okay?' he asked.

I could not answer, and out of respect he kept his distance from me.

Concentrate, I told myself. Eyes, look your last. This moment is a bonus. But I could not concentrate. My mind behaved in the way it wanted to. I heard the sound of a helicopter overhead, a telephone ringing, another bird crying. Only the snow did not make a noise.

'I'm sorry, darling,' I murmured, but he did not appear to mind. We were acting as though we had all the time in the world together instead of the few moments before the lid was closed.

The undertaker made a fresh pot of tea. I tried to focus on all the significant things I should tell Ben, all the things I had been too broken to say when I first saw him lying like this, but my mind remained a blank.

It was a miracle, but I finished the drawing. You know, I never even looked at it properly, not then. I suppose I knew instinctively, with the part of my brain still functioning, there would be the long years when I would do nothing else. So for now I put the pencil back in my bag. And the book. Then I stood up and whispered goodbye to my son. Just as I had on all those other times; holding back a little, smiling. Only this time I did not warn him to be careful. There was no need.

The man in the black suit was standing in the doorway once again. He was as colourless as the sky outside, only the dark suit seemed alive.

'Finished?' he asked.

I knew he was ready to close the lid. Reality trembled and waited to pounce.

'Yes,' I said. 'Finished!'

We might have been talking of a job well done. Ben did not move. I looked and looked and knew I would never look again.

'Bye, Ma,' he said. 'Thank you for the money, and the dinners were good.'

'Darling, it was my pleasure. Give my love to your father when you see him.'

And I went outside before the undertaker could stop me; out into the blurry landscape that had become whiter than when I arrived.

The footsteps and the tyre marks petered out as soon as I left the driveway and headed towards open country. I wanted to find the field filled with the black birds. I had no idea of time. The cold bit into me with surprising viciousness. A pair of black-and-white wings flashed past with a hard, rattling cry, sounding a warning. I could hear the muffled vibration of a gun, but it was difficult to tell from which direction it came. I turned off the road on to a snow-drifted path so crisp and clean that it took my breath away with its alien loveliness. Home was not a place I would ever be able to pinpoint again. The boundary would always be uncertain.

'You saw the possibilities, didn't you, Ben?' I said out loud.

It was a relief to be able to talk aloud with no one listening. The constriction in my throat was easing. What had been missing was the opportunity to talk to my son without fear of being overheard.

'You might have made a life here,' I continued. 'Although, in a way, you did, I suppose. It's all right,' I added hastily, before he could protest, 'I understand, you had to do what you needed to in order to survive.'

Poor Tara, I thought, but I couldn't say this. I didn't want to hurt his feelings while he was listening. Poor Percy, too.

'I have betrayed your father, Ben,' I said.

In the distance I heard a shot and the sky darkened as a whole field of birds took to the air. From this distance the sound was like an aircraft taking off; unbelievably loud, a landslide of crashing sounds that engulfed the shooting. I stood still, not knowing which way I should go. My feet in their thin tropical shoes were soaked and a few flakes of snow dislodged from the sky and fell on my face. My ankles and the bottom of my sari were wet. The voice came towards me from a great distance. I heard it calling my name, urgently. It was Eric.

'God! You must be freezing,' he said, hurrying towards me.

I lowered my eyes, not wanting him to see the expression on my face.

'This is private land,' he said. 'They told me you had walked out without saying where you were going.'

He stopped, and stared at me. Then he took my arm and helped me off the muddy wet field and on to the path. All around were the bodies of dead birds that I had not noticed before. Their grey faces weary, their eyes sodden with defeat.

'Come,' Eric said carefully. 'I told Ria I would fetch you.'

Once in the car he turned the heater full on and sat looking at me with an unreadable expression.

'Oh, Anula!' he said at last, shaking his head.

He went on saying my name over and over again. And then he was gripping me so I melted into his arms.

'What had you in mind?' he asked me gravely. 'I thought we had made a pact?'

It was impossible to explain.

'Did you think no one would care? Do you think I wouldn't care?'

He continued to hold me fiercely against him.

'It isn't a lifetime I have to offer you. It isn't happiness, even. The circumstances of our meeting could not be worse. But I am here, now, with you. I will bear witness to this event.'

I began to cry.

'You are not alone, Anula. Don't think that. If he were listening, don't you think Ben would be glad? That you have some comfort? That there is a small candle held out for you in the dark?'

I kissed him.

'All separation produces a wound, a rupture in the mind.'

He spoke very sadly. We drove back in silence. He held my hand all the way. The light was at its best. I suspected it could not get any brighter than this today. While I had been wandering in the fields the snow had begun to harden and the landscape was now a sharply defined, blinding white. Eric asked nothing of me. He did not even ask to see the drawing. His silence was like the landscape that flashed past. Only now, sitting on this coach I see how he knew, instinctively, what needed to be left untouched.

We came to the house where the terrorists had briefly lived. I had been shown photographs of the place, images of the bomb-making equipment, tins of chemicals; rubbish of sorts. All the windows were boarded up now. I would have liked us to stop, to peer in through the cracks. This place and the people in it were the reason Ben had been killed. He had never even known them. Ben's voice came to me clearly.

'Things happen, Ma, and people are killed. Nations rise and fall, not because of the men who think they are in control, but in spite of them! Remember Tolstoy?'

Finally we turned into the lane that led to Eel House. Eric switched off the ignition.

'I'll not come in. Ria is . . . she needs to be quiet. I've told her I'll see you tomorrow.'

Neither of us spoke. Tomorrow was the funeral. He leaned towards me and kissed me on the forehead. Then he kissed the palms of my hands and then the top of my head. He told me he would be thinking of me all night.

Ria glanced at me indifferently when I walked in.

'You'd better get out of those . . . clothes,' she said, pressing her lips together.

We were back to covertly hating each other.

'I have nothing else,' I said. 'Only the sari I want to wear to his funeral. Everything else needs washing.'

'Well, for goodness' sake give them to me to wash,' she said, irritated. 'And let me find you something to wear until these dry.'

She could not know, but I had pressed a photograph of Tara into the coffin before I left. The thought that it was lying there in the darkness beside him gave me some small comfort.

At eight the priest came. His first words set the tone of our brief and painful association.

'Ah,' he said, his kindly face unsmiling but full of warmth. 'How are you, m'dear?'

Then he enveloped me in a hug. Refusing any refreshments, he took my hands and led me step by step through what was to come. Ria sat quietly listening, but saying little, and in this way, what was to happen was agreed by the three of us.

'Tell me about the boy,' he said.

Instantly, as though it were yesterday, I saw Ben hurrying through the fields behind our house with an armful of blown eggshells.

Ria fetched the necklace he had made for her and even seeing this, remembering the other one he had given Tara, did not anger me as it had done before. The priest held the necklace in his large hands, marvelling at its delicate colours.

I could see Ria fold her pale hands together. She looked disapproving and ill at ease. I could see the blueness in her veins of her hands.

'Tomorrow, I want you to think of his life,' the priest said. 'I'm not trying to ignore what was done, I'm not trying to wipe out the injustice or belittle it. That is the job of your lawyer, Ria,' he said, looking at her now. 'My job is to help the two of you to remember him as he was. To celebrate his life. Okay?'

We both nodded. Connection hovered between us, bitterness stood back for a moment. Pain waited, pulsating quietly in the background.

'Tell me about the first time you saw him,' he said, turning to Ria. 'Tell me what you thought.'

So she told him what I had not known, how she had glimpsed Ben rising out of the water in her midnight garden, with the scent of flowers drifting in through the open window. She spoke as she had not spoken in all the days I had been with her, with a curious yearning and emotion at last in her voice. She had felt young, she said, that night, and for many nights after. I looked her full in the face and she smiled and made a gesture of depreciation. We looked at each other and then looked away again, connected for a moment.

'And now, Anula,' the priest said. The light from the fire flickered restlessly on his face. 'Of all the memories you must carry within you of your son, tell me one that is more significant than the others.'

I was concentrating hard.

'Maybe you need some time to reflect? Maybe you can tell me in the morning?'

I didn't need time to think. I had a photograph of it, I told him.

'We had been walking on the beach,' I said. 'In the days before the ceasefire ended we could walk undisturbed on the beach. It was Ben's birthday and my mother had made him a yellow, short-sleeved shirt.'

The stretch of beach near our home is like no other. Even now, with the hidden land-mines and the discarded, burnt-out army tanks, it was astonishingly wide and beautiful. Imagine what it once was like!

'Ben had strayed towards the water, moving closer and closer. Daring to go there without an adult.'

The waves that day were gentle, barely a movement. The wind was down, there were no kites in the sky and Ben walked as far as the water's edge. All around were catamarans pulled up high on the sand dunes. A few children played with a tyre hanging on a coconut tree. It was an ordinary afternoon in our costal town. My father was shielding his pipe, trying to light it against the breeze. The sky was a blistering blue. Percy got out his camera.

'Look at the fellow!' he said with admiration. 'See how fearless he is!'

At that moment, Ben turned and realised he was alone. We were high on the sand dunes and he probably couldn't see us for a moment.

'Mama!' he screamed, his face wobbling, and he began to cry just as Percy snapped him.

'Of course we rushed down the beach, laughing and waving. I remember scooping him up in my arms. I couldn't bear to see him cry. How could we have played such a trick on him!'

I remember his chubby, rounded arms, hotly wound around my neck.

'I have that photograph still,' I said. 'Even though the beach is no longer the stretch of paradise we once knew. And they are both gone.'

The fire had died down while I had been speaking. The priest nodded, waiting, giving me all the time I needed, knowing how this time could never be replaced. Outside, snow continued to fall unnoticed. Tomorrow we would bury Ben and a bit more of paradise would be lost.

That night I could not sleep. Hours went by. Occasionally I went over to the window and looked out, but there was never anything to see. Towards morning, a sound, heavy with meaning, woke me. It was a cock crowing. I lay rigid, listening, struggling to get my bearings, desperate to hold back the day. I had not thought of Tara all these weeks and now I thought of her. Tara was from another kind of life. I looked at my watch. It was seven in the morning. It would be midday at home. Tara would be at her father's shop and if there had been no trouble in the night she would be standing behind the till, staring out at the sea. She would be watching the glittering water, and waiting. I got out of bed. The sun glinted on the snow.

I washed and took out the sari I had brought specifically for this unimaginable day. Soft, white, like the whiteness outside, it was the sari I had worn last at my father's funeral. Then Percy and a young Ben had been by my side. Slowly I began to wind the cloth around my body, all thirteen yards of it, pleating it carefully. I took a long time over it, making sure the edges were straight and the bottom of the sari almost, but not quite, touching the ground. I secured the train over my shoulder with the pin Tara had given me. My hands were clumsy and slow. I was dressing like a person who hadn't been wearing a sari all their adult life. I put up my hair and after that I slipped on the black cardigan Ria had given me.

'Come,' I said out loud, to my reflection. 'Come, darling, let's go.'

There was no one about when I went downstairs and the first thing I saw was the newspaper open on the kitchen table. A small vase of some delicate white flower stood near it, trapped in sunlight. It was no ordinary day. A photograph stared out at me from the page. Confused, it was a moment before I recognised myself.

A moonlit night in Jaffna. A young man embraces his mother for the last time. He is about to leave on a long hazardous journey, fleeing to save his life . . . it read. Underneath, in capitals, were the words LIFE AND DEATH OF A REFUGEE. And then there were my words as I had spoken them to the journalist. There was a blurred photograph of Ben that I did not recognise, obviously taken here. I could dimly make out the river in the background and the trees appeared to be full of leaves. Ben was smiling.

'I took it,' Ria said, coming in unnoticed behind me. 'In August.' Her voice was a whisper.

'Look, I've brought you the rose you wanted,' she said. 'It's not fully open, but it was the only one they had in the village shop.'

She was dressed all in black and her short, severely cropped hair shone with an extraordinary sheen. She looked frightening and beautiful. It was too late for intimacies. The funeral was not for another hour. Shortly after we had drunk our first cup of tea, Eric arrived and I began to shake.

I remember almost nothing of the actual funeral. We drove to the crematorium where a Mass was said. I noticed the place was packed, but that was all. Eric and Ria flanked me, close enough to catch me, I suppose, should I stumble. But I did not falter and I walked up the aisle steadily to my seat at the front. Ben had died and been buried so many times since I had first heard the news. The priest told the story of Ben on the beach, but I'm not clear how much he said or what the reaction was. He talked about the tragedy of what had happened and the kind of world we lived in that forced people to travel huge distances from their homes. A shutter had gone down in my head again. We took communion, those of us who were Catholic; I seem to remember there were about three. It was all very civilised. A hymn was sung. Again, I'm unclear as to what it was. While they were singing I had one of the strange flashes, like a picture book, of the sitting room where Ben used to play the piano. But even that did not move me. We sang another hymn. I did not open my mouth for fear of what might come out of it. I found myself thinking of the snow and how its lightness had seeped in through the window the night before. The snow outside was affecting all the sounds inside, I thought listlessly. The hymn came to an end and the priest made the final address and there was music again. Everyone stood up and Ben's coffin began to move slowly away. Still all I did was stare, and it was then, with no warning at all, with only a small, barely audible sound, Ria fell forward in a faint.

The odd thing was that I felt almost better for it. The sight of Ria's grief made me feel I wasn't struggling alone. I suppose that was it. I could see people looking at me, although, even that was possibly only in my imagination. My mind was having thoughts of its own, running away with itself, acting in ways I could not have anticipated. I noticed as we picked her up that although she was very tall, Ria was as light as a bird. Someone brought her a glass of water.

'I'm all right,' she said faintly.

The bluish circles around her eyes were very obvious and ugly. They made the rest of her face even paler. We went outside and many people came to speak to us. There was the lawyer who I had last seen only a few days ago. He came up to me and shook my hand, murmuring condolences. The journalist who had written the article was there, too. There would be more articles in the days to come, she told us, as other newspapers took up the story. There were photographers taking photos of us, and standing a little way away, heads slightly bowed, were two policemen and a policewoman. Eric was speaking very softly to me. It was a moment before I understood.

'Just keep walking, darling,' was what he said as we were ushered into the waiting cars.

15

TEN O'CLOCK. M11 EXIT. HEATHROW. In the few days left to us, Ria withdrew completely. She had such an air of stunned and mistrustful defeat, of such private desolation, that I began to ask myself, had she had found out about Eric? I oscillated between fear that she might have found out and anger at her neglect of me. Didn't she know how much I was suffering? In Sri Lankan society, I wanted to tell her, nothing is more sacred than the relationship a mother has with a son. Blessed are the women who have many sons, I wanted to say. Whoever seeks to reverse the order of things in Nature will be cursed, was another saying that hovered constantly on my tongue.

Although through a supreme effort I was managing to stay silent, suppressed rage, like flash floods, surfaced on and off. Had it not been for Eric, I would not have been able to control it for long. The truth was both Ria and I were both waiting for me to leave Eel House. Very slowly, the last days of our enforced time together drew to a close.

We had both decided tacitly that I would leave the business of the court case to her. I had no money nor would I ever return to Britain. Even if my airfare were paid again, I could not apply for a visa before several years had passed. I was overcome by new terrible lethargy. I barely slept, was always cold and the food Ria prepared in her desultory way was so alien to me that I ate very little. What daylight there was took on a hallucinatory air, adding to my sense of dislocation.

The one person in all of this who made things bearable was Eric. While Ria hid herself in her study, unable or unwilling to communicate with me, Eric arrived each morning. The snow had hardened into ice and the weather had become so utterly cold that I had no escape but to wear the trousers Ria had put out for me. And so, each morning, in those last days while we waited for Ben's ashes, I would drive back to the farm with Eric. I sit on this coach now, free at last to think of him. I see it was good fortune that gave me Eric. In spite of my black present and hopeless future, even I can see, clearly, that he was my small portion of good luck. Brought to me by a flawed god in order to soften this body blow. It was the afterglow of all I had lost. He had loved me once more before I left. In all, we were intimate with each other five times. For a person like me, this was as strange and as beautiful as travelling to the moon.

The day after the funeral, with only two days left, at my request, Eric took me to look at the sea for one last time. He parked the car close to the front and we sat looking at the seagulls floating lazily above us. The overcast began to roll back and lift as if a blind was being drawn up. Underneath was a pale blue sky, clear as glass and with a greenish sheen.

'Shall we take a walk?' he asked.

There was hardly anyone on the beach, but today I felt it had too open an aspect for us to scatter the ashes. Eric agreed.

'There's another spit of land, further up the coast towards Dunwich,' he said. 'I think that might be better. Let me show it to you.'

The whole town had turned out for the funeral, he told me. I hadn't noticed.

At the edge of the salt marshes, we stopped. Behind us was the dark wood full of regimented trees, like an army. A thaw was setting in. Once it began, Eric said, the snow would vanish rapidly. Again he stopped the car, leaving the engine on so a little warmth came through. And now he fell silent, taking out his pipe, filling it slowly. Hopelessly, I began to cry. We would not make love again. He sat, letting me cry on, not touching me. Really I didn't know who I was crying for. Eric had offered me something that in the harsh, angry world I had come from, was astonishing, but it had never been intended to last. He would remain here, with his land, thinking of me often, loving me until he died. The knowledge brought no relief. Not then. Not now. Perhaps it never will.

I have no idea how long we sat in this way. Eric was in no hurry. He let me cry while he smoked his pipe, staring out into the marshes. Small black-and-white birds with spindly legs hopped about on the rough grass. A few seagulls called to each other across the water. The sun tipped their wings with gold. After a while, he suggested we stretch our legs a little. In spite of myself, I smiled. I had never heard the expression before.

He took me for a circular walk across the marshes. He had talked about this place on one of my visits to his house, but it was now that I saw its true beauty. In spite of all the crying I had done, or perhaps because of it, the air felt invigorating as we crossed the stile into the field. It was getting warmer. To our right in the distance was the Martello tower, silhouetted darkly against the expanse of snow-covered field and the sea beyond. The marshes, too, were deeply under snow, but here and there a few strands of scrub grass poked through. The sky was bright with the reflections of a sea almost out of sight and from where we stood we could see Eel House on the other bank of the river with more dark-spired trees behind it. Ria had told me it was here, from this point in the river, that Ben first swam towards the house. It was from here their fate was sealed.

Eric strode ahead quietly. The solitude of the horizon and the varying shapes of trees in the winter sky calmed me. Now that the snow was disappearing, everything was softened by a different set of colours. There were pale blues and brooding greens and a gentle rose-pink in the sky. A backdrop to the curlew's call. Too late, I understood the subtle beauty of this waterlogged colour. Then, in a flash of insight, I saw what this land meant to him. How his love for it had survived all else. The understanding that had come through pain was being coloured by love and in spite of my grief I intuited it would stay with me forever.

'This is the place,' I said out loud. 'This is where I want to scatter his ashes.'

Eric nodded. He looked pleased.

'You must tell Ria,' was all he said.

Yes, I thought, lulled by this unexpected calm, we were saying farewell. Since our last afternoon, lying naked – and, yes, I could say that word at last – I saw how we were taking leave of each other. Out brief light, I thought.

We walked on. A fragrance of neglect lingered on the fallen grass. The horizon was wide and haunting, loss trembled at the edge of my sightline.

'She's a fine girl,' Eric said, referring to Ria. 'Don't expect to see that at the moment. It's no one's fault. But that will change one day, I promise.'

'I won't be coming back,' I said quietly.

'Maybe not for a while,' he agreed.

Then he took my hand in his worn pale one and squeezed it. Neither of us spoke. Birdsong filled the air.

'Let it go,' Eric said.

He began to speak so softly that I struggled to hear.

'After Kevin died, I asked myself, why? Why had I bothered? The answer was simple but it took me a while to get to it. I saw that not to bother is not to live. Not to honour the dead.'

He stopped walking. The house was clearly visible now from the banks. Ria had put the lights on in the sitting room. In the summer, I supposed, the rushes and the reeds would grow high and screen it from view. In the summer there would be eels swimming into Eric's willow traps. In summer the light would go on and on forever. But neither Ben nor I would see any of it. Sadness settled on me like fine dust. The sadness of acceptance.

'So keep going,' he said. 'Ben was part of your life's experience. No one will take that away. Kevin is with me, still. That won't change, either.'

I thought of him, working the land through all weathers, head bowed, going through the motions of living. Grieving for the love that had been lost, letting the pain seep into the earth. We could promise each other nothing. The war at home would go on in some form or other, I would be denied a visa, I had no money. Eric was older than me; anything might happen. Best not to hope, we had said. Best to let it lie. Now I would have to put this into practice.

'I'll remember you,' he said. 'Every day, as I do the rounds. I'll think of you. When I scan the skies.'

I nodded.

'And you must think of this place. From your tropical home, you must imagine us getting through the days. That is what we will do. All of us. It will be all right, you'll see.'

I wanted to say something back to him. I wanted to tell him that I would never forget him and that, if I could ever get beyond this long sorrowful moment, it would be his help that I would remember. Love had come and gone time after time. This was life, I saw.

Later, as we drove back to the house, he told me a little more about Ria.

'When she was a child she used to come from London every summer to help her uncle on the farm.'

'Where is that farm now?'

'Oh, it got sold off. I bought some of the land. Another farmer absorbed the rest and Jack got his money. Eel House went to Ria because she'd always loved it. Much to Jack's disappointment. He wanted the lot sold and the money split. First time he didn't get his own way.'

He paused, looking angry.

'Ria used to be very different, then. Before her father died, she was always chattering. And she was always in the water, swimming all summer long. My wife used to say she was a little fish! She hardly ever swam afterwards.'

I tried to imagine Ria as a happy child and failed.

'When her father died, her mouth simply closed up. She was never the same.'

I waited but he had finished speaking.

'Nothing worked for her for years.'

Nothing worked for us, either, I thought.

'Then she met Ben.'

His words hovered between us. I knew he was pleading with me to see what it had been like for Ria. I was aware of my lack of generosity, but there was nothing I could do about it and I knew he wasn't judging me.

In this twilight world in which I had been existing for the last few weeks, there had been other moments like this. I had lived my life in small glimmers of light, brief illumination, like the fireflies at home; things shone briefly before fading from view. As to Ria, I saw no future there, either. We would never connect. The place I was in was so far below the surface it could not be called living.

'It's time for me to leave,' I told him. 'We have said all we can.'

'Perhaps, for the moment,' he agreed. 'Where you are just now has the appearance of being stationary, but it isn't. Not really, things will change. You will change and so will Ria. You will both see things differently.'

His voice was unbearable in its sad acceptance. I could not agree with him. Whatever changed, it would not bring back my son.

'You will survive this winter, I promise you,' was all he said.

He told me that he saw himself as living proof of this. But I wasn't him. And the thought of all the lonely years of existence was more than I could cope with. I wanted to tell him that where I came from there was no spring, but he had been extraordinarily loving to me and I could not hurt him.

'There were men sent to Siberia,' he said suddenly and for no apparent reason as he stared out at the frozen world. 'They built the Russian railways that exist even today. This weather makes me think of that.'

In a few days I would be flying over Siberia.

On the morning of the day we were to collect the ashes I woke to the sound of rain. Outside my window the scene had changed dramatically and the river, frozen for so many days, was flowing freely again. I could see grass, sodden and yellowed by days of snow, appearing here and there. A thin, watery sun had risen. I stared out, shocked by the change. I showered and dressed wearily. Everything was such an effort; I was interminably tired. All I wanted was to be back in Jaffna. I wanted to lie on my own bed in the stifling heat. I imagined curling up in a corner of it, in the tropical darkness, being left to die.

It is all I want, I told myself. At home I would be able to die in peace.

That morning Ria must have gone out very early. She came in as I wandered downstairs and the first thing I noticed was that she was wearing a bright red coat.

'Would you like some breakfast?' she asked. 'I'm driving into Ipswich at nine.'

I swallowed. The ground rose slightly and I could feel myself break out in a cold sweat. The thought of food was horrendous.

'I will come with you,' was all I said.

Memory fails me once again. I remember nothing of the drive to Ipswich except that the rain was melting the snow. We sat in several traffic jams; I was passive, like an animal waiting for the next blow, she hunched over the steering wheel, frowning. Once or twice she made reference to the solicitor. She had received letters; there was an application for a hearing, but before that some interviews had to take place.

'Do whatever you think best,' I said. 'I won't be here.'

'Yes, I know. Are you happy with that? I could phone you and send e-mails to anyone you know who has access to the Internet.'

We were sitting at another set of traffic lights and she waited, drumming her fingers on the steering wheel.

'Do what you think best. I trust you.'

She nodded and pressed her lips together. I thought that perhaps she was angry again, that she felt I was not behaving as a mother should. I sighed. The outside of the windscreen was filling up with large droplets of rain, but still she did not turn the wipers on. The lights changed and she woke from her daydream and cleared the windscreen. Someone beeped a horn politely and we moved off. The car was hot and comforting.

We collected the ashes and drove to the estuary where Eric's car was parked already. On the way, we stopped at the florist and I bought two red roses. Then we walked across the field. I carried the small box. Ria was still wearing her red coat. I had decided not to wear the white sari I had worn at the funeral. There was no point to be made, no one to impress with the fact that I was in mourning. We climbed the stile and immediately saw Eric in the distance. My heart flexed. He was wearing the same suit he had worn at the church. In the slight breeze the air held the faintest promise of warmth. What was lost was unrecoverable. A line of poetry ran through my head like music and, as I walked towards it, I saw the river was fast-flowing and high.

'The tide has come in,' Eric said by way of greeting.

His eyes were dark. He kissed both of us. Then he walked to the point where we could see Eel House clearly. It was the highest ground. I opened the box and we each took out a handful of the soft downy ashes of my son. Here was my world; here, in this box.

'Let's each go to whatever spot we want,' Ria said, and I nodded.

She walked away in the direction of the house and as I watched the pale light caught her hair. It seemed shot through with gold. I turned away and scattered what I held of Ben across the waters he had once swum. The river made a rushing noise as the breeze lifted the fine particles out of my hands. I watched them dissolve in the bright winter air. He is gone, I thought bleakly. Here, on this sodden grass, flattened by constant wetness, tomorrow there will be no mark of what was lost. I do not have enough life left to me in which to forget this, even if I wanted to. Overhead, a flock of birds moved slowly and steadily across the wide expanse of Suffolk skies; witness to all we did.

16

Ten twenty. Nearing Heathrow. So here I am, on this bus nearing the airport. The snow has melted; the fields have a blanket of soft grey light thrown on them. I cannot but marvel at how many shades of grey this country has. I will never pass this way again. Beside me, the Italian woman sits up, waking. I have been half talking to her, but she must have dozed off, uncomprehending. Who can blame her? Mine is a story that beggars belief. For the hundredth time, I think, although I am leaving, some part of me will remain. We are almost at the drop-off point and the passengers move restlessly. When he said his goodbye, Eric had held me while I cried. His lips on mine were warm and full of an aftermath of love. Yes, love. I can say the word without flinching, for it is true. We had shared a kind of loving that belongs to us alone. In spite of everything, it had been possible.

'I am honoured,' he had said, with old-fashioned courtesy, 'to have shared it with you. There is only one last thing I want to say. Maybe it will be of use . . .'

I waited, wiping my eyes.

'Don't try to run away from the grief. It will only follow you. The boy is at rest; now rest a little, yourself. Tell others how it was. And, if you can, when you return, write to Ria. I think it will help both of you.'

He asked nothing for himself. I saw his eyes swim in unshed tears. Until now, I had not thought of anything beyond the airport. Now I saw: leaving would be as bad as arriving. And there's Tara, I think. I have not spoken to Tara once since arriving here. I hadn't been able to ask Ria if I could phone her. By now, Tara will be in despair, waiting for news. I have a duty in that direction too. The Italian says something to me.

'What is your name?' I ask at last, arousing myself.

'I am Lucia,' she says. She sits staring ahead, her thick heavy face, in profile, strange and sad as cattle in a field.

A watery sun is struggling to appear. The coach speeds swiftly on. In all, with the traffic hold-ups, we have been travelling for nearly five hours. While I have been thinking, the landscape has changed. Now the flat fields that I have grown to love have gone and we are in the midst of silent grey towns, one no different from another. How did people live with such thick cloud? I think how life is, as fragile as the snow that has melted, and just as elusive. Ben had left me long ago. At the moment of his birth, leaving my body, slipping out, establishing himself in the world. Alone. We are always that, I think. I see my own lonely years ahead. What is in store for me? A lifetime of endless tropical sunlight. Nothing else, I think.

We are almost there. Now I see airport signs.

'What time is your flight?' Lucia asks.

'I have a three-hour wait,' I say. 'Terminal One.'

My legs feel hollow, now that the time has come to leave I do not want to go. I do not want to leave both of them. Despair clutches my heart. Now that the moment of reality is drawing close, I feel sanity slip slightly. I have suffered two deaths of the heart. Lucia is watching me from the corner of her eye.

'Come,' she says. 'I will accompany you. My flight leaves from Terminal Five, but it isn't until early evening. I will come with you and check in your bags.'

It is very nearly my undoing, this random kindness from a stranger. See, I wanted to say out loud, what a wonderful thing you have done for me, son. You have opened up the world. You have made it possible for me to see other places, meet other people, understand the world a little better. That counts for something, too, however terrible has been the way it was achieved. I want to believe it. But I cannot.

'Don't dismiss it,' Eric had said. 'It is his gift to you!'

Ah, Eric! Overhead there is the thunder of a plane and I see its under-carriage as it flies past. There are small dots in the windows. Humanity looking down on us.

'Come,' Lucia says, helping me off the bus when we finally stop. '*Andiamo*, let's go.'

Inside are officials. I freeze at the sight of them. All my life has been controlled by the power of the uniform, but Lucia is indifferent to them. My passport is checked.

'Your luggage, madam?'

'Only this bag,' I say, showing him.

He looks surprised.

'Travelling light,' he says, unexpectedly, his voice friendly.

I am taken aback.

'Yes,' I say.

'Not many travel so lightly on long-haul flights. You must be a good packer!'

He smiles and hands me my boarding pass.

'Watch the board for the gate number, madam,' he says, cheerful now. 'Have a good flight.'

'Thank you,' I say faintly.

He is young enough to be my son.

I say goodbye to Lucia.

'Here is my address,' she says. 'Next year, who knows, I will visit you in Sri Lanka.'

I smile. I am crying once again. She will not be allowed into Jaffna and I will never be allowed into Colombo, but it seems pointless to tell her this. So I agree that perhaps the war will stop next year. Perhaps, I say. Who knows?

And then, in the briefest space of time, moving as if in a bubble, unaware of the shops and the places to eat, the car in the centre of the mall being offered as a prize in a raffle, I am through to the

222

departure gate. My plane is ready for boarding. From then on it is exactly as it was before and I am herded from departure lounge through to departure gate. The plane stands on the tarmac. I had been stunned when I arrived. I had not seen the sheer size of the airport. Now I see there are hundreds of planes taking off, arriving, taxiing around. Lives being shuttled from one corner of the world to another. Mesmerised, I watch through the window, waiting for my passport to be checked. Ben is no longer part of this world and I am going home. Again I feel the soft touch of his ashes in my hand, like the down of his hair when he was born. Sadness, slow and beyond any kind of language, settles on me.

In my bag is the drawing I made. Ria had not mentioned it, and neither had I. When I left, she gave me the only two photographs she had of him. One was a picture of him, as she had known him, in that last, lost summer of his life. Smiling at the camera, staring at the sun, innocently searching for happiness. The other photograph was one I did not know he had stolen from me. It was of himself as a small boy, standing under the jak-fruit tree in the back yard of our post office. I was in it and so was Percy.

'It's yours,' Ria had said at the last minute.

We had arrived at the bus station and were sitting in the car. The heater was blowing warm air on my legs.

'Soon you will have real heat,' she said absent-mindedly.

'Don't you want to keep one of them?' I asked, surprised.

She shook her head, not looking at me.

'No, I have other things. Different memories, you know.'

She raised her head then and I saw the flash of her brilliant blue eyes. She was looking very pale, but then she smiled, slightly, and I saw that once, long ago, perhaps when she was happy, she would have been very beautiful.

'You must have them,' she said pressing my hand.

The seat-belt sign is switched on, the pilot calls to the stewardess.

'Cabin crew, check and cross-check doors,' he says.

The plane begins to taxi slowly towards the runway. We pass a hoarding that says BANKING FOR TOMORROW. The plane gathers speed, slipping easily into its position on the runway. Then, with hardly any hesitation, it is airborne, lifting and turning, flying. Briefly we see London sprawling below us, gun-metal grey and silvery. I take out the photographs from my handbag. At the time, I had thought she was unfeeling. But then, I thought, perhaps she had taken a copy. Now I am glad to have something that he had touched. Now I think her generous. Then we are climbing up, up through the dark rain clouds, banking and adjusting before we swing higher into the bright sunlight above.

Lydia

17

'You might as well begin at the beginning,' she says.

Her voice is softly modulated and I dislike it instantly. There is no sound in the room except for the clock ticking. I swallow. Okay.

'My name is Lydia,' I say. 'I'm fifteen years old, I'm at school studying history, geography, English. I want to read archaeology at Sussex University one day . . . is that the sort of thing you want me to say?'

'Well, it's a start.'

She is clearly not going to help me in any way. I feel my voice wobble. What craziness had brought me here? Oh, get on with it, I tell myself.

'My surname is Robinson,' I continue. 'It's my mother's name. Her maiden name; she never married.'

'Did your father not want you to have his name?'

I take a deep breath; and then I tell her.

'Until very recently I thought I was a donor baby,' I say, and I look her full in the face. There, I think, see what you make of that!

If I was expecting a reaction, I wasn't getting it. She's too cool for that.

'How do you mean, exactly?' she asks.

Cool, cool. Sophisticated bitch, Ms Know-all, I think. I hide my anger, knowing she would love to see it. These types always do. It gives them the perfect opportunity to say, 'Ah, look, she's screwed up!' Well, I'm not giving her the satisfaction, let me tell you.

This is all Miranda's idea. Miranda is my aunt. She's also my legal guardian, along with Uncle Jack. He's the man from hell. Anyway, they're supposed to be *looking after* me. They were the ones who took me in, were 'very generous to me', as the other rellies like to think. Maria Robinson, my mother – they all called her Ria – died in a car crash when I was thirteen. It was not her fault. It was the drunks in the overturned car in the middle of the road. She swerved to avoid them and hit an oncoming lorry. Trying to multi-task, she was, and failing. We girls are supposed to be good at it, but not my ma. Not this time, anyway. So she died and Uncle Jack was adamant: her ashes had to be spread over the estuary. I didn't care where they went. They could have spread them on toast, for all I cared! I was too busy thinking about what it would be like without her. I went into a black hole afterwards. It took a year before I even realised I was in one, and then I still didn't care about anything much.

But to begin at the beginning, I had what you might call a repressed childhood. It wasn't the 1950s or anything like that, but it might as well have been for all the skeletons in our family cupboard. When I was very small, Mum and I were close in the sort of physical way that mothers and very small children are. She looked after me, fed me, taught me to read, took me to the dentist for check-ups, even taught me to swim in the river at the bottom of our garden. She was dead keen on swimming, actually.

'I don't want you to get drowned,' was what she said.

She was a good, conscientious mother. I wasn't neglected, don't ever think that. Later on, she would always check my homework, make sure my hair was combed before I left for school, *and* she was always at home when I returned.

'Well, that was because she worked from home, wasn't it?'

'Yes, it was. But I mean she never went out at the time I was due back from school, never went shopping or visited her horrid friend. She was always there waiting, there was always food when I got in.'

I think for a moment, frowning. She used to ask about my day, how the maths homework was received, what the English lesson was like, that sort of thing. She never quite looked at me, never smiled. I can't say I noticed any of this at the time, but now I'm having to think about it I wonder if it would have made a difference? Well, it's no good worrying about that now.

'She never asked me about how I felt. She was scared to.'

The therapist, her name is Stephanie, looks at me. She has this trick of simply looking, saying nothing, trying to unnerve me. She almost succeeds. I wish I hadn't given so much away. And in any case, it was a bit disloyal to poor old Mum, who couldn't exactly defend herself. I shut up for a moment.

After a few minutes Stephanie breaks the silence. I s'pose she has to earn her money.

'Did she hug you? When you came in? Touch you?'

I can't believe I'm doing this, sitting here with this cow. I want to shout and cry at the same time. I feel the age-old rage envelop me. Then I feel weary. What the hell, the bitch can only get to me if I let her. Believe me, I'm far more cunning than she is. I'm not going to tell her how it really was between us. I'm not going to tell her how we communicated, without saying a word, or how I felt I understood *everything* about how she was let down.

'No,' I say calmly. 'We weren't a touchy-feely family.'

I make my voice as sneering as possible. Instinct tells me she'd like that expression. That's why I use it. Instantly she writes furiously in her pad, and I want to yell with delight. Bull's-eye!

'But,' I say, holding up my index finger, giving her a crumb, 'we were close in other ways.'

'How?' she pounces. 'Tell me.'

'Well,' I say, pretending to look thoughtful, resisting the urge to throw something at her, 'she would read her poems to me.'

This was absolutely true, as it happens.

'She used to read to me a lot when I was little . . . till I stopped her one night.'

I could see Stephanie trying not to ask another question, so I rewarded her for her silence.

Mum had read me one of her poems at bedtime.

'I wrote this before you were born,' she said.

I remember she'd been sitting on my bed with her arm around me.

'What was the poem about?' Stephanie asks.

'"*Too rushed to ask . . . / I have stolen something precious from you . . .*" Something like that . .'

'Did you know she was referring to your father?'

I glare at her.

'Maybe.'

'What happened then?'

Bitch. You know what happened. Miranda's told you.

'She started to cry.'

Stephanie is looking at me expectantly. Her face is a comic question mark.

'I pushed her away and told her I hated her poems.'

'What happened then?'

Nothing! Nothing! Nothing! Bitch!

'Did she read to you again?'

'Yes, of course – stories.'

'She never read you her poems again?'

I shake my head. I really want to kill this woman.

'There was another time, though, when she did?'

I hesitate. Actually, I'm quite tired.

'Yes.'

'Tell me.'

So I do. Who cares?

It had been an odd sort of day.

'Go on,' Stephanie says.

Blank-faced bitch.

There'd been no school, and I'd been over at the farm, helping with fruit picking. When I got back, hot and slightly cross because I was tired and starving hungry, my mother was sitting in the kitchen. I somehow knew something was wrong. She wasn't crying or anything. There was a letter on the table, I remember. A thick, fat, airmail envelope.

'What's that?' I asked idly.

Really I was more interested in finding something to eat. I began opening the pans and looking in the fridge.

'Oh, it isn't anything,' my mother said vaguely and, preoccupied though I was, I knew she was lying.

The moment passed, she offered to make me a sandwich. I caught a glimpse of a photograph in the envelope and then she put it away.

'Weren't you curious? After all, you were only eight or nine?' Stephanie asks.

'Well, I might have been, but I was really starving.'

She'd made me a ham sandwich, thick and full of freshly cooked ham, a little mustard, chunky bread, and I'd wolfed the lot down.

'She was a fantastic cook,' I say.

I haven't thought about that incident for a long time. But thinking about it now, I realise how edgy she had been for the rest of that day and for days afterwards. Unusually, she had read me the poem she was working on and then, that night, we had gone to the cinema together. Afterwards we had supper in a local café.

'I used to come here a lot before you were born,' she had volunteered.

I remember how her face had changed as she spoke. She had very blue eyes and they suddenly filled up with tears. I panicked and did what I always do. I changed the subject. Her face changed again. She looked frightened. And then we talked of something else. Later, I mean a long time later . . .

'How long?'

'I can't remember. I talked to my friend Sarah.'

'Your mother probably had IVF treatment,' Sarah had said.

Sarah knew about these things.

'You could be a donor baby!' Sarah had whispered excitedly. 'Think of that!'

'Well . . . I think she met him.'

'They do sometimes. Sometimes both parties strike a bargain. Meet once, do the deed, pay up and never meet again!'

It was possible, I remember thinking. Poor old Mum, buying a sperm to make a life! That's how much she must have wanted to have me. Sarah was looking expectantly at me.

'Well, what does it matter? I'll never meet him anyway,' I said.

'Oh, oh!' Sarah said, her mouth a perfect rosebud circle of interest. 'You do know what they do, don't you? They go to this clinic and . . .'

Sarah was allowed to watch far more television than I was. She was allowed to stay up and watch as many reality shows as she liked, whereas my mother thought they were disgraceful.

'You do know what I mean, don't you?' Sarah asked again.

'Yes, of course,' I said.

I didn't want the details or I might have punched Sarah. Poor old Mum, was what I was thinking. Anyway, I'd a vague idea, as we had once caught the local flasher Frank doing it to himself on our way home from school.

'Isn't it the case that your mother thought she couldn't have children?' Stephanie asks, butting into my thoughts.

'What's that got to do with anything?'

I glare at her. I just know she wants me to cry.

'Wouldn't she have *wanted* to talk to you about your father?'

'Maybe.'

'Weren't you curious, too?'

'No,' I lied.

Of course I was curious, stupid. I didn't tell her that one night I heard Uncle Jack, who was visiting us, shouting at Mum, saying, 'Why did you do it, then? Why couldn't you be like normal people?' Mum was crying like anything. They must have thought I was asleep. Anyway I didn't want her to cry like that, again. Who cared about the donor? And then, a year later, when I might have asked her, she was dead. Sarah moved to another area entirely, and that was that. I no longer wanted to be friends with anyone else in the way we had been friends.

'Did you see Sarah again, after she moved?'

'She came to the funeral.'

She had come back to Orford, quite by chance, on the weekend that my mother had been killed. One of her aunts lived in a village close by, Sarah and her mother were visiting her. We had texted each other a few days before. Both of us missed the other far more than we wanted to admit and we'd sort of planned what we would do when she came back. It was a Friday in June. Nothing special; hot, but not too hot. We'd had an exam in school that morning and I told my mother I would be back early.

'I'm going into Ipswich,' she had said. 'I've got to see the lawyer about something.'

As long as I could remember, my mother used to see a lawyer about something. When I was very small I used to have to stay with Jack and Miranda while she went up to London to see a lawyer about something. Both my uncle and aunt disapproved of these trips, and when she returned Mum was always bad tempered. I had no idea what it was all about. There were so many other pressing things going on that 'seeing a lawyer about something' never grabbed my curiosity. Anyway, that morning, before I left for school, she warned me she might be late. It was fine by me. As I hardly ever had the house to myself I looked on her absence that afternoon as a treat. So I didn't worry when there was no sign of her at three o'clock or at four. At five thirty Sarah rang to say they had stopped off at her gran's for tea but hoped to be at her aunt's house later that evening. I could hear from her voice that she was disappointed. We had planned a trip up to Eric's farm and we were going to take the smaller boat out on the river. We never did, of course. We never went up that river together again.

'When did you hear?' Stephanie asks, very quietly. 'About your mother?'

I say nothing.

'Lydia? When did you get the news?'

'At ten to six.'

They had rung. Then they came round. One policewoman and a policeman. I hadn't been scared. It was like reality telly. You don't get scared by reality telly. One half of me was watching the other half of me. Curiously.

'Detached?'

'Hmm, detached.'

They had asked me if my dad was in, first. Well, that was a laugh.

I wondered if he'd been traced and was in trouble. Would I disown him? Tell him what a shit he was for not giving a damn about Mum all these years.

The police invited themselves in and wanted to know if I was alone. I said I was, but that it didn't happen often because my mum was very careful to be there when I got back but today was different because of the exam and the lawyer and stuff.

'Oh, it doesn't matter, love,' the policewoman said. 'We're not worried about that.'

She seemed a tiny bit odd and suddenly, for no reason at all, I was afraid.

'What's wrong?' I asked.

'Is there any relative nearby?'

'No, just a good friend.'

There was no one. Only Eric, of course. Jack and Miranda and the cousins were in Sicily. It seemed the police had been to Eric's farm, but there was no one there. That was why they had then come straight here. I completely forgot to mention Sarah and her mother who would be over in Orford later that evening. In any case, I was thoroughly frightened now.

'What is it?' I asked again.

They knew, of course. They could see the panic in my eyes. I've often wondered afterwards what I must have looked like. Anyway, one of them sat me down and then took a seat next to me. The other sat on my other side and held my hand.

'It's your mum, love,' she said. 'She's had an accident.'

'Is she dead?' I asked.

But I already knew the answer to that.

The funny thing about bad news is that you never respond in the way you might have thought you would. It isn't a bit like reality TV. That isn't real at all; this was. I didn't cry, or faint. I didn't behave like a Gwyneth Paltrow or Kate Winslet. It was not my Oscar performance; no, I hardly made a sound. The policewoman was freaked out by it.

'You all right, luv?' she kept asking me over and over again. 'Would you like a glass of water?'

I shook my head as if to clear an obstruction.

'I don't want any.'

But she gave me some anyway and I sipped it. The water was taste-less, invisible, like whatever it was that was going on in my head. Actually, there wasn't anything in my head at all. I looked down at my feet and they seemed to have grown to enormous proportions. I frowned. I had no recollection of having taken my shoes off. What had I been doing before the police? I looked into the concerned face of the policewoman. She was about my mother's age.

'Can I see her?' I asked.

I saw her and the policeman exchange looks. I heard the crackle of their radio. Then with a clatter of wings a flock of geese flew over the river. They did this every day in spring and early summer. Then they stopped in the autumn and returned again the following year. Well, I remember thinking, a group of birds returned, but were they the *same* ones? The thought just popped into my head. I had no idea why. The policewoman was speaking again and I tried to concen-trate but her face was going in and out of focus. I must have looked a bit odd because she suddenly had her arm around me. Her face was very close. I could see she had a lot of open pores and the roots of her hair, near her ears, were all grey. I could see the weave of her uniform and smell a faint perfume that reminded me of cut grass in early summer. I did not cry.

They carried on talking to me and I must have answered because they nodded and asked me another question. I could no longer work out what they were saying but thought it best to agree. The policeman squatted on his haunches and peered at me as if he was trying to see inside my head. I felt laughter bubble up but I didn't let it out either. So there I was, not laughing or crying or speaking.

'She's in shock,' someone said.

I turned my head but there was no one else there.

'When will Eric be back?'

How did I know? Why weren't they asking my mother? At that, someone seemed to throw cold water over my face because I stood up calmly and told them I was ready.

We went out and got into the waiting car. I still didn't have a clue as to where we were going. The sun was setting in a nasty yellowish orange glow. I was surprised that I had never noticed before how tacky sunsets are.

'Why d'you say that?' Stephanie asks, interrupting my train of thought, making me angry again, just when I'm feeling calmer and enjoying the story.

I have never told the story in quite this way before, partly because most people know about what happened anyway. Most people don't want the bother of being reminded of me. Anyway, Stephanie is waiting. I ignore her question and continue. I'll decide what to answer and what not to.

'We drove to the hospital in Ipswich,' I say.

I had been to Accident and Emergency before; the time I'd got glass in my foot and the time I'd had the asthma attack and no one knew why. I'd been to the maternity wing of the hospital when Sarah's baby brother was born and the nurse let me hold one of the babies. But this time we didn't go in the usual way. This time we went along a long winding route, over speed bumps and past a zebra crossing where a group of people stared at the police car curiously. The car radio was crackling and the driver was talking into it. I couldn't understand a word they were saying. The policewoman kept squeezing my hand. She looked as if she was going to cry at any moment. I wanted to tell her it was my mother and not hers. No, really, it crossed my mind to say, look this isn't the telly. I suppose I was in a curious state of mind.

'We've sent a message to your aunt and uncle, love,' they told me. 'They're flying back on the first available flight home.'

Still I said nothing.

The driver stopped the car and got out. He went a little way away and began talking into his radio. The police took me into the squat building nearby. Nasty fir trees grew all around, screening it from the rest of the hospital. There was no one about as we walked towards the reception desk and the officer gave my name. I was aware of another exchange of looks, but I had this feeling of watching all this from a long way off, through the wrong side of my mother's bird binoculars. A telephone rang somewhere; there was a faint smell of disinfectant. I recognised it as being the same as when the school toilets were cleaned. People in green coats moved about, no one was speaking very loud, no one really looked at me. I walked between the two women feeling as though I was an alien. What would Sarah say? What would Mum say when she found out? And then we were in this room. I can't really describe it, except that I saw a bucket and a steel bed. Do you think it was a bed? Anyway, there was this thing on it, covered by a sheet. And a man went towards it and it was only then that I saw my mother's shoe, not quite off her foot but not quite on either, and her jeans, I saw, had been torn. They were her best jeans, I remember thinking. The thought was sort of fast and condensed and followed by two more thoughts. She was wearing the bracelet I'd given her for her birthday. And there was a gash across her bare arm that looked pretty nasty, and then . . . and then . . . I saw her face. Squashed and flattened and with a purple bruise that seemed to cover her forehead. Like the worst fall you could ever imagine having, like the accident that made you scream and scream.

'Mum,' I shouted. 'Mum, Mum!'

And then I fainted.

Before you start feeling sorry for me, let me tell you I'm not the nicest of people. Most of the time I hate everything and everyone. Last year at school one of my teachers wrote that I was a mass of insecurities and immaturities. She'd been reading books on psychology, I suppose. Stupid cow. What would she have been like if she had had to identify her mother's mangled body in the middle of the night?

'How did you feel about that? Tell me.'

That's the bloody therapist talking. Don't they just love their jobs? How does she think I felt!

'It wasn't like opening my Christmas presents,' I tell her.

Her face remains perfectly smooth. I wonder if she's had a facelift. Everything is so refined and airbrushed. Does she take her teeth out to have sex I wonder? I guess it's my immaturities that make me have thoughts like that.

'Tell me a bit more about your mother.'

'Like I said, everyone called her Ria. I thought she was beautiful. She was very tall; I'm going to take after her in this. What d'you want to know?'

'Tell me other things.'

'We *were* close but it wasn't obvious. Is that the sort of thing you want to know?'

I pause, remembering something else Mum had once said.

'Your father,' she had said, 'was not allowed legally into this country.'

Can you *believe* that? The bastard must have used her to get money, to stay here. Sarah said you hear about these people all the time. Anyway, Mum had sounded so sad when she spoke of Donor-man that, to be honest, I never wanted to see him in case I'd kill him. So I always changed the subject. Aunt Miranda used to have this saying, 'Least said, soonest mended,' and I thought so too.

'She was the most fantastic poet, really,' I tell Stephanie.

I'm having difficulty keeping the pride out of my voice, I know.

'Did the two of you fight?'

'No,' I say, reluctantly.

I had to look after her, didn't I? So I couldn't fight. I always used to envy my school friends who came to school bawling their eyes out.

'She's chucked me out, miss,' Chorley used to snivel to the teacher, and then everyone used to crowd round and offer sympathy. Even me. I could be relied on to do the right thing.

'Oh, Chorley,' I used to say, loathing the little coward, 'I'm so sorry you have to stay at your gran's for the night.'

At least the tart had a gran! We all knew she wouldn't go to her though but would spend the night with her boyfriend, but the teacher, being incredibly naïve, would ring Chorley's mother and try to patch things up between them. No one ever did that sort of thing for me, I'll have you know. Number one, I no longer had a mother to patch things up with by this time, and number two I was the sort of person no one dared to provoke. Probably the mass of insecurities was the reason for this.

'Were you hurt that no one noticed how you felt?'

'Hurt?'

Oh, please! What is this? Jungian or Freudian psychology?

'Am I making you angry?'

Laugh out loud. It's Jack and Miranda's money you are wasting, cow-face. Please ask me some intelligent questions. Silence. Looks like we're stumped.

'I don't want to ask you any questions you don't want me to.'

'I don't want to ask you any questions you don't want me to. Sorry!'

Another silence. I would whistle if I could, but my teeth are the wrong shape. Eric tried to teach me.

'Eric?'

'Yeah. He's my friend. He lived near us, at the farm. I used to work there in the summer.'

'Where is he now?'

'Still there.'

Idiot! He hasn't gone on a world cruise, has he! Concentrate, answer the questions.

'He knew my mother when she was a little girl.'

I'm as good as his granddaughter. He takes me eel-catching in the summer. We take the boat upstream in the early mornings. Sometimes we even sleep on the boat and then wake up very early when the sun rises. All the coots come out on the water making parping noises. As soon as they see us moving about they swim over, hoping for food. The sun rises above the mist, the willows rustle softly in the breeze and Eric makes us breakfast. Bliss! Bliss! I'm happy at last! Two rashers of bacon, two eggs, sometimes a bit of onion. And then tomato sauce and bread. You wouldn't think to see us sitting there so peacefully that the rest of the country is a mass of riots and unemployment. That terror stalks the streets of every town in Britain, that a crusade is taking place in Britain, just like in the Middle Ages. Seeing us there is a bit like reading *The Wind in the Willows*. Honestly, it's so peaceful. Afterwards we check the eel-traps.

'Tell me more about Eric.'

'He's old. Mum trusted him completely, so do I. He never repeats anything you tell him. Not a bit like Miranda and Jack, who are the biggest gossips in the world.'

'What sorts of things do they gossip about?'

I open my mouth to speak, then close it again. Is this a trap? Are my words going straight back to Uncle Jack? I don't like the sound of this question, so I ignore it. Uncle Jack is not my favourite person. Everyone says he feels guilty as hell about Mum, but I don't see any sign of it, myself.

'Oh, I don't know,' I say, making my voice sound vague.

There's a small pause.

'Lydia, whatever you tell me is in confidence. You know that, don't you?'

'You know that, don't you!'

Another pause.

'Are you referring to the fact that your uncle was part of a right-wing political party? And that he had to resign because there was some suspicion he was involved in the animal killings?'

I keep my face perfectly straight and open my eyes really wide. I know I can look innocent this way. I hate this woman almost as much as I hate Uncle Jack. And just for the record, I do think he was part of that business. One, he hates Muslims; two, there's no smoke without fire. I know Eric keeps telling me it was never proved and that he was really only having an affair with some friend of Mum's. Oh God, my mum was surrounded by betrayers.

'No, of course not,' I say, my eyes wide.

'You love Eric, don't you?'

Another stupid question. What does she think?

'No, I hate him.'

Her face is comical. Oh, how immature, she's thinking! Of course I love Eric. He loved us both. Now she's dead, Eric is all I've got. He understood everything. Why Mum was so repressed, why I behaved the way I did because I was trying to look after her. I was always the strong one. Being different makes you tough. I'd heard the stories about my birth. I mean, the way the midwife had said as she pulled me out:

'Oh, look, she's got a Mongolian blue spot! Is the father a foreigner?'

My aunt told this story to me, thinking it was funny.

'You had a blue spot on your bottom,' she said.

She must have told my cousins because they took it up and tormented me with it.

In fact, the 'blue spot' was at the base of my spine and it had faded by the time I was a week old, but the way the story went around the family you'd think I was marked for life! Eric heard Sophie laughing and teasing me about it and told her off. Then I heard him saying something to Mum and she cried and cried and Eric gave her a hug. And after that she tried to have one of her hopeful heart-to-hearts that I blocked again for fear she'd start crying. Oh God!

'Anyway, I'm over all that now.'

'How's that?'

Because Eric told me. Lovely Eric, rescuing me as always.

'He told me that a Mongolian blue spot was a birthmark that appeared at birth on children of Asian descent but faded quickly afterwards. It meant *nothing!*'

Why my aunt had to even mention it was a mystery to me. At least if she had to mention it, why couldn't she talk about its significance? Why make such a bloody issue of it in the first place?

'Did she make an issue of it?'

'She said later it was her way of trying to tell me about my father. Because Mum had told her she was scared of hurting me. So we were both trying not to hurt each other. I talked to Eric about it, obviously, afterwards. He said she blamed herself for not telling me when I was very small, but that in the beginning she had been so traumatised and frightened of damaging me that she couldn't. Eric said that sometimes grief works in strange ways, not how you'd expect it to, and that I shouldn't judge her. And when I freaked out over the Mongolian whatsit she clammed up completely. Anyway, it's all in the diary she kept. How much she loved him, how much she wanted me. It's all there; I've seen it. Now.'

Funny how everything ends up as my fault. I stop talking. It's strange, really, how circular the process of revisiting the past is. Nothing goes away. All the things that hurt long ago remain poisonously capable of hurting again and again. Like my aunt's joke.

'She didn't mean it in the way you took it, Lydi,' Eric said.

But it was too late by then; she was dead.

'She was frightened. Everything that had happened frightened her. She felt to blame on every count, don't you see?'

Somehow I was meant to be strong, understanding and magnanimous.

'You tell me, how was I supposed to manage that? I was thirteen, for God's sake. *Thirteen!*'

'So what did you do?' Stephanie asks.

I couldn't believe the question. She calls herself a therapist! I'm here under sufferance. Miranda and Jack are paying for the sessions at the moment. I'll pay them back, of course; as soon as the money comes through. That's the other thing, you see. When I'm eighteen I'll be rich. The insurance people paid up. The way it works is, you lose your mother by accident and you are given money to the value of that loss. I imagine someone sitting in front of their laptop, checking the chart. Accidental death of mother . . . £500,000. Accidental death of migrant worker . . . £1,200. Sorry, mate, that's your lot. But I'm jumping ahead.

'Go back to the beginning.'

Robot!

'What did you do when she was killed?'

Big question. 'I started giving everyone a hard time. I began to play up at school.'

'How?'

'Well, you know the war in the Middle East was getting on people's nerves. I wrote to the Prime Minister and told him that Uncle Jack was causing trouble for the Muslims in Britain. "Inciting racial hatred", those were the words I used!'

'Was he?'

'I dunno. Probably . . . who knows? I hate Jack. Anyway, I told him he was breeding a nation who would eventually destroy this country too.'

Stephanie raises her eyebrows slightly.

'Well? Look what's been happening. That woman was not the first suicide bomber in Britain, was she? Can't you see there's a trend here?'

'Tell me what happened after you wrote that letter.'

'Why are you asking me? You know. Jack's already told you.'

'No one's talked about you to me. I'm asking because I don't know.'

I've got her really riled. Hurrah!

Eric was the only one who saw what was going on. He came to visit Jack and Miranda. There was some kind of explosion between them. I could hear Miranda shouting and then Jack started. She had found out about his affair with Mum's loathsome friend. There'd been other trouble at home that day, anyway. Someone had come from some government office to talk to Jack! I giggle, remembering: their serious faces, my obvious lies, the way Jack tried to be calm when really he hated my guts for ruining his comeback to politics for good! Strangely I don't remember that time with any distaste, even though it got me into a lot of trouble. I remember it as the day the poison was sucked out of me. By lovely, wonderful Eric.

18

'Tell me what happened after you left the hospital that evening?'

We're on our second session together, Stephanie and I. Stephanie is wearing an orange shift dress. There is, amongst students of my age, a trend towards dressing in 1960s clothes. I suppose the trend has existed on and off for ages, but anyway I would say there's a great revival of the era just at the moment. Although she's certainly *not* my age, Stephanie is wearing just such a dress. For some reason the sight of her in this orange-and-black dress irritates me. I glare at her.

'Where did the police take you that night? You couldn't have been left on your own, after all.'

She's right, of course. They weren't prepared to leave me until I told them who I could stay with. Jack and Miranda were coming over on the first flight from Palermo, but that was eleven hours away.

'What about your friend Sarah?' one of them asked me.

I had stopped screaming. A doctor had seen me and given me something to take and I'd drunk some water. I was cold now, although it was a hot evening. A nurse brought a blanket and they put it around my shoulders. I felt like a homeless person. Had I given the matter some thought, I would have seen that of course I was sort of homeless; motherless, anyway. The policewoman was still at it, gently trying to get me to speak.

'Give us your friend's address, love, and we'll ring her parents. It's only until your uncle and aunt get here, it's not for long. Only, we can't leave you alone.'

Not after news like this, was what they meant. What did they think I'd do?

'What were you feeling?' Stephanie asks.

Jesus!

'I don't want to go to Sarah's,' I said.

The policewoman looked a bit taken aback.

'She's your best friend, isn't she?'

She was suddenly no longer my best friend.

'I want to go to Eric's farm,' I told them, calmly.

They must have thought I was pretty cool to be behaving like this. No tears, no emotion, well, not after that initial screaming fit. Someone had clamped up my throat, which incidentally was sore from the screaming.

'Can you really remember your throat being sore from all those years ago?'

'Yes,' I say, shortly.

What does she think? That I'd have forgotten it? I remember every single last fucking thing of that day. Everything, every fibre on the policewoman's uniform, the way the weave ran in the cloth, her teeth with a little fleck of lipstick. I think she was pretty shaken up by it all.

'So you went to Eric?'

We did. There was a bit of a wait. Eric had been over in Ipswich, too, that day, to some farmer's market or other. But the traffic had held him up on the ring road. He presumed it had been an accident. There was a black spot at the turning to Snape. He told me years afterwards that he'd thought some bloody idiot had been going too fast. It was what usually happened. It had never crossed his mind that it might have involved someone he loved. Anyway, he turned off at Snape and decided he would call by his sister's house for a cup of tea. By the time he left, after she had insisted he have a bite to eat, it was already dark. We were waiting for him in the lane, sitting in the police car. Whatever it was that I had been given at the hospital was taking effect and I had stopped shaking and was now feeling drowsy. The early evening had taken on an ethereal feel. Normally my mother would be cooking something. The television would be on, I might be on the phone to one of my friends, or I might, if it was a Thursday, be cycling back from my piano lesson.

'You play the piano?' Stephanie asked.

'I play jazz.'

'Just jazz?'

'Yes.'

Anyway, it wasn't a Thursday, nor was it any other ordinary day. I paused, thinking. In one second all my ordinary days had been destroyed. Eric was coming home to this.

'Here he is,' the policewoman said.

She'd been talking to me all this time. I hadn't said much, but she had kept up a steady stream of soft conversation. Like the brook at Withy Common, she'd been.

'Did you resent her?'

'No.'

She had realised quite early on that I didn't want her to touch me. I suppose they are trained to work these things out. Anyway, she just talked; giving me the facts, knowing this was what I wanted most. When she saw Eric's car, she turned to me.

'I'll have a word with him, love. Then you can come out, okay?'

I nodded, unable to speak. She got out of the car. I caught a glimpse of Eric, his long legs unfolding as he climbed out of his car. Then I saw Flossie bouncing around and I heard her bark once or twice at the policewoman.

'Be quiet, Floss,' I heard Eric say, and I imagined Floss sniffing the policewoman and then wagging her tail. I saw all these things without looking. I saw them in my head. There was a pause. A silence. Then I heard a sound, soft and muffled, not like any sound I had heard before. And then the policewoman was opening my door and helping me out and Flossie was running around in circles between my legs while Eric simply stood absolutely still, his shoulders hunched, staring at the ground. We must have seen each other at the same instance.

'Lydi,' he said, in his old, familiar voice, only now it was quivering and shocked.

I stop. Stephanie waits for me to continue.

'That's all I can remember,' I say flatly, knowing she wants more, knowing she's waiting for me to say that I ran to him crying. Or that he cried, or that the policewoman cried. I know she wanted a conclusion of some sort. But she isn't bloody getting one.

I don't recall a great deal more of the rest of that night. I think Eric and I clung together without saying too much. Eric absorbed the impact without any showiness. His face hardly changed. Tears rolled down his lined face without sound, he held me gently and then took me inside into his huge old kitchen where he sat me down beside the dying fire. I had known this place all my life. My mother used to take me there from the moment I had been born and set me down in my Moses basket on the dining table beside the fire. I had taken my first footsteps on these very flagstones. It was to this kitchen I had returned after my first day at school, hungry and full of excited news about my day. And now here I was again, sitting staring at Eric's hands as he deftly made up the fire. And my mother was dead. The thought had no meaning to it.

After a while, during which he sat in shocked, subdued silence, Eric offered the policewoman some tea. I suppose she felt uneasy about leaving us in this state; perhaps she was more used to people who cried and screamed, and perhaps our joint silence unnerved her. So she drank some tea with us before leaving. Promising to return the following day, urging us to eat something, hoping we would get through the night. And then at last we were alone together. Eric and I.

Looking back, I think Eric began to tell me the whole story on that very night. I barely understood, of course, but I think he wanted me to understand certain things before Uncle Jack returned.

'You will have to live with them,' he warned. 'Jack is your legal guardian.'

'I don't want to.'

He nodded, staring at the ground.

'It will be said that I am too old anyway, and the other side of your family is not an alternative.'

He had never said anything like that before. I registered his words, but all else was so overwhelming that I did not pick up on them. The full impact of what had happened was beginning to dawn on me by now and there was no room for any other thoughts. A little later there was the sound of a car and our local GP arrived, followed by Sarah's mother. I did not want to see her and so I went up to the spare room to hide while Eric dealt with the visitors. I was crying now, quietly and in earnest, although even through my tears I had the sense that what I was feeling wasn't really proper grief. That would come much later on. After the visitors had left, I heard Eric coming up the stairs. His footsteps were slow and weary. He was carrying a bowl of warm milk with bread and honey and he sat on the end of the bed and fed it to me.

'He really loved you!' Stephanie says, pointlessly.

I ignore her. There is nothing this woman can tell me that is of any use. I really don't know what I'm doing here.

'You'll have to live with them,' he said again, 'but your home is here. Any time, every holiday. Always. I shall tell them.'

I had always known in some subliminal way that Eric did not like Uncle Jack and Miranda.

'Had you ever wondered why this was?' Stephanie asks.

I shake my head and look at her pityingly. Didn't she know; that wasn't how children's minds worked, the fool!

'They were all there at the funeral,' I say.

Jack, Miranda, Sophie and Zach. My ex-friend Sarah, her parents; the whole of Orford, really. Except, of course, the bitch Heather, who couldn't come because of Jack. The policewoman, standing at the back, coming up to me afterwards to hug me. Oh God, everyone was there.

'You call her your "ex-friend". But she wasn't that yet, was she?'

'Sarah? Oh, she was. She was that instantly. From the moment my mother died, the relationship between us was uneven. She knew that. We both did.'

'But she still wanted to be your friend, didn't she?'

'She wanted to pity me.'

'Do you think your response was right?'

I give Stephanie a contemptuous look.

'What if it wasn't?' I say. 'The friendship could no longer work, don't you see?'

'What happened next?'

'It was almost the summer holidays.'

I had gone back to school briefly, but everything had changed in some strange and subtle way. The school and the teachers were sympathetic, the other girls tried to be nice to me, everything was as before. It was I who had changed. For the first time I noticed the way other families were made up and what difference it made to have an older or younger sibling. I saw that those of my friends who had complained about members of their family in the past – the younger sister who used all their make-up, the older brother who bossed them around – did not really mean what they said. Their complaints were fake complaints and the realisation filled me with bitterness. I was beginning to see that the world was not the place I had believed it to be.

But all this was still buried in me. I spent what was left of that summer living with Eric. There were a lot of loose ends to be tied up. It shocked me (and I tried to hide the shock) that such a momentous thing as a person dying could be dealt with so quickly. Eric knew what was going on in my head, but he said nothing. When he finally got round to talking about the past he told me he was simply biding his time that summer, waiting for the outer wound to heal before he disturbed the ashes of the past. So for the moment, all that summer, in weather that was unimaginably wonderful, I stayed at the farm while Eel House was packed up and rented out to tenants from overseas and Uncle Jack attended to the legal matters resulting from the accident. I understood vaguely that I was going to be rich when I grew up. I learnt this uninteresting fact from Sarah. She came once to visit me at the farm before going on holiday with her family. The visit was not successful. Eric was out checking his trees and Sarah and I had the run of the house. We decided to walk to the river the long way round. Without a word being said, both of us wanted to avoid the path that led to Eel House. I remember thinking with surprise that we could still read each other's minds even though we were only fake friends now. Perhaps this is always the case. Having known someone well, you never really forget the way their mind works. Anyway, by tacit agreement we went down to the river via the matchstick wood. In the past we had often walked this way, looking for the fossils that my mother said existed in this forest. We were no longer interested in fossils, of course. Sarah was a year older than me and she'd got herself a boyfriend. She began to talk about him now. He wanted to sleep with her, she told me, but she wasn't sure if she should wait a few weeks. She spoke seriously, there was none of the smutty humour of the summer before. So we were changed.

'There'll be lots of boys interested in you now,' she said.

I would be starting at a new school in London in the autumn when I moved in with Jack and Miranda. I had not wanted to discuss the move, hoping that if I didn't it might go away. For the first time I became aware of the concept of happiness.

'Children do not perceive happiness the way adults do,' I tell Stephanie. 'And I was now an adult.'

Stephanie says nothing. Her face is a perfect blank, waiting for me to continue.

'I remember that walk particularly vividly. It was the last time I ever saw Sarah,' I say.

'You're going to be very rich,' Sarah said as we reached the river and went over to where Eric had moored his boat. 'My mother says you will never have to worry about anything because the insurance money from your mum's accident will pay for everything.'

She didn't say it, but I knew she was thinking I was lucky. Sarah's father had been unemployed for years. Their family had lost all their savings in the depression of 2009 and later on their house too. And here was I, about to go to a private school paid for by the money from my dead mother's insurance.

'Your family does rather well from insurance, my mum reckons,' Sarah said, trying not to sound nasty.

I had no idea what she meant.

'Why didn't you ask her?' Stephanie interrupts.

I shake my head. It's difficult to explain the disjointed way in which we conversed with each other. Nothing revealed itself simply. Perhaps this had been my failing.

'Surely you were curious?' Stephanie asks.

I don't bother to reply.

All that hot summer's afternoon, with my mother not long dead we messed around on the river as though there was nothing different in the way we were. I noticed my legs had begun to turn a deep nut brown. Always in the past when this happened my mother used to comment on the way I tanned. I was secretly filled with loathing. I knew she was trying to make me feel proud of my Mongolian half, but I felt it was more important to her than to me. I just wanted to be like her. She herself was so fair that it took the whole summer for her to change colour, and even then she would have to be careful not to burn. At some point when the sun was at its brilliant highest, while we were moored under one of the willow trees upstream, a flock of birds were disturbed by some RAF planes flying overhead. They were going in the direction of Mildenhall airstrip, reminding us that we were a country on the brink of war with some Middle Eastern country or other, yet again.

'My brother's joined the army,' Sarah said, watching the planes until they disappeared. 'Mum's angry with him. She says he should have told us before he did.'

'Will he go to the Middle East, then?'

'Probably,' she said shortly.

I digested this fact. So her brother might die, too.

'Everybody might die at any time,' I told Eric that night. 'We are all skittles, waiting to be knocked down.'

The journey from childhood to being grown up had been quick.

'Before you go to London,' Eric said. 'I've some things I want to give you.'

I didn't want to go to London.

'You'll be back,' he said. 'It won't be for long. These private schools have short terms.'

The funny thing was, we didn't talk about Mum but it felt as if we were talking about her all the time subliminally. Sometimes one or other of us started to cry in the middle of a silence, as if we'd just been saying something about her.

The house was now packed up. The piano had been removed to

251

Eric's place because we didn't want the renters to use it. All my mother's stuff and the things I didn't want in my new room at Uncle Jack's house were being stored in Eric's attic. I felt glad that they were out of the way of my relatives' prying eyes even then. The summer wore on, a summer of outstanding weather.

'Always the way,' Eric muttered, 'during a war.'

I knew he was thinking about the other wars he had lived through.

'This is your home now,' he said on another occasion. 'Don't forget that. Your things are here, your piano. You've a bedroom here, too. So whenever you want, you can come over.'

We were shelling peas in the kitchen, with the back door open. It was the last day of August and although still light there was a feeling of slight change in the way it fell. Soon the nights would be drawing in.

'You'll have no one to talk to much,' I said, meaning when I left for London.

'Oh, don't mind me. I'll keep busy. And don't forget I have the house to keep me company.'

The farmhouse was a living, breathing thing to him in the way Eel House had once been to me.

'And will be again,' he corrected me. 'Your early years are there,' he said. 'Your ma's there. And others too.'

We had scattered my mother's ashes along the riverbank. Strangely enough it had been Jack's idea. It had pleased Eric.

'She'll be there,' he said. 'Walking along the path. Like she used to when she was a girl. Her father, your grandfather, used to tell her off. She was always coming home with some animal or other she had found in the river. Once she slipped and fell in! There had been a lot of rain at that time. But your ma was a strong swimmer. No water would get the better of her!'

He sounded pleased; as he should be, for it had been Eric who taught her to swim. My mother had been dead for three months by now and the strange thing was that the more time that passed, the worse things felt. Eric seemed to understand this for suddenly, with only one week to go before Uncle Jack came to collect me, he took me out in the boat. He had received a letter from abroad and wanted my advice, he said.

19

'And that was when you heard of it?'

'Yes.'

The sound of a lawn mower drifts in through the open window making it impossible for us to speak. Grass scents and piercing bird-calls fill the air. The light is luminous. Stephanie is watching me like a hawk. We have reached this point quicker than I expected. I dislike her less.

'Tell me?'

I frown. I am used to arranging my emotions like a row of shoes, all polished and ready to be worn, but somehow, never used. I don't care to be ordered about in this way. Watch it, Stephanie, I think.

'He took me upstream for a day's fishing. That's how I knew he had something important to say.'

Someone was flying a kite. It floated lazily in a hard, diamond-blue sky. There were no clouds, not even wisps of ones. When we had rowed out a little way to his favourite spot, we settled down and Eric cast his line.

'Imagine what it must be like in the tropics,' he said.

That was how he began. I watched a dragonfly hovering above the waterline. Small insects bumbled about. The sun shone like cut glass on the water as he told me this story.

'There is a small island in the Indian Ocean that once lay on the trade routes for the western world,' he said.

The Dutch had travelled there and the Portuguese in their fleets of sailing ships. By the time the English arrived there were gardens of splendour, irrigation systems of remarkable intricacy and forts built around the harbour. The English were enchanted by the sight; never had they seen such a perfect place in all their travels, never had they seen such wide sandy beaches, such blue hills, such smiling people. They set to work. They built roads, and astonishing narrow-gauge railways. They cleared some of the jungles and they planted forests of rubber trees to supply the world with raw rubber. They covered those blue hills with a soft cloak of tea bushes. Ceylon tea became the finest tea in the world and the English set the native people to work to help them keep it this way. But that was long ago, so long as to be now considered unimportant. Then the day came when the Union Jack was taken down and the English left for home again. A new flag of saffron and maroon was raised. The island of Ceylon was no more and the natives, without the masterly watch of the masters, began to fight. What began as a playground fight continues today, stopping and starting, rearranging itself, pretending to be over but continuing regardless.

'Tamils,' I said, for I had heard about them in the news.

'Not just the Tamils,' Eric corrected me. 'The government is made up of another ethnic group, much larger than the Tamils.'

'But that was all years ago, wasn't it?' I asked, puzzled.

'It's in remission at the moment. Not over, just waiting to mutate into another, deadlier form. These things don't just go away.'

I wondered why he was telling me all this. What had it to do with me? Opening my mouth to ask him, I was distracted by a large water bird wading into the river beside us, eyes intently on the lookout for fish. Then, in the gentle glare of that summer's afternoon, nearly three months after my mother's death, I listened to the story of a man who had once lived on the northernmost tip of the island of Sri Lanka.

His name was Ben Chinniah and he had grown up in a country

wracked by a sadistic civil war. This war had gone on for so long that there was no means of distinguishing myth from reality, statistics from propaganda, facts from fiction. The war itself was the thing that mattered, and all was fair in it. Ben Chinniah, Eric told me, was only about thirteen when his father disappeared, and by the time he was twenty-four it was clear that he would either have to go into hiding or leave the country. He was a fully qualified doctor and his desire to help people had not gone unnoticed.

'In a war,' said Eric, 'you must kill, not help one another.'

I supposed he was thinking about his son, Kevin. I had heard the story of Kevin from my mother when I was younger.

Ben Chinniah decided to leave his home. He had heard stories of others who had migrated successfully and so he began to save his money for his illegal fare for Europe. He wanted to come to England because, well, because for one thing he spoke English, and for another his country had a history of connections with Britain.

'Fool,' I said idly. 'Didn't he know how refugees are treated here?'

Apparently not, Eric said. He continued his story. It meandered slowly and sometimes confusingly across that long, hot afternoon. I was only half listening. In less than a week I would be beginning a new life in the outskirts of London. Everything about the old life had changed so suddenly that I had barely any time to adjust, yet in some ways I felt I had been living this new life for ever. Eric lit his pipe and the scent of tobacco rose and dispersed into the fine summer air. I tried to image the tropics he was describing, but I had never been further than Ely in my life.

'Imagine, Lydi,' he said quietly, 'what it would be like if you were going so far that you could never come back.'

Like death, I thought. A picture of my mother's foot with its shoe half off her foot flashed before my eyes. Then vanished again.

'A man lives his life and thinks he will go on living it, uninterrupted,' Eric said. 'But then it falls apart, like flesh from a bone, and he is surprised.'

Overhead another fleet of planes stopped all conversation with their roar. The noise disturbed the dragonfly and the heron. Both disappeared from view and did not return again that day as I sat on the gently rocking boat listening to Eric tell me who my father was.

'And you had no idea until that moment?' Stephanie asks.

I shake my head. None whatsoever.

'So why do you think she never told you?'

My head is beginning to ache. I shrug. Who knows, really?

'Eric said she had been frightened of my reaction.'

He thought she blamed herself for Ben's death. Guilt might have kept her quiet. Anyway, a curtain had been opened. I remember staring out at the landscape: the marshes and the meadow, the sun on the field where the horses grazed. Behind us was my old home, hidden by a bank of trees, and in the distance, hardly discernible, was the sea over which my father had come.

I asked Eric to take me to the spot where he had been killed. We drove across to the marshes later that day. The tide was low by now as we waded across to the field where it had happened. From here I could see the window of what used to be my mother's study. She would have had a clear view of the river and the field beyond it from here. But she had been downstairs in the kitchen, trying to get rid of Miranda and Jack, wondering where Ben had got to, thinking it was getting late. It was summer then too and the reeds would have been high. She wouldn't have seen him running across the field from the kitchen. All she would have heard would have been a shot. She would not have understood where it was coming from. She might have been smiling, talking to Miranda. He had run, with his head down, carrying his rucksack on his back. Maybe he knew he was already a hunted man. Possibly he thought they were after him because he had no proper papers, or because he was working, illegally. No one except the police would have known the truth of it. So he ran, with his head down, innocently, heading for cover in the thicket of matchstick trees. He would have been all right had he crossed the river and made it to Eel House. Had he done so he would have been safe. But he must have stumbled in the long coarse grass. As she watched, two men emerged from the other direction. They were waving their arms and their voices carried faintly across on the breeze. Instinctively, she had known something was wrong and she had hurried out through the door, leaving Jack and Miranda calling out to the children. Later she would run away to her special part of the beach and they would send out a search party for her. Of course, by that time she was at Eric's farm, inconsolable with grief. But in that first instance, all my mother did was scramble across the narrow gap in the hedge and into the field. By the time she reached him, he was already dead.

Eric told me that although the lawyers had tried there had been no compensation for the mistake. My father had been an illegal immigrant and as such had no right to any police compensation.

'It was some months before your mother realised that she was pregnant with you,' he told me. 'And by then the fight had gone out of her.'

We had gone into the field after that and he showed me the exact spot where Ben, my father, had fallen; never knowing he was to be my father. With my mother not yet my mother. The field was full of small speedwell flowers and a few daisies. From this point you could see the house very clearly. It was so close; he must have thought he could get across the river and reach it before they could catch him. He must have run as fast as he could, desperately trying to reach the safety of Eel House and my mother. I stared helplessly at the ground thinking of how he must have bled and the way the police officers would have gathered round. I had seen farmers gathering in this way to look at the animals they had shot. I lifted my head to find the patch of sky he would have seen as he lay dying. It was nearly evening by now, long after the time when it happened. The light was leaving the sky in the quick way of late summer but there were still some slivers of brightness here and there. The world had been changing and changing for months and now it had changed again. It would never stop changing, I thought. We were at war. Soon, it was predicted, there would be another world war. The war to end all wars, was what the media said. Hadn't they said that once before? Yet a man can die with the glow of a receding sun in his eyes without knowing he had a child. I thought of the grief this simple act had brought with it.

I thought of the silence that had bound my mother, stopped her from telling me the truth. And I had a sudden picture of Mum reading that poem and me, pushing her away.

'Never mind, now,' Eric said. 'Things happen in spite of the best intentions, sometimes because of them. You were only a little girl.'

He gave me a hug.

'I often talked about it with her,' he confessed. 'She told me she had tried many times, but you always looked so terrified that she was frightened of losing your love. She was a timid woman, you know, Lydi. Life had taken everything away from her She didn't want to lose you, too. She had been told by someone – I think it was your aunt – that she should wait until you showed a natural curiosity.'

'And I was never going to show that!' I said.

Eric looked at me sadly.

'I thought I was a donor baby. Belonging nowhere.'

'Is that what you felt?'

I nodded, speechless.

'Just like your father did. Rootless.'

He had hoped the place where I grew up would be enough for me.

'You had your home,' he said. 'And your ma and me and the farm. I hoped that would do. But it was just a hope.'

I saw I had been rootless too, for a long time, years, probably, since I had been very little. The teachers used to say I was a restless person. Suddenly I saw why. Love, or at least the hope of it at my concep-tion, was what I had longed for. Why else continue? What was the point?

I stop speaking. The lawn mower has long since finished cutting the grass. Stephanie reaches up and opens the window, letting in a pale golden evening sun. I have gone well past my hour, but she has not stopped me. We sit for a moment in silence. Her face is in shadows and I cannot easily see the expression on it.

'So now you know,' she says, finally.

I nod. I find I am exhausted.

'And . . .' her voice trails off. 'What now?'

There is one more thing.

'It will have to wait,' Stephanie says.

I imagine her voice has become less harsh. Perhaps my story has affected her after all.

'Do you have a photograph?' she asks. 'Of Ben? Perhaps in amongst your mother's things?'

I tell her there was nothing in my mother's papers, nothing in any of the places Eric and I had looked. Whatever happened that summer had gone unrecorded by any camera. I don't even think my mother had owned a digital camera, I say. But I have seen a photo of him.

'Bring it with you for your last session,' she says.

May 9th. Fourth session.

He showed me the letter that same evening. We had just had supper. Neither of us ate very much. It was hot and we were both in some state of shock. After we had finished, he cleared the table. Flossie was running about outside barking at an invisible cat and all the stars were beginning to come out in a wide and cloudless night sky. The moon was rising slowly through the trees, shedding a watery light. Eric put a bowl of plums out for us to eat and I got some ice cream from the old freezer. There was a companionable silence between us. We had lived this way for months now. In some ways it was no different from the days when Mum was alive and I would have sleep-overs at the farm to give her a rest. Her presence was very near tonight as we sat under the stars. But there was more to come.

'I have something here that belongs to you,' he said, and he handed me two photographs.

In both of them was a man, about my height, hand shading the sun from his eyes, smiling at the camera. It was as though I was looking at an image so like myself. Later, when I was alone in my room high in the attic of the house, I re-read the letter. Eric had handed it to me saying it was mine by rights.

My Dear Eric, I read out loud to Stephanie.

You will be surprised to hear from me after so long. I fear that you might not want to be reminded of me and I take a risk writing this. I was always one to take risks with you, Eric. I can tell you exactly how long it has been since we spoke. It is almost sixteen years. Long, painful years for me in every imaginable way. From the moment I left you and the deep winter your country was in I was catapulted back into the reality of my own life and the terrible events that surrounded it. I planned to write to you and to Ria. I planned to say those things I had been unable to voice during my visit. I had every intention of revisiting our shared secret, the love you gave so freely, wanting nothing in return. How clearly, how painfully I remember it. Thanking you is hardly appropriate. To tell you that you saved my life does no justice. So why didn't I write? I could not. The truth of my situation is simple. To get over a death such as the one I have had to come to terms with takes time. All the years of a person's life twice over. Ben was twenty-five when he died and only sixteen years have passed, so by that rule I still have many more years before I can hope for any respite. Writing, even thinking of you in all my sorrow was not an option. I suspect I hardly need to tell you this, Eric. I know you will understand. I know what kind of man you are, how far finer a person you are than anyone I have ever known. Mine was a long slow and painful journey to understanding. I've had to come to terms with who I am, how this war has shaped me. You were right when you said we need never meet again. I thought you cruel at the time and it was only much later that I understood.

I returned home to an apparent end to the civil war in my country. I say apparent because the government was proclaiming it had destroyed the Tamil strongholds in the North and the East. But in fact all was the same old chaos. The one outspoken journalist who unreservedly supported the underdogs in this country was assassinated by the army; hungry, powerful thugs are the new ruling class. We, as a people, have had no one to turn to for years. There was nothing new in this except that, for me, it no longer mattered whether I lived or died. You see, Eric, what I had discovered was that violence is not particularly endemic to this place alone. In Sri Lanka the violence we witness daily goes on openly whereas, forgive me, in your country it seems to me the violence is hidden. Coated in sweet words, committed and then apologised for with apparent sorrow, but committed anyway. In the name of democracy, or freedom, or the war on terror. In the long nights that I have had to endure since leaving you I have been thinking of this terror that our various governments pledge to fight. Who is he and what face does he have? I find it impossible to comprehend that Ben's face represented terror to the people who killed him. I find it impossible to imagine that a face so loved could be mistaken in this way. But there it is. As you can see, the events of that time go round my head for all eternity. I fear they will not cease until I too cease to exist.

On my return to my home town, after a journey of interminable difficulty (can you imagine it, first the long, uncomfortable flight, then being manhandled at the airport in Colombo, then the journey by jeep to Elephant Pass and the danger at every army checkpoint when my documents were examined, and then the road blocks that went on and on) I arrived at my house to find people gathered around. Part of the house had been ransacked and broken into and many of my things had been stolen. Tara was waiting for me, along with two of my friends. They told me the priest had disappeared days after I left. They told me it was because the authorities believed he had helped Ben to leave the country in the first place. Can you believe it? Ben was dead and they were punishing the priest for something that no longer mattered anyway!

Returning home was far more painful than I could have imagined. I was returning to a country that was a foreign place. England and its frozen snow, its terrible emotions, were large within me. I could not shake them off, and as I wandered through the small rooms of my house and out through to the garden it seemed to me that the lush tropical life and the heat of the sun was now completely in monotone, while my memories and I existed in colour. Tara saw instantly that the change in me was irreversible. Tara was nobody's fool. She had always been able to read people as though they were books. It is her special talent. The three weeks had been a lifetime for her, too. Her lovely face was furrowed and pale, and I saw within it what time would eventually do to it. We faced each other warily. There were things we could no longer discuss. I had been to claim my son. Even though I had not been able to bring him back home with me, still he remained my son. What of her? The unspoken agreement, made in that other life, seemed elusive and insubstantial now. She tried telling me this; we tried honesty and then saw that the time for honesty had passed. What was left?

Why am I telling you this now? Firstly, Eric, because I want you to know I did not forget you. That I was unable to write had no bearing on how often I thought of you. I want you to understand that there has not been a single day when secret thoughts of you didn't fill me with longing. Grieving for you on top of losing Ben has been a private and complicated thing. Just as you always told me it would be. What cannot be discussed cannot be cured. With no one to tell, the agony has gone on and on. Old age does not diminish emotions. Who ever thinks that has never grown old! The truth is, I will never get over you. Tara was a constant reminder of Ria, and every time I thought of Ria I felt I was withholding things from Tara. My mind was in so much torment that I no longer knew what to think. In the end I just lived each day, rising with the light and laying my head down with the night. In between, I did what was necessary to stay alive and in this way time inched past. The events that I had witnessed replayed themselves over and over again in my mind, each time a little more desolate than the last. But you must not think I forgot you. I saw snow in my dreams, falling endlessly. I would wake in the hot, dead nights and hear the sound of water birds. It does not cease to amaze me that when one really wants to die, as I so often did in the years that followed, it becomes an impossibility. Why is this so?

For a time there were no more disappearances and people began *to hope that torture was a thing of the past. The rebels had been defeated, the army controlled the area now and we Tamils remained, penned in like animals in what were once Tiger-controlled areas. This was peace, as the government described it. At some point in the years that followed, Tara went mad. It happened after the soldiers raped her. Yes, Eric, the soldiers who were guarding us 'for our own good' were often unable to resist doling out some extra punishment for our past 'crimes'. It was, you understand, all part of the peace process. It was a price we were expected to pay, uncomplaining. In any case, who was there to complain to? The government? The police? Young women were the main target of the peace operation. Tamil girls are prettier that their Singhalese counterparts, they are easier to find. Tara was always going past the checkpoint on her bicycle. It was the only way to reach the shops. One morning she set off as usual but this time a young soldier stopped her and took away her pass. There was something wrong with it, he told her. A couple of other soldiers came out and looked at it. They agreed. She was asked to step inside the office. She protested, saying the pass had been fine yesterday, what could be wrong with it today? The soldiers grinned. Today is different, they told her. Inside, she was taken into a room that had no windows and asked to wait. A man came in and handcuffed and gagged her. Then he raped her. After that another man came in and another. She was not released until early afternoon. By the time she got home she was already beginning to lose her grip on reality.*

At the time I badly wanted to write to you. Tara was my last link with Ben's life in this place. She was important to me. But then I thought of Ria. Once again all my difficulties, the impossibility of understanding what had happened between Ben and her, stopped me. Call me a coward, Eric. I am ashamed that I could not overcome my feelings towards Ria and write to you. But I have learnt to admit to what is impossible for me to do. Some months afterwards, Tara committed suicide. I did not weep at her funeral. I no longer am able to cry.

Recently I moved from the town of Jaffna. The government was offering Tamil civilians the chance to relocate. It was a move to show the world that they were fair and reasonable people. The world, of course, couldn't care less. It was too busy culling people in other parts. Sri Lanka was a place that had been something once briefly long ago and now was no more than a full stop on the atlas. In the great scheme of culling that was taking place around the globe, what went on on our island was as nothing. Anyway, I was paid a visit by a Tamil official who worked for the government. He used to be a friend of my husband, Percy, but the necessity of survival had changed him. I did not blame him; I merely observed the process of survival. I am a hard woman now, Eric, I observe many things that cannot be talked of. Anyway, this man said that the council felt I needed a change, I had endured a lot at the hands of the white imperialist bastards. This was the way they washed their hands of the tragedy of what was done to my son. The man told me that I could move to the east coast if I wished. There was a job in a community centre for someone who could read and write in English. I decided to take it. There was no reason for me to stay in the old house. All my memories are dispersed around the world, lifted by the winter breeze in beautiful, (forgive me) but terrible, Suffolk. I am therefore free to go wherever I wish. It was at this point that I realised how I had been freed from desire. This is what first Percy and Ben have done for me. They have released me at last, I thought. At this I broke down and began to cry. The Tamil official looked at me stonily for a moment. Then I saw that there were tears in his eyes, too. I will never be vindicated like you are, he said, very, very softly, in old-fashioned Tamil. I have made choices. I told him that most of us had to make choices. The thing was that the choices we were offered were unworkable. That is what has come from the destruction of our spirit, he told me.

So after that I left and moved towards Batticlore, to another view of the sea, to a different shoreline, taking my memories with me. Often I would think of you. Every time I watched a flock of birds gathering to begin their long migration across the seas

I thought of your marshlands and sometimes I felt your presence walking beside me, comforting me in my loss. But still I was unable to contact you. Life had silted up my feelings. One day I was walking along the beach and I heard church bells. The wind must have been in the right direction, I suppose, but as I watched the waves I remember the story of the fifty-two bells under the sea in Dunwich. I had forgotten about that particular story.

Time passed. I learnt office skills. I learnt to use a computer. I was working for a counsellor who worked with various victims of the war. The service was government-funded. These days, everything is government-controlled, because of the government's desperate need to be seen as decent and law-abiding. So we have organisations set up to heal our wounds and make us whole again. In this way we mastered the art of pretence.

After a year, foreign people began to trickle in, working as volunteers in these agencies. They were never allowed to be alone with the clients, but at least they were allowed in. One such person came looking for me with your letter. It had taken her months to find me. I had moved and moved again and the trail had grown cold, but in all this time she had not lost your letter, nor had she stopped looking for me. She was of course the journalist who wrote the piece about Ben after he died. I did not recognise her, nor she me. We had both changed. But then she began to tell me this story about a woman who had come to Suffolk to identify her dead son.

'I have a letter for her,' she said, 'from someone who knew her. He's desperately trying to get in touch with her.'

I felt myself grow cold as I listened.

'I am she,' was all I could manage to say before I began to weep.

Later, when she gave me your letter, I was stunned. She sat with me as I read and re-read it. It was almost impossible to comprehend. Joy was filling my heart, joy such as I had known only once, when Ben was born. This child? His child, you say? Are you quite certain? The letter is almost two years old. Could it be a mistake? Is it some cruel hoax to break me further?

Lydia! Little Lydia! My Lydia! The journalist had one last thing for me. It was in her suitcase at the rest house. She had kept it separate from the letter, she told me, for fear of it getting damaged.

'Wait,' she said, smiling at me. 'I'll be back this evening. I'll bring you something else.'

I waited in an agony of suspense, unable to concentrate on anything. My supervisor was surprised and wondered if I was sickening with dengue fever, but it was a different sort of fever I felt. Later, after work, I went home to my small government flat. Outside, the sea moved restlessly. The monsoons were almost upon us. The world news was not good. America was on the brink of war with the Middle East yet again, Britain looks set to be drawn in, everyone says. There will be more deaths, more mutilations, more grief. Nothing would stand in the way of this systematic culling, but I no longer cared.

The journalist returned when it had got dark. The monsoons had broken and the air was wet and cool. She handed me the photograph of Lydia. She looked so small, so beautiful, standing there next to an older Ria. And in her face was my son.

The letter ended there. At the bottom was a postscript in which Anula Chinniah had hastily scribbled an address and a promise that she would now move heaven and earth to get a travel visa to come to the UK. She hoped to see him soon, for she would not rest, she told him, until she could set eyes on me.

20

JUNE 1ST. I AM STANDING BY the arrivals board at Heathrow's Terminal One. It is late on a summer's night. I am almost sixteen years old. It has taken me this long to get to this point. I stand impatiently waiting for a plane to arrive. The board flickers and somersaults, its many eyelashes flutter and flutter again, and the information I have been waiting for is displayed at last. Landed! I turn towards the automatic doors and move closer to the barrier. I am alone. Eric is waiting in the car park. We are going home to Eel House together afterwards. Both of us thought I should do this thing alone. But now I am here, I wish he was with me. It's too late. My hands are clammy, I keep swallowing nervously. People push against me as they jostle to get a better view of the arrivals. There is an air of anticipation amongst the crowd, an intake of collective breath each time the automatic doors open. I would have liked to watch the plane as it landed, but it is forbidden to do so for fear of yet another terrorist attack. These attacks are regular occurrences now. People don't even bother to call them 'terrorist' attacks, for they could be done by anybody who feels like causing a disturbance. Britain is no longer a law-abiding country and everything in the airport is designed to stop people hindering the safe passage of others in and out of the country. Uncle Jack told me that once long ago there used to be a viewing area, but security is too tight for that to be permitted now. We live in suspicious times.

This new war we started is getting worse. The future is uncertain. At the end of my last session, Stephanie said all futures were uncertain. That was the nature of the future. But she also felt it was a time of optimism for me. It was the first time she volunteered anything other than a question. I no longer dislike her.

On my last session, I overstepped my allotted hour with her. It had become a habit and she made no move to end the session. It was my last consultation. I didn't feel I needed any more, neither did she. We sat in silence. I felt exhausted and drained of energy. It was the first time that I had ever told this entire story to anyone. Even Eric had only got bits and pieces, odd bits of conversation, threads.

'Tomorrow,' I said out loud, 'I'm going to Heathrow to meet the woman who is my grandmother. She will be returning after an absence of nearly seventeen years!'

'How old is she now?' Stephanie asked and I shrugged.

'I don't know. In her seventies, I guess.'

'Are you nervous?'

No, I wasn't nervous, I was . . . I paused, unable to define the feeling of lightness I felt at the thought of the woman I planned to meet. All those elusive feelings that had never made sense, my withdrawn mother, the way it used to seem that she was simply waiting to die, all of this was beginning to make sense. I had lived under an opaque sky for most of my life.

'What do you think it was like for her?' Stephanie had asked.

I looked at her. Poor old Stephanie. Why had I hated her so much? The rage that had swept over me throughout my childhood had abated. Perhaps, I thought, spelling it out was part of what we must do.

'I think she was frightened by more or less everything. She knew my father had had someone else he had left behind at home, perhaps she never knew for certain who he really loved. Also she must have felt guilty about his death. After all, she was the one who asked him to bring his stuff over to Eel House. She must have gone over everything a million times and wondered, "What if . . .?"'

Stephanie nodded. In all our sessions, she had not smiled once. But she smiled yesterday.

'What will you do now?' she asked.

'Well,' I said slowly, 'tomorrow when the sun has almost set I will be at Heathrow. There I will search the arrivals board for the last flight in from Colombo.'

I grinned. I've never had a gran before! I tried to imagine her boarding the plane, waiting patiently for the long flight to end, wondering what it was going to be like at the other end. She would remember how she had arrived. It would be impossible to think of anything else, of course.

After reading Eric's letter, I had written to her. Then, fearful that the letter would not get through, I got the name of the place where she worked. It took a while to trace her, but eventually I did. And then I rang her. It was late afternoon in Batticlore, barely midday here. I had not long woken up. To tell you the truth, there had been an end-of-exams party the night before and I was a bit hung over. I heard her voice for the first time with a backdrop of other sounds. I have never been to the tropics and somewhere faintly behind her voice I could hear the sound of a bird cawing.

'Lydia?' she asked, in a way I had not heard my name said before.

I laughed and asked her if that was a crow I heard.

'Anay, darling,' she said, and she began to cry.

Before we finished our conversation she had one last question for me.

'Why do such terrible things happen?' she asked.

It was the last thing I told Stephanie. Then I stood up and she shook my hand.

'Good luck,' she said. 'I hope it works out.'

When I got down the stairs and made my way outside it was still light and there was a light breeze. Birds were calling to each other in the tradition of this time of year and the air was damp and full of spring promise. Why do such terrible things happen?

I have a boyfriend. We get on very well, we don't have any secrets. Our problems are different; our problems are this war and what this will mean to us. There's talk of conscription being brought back. Lately the world has shrunk and speeded up at the same time. It is possible to annihilate a nation very quickly, but making another one is fast becoming an impossibility. Viruses multiplying in one part of the globe can travel in hours to another place and kill vast numbers of people. These are some of the things we worry about most. Our fears are no longer the war on terror but the war the planet is raging against humanity. It is too late and we are the ones left with the mess of others. And as to foreigners, illegal immigrants, asylum seekers, they are a thing of the past. It's very simple. Anyone entering the country, any Western country, without the proper documentation is simply caught and shot. It's Home Office policy, you know. Each nation looks after a small proportion of its own. The politicians tell us it's easier this way. Collective conscience is a thing of the past. A laughable matter. The way we live makes for a much cleaner war, so they say.

While I have been lost in thought, a small crowd has gathered around the barrier. They are probably waiting for different planes. There is one from Dubai and another from Sydney. A youngish man, slightly older than me, smiles.

'You waiting for the Qantas flight?' he asks.

I look at him and already I know he is not Indian, not Pakistani, not from Bangladesh. I know, from my research, that he is a Sri Lankan.

'No,' I say, also smiling. 'I'm waiting for the plane from Colombo.'

'Oh, Colombo!' He seems delighted. 'So am I. My wife is on this flight. You know it has taken me a long time to get her a visa.'

I feel a small thrill of triumph at my detective work. So I was right, he is Sri Lankan.

'You have a friend on the flight?'

I marvel at his friendliness.

'Yes,' I say, carefully, 'a Tamil.'

He doesn't bat an eyelid.

'Ah, the Tamils. It's terrible what has happened to them. I am a Singhalese but I'm ashamed at what we did to the Tamils.'

I nod. The man looks and sounds genuinely sorry. How does a nation appear so charming individually yet behave so monstrously collectively?

'Have you been to Sri Lanka?'

'Not yet,' I say, and realise that on some level I have been considering the possibility. The man is very friendly. He tells me about his wife who has been working as a nurse in a trauma centre but now that he has got a job here in London as a doctor in a teaching hospital he's been able to bring her over.

'I don't want to live there,' he said tentatively, looking over his shoulder nervously. 'I am ashamed at the way a succession of governments have behaved. I don't want to be part of it.'

I nod. I want to tell him that the woman I am meeting is my grandmother. That I am the legacy my father left for her. That knowing my parentage has at last made me feel whole, that I already love the country and want to do what I can there. But at that moment the automatic doors open and passengers pour out. Most of them have mountains of luggage perched precariously on trolleys. I watch them move towards us, searching the crowds, smiling recognition. There is a flurry of voices in greeting, rising above the public address system and the canned music. I stand anxiously watching and waiting while the man beside me goes forward to embrace his wife. He turns and sees me still standing there, still waiting.

'No luck?' he asks, and then he introduces his wife.

I am hardly listening, there is a constriction in my throat. I must not cry. What if she is not on this flight? What if they prevented her boarding? What if something has happened and she has died of a heart attack? She is old; I don't know how old, but she is my grandmother, for God's sake, she cannot be that young any more. I feel the palms of my hands sweaty with fear. She is my only link with the past. What if we never meet? The kind Singhalese man is talking to me.

'Don't worry, she's probably having to stand in a queue to have her visa checked. I'm sure she'll be along soon.'

'There was a long queue,' his wife says, moving her head from side to side, smiling a wide smile that fills her face.

Her voice reminds me of Anula's and I feel tears gather in my eyes. I am certain something has happened. The Singhalese man means well, but I wish he would go away. I want to be alone to deal with yet another blow. I feel desperate. This meeting must happen. Go away, I think, please, leave me alone. I glance up at the arrivals board and in that moment as my eyes move from it the automatic doors open abruptly and a lone woman comes out. She is dressed in white and has no luggage other than a small holdall. She is very small. And thin. Stopping, she searches the crowd in front of her. I see the future is in her beautiful face. I see her lips moving as she forms my name, and suddenly I push through the waiting people.

'Grandma!' I cry. 'It's me! Lydia!'

Acknowledgements

There are two people that I need to thank above all others: my agent Felicity Bryan for her unwavering support, (as always) and my editor Clare Smith, whose extraordinary understanding has been instrumental in my continued development as a writer.

I would also like to thank the entire team at Harper Press who work invisibly behind the scenes on my behalf, in particular, Essie Cousins and Sophie Goulden.

Similarly all those at the Felicity Bryan Agency. Thank you.

And finally, thanks to my friend Dave King who gave me many hours of his time discussing the methods of forensic science.

Ideas,
interviews
& features ...

A Writing Life

When do you write?
On and off all day when I'm not teaching or cooking!

Where do you write?
In my small study crammed from floor to ceiling with visual sources.

Why do you write?
Because it makes me happy.

Pen or computer?
Computer, but pen in endless Moleskine notebooks, too.

Silence or music?
Non-stop music on my iPod!

How do you start a book?
With a first sentence.

And finish?
With an enormous sense of exhaustion and relief.

Do you have any writing rituals or superstitions?
I always pick four or five pieces of music that suggest the atmosphere of the book I'm working on first.

Which living writer do you most admire?
Orhan Pamuk.

What or who inspires you?
My husband.

If you weren't a writer what job would you do?
I guess I'd be a painter.

What's your guilty reading pleasure or favourite trashy read?
Can't read trash, it drives me demented. ■

Author photograph © Alistair Tearne

LIFE
at a Glance

BORN
Colombo, Sri Lanka, 1954

EDUCATED
London; Oxford (MA, Ruskin)

CAREER
Painter and filmmaker. Currently holds an AHRC Fellowship in the Creative and Performing Arts, Brookes University

FAMILY
Married. Three children

LIVES
Oxford

Picturing Place

by Roma Tearne

EARLY IN SEPTEMBER 2000, long before I conceived the idea for the novel *The Swimmer*, I visited an exquisite little exhibition. It was called, simply: 'Constable's Clouds'. I had come across a small notice in a newspaper that said it should not be missed.

Constable, that giant of British landscape painters (he was born in 1776 in the village of East Bergholt, in Suffolk), is an artist whose name is known throughout the world. Even if you have never seen an original painting of his, you will be familiar with their reproductions. You may not be able to name *Flatford Mill* or *A Lane Near Dedham*, but the strongly cast shadows across the path, the distance beyond where the church is seen, the rooks flying around the famous tree, are all images that are lodged in our imagination.

The first time I saw a Constable was not at the Tate but curiously on the lid of a biscuit tin in my grandparents' house, in Colombo. The biscuits from England had long gone but the picture stayed vaguely with me, filed away in my visual imagination as being something 'English'. It was my very first introduction to Suffolk.

In 1814, in order to capture the subtle changes of chiaroscuro, or light and shade caused by cloud movement, Constable had decided he needed to adopt the approach of *plein-air*, or outdoor painting.

'Chiaroscuro,' he wrote, 'may be defined as

the power which creates space; we find it everywhere and at all times in nature.'

For four years he would set up easels and canvases in the fields and lanes around East Bergholt and on the banks of the River Stour in order to observe the long shadows created by clouds as they drifted across the distant fields. By immersing himself physically in his environment in this way, it was possible to capture the very essence of the landscape of his childhood. Memory was in all he beheld.

The same is true for all of us today. If you wish to understand the landscape of Britain, it is important to walk within it; to investigate its hedges and ditches, its bridle paths and spinneys. To smell the air and stare up at the sky where streets of cloud formations can change the way the land looks in seconds. For many years this was exactly what I did. I was completely unaware as I subliminally absorbed aspects of the landscape that, one day, I would draw upon these sights and sounds, the call of the seabirds, the patterns of clouds, for my novel, *The Swimmer*. Research and its eventual application do not run seamlessly together and it was years before the Suffolk coastline and my characters finally met. ▶

The Witness.

DUNWICH RUINS.

◄ Meanwhile an accidental find sent me in another direction. W.G. Sebald calls it the 'invisible traces of memory' and the trigger for me was in an old book of maps, found in a musty second-hand bookshop in Aldeburgh. The unexpected is always present, everywhere. One only needs to be alert to its possibilities. The photographs that dropped out of that book of maps were curious in their anonymity and their sepia stillness. An onion field after harvest, the face of a Suffolk child. A forest on the borders of Suffolk with tall matchstick pines, a house (which eventually, when I located it, became 'Eel House' in the novel), a Suffolk summer, a view of the Fens and many more. There is something thrilling about finding photographs like these in the place where they were taken, something full of life that has vanished from the anonymous gaze. Who were these people who loved these views? What passion prompted them to photograph such ordinary-looking spots?

I decided to investigate further, try to find the places themselves or, if not, similar ones.

Travelling through the Suffolk landscape with these images, I was struck by the fact that they represented a tangible presence of absence. Of course, I never found the exact spots, for language is the thing that halts erasure and there were no written clues. Thus the photographs became images of loss, incapable of giving up their stories of landscape and inhabitants. All I had were fragments of a hesitant narrative, the possibility of a vanished world.

As I followed the dry bed of a winter stream, listening to the death rattle of last year's reeds conducting my own *plein-air* exploration, I remembered W.G. Sebald's haunting words: 'The preoccupation with making something out of nothing … is after all what writing is about.'

Tucking the photographs into my sketchbook, staring at their creased and blurred surfaces, aware of the date when they were taken, I could only be amazed at this sole surviving vestige in an unknown piece of land. How does something so small, so fragile, so inconspicuous, survive intact for nearly a hundred years? ■

Reading Group Questions

WHETHER YOU LOVE a book or loathe it, one of the pleasures of reading is the discussion books regularly inspire. Below are a few suggestions for topics of discussion about *The Swimmer* . . .

The Swimmer is set predominantly in Orford, Suffolk. What do you think this location brings to the novel? Do you think the author has successfully created an arresting sense of place?

The book is divided into three parts: Ria, Anula and Lydia. Do you think this is an effective tool for breaking down the novel? And do you think the author has successfully managed to create a distinct voice for each of these characters? If so, how?

Ria and Ben's romance is an unconventional one; they are eighteen years apart in age. Do you think this age gap plays a significant part in the nature of their relationship, or would you argue that it is not an important factor?

The meaning of home is one of *The Swimmer*'s central themes. In what ways is this tested throughout the course of the novel? What other themes, in your opinion, are significant in this book?

Before Ria speaks to Ben, she knows him simply as 'the swimmer'. Do you think this is a powerful title for the book?

How significant is the character of Eric? What are your thoughts on his relationship with both Ria and Anula?

The issue of illegal immigration is woven into *The Swimmer*. Has the book shed any light on this topic, so often at the forefront of the media? Has it helped shape your understanding of what it might mean to be an illegal immigrant today?

Ria and Anula are women from two very different backgrounds, who both love Ben – one as a lover and the other as a mother. In what ways are these women similar? In what ways are they different? How does their relationship evolve throughout the novel?

Ben's death is a huge tragedy, with major repercussions. Was his death something you expected or did it take you by surprise?

Set in the twenty-first century, *The Swimmer* is a work of contemporary fiction. What other genres do you think it could be described as?

How satisfied were you with the novel's conclusion?

If you Loved This,
You Might Like . . .

Hungry for Home
Cole Moreton

This is the tragic story of an Irish island and the dramatic events that led to it being abandoned. Moreton takes you through the lives of three generations, exploring the notion of home and its meaning for the characters.

Every Move You Make
David Malouf

This collection of short stories provides the perfect introduction to this talented Australian writer. Malouf illuminates the extraordinary moments in ordinary people's lives.

The Summer Book
Tove Jansson

A classic book focusing on the relationship between the little girl Sofia and her wilful, yet wise grandmother as they spend the summer together on a remote island off the coast of Finland.

Tess of the D'Urbervilles
Thomas Hardy

In one of Hardy's last novels, Tess details the loss of innocence and ultimate destruction of a young girl. Tearne is inspired by Hardy's use of landscape and light.

Have You Read?

Other books by Roma Tearne

Mosquito

When author Theo Samarajeeva returns to his native Sri Lanka after his wife's death, he hopes to escape his gnawing loss amidst the lush landscape of his increasingly war-torn country. But as he sinks into life in his beautiful, tortured land, he also finds himself slipping into friendship with an artistic young girl, Nulani. Friendship gradually blossoms into love – only to be torn apart when tensions in the troubled country erupt into violence.

'Heart-rending . . . readers of this powerful novel cannot fail to be moved'   *Spectator*

Bone China

An epic novel of love, loss and a family uprooted, set in the contrasting landscapes of Sri Lanka and immigrant London. Grace de Silva, wife of the shiftless but charming Aloysius, has five children and a disintegrating marriage. But civil unrest is stirring in her native Sri Lanka and Christopher, the youngest and the rebel of the family, is soon caught up in the tragedy that follows. As the decade unfolds against a backdrop of increasing ethnic violence, Grace watches helplessly as the life she knows begins to crumble.

'Probing loss and memory amid violence and displacement, her novels have affinities

TOP TEN *Favourite Writers*

George Eliot
Thomas Hardy
W. G. Sebald
Vladimir Nabokov
Orhan Pamuk
Virginia Woolf
W. B. Yeats
Dylan Thomas
Seamus Heaney
Czeslaw Milosz

17

with Romesh Gunesekera's groundbreaking
fiction' *Guardian*

....

Brixton Beach

When family tragedy strikes, Alice Fonseka, a
dreamy, artistic child with a Singhalese mother and Tamil father, leaves the beautiful island
of Sri Lanka. Unable to bear the injustice of
what has happened, her family heads for
England. There, in the cold, urban landscape
of London, Alice grows up, creating a life for
herself, with all that this means: struggles, a
home in London – and a blossoming of the art
through which she expresses herself. But there
is much she cannot find. Understanding.
Peace. Lasting love. She has nearly given up
when, unbidden, it blooms brightly. Then on
the clear summer morning of July 7, 2005,
violence crosses her path again . . .

'Rich and satisfying, and written with a
painter's instinct for the beautiful' *The Times* ∎

Find Out More

romatearne.com

The author's own website, where you can find
information about both her writing and her
painting.

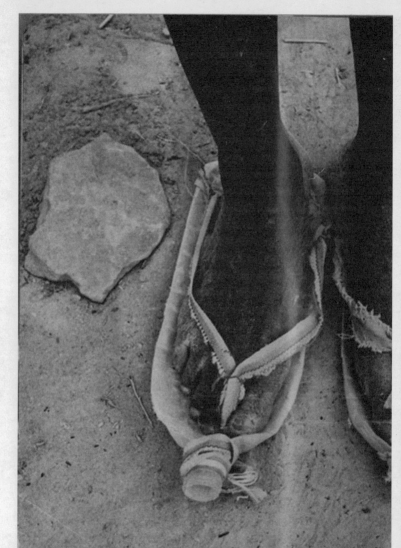

life and death of

a stowaway